The Wound of Words

Deborah Makarios

© 2020 Deborah Makarios   OI
deborah.makarios.nz   MAKARIOI

A catalogue record for this book is available from the National
Library of New Zealand.

ISBN (paperback): 978-0-473-51621-5
ISBN (ebook): 978-0-473-51622-2

Front cover typography: Evelyn Doyle
https://evelyndoyle.com

Cover image: ArtTower (CC0 license)

To my husband
and my father,
both men with excellent beards.

Contents

The wound of words
is worse than
the wound of swords.
***
Arab proverb

Unwelcome Home

"She's coming!"

The pageboy skidded through the courtyard gate hard on the heels of his shrill cry. Already a half-numbed footman was turning to bang on the great iron-bound door, the prearranged signal to the rest of the servants waiting in the warmth within.

Andrei's heart leapt at the page's call. At last! He whistled to summon his fellow stablemen and turned back to see the indoor servants forming a nervous but strictly hierarchical line down the front stair, under the major-domo's watchful eye. Housemaids on the left, footmen on the right, with outdoor staff lurking respectfully along the great grey façade of the Little Palace. It was only a week after Midwinter, despite the sunshine, and the biting chill reddened their cheeks in moments.

Andrei pulled the furred collar of the coat that marked him as Assistant Coachman closer about his neck, thankful for the turn of events that had promoted him to a position with a warmer neck. Coachman always said he should grow a beard like all the other men had, but what's the point of your father leaving you a silver razor as an heirloom if you don't use it? His father had never had a beard, and anyway, think what a fool he'd look while it grew in.

A faint fizzing hiss sounded through the still air: her Imperial Highness's carriage, mounted on sleigh runners for her

Midseason travel. Faint twitches of aprons and cuffs into perfect order could be seen fidgeting down the line of servants.
Three of the imperial greys swept through the gate, drawing
the silvery carriage with ease. The elderly head coachman in
his fur-lined coat pulled the horses up with apparent uncon-
cern, yet the carriage door came to rest precisely at the foot of
the stair.

Andrei stepped forward to take the lead horse's head, but
his eyes were fixed on the empty air so soon to be occupied by
the woman he loved. The head footman leapt to open the carriage door, and Andrei could have sworn every man, woman
and child present held their breath. Only the horses seemed
unaffected; they'd had a long run and were eager to reach the
stable they scented so near.

Out came an exquisitely smooth golden head, and Andrei
could almost hear a sigh of relief drift round the courtyard.
Duke Maxim was here; the scene to follow could not become
too unpleasant with such an urbane man in attendance. He
turned, giving Andrei a view of the aquiline profile and elegant moustache that had half the girls in town sighing for him,
and extended his long arm back into the carriage.

The lead horse became uneasy, flicking its head up and
down, and Andrei tightened his grip. A mittened hand came
into his view, resting in Duke Maxim's arm. A dark furred
hood followed, falling back to reveal Her Imperial Highness
Valeska Kira, only daughter of Czar Kiril. The duke smiled at
her, and she smiled back, gazing into his face, for all the world
as though they were newlyweds back from a honeymoon, not
cousins back from the season's royal duty tour.

Andrei craned his neck, but only two figures were visible.
Where was Bronya? She had to be here! Valeska Kira wouldn't
be travelling without her maid... He caught sight of a blue
cloth hood peeping out from the carriage door, and relaxed.

Valeska looked away from Maxim at the house and at the
people lined up outside it. She froze, and the tension in the

air tightened to breaking pitch. Andrei waited impatiently for Bronya to step out of the carriage.

"What is the meaning of this?" Valeska's high, clear voice rang off the frosty stones. "Why are we here?"

The major-domo stepped forward with a measured tread and bowed. "Welcome to the Little Palace, Your Highness."

Valeska turned to fix the old coachman with an icy blue eye. "Why did you drive me here? I gave orders for home, you may recall."

Coachman bore the brunt of that cold displeasure without giving an inch, and Andrei had to admire him for it. There wasn't one man in the stables who'd be in his boots right now, not for all the benefits the position conferred: title, pay, furred coat and all.

"The Czar's orders, Your Highness," he said, keeping his eyes respectfully on her feet. Anything to avoid that gaze.

Valeska drew in the cold air with a little hiss, and turned to where the major-domo was speaking again at her elbow.

"His Imperial Majesty has bethought him of the propriety of your assuming your own household, now that you are of age," he was saying unctuously, although Andrei saw he wasn't meeting her gaze either. "The Little Palace has therefore been reopened and..."

He found he was addressing the side of her head and fell silent.

"Maxim," Valeska said in a low and urgent voice, her eyes like sapphires in the snow in that white face. "Maxim!"

"Don't alarm yourself, my dear," Maxim said, his fine voice echoing off the grey bulk of the Little Palace. "Perhaps—"

"He can't do this to me! *She* can't do this to me," Valeska muttered.

"Let us not jump to conclusions," Maxim cautioned.

"I am not jumping anywhere," Valeska retorted. "I am going home."

Andrei frowned. If she left, Bronya would leave too, and she hadn't even noticed him yet.

Valeska turned to climb back into the carriage, and paused, eyeing the coachman. The regular puffs of breath appearing before his face suddenly ceased.

"The horses must be fatigued," she said. "As must you."

Andrei's blood surged. This was his chance! "I can have fresh horses harnessed to the little sleigh in three minutes, Your Highness," he said. "And I will gladly drive you wherever you wish to go."

She gave a sharp nod, and he beckoned the stablemen into action. Three minutes he'd said, and three minutes it had better be.

"But Your Highness must be fatigued also," the major-domo was saying. "Will you not come in and rest, perhaps take tea, before you depart?"

"I will wait in the carriage," Valeska said flatly, and Bronya's gloved hand appeared to help her in. Maxim was beckoned after, and the door firmly shut.

❄   ❄   ❄

The Great Palace was on the other side of Istvan from the Little Palace, and just for once Andrei was glad of it. There had been many weary to-ings and fro-ings with the wagon in the last two weeks, since Valeska Kira had left on the Midwinter tour, but today the sun was shining, the horses were fresh, and Bronya was perched beside him on the driver's seat.

Heads turned, eyes stared, talk buzzed as the glittering sleigh skimmed down the street between nobles' palaces and fine merchants' establishments. You didn't get this sort of reaction with a plodding cart-horse drawing the wagon to market.

"Take the back streets," Valeska said suddenly, and then, in a lower tone, "I've had enough of being stared at lately."

"Yes, Your Highness!"

Andrei deftly turned the sleigh down the first side street of sufficient width, a grin spreading across his face. The back streets weren't much to look at, being mostly crammed with unpretentious houses and unprepossessing shops, but what did he care? Back streets meant an indirect route, which meant longer at Bronya's side. True, they couldn't talk—more than his job was worth, Coachman had told him—but they were together, and that was enough for him.

As the sleigh drew near the Great Palace, Andrei spotted trouble: the gates were shut. He could guess why—the Czar had not been Valeska's father for sixteen years for nothing—but there wasn't much he could do about it. Do your duty and keep your mouth shut, that's what Coachman used to say, and he'd been in the imperial service sixty years.

Andrei drew the horses up to the gates.

"Open for Her Imperial Highness Valeska Kira!" he called, hoping fervently that he would not be called upon to contribute any more to what would undoubtedly be an awkward conversation.

The gatekeeper sidled out of his little booth and fixed his gaze high above the trees.

"My orders are to keep the gate shut," he said.

Andrei wondered what he should do next, but the decision was mercifully taken from his hands.

"I have come home. Open the gates," Valeska said in calm, measured tones, and the hair on Andrei's neck stood up.

"My orders are to keep the gate shut," the gatekeeper said, not daring to lower his eyes.

"Surely," Duke Maxim broke in diplomatically, "there is no harm in allowing Her Highness to see her father, and report on the errand on which he has sent her?"

"Allow?" Valeska hissed. "Errand?"

"My orders are—" the gatekeeper doggedly began.

"This is my home," Valeska snapped at him. "How dare you stand in my way?"

"My orders—"

"Those are my rooms," Valeska went on, gesturing to the corner of the massive block of the Great Palace. "Since the hour of my birth—" She broke off. "Who is that up there? What are they doing in my rooms?"

The gatekeeper hunkered into his coat. "The Royal Nursery is being prepared for the forthcoming heir."

"I am the heir;" Valeska ground out, "my father's only heir."

"But you're a grown lady now," Maxim said, though his tone seemed to suggest otherwise. "The nursery is hardly your place. I dare say the Czar has simply arranged for you to stay at the Little Palace while the Czarina's suite is refurbished." He lowered his voice. "After all, it has been some years now since your mother passed away."

The gatekeeper bore the expression of a man who has found his hands full of someone else's dirty work, and is becoming more and more convinced that he is not paid enough for the job.

"The Czarina's rooms are at present occupied by the Czarina," he said, scrunching himself further into his coat and clearly wishing he could disappear.

This produced a moment of dead silence from the back of the sleigh as Bronya clutched at Andrei's arm. And then they were all talking at once, Valeska's high clear voice, Bronya's low sweet one, and Maxim's like a golden trumpet over all.

"The Czarina? What do you mean? Who?" he demanded. "Speak, man!"

"The Czarina Svetlana," the gatekeeper said, eyes on the sky as though looking for an eagle to swoop down and carry him away. "Lately united to His Imperial Majesty Kiril."

And soon to bear his child, Andrei finished silently. He waited for the storm to break behind him, but after a long, deathly silence came only the words "Turn the sleigh."

"Yes, sir," Andrei said, only too glad to have something to do, and that something removing him from the unpleasant scene. Or at least part of it, since he was obliged to carry a large part of the late confrontation—and that the most distressed part—away with him.

The Great Palace's drive was designed with the idea that arriving vehicles would turn in the enormous sweep of courtyard in front of it, but little thought had been given to turning at the gates. Andrei pulled off the feat quite neatly, ruefully reflecting that his passengers wouldn't even have noticed.

"The Little Palace," Duke Maxim snapped, once the turn was complete.

"Anything but that!" Valeska countered.

"You must! It is hardly consistent with the dignity of an imperial princess—or of a duke—to plead with menials at the gates. Like a beggar!"

"But—" Valeska ground her teeth. "To be turned away from the doors of my own home!"

"To appear powerless is to be powerless," Maxim continued. "You should have known better than to begin a confrontation which you could not be certain to win."

"I can't believe he's actually married her," Valeska said in a toneless whisper, barely audible above the hissing of the runners. "A mere laundress, and vulgar besides!"

"You should have seen the danger," Maxim said. "If you had given me a more accurate idea of the situation, I would certainly not have accompanied you on the Lake visit, and all this might have been prevented! If I had only been there to put the right word in his ear at the right time! You know as well as I do this is the madness of a moment. A laundress as Czarina? Ridiculous! You have made a slip from which you may never recover!"

"Maxim! How can you be so cruel? You know I would have told you if I'd had the slightest—I never dreamed that he could have lowered himself in such a way."

"Oh, my dear," Maxim said, his voice suddenly gentle and caressing. "You know I have always been entirely partisan in my support of you, and my passion for the cause may have led me to speak unguardedly. You will not breathe a word of what has passed?" he suddenly demanded, his tone changing again like lightning.

"No, sir," came Bronya's low tones.

"No, sir," Andrei snapped, glaring at the road ahead. As if he needed to ask! Bronya was Valeska Kira's personal maid, wasn't she? Personal and confidential, and you didn't reach those kinds of heights in your profession by having a flapping mouth. Nor did Assistant Coachmen.

The sleigh pulled up at the foot of the Little Palace's front entrance, precisely where the carriage had stood less than an hour before. Maxim climbed out, helped Valeska down, and ushered her weary form within, Bronya hurrying after. Not a word from Bronya; not a look. Andrei heaved a sigh and drove the sleigh slowly round to the stables.

Personal and confidential maids didn't get much time off, Andrei knew, but in the few brief conversations he'd managed to have with Bronya—at servants' dances and the like—he'd learned she liked gardens. Hoping very much she still liked them at this time of year, he spent the afternoon hanging about in the one part of the garden which was visible only from the service wings, and therefore permissible for servants to use.

He was jumping from foot to foot in an attempt to keep warm, and brooding on the possibility that Bronya's position might allow her access to the parts of the garden Valeska Kira herself would walk in, when the heavy side door creaked open.

"Bronya!"

"Oh—Andrei." Not very enthusiastic, but at least she didn't go back inside.

"Are you all right?" he asked anxiously. "You look a bit tired."

The next moment he could have slapped himself. Of all the things to say!

"I don't—I mean—"

She gave a weary smile, and his heart turned over.

"I'll go away if you like," he offered.

"Have you been waiting to see me?" she asked, a hint of that smile peeking out the edge of her hood.

"Yes," he said boldly.

"And got thoroughly chilled, I dare say," she said.

He grinned. "You wouldn't be so unkind as to make me go and warm up, would you?"

Bronya's smile vanished. "No more than you deserve, I dare say. Offering to take Valeska to the Great Palace like that, knowing the reception she would face!"

"I just wanted to be near you," Andrei said honestly. "Anyway, from all I've heard, the princess is hard enough to cope with anything."

"You haven't heard very much, then," Bronya said, and turned away to stroll along the frosty path.

Andrei was beside her in a step. "So tell me more."

"You really want to know?"

"If it's you telling me."

Bronya rolled her eyes, but moved a little to one side, allowing room for Andrei to stroll down the path beside her.

"I would be dead if it wasn't for her. Do you remember the Lady's season, oh, it must be ten years ago now?"

Andrei scrunched up his face. That was before he came to Istvan, but... "The year the wells froze over?"

"That's the one."

"I remember dropping rocks down the well-shafts to see if we could break the ice."

"I was living on the streets," Bronya said softly. "I'm an orphan, you know. And I would have frozen to death if it hadn't been for Valeska. She was out for her daily drive, muffled up in so many furs you could hardly see her, but she made the driver stop when she saw me, and she asked me my story, and then," Bronya laughed, "then she ordered me into the sleigh, and took me home to the Great Palace to be her companion."

Andrei blinked. This was a side of the princess he had definitely not seen.

Bronya sighed, a great white plume drifting up into the grey air.

"It's not the past that's weighing on you, is it?" Andrei guessed shrewdly.

She turned startled eyes to him.

"If you ever want to talk about it," Andrei said, "you know I'm always here for you. A problem shared is a problem halved, right?"

Bronya smiled again, and it was the smile you'd give a child.

"That's sweet of you," she said, "but no. Sometimes a problem shared is just a problem spread."

"But—"

"I must go," she said, turning back towards the door. "My lady will be needing me soon."

She gave him that smile again, and disappeared through the door.

Andrei hunched into his coat and paced up and down. All right, Valeska Kira wasn't the cold-hearted monster some made her out to be—or wasn't always. And clearly, Bronya was loyal to her. All to the good—he admired loyalty—but equally clearly, she didn't take him seriously as a suitor. Not at all. Somehow, he would have to change her mind.

Andrei darted across the street, nipped under the noses of two plodding dray-horses, and rapped smartly on the door of the Howler station. Purely as a matter of form, since the door was always open, even on the coldest days when snow drifted in.

"Pyotr!" he called, dancing up to the long wooden counter in an effort to keep warm.

An old coat in the corner pulled itself together, and revealed itself to be Pyotr, the senior Howler at the local station. He was dressed for outdoors, which Andrei supposed he was, in a sense. He shivered.

"Ah, Andrei! Come to do business?" Pyotr asked, adjusting the tiny glasses on his round nose.

"You know that old brush—valuable antique brush, that is to say—which I asked you about before?"

"The last time you were stony broke?" Pyotr asked with a mischievous beam.

"I am *not* stony broke," Andrei said. "I have money in my pocket, I'll have you know, just not enough for the...investment I want to make."

"Dear me! An investment, is it? What heights stableboys rise to these days."

"Assistant Coachman now," Andrei corrected. "With the princess moving to the Little Palace and a bigger staff employed, I've been promoted."

"And you're overspending your increased wages already?" Pyotr asked, eyebrows raised.

"The increase has barely begun," Andrei said. "And this can't wait. So about this brush..."

"I've had a nibble of interest," Pyotr said. "A would-be buyer, in fact—an old widow-lady down south."

Andrei hesitated. An old widow-lady down south could be construed as his Granny Sonechka, and he didn't want her hearing about this. Not that there was anything underhanded in it, he would just rather she didn't know.

"How far south?"

"Right down by Summer's Meadow," Pyotr said, heaving what could have been a nostalgic sigh.

Andrei relaxed. Much further south than Granny, then.

"My cousin's wife's sister's boy runs the station down there. They've all the luck, that branch of the family, let me tell you. Been years since I saw the place. I keep telling myself it's time I paid a visit, but there! business is too good, and I mustn't complain. Now, then, where were we?"

"The buyer," Andrei prompted.

"Oh, yes. Well, she's offering two and a half eagles, which seems a fair price, considering the condi—"

"I'll take it," Andrei said instantly. He undid the top button of his coat to scuffle in the inner pocket, and the cold air dived in like an eagle plummeting on its prey. "Here you are."

He handed across the old bone-backed brush. Not without a twinge, for it was an old familiar friend, but he wasn't one to sacrifice the future to the past. He needed those two and a half eagles, and the sooner the better.

Pyotr took it, automatically turning to the light and scrutinizing the brush carefully.

"The brush hasn't changed since you last saw it, Pyotr," Andrei said.

"No offence, Andrei, just a matter of business. I've got my reputation to think of, after all. What good would the Howler network be if you couldn't trust us, eh?"

"Yes, all right, all right!" He jigged in place, wishing the old man would get a move on. The silversmith shut up shop early, the days being as short as they were, and he didn't want to miss him.

"Now then." Pyotr carefully placed the brush on the battered old counter, and withdrew from a concealed drawer two eagles and a 'wing', a half-eagle coin. They clinked as he set them down beside the brush.

"I receive from you this bone-backed brush, for the agreed price of two and one half eagles," Pyotr said, his voice taking on the sing-song intonation of long-familiar words oft repeated.

"Yes, yes."

"The two and one half eagles I pay to you today in trust; the brush shall be sent by the Howler courier network until it reaches the final station."

"Pyotr, I know all this!" Andrei said desperately. "Can't you just give me the money and—"

Pyotr looked over his glasses severely, and Andrei gave up the struggle, letting the old man maunder on through all the terms and conditions of the transaction, while his mind shot away to the silversmith's shop and perused the wares for sale. Two and a half eagles—that would buy something fairly impressive, he was sure.

"—the last purchaser shall have the space of one day to reverse the transaction, unravelling the chain in all its particulars." Pyotr seemed to be winding down, so Andrei flashed him a grin in hopes of staving off further details.

"I hope you're not making any decisions you'll come to regret," Pyotr said, as he finally—with infinite slowness it seemed to Andrei—took up the coins and held them out.

"I never regret anything," Andrei said, seizing the coins and dashing out the door with a quick "thanks!" flung over his shoulder.

The silversmith's shutters were still open. He was in luck! Ten minutes later he was speeding through the dusk towards the Little Palace servants' hall and a hot dinner, a precious little bag tucked carefully into his shirt for the safest of keeping.

❄   ❄   ❄

Bronya stepped out into the thin sunshine of the side garden and leaned against the wall with a sigh.

"Bronya!"

She looked up and saw Andrei waving from among the close-clipped hedges.

"Here again?" she asked, coming slowly down the steps. "If you carry on like this, the horses will forget what you look like."

"Come for a stroll," Andrei suggested, proffering his arm and disregarding the slight on his horses. "Nothing like a bit of brisk activity to chase the worries away, Granny always says. Anyway, there's something I wanted to talk to you about."

She took his arm, but the little worried wrinkle stayed on her smooth broad brow.

"But is there something you want to talk about first?" he asked. If ever there was a woman with Something On Her Mind, Bronya was she. And oh, how he wanted to know what it was! Particularly as he was absolutely certain it wasn't him.

"I can't," she said.

Which wasn't exactly a no, he noted.

After only a few scrunching paces across the gravel, her arm in his as tense as ever, she spoke again. "Well? What's so important?"

"You know the sun makes your hair shine like gold?" Andrei asked, his attention suddenly caught by the band of gold showing at the front of her warm hood.

"You asked me to walk up and down in a freezing garden, just so you can tell me my hair is yellow?" she asked, and there was rather more exasperation in her tone this time.

"Not at all, and that isn't what I said," Andrei said, returning to the business in hand. "I have something for you."

He drew out the little leather bag and ceremoniously presented it to her. She opened it, and a little stream of sparkling silver flowed out onto her gloved palm. It was a snowflake, hanging on a fine silver chain.

"Andrei!"

"Do you like it?"

"It's far too good for the likes of me, and I'm sure you shouldn't have," she said, giving him a half-heartedly reproachful look.

"Nothing is too good for you," Andrei said firmly. "Let me help you put it on."

"What will Her Highness think of her maid wearing fine silver jewellery?" Bronya asked, but she dropped her hood and lifted her heavy bundle of hair out of the way.

"She's got other things on her mind, from what I hear. Courting and so on." His hands were rapidly numbing out of his gloves, and he fumbled with the tiny clasp. At last he got it. "And while we're on the subject—"

A frazzled-looking housemaid popped her head around the door. "Bronya! The duke's gone and Her Highness is calling for you!"

Bronya gave Andrei's arm a quick squeeze and darted up the stairs without a backward look.

"She says she's fine," the housemaid hissed to Bronya, her voice carrying across the cold air, "but she looks worn to a shadow, and if you ask me, she's been crying."

Andrei watched the door close behind them, and wondered if other men had these kinds of problems when trying to propose. At least Bronya hadn't refused the necklace. She wasn't the sort of girl to take gifts from a man she had no further interest in. So there was hope still!

Suddenly aware of how cold he was, Andrei did a couple of cartwheels along the gravel walk and ran back towards the stable block to get warm.

❆   ❆   ❆

Two days later, Andrei was sitting at his ease in the stables, watching the grooms play dice, and wondering what it was that was weighing on Bronya's mind. Something to do with Valeska, he was pretty sure, and from what he could judge of Bronya's demeanour, something more—something worse—than Valeska having a new home and a new step-mother.

His ears caught the high trink of harness bells. *Lots* of harness bells. Seizing his coat, he ran to the courtyard, struggling into the sleeves as he rounded the corner. And no sooner had he arrived in the snowy courtyard than the three most magnificent horses he had ever seen swept through the gates, drawing the Czar's favourite racing sleigh behind them.

Andrei rushed forward to take the lead horse's head, wondering if this was Duke Maxim's doing. He was trying for a reconciliation between the Czar and his daughter, according to servants' hall gossip. But no—Duke Maxim wasn't the sort to leave things to chance. If he'd arranged for Czar Kiril to pay a visit, he'd be here himself, and Valeska would have had the whole household tuned to breaking point for the importance of the visit. There would have been orders, and all the stable staff brushed, polished and in perfect array, awaiting His Imperial Majesty's arrival.

Instead of which, there was just Andrei, holding the horses, and a rather flustered-looking major-domo being thumped on the shoulder by the brawny Czar as he pushed through the front door. Unlike his daughter, the Czar was not overly fond of formality and the distinctions of rank. Which may be why he'd married a laundrymaid, Andrei speculated, keeping the dangerous thought behind his teeth.

"Long stay?" he asked the Czar's lean little jockey of a driver, while stroking the lead's silken nose.

"Search me," the driver replied with a grimace. "We were out on the flats racing with some of the lads—" for thus did he refer to the cream of the nation's aristocratic youth, "—and halfway through a race His Majesty pulls up and tells me to take the reins and drive to the Little Palace."

"Halfway through a race?" Andrei echoed. Who on earth would drive off halfway through a race? "Must have been confusing for the sleighs behind!"

The driver grinned. "Might not have been that many to be confused, if you take my meaning."

Andrei stroked the long nose again and sighed for such exquisite creatures to drive. The inhabitants of the Little Palace stables were perfectly respectable stock, but no one had horses like the Czar. Not even his daughter.

"Look, he's been gone a while," Andrei said. "We don't want them catching a chill. How about we settle them into the stables for now?"

The driver shook his head regretfully. "More than my job's worth not to have them ready at the drop of a hat. He's not one to stand about waiting, is Czar Kiril."

"We could at least get them under cover," Andrei argued. "They'll be better off in the warm, even if they do have to stay in harness."

The driver looked at the front door, still firmly closed. "All right, then."

Andrei stepped aside, an arm extended to show the way, and the Czar's driver started his team with the subtlest of motions. The light racing sleigh was just whisking through the archway to the stable court when there was a roar from the building behind. Andrei spun round. The roar was followed by a piercing scream, the crash of broken furniture, and the thin tinkle of broken glass.

Andrei broke into a run and burst through the front door, something that would have earned him a serious dressing-down from the major-domo under ordinary circumstances.

The inside of the palace was not very familiar to Andrei— people who smelled of horses were supposed to stay outside— but he found himself in a stream of agitated servants hurrying across the entrance hall and down a wide corridor towards the back of the palace. The roaring voice grew louder, or at least, nearer.

The woman in front of Andrei came to a sudden stop, he halted himself, and was promptly barged into by the man behind. He peered down the corridor, his eyes still accustoming themselves to the relative dimness indoors. Over the heads of the pressing crowd, he could see a tall, elegant door, painted in cream picked out with gold.

The door was closed. He wriggled his way towards it, and as he did so heard further destruction within—china, by the sound of it. There was a whimper, too, but it sounded too clear to have come from the room within. He pushed closer, and found Bronya close to the door, tears in her eyes and the major-domo's firm hand on her shoulder.

"Please let me go to her," she whispered.

"Both His Majesty and Her Highness commanded that they were to be uninterrupted," the major-domo replied, pitching his voice low so that it would not be heard within. "If you open that door uninvited, you must seek employment elsewhere."

Bronya bit her lip, and Andrei reached out and touched her arm. She turned, and smiled through her tears. His heart turned over, and he longed to gather her into his arms and solve all her problems. He just had no idea how.

"If you are called for, you may enter," the major-domo told Bronya, unbending a little. Not a bad old fellow, Andrei decided, even if he was as formal as a funeral.

She pressed herself against the door, listening for the faintest hint of a summons. The roaring was more like ordinary shouting now, and the smashings had stopped. Valeska's voice could be heard from out here in the corridor, high and a little quivery, but decidedly defiant.

Secretly, Andrei was rather relieved to be banned from the room. Nothing so embarrassing as someone else's family fights, especially if they were your employer. But it had sounded rather violent...

The Czar's deep, rough voice shouted one or two rather incoherent remarks, and the door suddenly flung open. Andrei hauled Bronya back before she could fall through the doorway, and discovered to his horror that it was full of angry red-faced czar. He flattened himself obsequiously against the wall. The corridor emptied as if by magic, people melting away through any door or passage they could find.

"What are you doing here?" the Czar demanded.

For a horrible moment Andrei thought the Czar meant him, but with a surge of relief realized the Czar's driver was the man standing behind him, who began to stutter excuses.

"Sleigh! Now!" the Czar ordered, and barrelled towards the hall, the driver skittering ahead of him like a mouse before a large ramping cat.

"I'd better go," Andrei whispered to Bronya. As he slid cautiously along in the Czar's wake, he heard Valeska's voice uplifted behind him.

"Tell the footmen to clear this room, Bronya, then come to me in the library and take down a note to Duke Maxim."

He'd bet every coin he had—which admittedly wasn't many at present—that she had been the source of that terrified scream, but there was no trace of it now. She sounded cool and clear and in perfect control.

But then, her voice dropping and hoarse, came three more words. "I need him."

Rumour and Reversal

Andrei carefully slipped past the Czar as he stamped about on the front steps calling for his sleigh, and ran for the stables. Before he had reached the far end of the courtyard, he was compelled to dive aside as the three exquisite beasts charged past, their driver's face set in grim determination.

Picking himself up and dusting the snow off his coat, Andrei considered his future. He had never wanted to be anything but a coachman, ever since he was a tiny scrap of a boy back in the village. His grandmother had pulled in a few favours and got him a place here in town, and by merit he had risen to the status of second in command (from a total staff of two) in the Little Palace stables.

He had been just about to resign himself to never driving anything more splendid than a fat cart-horse taking the cook to market, when the Little Palace was suddenly turned into a working palace again, and he found himself second in command of a staff of no fewer than eight.

Undoubtedly, he'd moved up in the world in the most satisfactory fashion. But the pinnacle of any coachman's career, only to be dreamed of by most, was to be Head Coachman to the Czar. Not so much for the status—coachmen weren't snobs, or at least not about people—but for the quality of the animals themselves.

It was now dawning on Andrei that to be the Czar's coachman would, of necessity, involve a certain amount of interaction with the Czar himself, and that this would not form one of the benefits of the job. And yet...those horses!

"Andrei!"

He spun around so fast he nearly fell over. Bronya, without coat or gloves, was darting after him, a note clutched in her blue fingers.

"Please, will you take this to Duke Maxim?" she asked as she reached him, holding out the note.

"Of course—at once! But go inside, you'll—look, your hands are blue!"

He took the note and watched to see her turn back towards the door before he ran and slithered on.

The stables were all abuzz when Andrei reached them, and as he saddled a horse, one of the grooms detailed all he'd seen to those who'd missed the excitement.

"White as the snows, she was, and with the red print of a great big hand on her face."

This occasioned some hisses of indrawn breath and shakings of heads, but only the head coachman, old enough to be the Czar's father, felt free to comment.

"Always been that way, from a lad, he has. Free with his hands—"

"And other parts, from what I hear," muttered one groom to another, who sniggered.

Coachman eyed them disapprovingly. "You want to be less free with your tongue, my lad," he said austerely, "or you'll find it's got you into trouble it won't get you out of. The Czar won't trouble himself using the flat of his hand to the likes of *you*."

"Reckon she gave as good as she got?" the loose-tongued groom suggested, stationing himself at the door ready to open it for Andrei's departure.

To Andrei's surprise, Coachman chuckled. "She's not one to descend to fisticuffs, but a sharp enough tongue she has, and that's one weapon His Majesty's never got the mastery of. Why, on this very last trip, we were ambushed by a road-robber, and she—out of the trees he jumps, cutlass drawn, and before I can think or blink, up she stands in the carriage—the top was down, for it was a fine day, that day, at least till the fog came up in the afternoon—up she stands, and gives him the rough side of her tongue and sends him scrambling. And all done without a word that a lady oughtn't to know, what's more!" he added, with a stern look at the loose-tongued groom, who was clearly preparing to say something vulgarly suggestive.

Andrei swung himself into the saddle, the groom swung the door open, and they were off. It wasn't far to Duke Maxim's palace—not with a horse like this under him, anyway. It would have been a dull trudge on foot, but he was almost sorry to arrive at his destination so soon.

There were, even in this exalted street and this icy weather, a band of children playing outside. He eyed them carefully, and made his choice. It was an easy choice: most were making faces at the impressive and impassive footmen at the door, a few were staring at him, but only one was staring at the horse.

"Would you like to hold the horse for me?" he asked the rotund little figure.

"Yes please!" an excited little voice piped. "I'm Duscha," the voice continued, thus giving Andrei his first clue that the person inside the bundle of boots, coat, and muffler was a girl.

"Stand right there, Duscha," Andrei said, sliding down and handing her the reins. She didn't seem at all alarmed to be right in the path of a towering animal whose belly she could almost have walked under without ducking.

"I'm going to be a coachman when I grow up," Duscha said confidently, taking a better grip on the reins with her tiny mittened hands and fixing the horse with an eye born to command.

"Well, don't steal my job while I'm gone," Andrei said with

mock severity, and left her giggling.

The footmen eyed him dubiously, but opened the door with pleasing swiftness when he informed them he had a personal message from Her Imperial Highness Valeska Kira to deliver. He was ushered into a gilded echoing hall where twin roaring fireplaces billowed forth heat.

"Wait here," the duke's major-domo instructed, and withdrew.

Andrei was only too pleased to wait near such splendid fires. But all too soon Duke Maxim strode in, the major-domo presented Andrei to his notice, and Andrei presented the note to the duke.

He opened it at once, tearing it open impatiently. His eyes narrowed as he read, and his nostrils flared slightly. Then he crumpled it up and tossed it on a nearby table.

"No reply," he said. "See him out," he added to the major-domo, and strode away.

The next moment Andrei found himself outside the grand front door, between the two footmen, wondering just what he was supposed to say when he returned.

❄   ❄   ❄

Bronya met Andrei in the Little Palace courtyard as he trotted in. She'd been waiting just inside the door for the sound of hoofbeats, was Andrei's guess. She lifted an anxious face as he brought the horse to a halt.

"Did you—was he there? Did he get the note? How soon will he be here?" she asked, wringing her hands.

Andrei sighed and dismounted. "Yes, he was there, and yes, I gave the note to him in person. He read it straight away."

"And then?"

"And then he said 'no reply.'"

Worry flooded Bronya's large dark eyes.

"I don't know what the note said, of course," Andrei went on, "but he didn't seem happy to get it. Almost...offended? I don't think he's coming."

Bronya burst into tears, and before he knew what he was doing, he had an arm around her and she was sobbing all down the front of his coat.

"Oh, Andrei, I don't know what to think! I'm so worried!"

"You think he's too old for her—or not interested?" Andrei asked.

"It's not that...he seems attentive enough. If you saw them together!" She gave a little hiccuping laugh through her tears. "Such a fuss about placing her chair just so, moving it twice so she wouldn't get too close to the fire, telling her not to worry about things with her father, he'd handle it all for her, she wasn't to do a thing..."

The gossip was right, then, at least about that.

"So what's wrong?" he asked, drawing her a little closer into the shelter of the gently steaming horse.

"There's..." Bronya bit back a sob and dropped her voice. "There's something wrong with Her Highness's hands."

"Frostbite?" Andrei suggested with a shiver.

"They're both curled up into little fists."

"So she's angry about something. It wouldn't be the first time."

"All the time, Andrei! Ever since—even when she's asleep! I've suggested calling for a physician, or at least a healer, but she won't hear of it! It's...it's not natural."

"Well, if she won't see a healer there's nothing you can do about it, so why worry? It'll be the duke's problem soon anyway. This isn't your responsibility."

"But *she* is!"

Andrei shook his head in grudging admiration. "You're too loyal for your own good, Bronya. She has to live her life; it's time you thought about living yours."

She didn't look convinced.

He took her hands. "There's nothing more you can do," he said gently.

"There might be," she said, and suddenly pulled herself together. "I can't tell you more—I shouldn't have told you this much."

"I won't betray your confidence," Andrei said. "But I'd better get this mare back to the stables before she catches a chill."

"Of course—thank you." She dried her eyes and hurried inside.

Andrei led the mare away briskly, wondering furiously what in the four seasons was going on with Valeska Kira—and what the "more" was that Bronya was still not telling him.

❅   ❅   ❅

The hours passed, and the duke did not come. At last the old coachman cleared his throat and hauled himself out of his chair. "Time you were harnessing the horses for Her Highness's drive."

"In this weather?" Andrei asked incredulously. Freezing cold still, and a storm coming up, if he was any judge.

Coachman gave a leathery cackle. "Clear to see you haven't been long in royal service. It doesn't matter if the lady's likely to go or not. She still wants to be offered the opportunity. Mind you," he added, easing a crick out of his back, "I can call to mind days the late Czarina took her drive when the Coachman could hardly see past his horses' ears."

He went off to dress himself in the formal uniform demanded by the occasion, and Andrei hurried to obey, pulling a couple of the grooms away from their game.

Valeska Kira was carrying on like nothing had changed—like she still lived at court. He'd even heard rumours from the indoor staff that there had been Words Passed over a mere matter of luncheon being served three minutes late. Was that what was bothering Bronya? He didn't see how it fit with the hands, though.

The harnessing complete, Andrei put on his coat to take the sleigh round to the courtyard where Coachman would appear in all his splendour and take command of it. The wind was chill and the sky leaden, but no fresh snow was falling yet. Andrei pulled up outside the door and went to hold the leader's head. Coachman appeared and stood at attention at a dignified distance from the sleigh. The front door opened, and Her Highness came out, a great furry hood obscuring most of her face. Bronya, rather less sumptuously furred, was in close attendance.

The coachman bowed, Valeska acknowledged him with an incline of the head, and all was proceeding according to the pattern of time immemorial, when Andrei's ears caught the hiss of runners on snow, and the duke's equipage came briskly through the gate. Maxim's driver hastily reined in his horses when he saw Valeska's sleigh already at the front door, but he was adept, and managed it without putting his noble passenger off balance.

Maxim descended in a single dashing stride, his tall boots squeaking on the thin layer of settled snow. What he spent on his clothes Andrei didn't like to think, but there was no denying he cut a fine figure, with his narrow breeches, long silken waistcoat and matching topcoat. His hatless head rose out of a swarm of black furs which he slipped off and flung behind him into the sleigh. Very effective look with that sleek head of golden hair, but looks weren't everything, as Andrei's Granny used to say. His ears must be absolutely freezing.

"My dear cousin," he greeted Valeska, who was still poised at the foot of the steps. "What seems to be the trouble?"

Valeska hesitated, looking from the approaching duke to the waiting sleigh before her.

"Perhaps you would join me on my drive?" she suggested.

The duke gave an exaggerated shiver. "My dear Valeska, I've just been for a drive—here, to see you. I was given to understand it was important. Of course, if you have better things to do..."

"No, not at all," she hurried to assure him. "But I—I thought you weren't coming."

He arched a brow, glinting in the sun. "Thought? Hoped, it would seem, since you are bent on departing yourself."

"I always take a drive at this time of the day, Maxim, you know that. Just like Mother did."

"Your mother was always ready to welcome her friends," Maxim said in a gently reproving tone.

It must be hard, Andrei brooded, losing your mother young and having people all around you who knew her longer than you did. Of course, he'd lost his own mother young, but at least Granny never compared Andrei to her late daughter-in-law. "Just like your father," on the other hand, passed her lips several times a week, on average.

"Of—of course," Valeska faltered. "But..."

"But you are, after all, your father's daughter," Maxim said. "I quite understand."

"No—Maxim, that isn't what I meant at all. Of course I won't go."

Coachman receded into the background with dignity.

"Nonsense," Maxim said crisply. "It's clear you have every intention of going, and I have no intention of preventing you. I came here to help you, not to bully you into doing whatever I say."

"Maxim, I—" Valeska began, but already Maxim was handing her into the sleigh. Bronya followed, her movements disjointed as though half of her was trying to stay behind.

"You there," Maxim said, his eye falling on Andrei. "What are you doing standing in the way? Take the reins and be off with you."

Andrei gave a wild-eyed glance across the courtyard, but Coachman wasn't stepping forward to take his place, and he didn't dare disobey.

He leapt back onto the driver's seat, flourished the whip above the horses' heads, and whisked away through the court-yard gate.

No one had told him where to go, but his instinct suggested Valeska might prefer to be away from crowds. The flats just outside Istvan, where sleighs were raced, seemed indicated. An awkward silence prevailed until they reached the open country at the edge of town.

Valeska's commanding voice cut across the crisp air. "Drive fast."

"Yes, Your Highness!" Andrei needed no second invitation. Of course, he shouldn't go *really* fast, not with such an impor-tant lady in the sleigh, but—

"Faster!"

Andrei succumbed to the temptation to see what these beau-tiful beasts could do, before Valeska Kira got over whatever was making her behave so unlike her usual self. He was re-warded with the exhilaration of going faster than he'd ever gone before, the wind tearing at his face, the horses moving like a single twelve-legged creature. They whipped across the flats.

At last against the wind came Valeska's words, "The Little Palace."

Andrei turned the horses in a smooth arc across the snow and set a course for home. Funny she hadn't just said "home," but then—

"At a dignified pace," Valeska added.

"Yes, Your Highness."

The old Valeska was back, then. Pity.

❄   ❄   ❄

The only way to find out what was going on, Andrei de-cided, was to do a bit of investigating on his own account. Bronya was so loyal she wouldn't tell him a thing, and even if she did she'd feel awful, and he didn't want that. But that didn't mean that he couldn't look into things himself, without her knowing.

The next day, therefore, Andrei went to see a healer. She seemed rather an intellectual sort, and he hoped she wouldn't see through his story too quickly. Town healers seemed like they all wanted to be physicians, even though everyone born below the Silver Step knew physicians were as likely as not to polish their patient off altogether.

Putting on his most innocent, fresh-up-from-the-country look, Andrei explained it was his little sister who had the problem. The healer, not unnaturally, wanted to know why he hadn't brought her with him.

Andrei had foreseen this, and glibly rattled off his story: she was at home in the village; their local healer wasn't much good but they didn't want to offend her by openly seeking other help. He was coming up to town on the freight wagons anyway, so he thought he'd at least come and ask.

There was still a certain dubiousness in her eye, but the healer agreed to hear his account of the symptoms, so he took heart and described the problem with Valeska's hands as best as he could, without having actually seen them.

"No recent injury?"

"No, nothing like that."

"Even an injury to another part of her body could cause these symptoms. Head or neck injury, particularly."

Andrei shook his head. If Valeska had been injured, Bronya would have been fretting about that, and anyway, why would Valeska hide an injury? No injury.

"Any sign of similar contractions in the feet?"

"I haven't noticed any," Andrei said honestly. She still fit into her dainty little boots, so there couldn't be anything too major there.

The healer pursed her lips. "How are her water and earth?"

This Andrei took in his stride, having heard his Granny, a

healer herself, wield the same question a hundred times, gen-
erally when she felt herself not to be getting a grip on the diagnosis.

"Just as usual," he said firmly, then added "so Mother tells
me."

The healer said "Hmm," and stroked her chin thoughtfully
while gazing at a piece of blue glassware on the table that
served as desk, bench, and examining table.

Andrei tried to look hopeful and impressed.

"And her age—sixteen, you said?"

Andrei nodded.

"Most likely temper, then," the healer said authoritatively.
"Girls get it in their heads to be the centre of attention at that
age, and one way's as good as another."

She got up and started bustling about, collecting a little box
of waxed paper and a tiny scoop and fetching a green glass jar
off a shelf.

"Tell your mother to try her on hot and cold plunge baths,
alternating, and if that doesn't cause her hands to uncurl, try
a dusting of this rose-hip preparation down her spine."

Andrei took the box, paid his coin, and thanked her. He
found himself out on the street again, staring at the little box
in his hands. If he wasn't mistaken, that healer had just pre-
scribed him itching powder. He put it in his pocket with a
laugh and sauntered down the street, debating whether it was
even worth suggesting it to Bronya. He couldn't see Valeska
Kira laughing it off.

As he came abreast of the Howler station, he found a crowd
spilling out the door, forcing passers-by to descend into the
muddy squelch of the street proper.

"What's going on?" he asked a man at the back of the crowd.

"That's what we'd all like to know," he answered solemnly.
"Strange doings afoot, it seems! Boba's telling, listen!"

His curiosity piqued, Andrei hung about until he could
squeeze through the door and find out what exactly the un-

seen Boba was saying. The tale was well and truly told by then, of course, but Boba—a Howler courier, by his uniform—was by no means averse to having a fresh audience.

"I take my run out to the south and west, as you know," he said, "and there was I at the relay station, waiting for hours, when finally Toma staggers in. I give you my word, I thought he'd been set upon at first, but once I got him in and his coat off, there wasn't a mark on him. He just sat there and shivered by the fire for an hour, and finally he speaks."

The room waited, hanging on his every word. Half of them had heard it before, of course, but it seemed they hadn't sucked the full horror out of the tale on the first telling.

"He tells me he was leading his horse along the forest path, seeing as it had got so dark already, and he collided with a wandering man—'or I thought it was a man,' he said to me. 'Two arms and legs and all, just like you and me, but Boba,' he says, his eyes wide with the horror of it, 'he hadn't no head.'"

A murmuring shiver ran round the room.

"'No head?' says I. 'Come now, Toma, how's a man to walk around anywhere, forest or not, without a head? It's against nature,' says I. 'It's dark out there in the forest, as you say. Likely you didn't see right, that's all.' And he gives this little laugh which I swear I'll hear to my dying day, he gives this laugh and he says, 'Oh, I saw his head all right. It was a solid block of wood, is what it was.' Now, that's another matter altogether, and so I said. 'Many's the man whose head could be a block of wood for all his brains, or his looks, if it comes to that,' I said. 'No use frightening yourself half out of your wits because you meet an ugly fool on the path. Us Howlers aren't bred from chickens, you know.'"

Pyotr made approving noises from behind his counter.

"And he looks at me," Boba went on, his voice dropping, and his hearers leaning in, "and he gives that mad laugh again, and says, 'how many ugly fools have faces of bark, Boba?' and he holds out his hand...and there's a fragment of bark, clutched tight in his hand, so tight it's drawn blood."

A long sigh went round the room. Boba was well known as a storyteller, and he certainly had material worthy of his powers today.

"Are you sure it was his own blood?" Andrei asked, and had the satisfaction of hearing groans of horror echoing round the room.

"No, young man, that I am not," Boba said solemnly.

"What's all this?" said a fresh voice, and Boba turned to tell his tale again. Andrei felt a pluck at his sleeve.

"Pyotr? Don't tell me you've got a story to tell, too."

The Howler man frowned, a little wedge appearing at the top of his nose. "I've got a story all right, but you won't like it."

Andrei sucked in a breath as the draft from the ever-open door went down his neck. "Don't tell me..."

"A reversal. Sorry, lad, but there it is. Hand over, and we'll none of us have to think of it again."

"But it's been ages! Are you sure it was done in time?"

Pyotr drew himself up, and the light glinted off his little spectacles. "Is it my integrity or that of my fellow Howlers you're questioning?" he demanded. The Howler clan prided themselves on their integrity; indeed, the whole system ran on it. *Honest as a Howler* was practically proverbial.

"I didn't mean—"

"You ought to be sure what you do mean before you go opening that big mouth of yours," Pyotr said sternly. "It was done within the day—matter of fact, the old woman at the other end started it back inside of an hour. But a long chain there and back, you've got to expect it to take some time. All fair and above board, and I'll thank you for the two and a half eagles you owe me. Then you can have your brush back."

"The thing is," Andrei said with a winning smile, "the thing is, old friend—"

"Don't call me your friend," the Howler man said unsympathetically. "People only call me friend when they're planning on cheating me, and I hope you aren't intending to do that."

"Of course not!" Andrei said hurriedly. "It's just...I don't have it on me just now."

"Don't have it at all, more like!" Pyotr eyed Andrei closely. "I hear you've been seen shopping for an item much too pretty for your neck—a not unrelated fact, eh?"

Andrei blushed, and hoped it would be put down to the nip in the air from the open door.

"Let's hope she's understanding about giving it back, then, because—"

"No! I don't ask for gifts back," Andrei said hotly. "I'll get the money some other way."

"Better make it soon," Pyotr advised. "No one owing to a Howler man can use the Howler network—"

"I know, I know!"

"—and no one's Granny is going to be getting a little something from his weekly pay without the network."

"All right! You don't need to tell me; we all know how it works!"

"No one's above the Lore, lad. I'll be seeing your two and a half eagles by tomorrow's close, then."

"Tomorrow?"

"That's what I said." Pyotr turned his attention to another customer, and Andrei turned away, his mind racing through fog.

Boba was hotly rebutting the recent arrival's suggestion that Toma's monster was no more than a tree combined with a certain quantity of recently imbibed alcohol. Howlers weren't ones to drink to excess, he said, earning nods from around the room, and certainly not while on duty. And what was more, he'd never yet heard of a tree that walked around and groaned, and he hoped he never did.

This was immediately taken up by the listeners. Groans? He hadn't mentioned groans before.

"Wordless groans," Boba said firmly. "As though it willed to speak but hadn't a tongue."

Andrei gave a wordless groan of his own, startling a nervous fellow by the door, and passed out into the street.

Two and a half eagles. By tomorrow.

❄   ❄   ❄

Late that night, Andrei lay fretting on his straw mattress, huddled under a thick scratchy blanket. If he scrunched himself down just right, he could see out the tiny window to the main bulk of the Little Palace. There was a light still burning in one of the upstairs windows. That much illumination in a room late at night—it had to be Valeska's chamber. Not that he cared a straw for her rest, but if she was still awake, Bronya was likely with her. Just over there...

Warmed by the glow of the fire and lit by half a dozen candles in silver mirrored girandoles, Valeska Kira sat in a low-backed chair and let Bronya brush her long dark hair. Bronya worked in silence, as was usual, keeping her eyes on her work. Valeska watched her in the dressing table's large mirror.

"It's a wonderful thing to be loved, Bronya," she said, breaking their accustomed silence.

"Yes, my lady," Bronya said, rather startled. The duke's arrival early in the morning with a large bouquet—at this time of year!—had resulted in a rather emotional reunion, and if Valeska had apologized for perhaps more than her fair share of the falling-out, well, it was none of Bronya's business. As long as Valeska was happy...and she'd certainly looked happy today, basking in Maxim's assiduous attentions.

"And to love in return," Valeska continued, "provided that the object of one's affections is suitably worthy."

"Yes, my lady," Bronya said, and when this did not seem enough, added "The duke is a fine man."

If there was a lack of warmth in her tone, Valeska did not heed it.

"He is...superlative," she murmured, a little smile toying round her lips. "Indeed, Bronya, I could hardly imagine a more perfectly suitable man. He is, perhaps, a little older than I, but a true lady knows how to value wisdom and experience."

"He's very handsome, too," Bronya put in, hiding a little smile of her own as she carefully parted Valeska's hair in two.

"A consideration," Valeska allowed, "though hardly a prime one. Maxim has charm, which is something more; he is diplomatic, shrewd, mannered—the perfect courtier. And who else in the kingdom even approaches me in birth? His father was a second cousin of my grandfather, the late Czar, you know."

Bronya made a tactfully indistinct murmur and began to plait the long dark hair down one side of Valeska's head. As always, she marvelled at the perfect posture which held her lady's head high, without a hint of sag or slump, from the moment she sat up in bed in the morning to the moment she laid her head on the pillow at night.

"While it is an excellent match for Maxim," Valeska said, still gazing reflectively in the mirror, "it cannot be said to be beyond his deserts. Nor do I think I am lowering myself by the match. In fact," her lips twisted wryly for a moment, "it could be said that I am fortunate in the match too. Just imagine—if Maxim had married in his early youth, I should have been condemned to spending my life alone. For who else is there that I could possibly marry?"

Bronya bound the first plait with ribbon, silently reflecting that if Maxim had married in his early youth, Valeska would probably be engaged to his son by now.

"I may be young," Valeska's voice went on, calm and even, "but I am not a fool. I know perfectly well that a lady of rank does not marry solely to please her own inclinations. A peasant girl may marry without considering the position of the man of her choice, but those born to a higher Step may not."

A laundress might very well consider the position of the man of her choice, Bronya thought, if she wanted to be Czarina, but she didn't say so. Duke Maxim wasn't the only one who knew how to be diplomatic.

"What a good thing it is," Bronya said with a warm smile, "that your inclinations run in the direction of such a suitable man."

"Fortunate indeed," Valeska said. "But I am well aware—as must you be—that not everyone shares my good fortune. I understand that one of the stableboys has been showing you rather more attention than necessary."

"The Assistant Coachman," Bronya said, not meeting Valeska's eyes in the mirror.

Valeska dismissed this distinction with an airy wave. "An outdoor servant regardless, Bronya. Beneath you."

"Beneath a child of the streets?" Bronya asked, trying to make light of the matter.

"Bronya," Valeska said severely, "you have been brought up at court. You may be a servant, but you are the personal servant of the heir to the throne. A titled husband is not out of the question. A servant smelling of horses is."

It was true, Bronya reflected as she tied the ribbon round the second plait. Andrei did smell of horses. It was a warm, dry, salty smell, a strangely comforting smell.

"I shall have the major-domo speak to him," Valeska said firmly. "You will not be troubled further with his attentions."

"Yes, my lady," Bronya said, not being in a position to say anything else. She held the thick velvet dressing gown as Valeska slipped out of it and helped her lady into bed.

"Maxim's coming again tomorrow," Valeska said. "He said he has something very particular to say to me."

Judging by the barely restrained excitement in her tone, Valeska was in no doubt as to what this very particular speech might be.

Bronya extinguished the candles one by one, leaving the

room lit only by the glowing coals in the fireplace, and slipped out the door. Her eyes were prickling. Tiredness, she told herself. Or perhaps she had extinguished the candles clumsily, and the smoke got in her eyes. Nothing to do with Valeska's well-meant and caring advice. Nothing at all.

Across the stableyard, Andrei saw the light behind the curtains slowly dim. He sighed, and settled himself to sleep. Two and a half eagles by tomorrow's close.

Two and a half...

Bronya...

Dawn came, bringing Andrei no illumination in the matter of the two and a half eagles. It did reveal to his sight yet another problem to deal with: the water in his bedroom ewer had frozen over again. Andrei sighed, shook it to be sure it was part liquid, and poked at it gingerly with his cherished silver razor. No good. He folded the razor again and slipped it into his shirt pocket, wincing at the cold biting his skin through the thin linen.

Andrei clattered downstairs to the stable block's main room. It was stuffy and smelled of horses, to be sure, but it was the one place in the building you could be sure of being warm.

"Morning, Coachman," Andrei said respectfully.

The old man coughed vigorously in his blankets. Slept here all night, by the looks of it, and with that cough it was probably just as well.

"You're late," he said.

"My water's frozen again," Andrei said, putting the ewer down by the little coal stove and taking a seat beside the coachman's makeshift bed. "That's the one thing I hate about win–" A large leathery hand clapped over his mouth.

"Never speak ill of the Lady," Coachman said in a gravelly undertone. "Never by name, you hear me?"

Andrei nodded, since speech was at present impossible. Might as well humour the superstitious old fellow.

"Good," Coachman said, and coughed long and hard, spitting at last into a small bowl beside his makeshift bed. "It's turned colder in the night, but it's crisp yet. Her Highness'll want the sleigh out this afternoon as always, and I can't be sure of keeping this cough under."

Coachman would split himself before he'd do anything so against his code as intruding his ill health on Her Imperial Highness.

"You'll have to do it," Coachman concluded, and Andrei's heart leapt. Another chance to drive something swifter than a cart-horse—and with any luck, Valeska Kira would be wanting another whip across the flats.

"And mind you do a proper job of it!" Coachman warned.

"I'll take as much care of her as if my life depended on it," Andrei said, springing to his feet.

"It probably does," the old man said dryly, but Andrei was already rattling his wash-water around the jug and dashing from the room.

Once upstairs in his own little attic room, he carefully wedged his piece of broken mirror at the right angle, worked up some foam before the water could freeze again, and, removing his now warm razor from his pocket, began most carefully to shave. And it was as he glared at his contorted half-foaming face in the mirror that it hit him. Coachman! Of course—he'd know what had happened. And he'd talk, if Andrei approached him the right way.

His shave completed, Andrei went to butter the old coachman up. He was a bit cranky to begin with, but never one to miss a chance of telling the younger generation about the good old days. With care, Andrei drew him on to the subject of the recent Lake trip, and the excitement with the road-robber. This led to a discourse on how the roads weren't kept as they used to be, nor were young carriage drivers prepared to cope with

the vicissitudes and dangers of the roads as they had been in
his younger days.

Andrei wasn't sure why they would have needed to be prepared for such eventualities in Coachman's day, if the roads
were as safe as he said, but he didn't want to miss his chance
at posing the question he'd engineered the whole conversation
for.

"Did the princess shake her fist at him, or point accusingly,
or anything like that?" Andrei asked, as casually as he could,
"or was it purely the power of her words that scared him off?"

The coachman snorted. "How would I know, lad? I don't
have eyes in the back of my head, do I?"

Well, there went that avenue of enquiry. The only person
in the Little Palace—apart from Bronya, who'd never say a
word—who was with Valeska for the whole journey, and he'd
had his back to her the whole time.

The stable door creaked, opening just far enough to allow a
pageboy to squeeze himself through the gap.

"Her Highness wants the sleigh?" Coachman asked, automatically heaving himself to his feet.

"No—it's Andrei," the pageboy said. "And not Her Highness at all."

"Make yourself clear, can't you?" Coachman demanded tes-
tily, creaking back into his chair. "Aren't pages hired for their
wits? My old cart-horse could deliver a message better."

The pageboy rolled his eyes—taking care that Coachman
could not see him do so—and tried again. "The major-domo
wants to see Andrei."

"Assistant Coachman to you," Andrei said, swapping his
grandfather's warm but shapeless coat for the more formal
jacket before following the pageboy out of the stables, across
snowy paths, and into the depths of the Little Palace's service
wing. The pageboy delivered him to the door of the major-
domo's office with a pert word, skipping away before Andrei
could mess up his perfectly smoothed hair for him.

Andrei knocked and was bidden to enter. The major-domo was sitting in a heavy chair, as befitted his station, behind a large plain table covered in papers.

"Andrei," the major-domo said, with a rather more human tone than he'd ever been heard to use in the presence of Valeska Kira. "Sit down, will you?"

Andrei did so, his mind racing. This wouldn't be about the eagles—Howlers were discreet, unless provoked to be otherwise—and it wasn't likely to be another raise in his pay. A horrible thought gnawed its way into his mind. Had someone found out about him driving Valeska so fast the other day? Was this the sack? But no, you weren't likely to get the sack for obeying your lady. Not unless the Czar had given orders to the contrary, and *that* didn't seem likely.

"Enjoying being part of a larger household?" the major-domo asked.

"Er, yes," Andrei replied cautiously. This didn't sound like the sack. Not yet, anyway...

"Particularly as it involves having more young women about the place, eh?" the major-domo said jocularly, leaning back and folding his arms across his black silk waistcoat.

Andrei grinned, and the major-domo chuckled.

"Known Her Imperial Highness's maid Bronya long?"

"A couple of years," Andrei said, stretching the truth nearly to breaking point. He'd seen her two years ago at one of the periodic servants' dances, and had managed to actually dance with her a year later, which was the first time they'd ever spoken. Not that she'd been far from his mind in the meantime.

"Mm." The major-domo leaned forward again, his expression more serious. "Fond of her?"

"Very."

The dark eyes across the table scrutinized him under bushy brows. "Plenty of other girls in the imperial service—and out of it."

"None like Bronya," Andrei said firmly.

The major-domo sighed. "Well, it may be, and it may not. The point is, she's not for you. You're not to speak to her again."

"What?" Andrei stared, his mouth hanging slightly open. The major-domo couldn't say who Andrei was and wasn't allowed to talk to, could he? Or marry, if it came to that!

"Her Highness had a word with me this morning, and bade me have a word with you. Which I have."

The major-domo stood, indicating that the conversation was over. Andrei didn't notice.

"But...doesn't she want Bronya to be happy?"

The major-domo sighed again and leaned on the table. "People have different ideas of what makes for happiness. Valeska Kira values Bronya a good deal, and she has no particular reason to think highly of you. It's a blow, I can see," he went on, his voice gentling a little. "But those in service can't always act according to their wish. You're still young. You'll get over it."

Andrei got to his feet in a daze and somehow found his way out through the door. Get over being separated from Bronya? Never! He wasn't going to change, and if Bronya wanted him, he wasn't going to let Valeska Kira stand in the way, not if she was seated on the Throne of Seven Steps and all.

He stumbled out into the little garden where he had talked with Bronya, and the cold cleared his mind in a moment. That was it. Valeska had to change her mind. He had to find a way to make her change her mind. Perhaps if he pleaded with her this afternoon—no, he wasn't exactly silver-tongued, and she wasn't easily swayed. Nor likely to listen to a servant she paid little more heed to than she did the horses he drove. But somehow... Today was his chance; he might not get another. Somehow, he had to change her mind.

The day crept slowly by, Andrei moving as in a dream around his daily duties, accepting with indifference Coachman's scolding for his unaccustomed slowness. Duke Maxim's driver arrived, delivering his master to dinner with the princess, and as the hours wore on it seemed less and less likely that the duke would depart before Valeska's accustomed drive.

Andrei's heart began to thump. What if today of all days she decided to stay in? His one chance, gone! Not that it would do him any good if he couldn't think of a way to make use of it.

No message came to countermand the standing order for the sleigh. At the usual time, the sleigh was drawn into position, and the horses led out for harnessing. And as Andrei's hands moved about the harness, checking here, buckling there, the idea came to him. His lips curved up, and his hands moved faster. He'd only need a minute spare, and with any luck the duke's presence would slow things down just a little.

Mere minutes later, three perfectly harnessed horses, white against the grimy snow, drew the delicate silvery sleigh out of the stable alley and along to the main courtyard gate. A handful of children were playing in the street as usual. Andrei grinned, slowed the horses to a walk, and beckoned to a small boy in a grubby blue jacket engaged in a slushball fight.

"Andrei!" The little boy slid expertly across the icy patches towards the sleigh. "Do I get a ride?"

"Maybe another day," Andrei said. "I'm on Her Highness's business, you know. But I've got a job for you…"

Out of the Frying Pan

The front door opened just as Andrei pulled up outside it with a little spray of ice. Just in time. Bronya eyed him narrowly as she helped Valeska down the steps. He grinned back. Valeska Kira was hanging on Duke Maxim's every word; she hadn't noticed a thing. Maxim handed her solicitously into the sleigh, her mittened fist resting like a ball in his hand. Once Bronya had her lady well tucked in with furs and lap robes, she took her own seat at Andrei's side.

"Shall we?" Duke Maxim said, his fine voice sounding clearly in the freezing air.

Andrei knew his cue and started the horses with a flourish of the whip over their heads. A good driver's whip never needed to make contact with the horses at all. He turned them neatly, circling the courtyard to leave by the same gate. The remaining boys cheered and jumped up and down on their slush heaps.

Andrei drove at a dignified pace down the larger streets, heading by degrees for the edge of town. A scattered few bowed and curtsied as they passed. Her Highness's favourite place to drive, he had been reliably informed by Coachman, was not the flats, but the low hill overlooking the palaces and huddled streets of Istvan. It was carpeted in snow, and stands of snow-capped evergreens dotted its sides.

The route Andrei chose was perhaps a little less than direct, but with any luck the two in the back would be too wrapped

up in each other to care, or even notice. He couldn't afford to
reach the hill too soon.

Valeska took a deep breath as they left the city behind, and
let it hiss slowly away. "So nice to be out of the city," she observed to her companion. "As far away as possible from *that
woman.*"

Andrei kept his eyes straight ahead, and pretended to be
deaf in the approved manner.

"Don't even demean yourself to think of her," Maxim advised.

"What else have I to think of, shut away as I am?" Valeska
asked. "Except for you, of course..."

"You'd rather I brought you court gossip?" Maxim asked
with a faintly disapproving note. "The same old feuds and
scandals, hashed over and over again? Not to mention the
chatter over the laundress's first grand ball this evening—
hardly appropriate in her condition."

"A ball?" Valeska's voice sharpened.

"But haven't you—? My dear cousin, you don't mean to tell
me you haven't been..."

"Not invited," Valeska said, in tones which made the frosty
air seem mild. "Not that I would attend such a demeaning
event if I were. He won't even see me, Maxim."

"Perhaps he is concerned for your safety," Maxim suggested,
though even he didn't seem very convinced. "Across town by
night..."

"He didn't seem so concerned for my safety when he sent
me to make the Midseason visit to the Lady's Lake," Valeska
said bitterly. "I believe he would have been content to send
me off with no protection but the old coachman, if you hadn't
volunteered to accompany me."

"As I recall," Maxim murmured, "there was no threat you
were not perfectly capable of counteracting yourself."

A tactful reference to the road-robber she'd yelled at, Andrei
guessed.

"Threat? I would have died of boredom without you," Valeska said, a little humour creeping into her voice. "No one but that mindless flirt Lala Bora to talk to!"

That must be Valeska's temporary lady-in-waiting, acting as chaperone for the trip. Bronya counting as "no one" again, Andrei supposed grimly.

"Now don't say that," Maxim scolded. "You talked to the peasants in practically every village we passed through."

"True," she conceded, "but one can hardly have an intelligent conversation with someone who goggles at one when one speaks and gets utterly tongue-tied when they try to speak themselves." She sighed. "If you didn't come to see me every day I believe I'd die of boredom even now. I'm so entirely cut off from everything, Maxim."

"So you say," Maxim said, with a sudden edge to his voice. "But you do not seem to lack for amusements. Why, you drive out every day!"

"Alone," Valeska said bleakly. "A solitary drive each afternoon is hardly the height of a social whirl, Maxim. I never meet anyone!"

"And who did you meet yesterday?" he enquired. "I hear you were at the silversmith's for well over an hour."

"How did you hear about that?" Valeska asked, a shade defensively.

"You are Her Imperial Highness Valeska Kira. You must expect your movements to be noted," Maxim said smoothly. "I note you do not answer my question as to who you met there."

"No one, Maxim! I was shopping, that is all."

"For over an hour, in the one little shop?"

"I couldn't decide what to buy. I wasn't sure what—my friend would most like."

"Mysterious friends without names," Maxim said, "and this from a lady who claims to be friendless?"

Valeska tried to laugh. "Not nameless at all, Maxim. You must trust me a little."

"Yet it would appear that you do not trust me at all," he said coldly, and began to speak in a rather distant voice about the latest trivialities of court gossip.

Gossip was a favourite recreation in the servants' hall, but Andrei had never seen the attraction: endless words about people you didn't know, weren't likely to meet, and wouldn't care for if you did. He turned his attention to the driving ahead. They were coming to a more heavily wooded part of the hill now, where the branches bent slowly down under the accumulating weight of snow, before the weight bent them too far and the snow would slip off in a miniature avalanche.

There was a quick flash of blue in the trees ahead. Andrei braced himself against the footboard. As they went under the trees, a sudden fall of snow from a branch high above dropped right in front of the sleigh.

The startled horses reared and plunged. Two tried to veer left, but the right-hand horse shied right, and then they were running wild, all thought of pace and gait forgotten. Valeska screamed, and Bronya would have been thrown backwards into the body of the sleigh had she not clutched at Andrei's arm.

This was his moment! With a calm panache which he hoped was noticeable to the pair in the back, he masterfully gathered in the reins, stood up in his seat like a charioteer of the old days, and brought the horses gradually to a halt.

He turned to his passengers, bowed as deeply as his thick coat permitted, and said in his most impressive voice, "I trust Her Highness is unharmed?" At her shaky nod he bowed again, and added "Please excuse the delay while I see to the horses."

He leapt down with a limberness the old coachman hadn't shown in years, and laid a soothing hand on the nose of each trembling horse in turn, checking over their harness as he did so.

"Maxim..." Valeska's normally autocratic voice had an unaccustomed quiver.

"Calm yourself," Maxim said. "You see the driver is entirely master of the situation."

Andrei hid a smile as he bent to check on the sleigh's ornately carved shafts. Valeska Kira had no particular reason to think well of him, eh? Well, the shafts might be a day or so closer to their eventual demise, but there was no real damage, and the Czar could certainly afford to buy his daughter a new sleigh when needed. Perhaps even a better one...

Jumping back into his place, he took up the reins and waited for orders.

"The Little Palace," Valeska said, the wobble already firmly eradicated from her voice.

"Of course," Maxim said. "Straight to the samovar—you need something hot and comforting after your shock."

Andrei took a shortcut back to the Little Palace, avoiding the possibility of running into crowds on the wider streets. As Valeska descended, Maxim and Bronya fussing round her, the small boy in the dirty blue jacket appeared from the back of the sleigh.

"Hoy! What do you think you're about, boy?" Maxim demanded sternly.

"Don't shout at the poor child," Valeska said. "Were you riding on the runners?" she asked the little boy, who snatched off his cap.

"Yes, Your...Your..."

"Highness," Bronya murmured.

"Highness," the boy finished with an abashed grin.

Valeska was by now almost smiling—an unfamiliar expression which made her look more human than usual. "It's very dangerous, and you must promise me not to do it again," she told him. "You might have been badly injured when the horses bolted."

"Oh, I didn't get on till after that," the boy said cheerfully. "Didn't I do a good job with the snow?" he asked Andrei, who glared at him. "Jumped on the branch at just the right moment, din' I?"

"Do you mean to say," broke in Maxim, "that you engineered that—that accident?"

"Wasn't an accident," the boy protested. "Nobody got hurt. Not with Andrei driving. He's the best! Don't forget," he told Andrei, "you owe me a hot pie."

A silence fell, during which the boy finally caught Andrei's eye.

"I mean, um..." he faltered, and stopped.

"Bronya," Valeska said icily, "take this child to the kitchens and see he is given a hot meal. Maxim, send this reckless fool packing. He is not to come under this roof again."

She swept into the hall and the door was closed behind her. Andrei caught Bronya's eye, and wished he hadn't. Words hovered on her lips, but Maxim broke the silence first.

"You heard Her Highness," he said. "No doubt your young friend here will see your things are sent on."

"Where?" Bronya asked bitterly.

"I don't like to see a talented young man's life blighted by one foolish decision," Maxim said easily. "Thought you'd impress the princess and gain a reward, eh? Well, we were all young and high-spirited once. Take this card to the Four Corners coach inn—I've done a favour or two for Fredek in my time; he'll take you on."

"Thank you!" Bronya said fervently.

A cab driver? Him? With a ricketty old cab and an even rickettier old nag to draw it? Andrei opened his stiff lips to protest but caught Bronya's eye again, and forced out "Thank you, sir," instead.

"No need for Her Highness to hear about it," Maxim added pleasantly. "And now I'd better be getting along to that samovar before I'm missed." He ruffled the little boy's hair. "Mind you stay off runners in future, lad."

The little boy glared at Maxim's retreating back, flattening his hair and jamming his cap back on.

Bronya drew a big breath, and Andrei braced himself.

"You fool!" she said, and it was plain that this, though delivered with a wealth of meaning, was but a preliminary salvo. "What on earth possessed you to risk the life of the heir to the Throne of Seven Steps? And her cousin as well!"

"I didn't!" Andrei protested. "I wouldn't! They were perfectly safe—they aren't even bruised!"

"Andrei's the best coachman in the world," the little boy said, clearly anxious to regain his lost favour.

"You stay out of this," Bronya snapped, and the little boy closed his mouth and opened his eyes very wide. "He's not a coachman at all, thanks to his tricks!"

"Bronya, I only did it for you!"

"For *me*?" she said incredulously. "How is—"

"So Valeska Kira would think better of me—not forbid me to talk to you. See you. Court you," he added despondently.

"You thought this—" Bronya broke off, apparently lost for words. But not for long. "You thought *this* would persuade Valeska you'd make a good husband for me?"

The little boy's eyes grew rounder.

"You don't *think!*" Bronya went on. "You're reckless and foolhardy and—"

"Bronya—" Andrei tried.

"Don't you Bronya me! A woman marries to gain a husband, not to have one more child about the place!"

"Marry me, and I'll treat you like a princess," Andrei tried desperately.

Bronya snorted. "You already did treat me like a princess—nearly broke her neck and mine," she retorted. "All I want is a man who'll be responsible," she continued in calmer tones. "Prove you can take responsibility and I might reconsider. After all," she added, "a princess is allowed to set her suitor a challenge, isn't she? There's yours: grow up."

"Ooo," the little boy began, but retired precipitately behind Bronya's skirts when he saw the look in Andrei's eye.

"Time you were packing your things," Bronya went on. "Oh, and you'd better have this necklace back too," she added, her hand going to the collar of her coat.

Andrei hesitated, but only for a moment. "It was a gift," he said. "Keep it."

As he started the horses back towards the stables, face grim, a small snowball exploded on his shoulder.

"Hey mister," a little voice called, "don't forget you still owe me a hot pie!"

❄   ❄   ❄

The samovar was just coming to the boil as Maxim entered the drawing room. Once the waiting maid had filled the teapot, Valeska bid her depart. "Duke Maxim will pour."

"Anything for a drop of something hot inside me," Maxim said agreeably. The maid bobbed and disappeared. The tea duly poured, Maxim settled back in his chair, stretching out his long legs to the fire.

"Now that we're alone," Valeska said demurely, "wasn't there something you wanted to say to me?"

Maxim looked blank, and the hint of a frown crept across his fine forehead.

"I remember you saying yesterday," Valeska continued, keeping her eyes on the delicate cup carefully held between her two little fists, "that you had something very particular to say to me."

"So I did," Maxim said, his voice low and resonant. He set the cup down.

"Yet you haven't said it," Valeska said, now looking at his cup instead of hers.

"Do such thoughts need to be given utterance," Maxim asked softly, "when you understand me so well?"

Valeska's cheeks blossomed pink.

"You know what I would say," Maxim said. "You understand me as none of the shrill and shallow court ladies have ever done."

"Oh, Maxim." Valeska looked up with a brief and brilliant smile, but her lids drooped again.

"You do not seem as joyful as I had thought you might," he said, a hint of reserve creeping into his voice.

"Oh, I am! But...when? My father..."

"This must remain our secret for the present," Maxim said, taking her cup and setting it aside so as to be able to take her hands in his. "You must trust me to open the subject with your father when the time seems right. I would not, of course, do anything to jeopardize your position. You know that. He must give permission—what reason could he have to object?"

Valeska sighed. "No reason, of course, you are right. Yet..."

"Yet what? You do not trust me?"

"I do! But I have waited so long to be happy. How can I believe at last that my waiting is at an end?"

Maxim bent forward and kissed her hands. "How can you doubt it? After all I have done—"

He broke off as the door opened and Bronya entered.

"Oh, I beg your pardon, my lady, sir," she said, blushing, and began to withdraw.

Maxim was already on his feet and standing casually with an arm draped along the mantelpiece.

"Bronya!" Valeska called, as the door was about to close.

"My lady?"

"Has that person been removed from the premises?"

"Yes, my lady."

"Good. You may go. I will ring when you are wanted."

Bronya bobbed a curtsy and left, closing the door carefully behind her. She ought to rejoice in her lady's happiness, she told herself as she walked slowly away. At least someone was happy... Her hand went almost automatically to where the silver snowflake lay hidden under her dress, and she sighed.

❄   ❄   ❄

Andrei huddled into his grandfather's old coat as the thin wind blew occasional stray snowflakes down his neck. He tried not to think about the thickly furred coat of the true coachman; tried to ignore the creak of the shabby sleigh beneath him.

The line of sleighs leading to the Czar's palace started and stopped, started and stopped. The single horse under Andrei's command huffed, a little white cloud in the chill air. The fat old mare wasn't that bad a horse, Andrei told himself—as long as he didn't compare her with the imperial beasts.

He was lucky, he supposed: having Duke Maxim's patronage meant he was spared the worst horse with the worst sleigh which as new boy he would otherwise be doomed to driving— if he was allowed to drive at all. Manure didn't shovel itself.

Still, he was never going to strike Valeska Kira as a suitable husband for Bronya while he was driving fourth-rate nobles to parties. Anyone who was anyone had their own equipage, and by the looks of it, every single one of them was in this line. Andrei's horse clopped on as the sleigh in front moved up.

Andrei sighed. Here he was, practically the best driver in the land, and his horse could do the job without him. And his neck was cold. And that blasted packet of itching powder had come open in his pack and spilled all over his spare shirt—which he'd been told to put on before he went to collect the fourth-rate noble. He squirmed uncomfortably.

Still, there was one comfort: things were so bad for him now there was nowhere to go but up.

At last they creaked into the palace courtyard—more or less a square in its own right—and came to a halt at the foot of the grand stair. A footman handed the extremely minor nobleman out with a flourish.

"Over there," another footman directed, and Andrei nodded, followed the line of empty sleighs around the edge of the square, and parked up. Jumping down, he pulled the blanket off the floor of the sleigh and draped it over his horse. No sense in them both freezing.

The mare whickered in a pleased manner and tried to nuzzle Andrei's neck. As her chin was still covered in the frozen condensation of her breath, this friendly gesture was less than warmly received, but Andrei dodged her nose and huddled up against her neck for warmth. At least he was out of the wind now, and was free until his fourth-rate passenger left the ball—at whatever hour that might be.

Around him, drivers were settling in for a long night, some rolling themselves in blankets for a bit of shut-eye, others bringing out playing cards or small flasks. Andrei wasn't interested. Not that he minded the risk, but if you wanted to be a successful gambler, you had to be good, and to be good you had to work at it. Andrei was only interested in being good at one thing, and cards wasn't it. And if you weren't going to be good at something, why bother with it at all?

There was a good deal of shop talk, in which Andrei joined, gritting his teeth against the inevitable jokes about his change of employment.

"I like your horse," one liveried fellow said, choking himself on a mouthful of liquor at the thought of his forthcoming witticism. "Was she your grandmother's?"

"Laugh all you want, Pavel," Andrei retorted, "I'm still a better driver than you." He was. And if he got a chance to prove himself, there was hope for him yet. Nowhere to go but up...

"Oh, really? Going to win races with that old nag, are you?" Pavel jeered.

"I didn't say I had a better horse, you cloth-eared idiot," Andrei said. "Give me my pick of horse and sleigh and I'll beat you on any course you choose."

The huddled grooms and drivers jeered at Pavel in his turn,

who turned red and shoved his flask back in his pocket.

"I get first choice," he demanded.

"You'll need it," Andrei said. He knew Pavel. An eye for the flashy, certainly, but it wasn't the look of your equipage that won you the race. Pavel wouldn't be able to pick a winning horse if he waited at the finish line.

"Twice around the courtyard," Pavel said with an unsteady wave of his arm. "Finish line at the foot of the stairs, where that band of light is."

The great front doors stood open, their gold trim leaping and flickering in the flaming torchlight which poured out in a stream across the cold dark courtyard.

"Go on, then," Andrei said. "Choose your team." There wasn't a driver present who wouldn't loan his equipage for a race like this. Not unless his horses weren't up to it, and then he'd be taking heat from the other drivers for bringing them out. Especially on a night like this.

He checked on the old mare, who seemed to have settled into a contented nap. He didn't need to watch Pavel's strutting up and down selecting his sleigh—he was pretty sure he knew which rig Pavel would go for, in any case, and he knew for certain which one he'd choose himself.

Pavel made up his mind at last, choosing, as Andrei had suspected, the matched whites of one of the more ostentatious young noblemen—one of the Czar's racing "lads". They weren't bad horses, to be sure, but he knew for a fact that the gelding on the left had been picked to make a set with the others. He looked like a thousand silver eagles in the light of the moon, but this was a race, not a beauty parade.

"I'll take Tibor's bays," Andrei said, and Pavel sneered.

"I'm not surprised the princess fired you," he said, "with low-class taste like that. Tibor doesn't even drive for a noble!"

It was true that Tibor's rig was, in comparison with Pavel's choice, extremely plain, being made of light wood with practically no ornamentation. Pavel's chosen sleigh, on the other hand, could have passed for the carriage of the moon, so encrusted was it with silver. Which, naturally, added a great deal of weight. It was no contest—Andrei could win this sitting backwards with his eyes closed.

They took one turn around the courtyard side by side and slowly, to warm the horses and check the way was clear. The last of the fashionably late had made their appearance, and the courtyard was left only to the drivers. The Czar's head coachman took it upon himself to drop his sash as a signal to start, and they were off.

Andrei looked back as he completed the first circuit of the courtyard. Sure enough, the gelding was giving Pavel more trouble than he knew what to do with. It was hardly even a race any more, for all Pavel's shouting and cracking of whip. Andrei eased Tibor's horses—no sense returning them blown—and grinned.

No sooner had he turned the last corner than he got to his feet on the driver's seat, turned around with the reins behind his back, and bowed graciously to the crowd of drivers and the sweating, cursing Pavel. The band of light flashed across Andrei's face and he braced himself, rising from his bow as he reined in the horses.

Showing off, yes, but you never knew who might be watching, who might be impressed. He had to take—or make—any chance he could get.

Movement caught his eye above: the glazed inner doors swung open, and a majestic figure stepped forth, a strain of music floating around him. The Czar? No—the bulging uniforms at the door weren't saluting. The figure turned, and Andrei recognized in his magnificent ensemble the uniform of the imperial major-domo.

"You there," the major-domo boomed, crooking a finger at Andrei.

"Me?" Andrei asked, adding a finger pointing at himself in case his meaning was unclear.

The major-domo nodded impatiently. "Bring your whip," he added as Andrei looked about for a place to stow it. "And get a move on—His Imperial Majesty is calling for you."

This seemed unlikely—had he been mistaken for someone else?—but he didn't argue. Hopping down, he handed the reins to Tibor and ran up the grand stair, reaching the top just as Pavel finally reached the foot and wrestled the restive horses to a halt.

Andrei followed the major-domo through the great doors and into a world of dreams. Gold and glass everywhere—or was that crystal? Andrei wasn't clear on the distinction, but everything he looked at gleamed or glittered or both. And it was blissfully warm after the chill of the midnight square, with roaring fires in every room they passed through and galaxies of candelabra tipped with fire overhead.

Wooden-faced footmen watched them pass; occasional ball attendees drew out of their way with anxious faces. A qualm crept into Andrei's heart. What if it wasn't a mistaken identity? What if the Czar *was* calling for him—calling for him as the near assassin of his daughter? Nothing like a bit of danger to make the heart grow fonder... Andrei's skin prickled with goosebumps despite the warmth of the grand rooms through which they passed. All it would take was a word from the duke and he was dead meat.

But then why did the major-domo insist on him bringing his whip? An unpleasant image appeared in his mind's eye, of the Czar flogging him with his own whip—in person!—before handing him over to the executioners.

Andrei summoned his courage to ask the major-domo why he had been called for, but his mouth was too dry and no sound emerged. Being personally flogged by the Czar was a kind of distinction, he supposed, but scarcely the sort he'd been hoping for. And with his luck, the Czar would just hand the whip to one of his footmen, and where was the distinction in that?

The music grew louder, and they entered what could only be

a ballroom, full of dozens of dancers swirling—with painfully tense expressions. Thus proving that being noble didn't mean you had more fun, Andrei supposed. As they passed down the great room, Andrei caught sight of the Czar's big red bearded face over the heads of the crowd. Sitting down, but still towering over everyone. That was thrones for you.

As they arrived at the foot of the throne's seven great steps, the major-domo coughed genteelly and bowed as deeply as his impressive belly allowed.

"A driver, as requested, Your Majesty," the major-domo said.

Andrei caught only a glimpse of the upper steps before he too was bowing deeply. His relatively thin coat formed no obstacle to the deepest reverence, and his head went down almost to the stone step which formed the base of the whole awe-inspiring stair. His heart pounded with relief. *A* driver. Not *the* driver. He might survive the night after all.

"You've been all night about it," said Czar Kiril, his words carried on a wave of alcohol fumes.

The major-domo didn't argue the point.

"Are you loyal to your Czar?" Kiril demanded of Andrei.

"Yes, Your Majesty!" Andrei hastily replied, bowing again for good measure.

"Stop going up and down like that," the Czar complained. "You're making me feel sick."

Andrei stood bolt upright, his eyes fixed respectfully on the gem-encrusted step on which the throne itself stood. Head height for him, being a tall lad, but also the level of the Czar's enormous highly-polished boots. The last thing he wanted was to be blamed for the Czar getting dizzy and falling off one of the cliff-like sides of the Seven Steps. It was a long way down.

"You have your whip?" the Czar continued.

"Yes, Your Majesty!"

"Good! Take it, and flog this insolent wretch to within an inch of his life. An inch!" the Czar cried, flinging out an arm. A knot of attendants parted, revealing the figure of Duke Maxim.

"Sir," Maxim began evenly, but the Czar was not having it.

"You know where she is—the mother of my son!" he bawled down from his perch, veins bulging on his reddened neck. "Miss her own ball? Never! It is some evil you have plotted!"

"I must beseech Your Majesty to remain calm," Maxim was saying, in the teeth of all the evidence. "Think of your... health."

"You dare!" screamed the Czar, leaping to his feet. And then, before Andrei's horrified eyes, he changed. Tall already, he reared his head to at least eight feet, his skin going a darker red and becoming thick and leathery. Bony protrusions sprouted around his face, but the eyes that looked out of that dreadful face were still horribly human—and so was his voice.

"Flog him!" the great red mouth cried.

Andrei staggered forward, thanks to a discreet shove from the major-domo. A couple of burly footmen took Maxim by the arms and turned him away from the Czar.

Befuddled with terror, Andrei wondered briefly why everyone seemed to be carrying on as usual—even the orchestra kept playing, the dancers carrying on their travesty of a society ball. Carrying on as usual. Perhaps it was, Andrei thought with a shudder, and pulled himself together.

No use hoping this was all a dream. His imagination might have furnished the great hall at a pinch, but all those ladies' dresses? Never. He braced himself. To flog one's patron was unforgivable, but to disobey the Czar of the Seven Steps— impossible.

Andrei took a deep breath, and carefully placed his feet, estimating the distance. A little closer—no, a little further. He coiled his whip, shook it out, coiled it again. Another deep breath, another sidle to allow space for the backswing.

"Now!" the Czar-monster roared, planting one of his great black boots down on the golden step.

Andrei let the whip's long lash fall loosely against Maxim's back. His arms were weak with terror, and if there was one way to escape this nightmare alive, it was to flog the duke so lightly that he would take no harm and be merciful in return. But then, what noble alive would forgive the shame of being beaten by one so many ranks below? Andrei gathered the whip in, hands shaking.

"Harder!" the Czar-monster bellowed, descending another couple of steps to stand on copper. "Or are you in league with this traitor too?"

Hoping the duke's coat and long satin waistcoat would provide a measure of padding—fortunately the Czar hadn't ordered him stripped for the whipping—Andrei struck a tiny bit harder.

The Czar-monster uttered a roar of rage, plunged down the remaining steps in one great stride, and snatched the whip out of Andrei's hand. "Conspirator!" he shouted, flecks of foam falling to his beard. "Is this how you obey your Czar?"

Andrei backed away, eyeing the wall of glass doors which ran down one side of the ballroom. A quick review of his path through the palace suggested they opened eastwards—far from the old mare, but he could get into the gardens...

"Traitor!" the Czar-monster repeated, advancing on Andrei with the whip.

"No!" Andrei cried desperately.

"Treacherous liar! Kill him!"

Andrei was staggered for a moment. He couldn't possibly kill the duke! But as another squad of muscular footmen moved towards him, he revised his opinion. It wasn't the duke's death Czar Kiril had in mind. Definitely, time to visit the gardens.

Andrei ducked and swerved onto the dance floor, dodging through the still grimly dancing couples. The ladies screamed as the footmen ploughed through the formations behind him.

Flinging open the first door he reached, Andrei plunged into the night, the cold air seizing his throat in a gasp. The light flooding through the windows behind him revealed a wide terrace, which gave on...darkness. An iced-up fountain loomed beyond, its base lost somewhere in the shadows below.

Hoping very much it wasn't too deep a drop, Andrei vaulted over the edge and landed heavily in a rather prickly hedge. Scrambling free, he spared a moment to look behind him as he ran. The footmen did not want to spoil their lovely uniforms, it appeared—they were detouring via the stairs.

He smiled smugly to himself, dodged round the fountain, turned north—he must get away from Istvan at all costs—tripped over a low shrubby thing, staggered, recovered, and ran on, the gravel walks and frosted garden beds crunching and squeaking beneath his boots. They'd never catch him now. All those muscles might look impressive, but they weren't built for speed.

From the terrace, Kiril's great voice bellowed "Archers!" and Andrei stopped smiling. There was no outrunning an arrow. He ran faster, the chill air slicing at his windpipe as he gasped for breath. Must get away before the archers assemble...

Far too soon, there came the twang of bowstrings, the whistle of a flight of arrows, and then a sudden pained cry. Andrei was pleased to find it wasn't his. A quick look back showed him the terrace ablaze with light and lined with archers, the Czar-monster's head still towering above them.

Closer—uncomfortably closer—were two footmen hauling a third to his feet. There was an arrow in his arm, and for a moment Andrei thought they'd mistaken the unfortunate front-runner for himself.

But the Czar, it seemed, was not deceived.

"After him!" he roared, in a voice that split the night.

A moment later came the graunching sound of stone on stone, followed by a series of deep, earthshaking thumps. Andrei didn't look around. Then came a chorus of surprised yells from the party of footmen. Andrei didn't look around. The thumping continued, and did he dare suppose it was drawing nearer?

Andrei looked, disbelieved, looked again, and wished he hadn't. He put on a fresh turn of speed, his hair doing its level best to stand on end.

Thumping through the gardens behind him was the large stone fountain.

Homeward Bound

Even supernatural terror can only drive the body on for so long. Andrei's limbs shook, his gut twisted, and his back sagged into a bowed shamble. He reached a low parapet, rolled himself untidily over it, and dropped his full height or more into longish grass.

This must be the border between the extensive palace gardens and the parklands beyond. Outside of town by anyone's measure. With any luck, that fountain thing would go no further.

Andrei braced himself for an attempt to get to his feet and rolled over with a groan. The base of the fountain slammed into the ground beside him. Andrei was flung into the air and landed asprawl on the rim of the fountain's lower bowl, fetching himself a crack on the head as he did so. The stars rushed at his head, and then the darkness was absolute.

There was a sickening jerk and a blaze of light, and he was conscious again. He was lying in a fountain, mercifully dry, and his head hurt, and everything kept moving, and what on earth had he been doing last night? He peered muzzily over the lip of the bowl at the view lurching past, and it all came back to him.

With a turn of speed he found impressive in hindsight, Andrei launched himself out of the fountain and was away across the snow-dusted fields, deserted in their winter sleep. If he could just reach that line of trees...

He did, and promptly emptied his stomach underneath the nearest. He couldn't tell the thumping from the pounding in his head, but they both seemed to be subsiding. Eyes closed, he let his head drop to rest on the carpet of pine needles under the neighbouring tree. Relief washed over him, followed by a splash of icy water.

Andrei sat up with a yell, and clutched his head with another, much quieter, one. There before him stood the fountain. He could see behind it the circular impressions left as it changed course across the fields. He frowned at it, and tried to think.

"You're following me," he said at last. "Because *he* told you to?" His skin crawled at the thought of the enemy he'd made last night. *Enemies.*

He frowned. "Wait a minute!" He straightened up suddenly and wished he hadn't. Subsiding back against the tree, tenderly holding his head together, he eyed the fountain suspiciously.

"You caught me last night," he said cautiously, "but you didn't take me back to *him.*"

Inasmuch as it was possible for a fountain to look embarrassed, this one did. The stone wreaths decorating the upper bowls seemed to droop bashfully. The great muddied foot of the fountain even seemed to scuffle in the dirt, like a small boy being scolded.

"You just kept going," Andrei continued, since the fountain didn't appear to be trying to cart him off again. "For miles!" he added, realizing that the shadow in the blue distance was the central plateau on which the capital stood.

"Almost as though..." Was that even possible? "...you were running away?"

The fountain stopped shuffling—froze, in fact.

"What makes an imperial fountain want to run away from home...er, garden?" Andrei asked, feeling more ridiculous every moment.

The fountain leaned vertiginously towards the first tree in the line, spewing a mix of water and ice from its upper reaches to lie melting on the ground next to Andrei's own mess.

Andrei stared, baffled.

The fountain righted itself, then leaned back slightly. An arc of water came out amidships and left a wet mark down the side of the tree, just like—

"Oh!" Andrei said, and the arc of water stopped. "So... you're running away because people piss on you? In you? And puke," he added as the fountain briefly repeated its first performance. "Fair enough."

He leaned his aching head against the tree and considered the possibility that the crack on his head was harder than he'd realized. Here he was, sitting under a tree in the middle of who knew where, talking to a chunk of moving masonry about the trials of being a garden fountain.

On the other hand, he had seen the fountain moving before the crack on the head. And that wasn't all he had seen. Andrei couldn't stop his mind replaying the transformation he had witnessed, and he shuddered. No wonder Bronya was worried. There was something strange going on in the imperial family. Something very, very wrong. But what could he do about it? Nothing. He was a driver, not a magic expert.

Except...he wasn't a driver. You can't be a driver without a rig, and here he was with nothing to drive but his own two feet. And where was he going to find decent employment, now that the Czar himself—and Duke Maxim, most likely—were out for his blood?

Suddenly feeling exposed despite the windbreak at his back, Andrei got to his feet and started along the line of trees edging the field.

Thump.

He turned. The fountain wasn't moving, but it had moved— that was clear from the broken branches of the trees.

"Stop following me," he said, and a few paces later, "Shoo! Go home! I mean, go—anywhere you like, just stop following me!"

Thump.

"After him!" the Czar had said, and after him it appeared this fountain intended to go. He supposed he should be thankful that the Czar hadn't thought to add "Bring him back."

What was he going to do? Even if he could elude the Czar, no one was going to hire a driver who came with a stone nightmare at his heels. Andrei heaved up a sigh from the soles of his boots. He was going to have to go home to Granny.

She was a healer, and that was a bit like magic, wasn't it? Maybe she would know what to do, and at the very least, she'd hide him from the Czar. Who, for all Andrei knew, was having his soldiers follow the trail left by the fountain in the night. Andrei went hot and cold all over at the thought and broke into a weak run.

He hadn't run very far, however, before he realized that he didn't know which way to go. He had to find out where he was—which meant he'd have to talk to someone without them noticing the fountain following him round like an oversized dog. He groaned, and then, because there was no other way, he went on.

Half a day later, Andrei had learned a number of things. He knew his chances of outrunning the blasted thing (none), the odds of being able to outmanoeuvre his pursuer (also none), what happened to a modestly-sized tree which the fountain landed on (kindling), and the exact pitch at which a farm girl surprised by a thundering fountain screams (quite remarkably high).

Having exhausted himself running away from whoever might respond to the farm girl's scream, Andrei found himself forced to bargain.

"Look," he said, still bent double and wheezing, "you're going to have to stop scaring people, or I'll starve to death, and what will you do then?"

The fountain did not appear to be overly concerned with this possibility.

"You'll have to stay by my graveside forever," Andrei improvised, "and the next thing you know drunkards will be pissing in your bowl again."

The fountain uttered a low, gurgling growl, like a bear gargling ice.

"Try to keep at a distance," Andrei said, "and if anyone sees you, you freeze, understand?"

A little blip of water shot up from the tip of the fountain and down again. Andrei decided to take this as agreement.

"Well, mind you do," he said in his best imitation of Bronya's manner with the pageboys, and walked on.

He tried not to reckon up the number of meals he'd missed. No breakfast, no lunch, nothing warm in his belly to shield him against the chill. His coat wasn't thick enough, either. But at least his feet were warm. Get yourself some good boots and thick socks, Granny always said, and you'd be right. His boots were the best he could buy, and the socks were knit from the thickest wool he could find, from hardy grey northern sheep. One of the grooms had teased him for knitting, "like a girl," and been bawled out by Coachman.

"If you'd learned your hands to knit, maybe you wouldn't be such a clumsy clod with your tools!" the old man had snapped. Coachman had always knitted his own socks, it turned out, until the rheumatism had stiffened his hands beyond any use but holding the reins. Andrei smiled at the memory, and tramped on.

Fortunately, it was not long before he spotted another sign of human habitation. As he drew nearer, he saw how battered the buildings were, and his hopes cooled. Battered could so easily mean abandoned, and abandoned meant no food. But as he entered the yard, he heard noises in the ramshackle barn, which resolved themselves into a heavily-built man carrying a pitchfork.

"Good day to you!" Andrei said, with all the renewed cheer of a hungry man faced with the prospect of food.

"What was that thumping?" the farmer asked, eyeing him suspiciously.

"Thumping?" Andrei affected a blank look, but the farmer was no longer looking at him. Andrei turned to see the fountain in the corner of the yard. He'd told the blasted thing to keep its distance!

"What's that?" the farmer demanded.

"It appears to be a fountain," Andrei said. "Quite a taste you have in—"

"What's it doing there?"

"It does seem odd," Andrei agreed, the risky joy barrelling through his blood. "I would have put it in the centre of the yard myself—but the corner you've chosen is fine too," he added hastily.

There was a long and perilous silence while the farmer made up his mind.

"It was the wife's idea, that," he said, to Andrei's relief. Because who would admit that he'd never noticed a nine-foot-high three-bowl fountain in his yard before? Mad talk. "What brings you here?" he added gruffly.

"Lost my bearings, I'm afraid," Andrei said cheerily. "I was heading to Monik and..." From the look on the man's face he knew he was nowhere near home.

"You *are* lost," the farmer said. "Quickest way is south back to Istvan and out from there."

"Between you and me and the fountain," Andrei confided, "I'd rather avoid town altogether."

The man's face darkened in suspicion.

"A matter of a lady I'd rather not cross paths with just now," Andrei added, thinking of Bronya. She'd skin him.

The farmer broke into a rusty chuckle. "Heh, heh! Young feller like you! I bet there is. You'll need to bear southwest, then, I'd say. You'll reach a village each day if you keep up a good pace, and folk are hospitable. We had some crazy young noblewoman come past just yesterday—grand looker, she was, peeking through the grill on one of them ancient old boxed-in sleighs they used to have, back when proper ladies never stuck their heads out of doors. Her man came and asked for a bite and water for the horses—we were glad to oblige. Will you take a bite before you go on? The wife'll have it ready any minute now."

To this Andrei readily assented, being rather hollow about the middle, and he paid for his meal with all the city news he could think of that wasn't downright seditious. "By the by, the Czar's become a monster" wasn't the sort of gossip simple country people wanted to hear, and with the Czar's portrait literally hanging over him, he didn't dare. He didn't mention the Czarina's disappearance, either. The mere fact of her being Czarina was scandal enough without adding unexplained disappearances.

When they emerged, the fountain was gone. The farmer kept looking at the corner where it had stood, blinking, squinting, looking away and then back again.

"Did you... Was there..." he began, and fell silent.

"Was there what?" his wife asked.

"Nothing," he muttered, looking sideways.

"Well, I'll be on my way," Andrei said cheerfully. "Many thanks for the meal."

"And to you for the news," the woman said. "It's not often we get it so fresh. Lady be light on you!" She elbowed her husband, who tore his eyes away from the fountainless corner.

"Eh? Oh, yes. Lady b'light," he said absently, his eyes already sliding back.

The traditional winter benediction. You didn't hear it so much in the towns, Andrei thought as he set off to the southwest with a new spring in his step. His belly was full, his way was plain, his hopes were high and—thump.

With a sigh, he turned. "Very clever," he said, and the fountain looked smug. "And since you can obviously move quietly when you want to, how about not jarring the spine out of my body with every step you take?"

The fountain looked embarrassed again, and crept forward in what almost passed for a glide as Andrei walked on.

He sighed. Winter was all very well when it was outside and you were inside, in a warm hay-scented stable full of horses—or even bundled up in furs, racing along in a sleigh, but there was nothing in this muddy icy mess to be enjoyed. This was no more than a trudge, and a slow, dragging trudge at that, with the mud on his boots growing heavier with every step.

"Stupid winter," Andrei muttered rebelliously. Coachman wasn't here to know or care.

The thin sunlight faded out as the clouds built up across the wide emptiness of the sky. Cold earth, dark sky, and thin biting flakes on a sharp wind between. Andrei huddled into his inadequate coat, and trudged on.

The hair on his neck started to stand on end—and was that a beard coming? At least he had his father's razor in his pocket still. He patted it, which gave him some comfort, but nothing could erase the chill in the wind, or the unnerving knowledge that somewhere close behind him was an enchanted fountain that could crush him like a bug—and now he couldn't hear how close it was.

Andrei wasn't a nervous type, but the memory of last night's abduction was hard to shake. The fountain could just scoop him up at any moment, and... He stopped dead, his mind sparkling. Well, after all, why not? He was the greatest driver in the land, was he not?

He spun on his heel, repressed a yelp at finding himself nearly nose-to-wreath with the middle bowl, and stepped backwards with what he hoped was dignity.

"Look," he said in his most persuasive tone, "if you're going wherever I'm going anyway, do I really need to walk?"

✳   ✳   ✳

Valeska Kira paced up and down the elegant drawing room, back and forth, back and forth, as Bronya read aloud.

"Was that a sleigh?" Valeska demanded suddenly, cutting across Bronya's smooth flow of words. "Why isn't there a sitting room at the front?"

Rightly deciding that this was not a question to which her lady required an answer, Bronya remained silent. Valeska hurried to her favourite chair, placing herself for the most pleasing appearance as the visitor arrived.

The door slammed open.

"Father!"

Not the guest she was hoping for, Bronya noted.

"Where is she?" the Czar demanded.

"I haven't the least idea what you're talking about," Valeska said.

"My Svetlana did not come to her ball. She has vanished— completely!"

"I'm not surprised she left," Valeska observed.

"You know where the Czarina is!" the Czar growled. "You did this, as you did—" He caught sight of Bronya. "Other things," he finished darkly.

"I have nothing to reproach myself with," Valeska said, ostentatiously turning her head to gaze out the window to the garden. "Nor would I demean myself to have dealings with that woman. I don't know how Maxim could even bear to speak to her."

"You were in it together, then!" her father roared. "You and that rat have plotted together to steal my woman!"

Valeska merely yawned delicately, one dainty fist held politely to her lips.

"My son's mother!" the Czar shouted, stamping his booted foot on the flowered carpet.

Valeska's head turned back from the window with an almost audible snap. "Your son..."

"I know she carries a son," the Czar said proudly, and some of the tension left Valeska's figure.

"So you have been plotting with that degraded son of a golden milksop," he continued. "I knew it! I should have had him flogged harder!"

Valeska went pale. "You did what? How could you!" She rose. "Let me go to him!"

Kiril laughed. "Good luck finding your precious rat! He's gone to hide in some hole. But I'll find him. And her! I won't be robbed of my son. My *heir*," he added. He flung out of the room, slamming the door behind him with such force that the mirrors rattled and a small china figurine toppled off the mantelpiece, smashing on the marble hearth below.

"Bronya," Valeska said in a strangled voice, turning to look out the window again, "call my major-domo. I want all the men of my household out searching for the duke. My father must not find him. Quickly, now!"

❄   ❄   ❄

Andrei left the approach till after dark. He'd had enough in the last three days of dealing with people's reactions to his stone companion—an enjoyable game of wits at first, but one he quickly tired of—and he could find his way to Granny's house blindfolded at midnight in a snowstorm if he had to. Bad enough being seen with the stony lump in strange villages; he didn't need funny looks round his childhood home.

He slipped down the unlit stone-paved road, aware of the fountain only as a surprisingly gentle tapping of stone on stone behind him. He knocked on the old familiar door, and waited. Granny Sonechka was used to being knocked awake by people whose emergencies arrived at an untimely hour. She slept with one ear open, she always used to say.

Footsteps sounded within, and Andrei automatically stood up straight (Granny was a stickler for not slouching), and prepared to try to explain himself. The door opened, just the width of a face. An unfamiliar, sullen face, with thick black hair hanging low over suspicious eyes. A face much higher than he'd expected. And younger—a few years younger than Andrei himself, even. The greeting died on his lips, but his mouth stayed open. Who was this girl? He groped for words, but she beat him to it.

"Is your wife in labour?" she asked coolly, and this completely derailed him.

"What?" he yelped. "I—um, no—I—I don't have a wife." A horrible thought assailed him. What if this *was* Granny, dreadfully altered like the Czar? But she clearly didn't recognize him...

"We don't do love philtres," the girl was saying, in that same level, practical tone.

Andrei blushed to the roots of his hair.

"Or beard elixir," she added. "You just have to wait for it to grow in."

"No, I—I shave," Andrei protested.

"Then what are you here for?" she asked, the hint of suspicion darkening on her face again. The movement of her shoulder suggested she was reaching for the stout stick Granny always prudently kept behind the door.

He couldn't just ask her if she was his grandmother under a curse. She'd definitely whop him then, Granny or not. As he struggled for what to say and words to say it with, a sharp voice called from within.

"Who *is* that?"

Andrei almost melted on the doorstep with relief. "It's me, Granny," he said, finding words at last.

The door opened wider to reveal a round little woman bundled in shawls. Her dark eyes snapped.

"And what do you think you're doing keeping my girl standing at the door half the night, with the cold rushing in?" she demanded. "Get yourself in and lean down so I can get some warm back in my hands boxing your ears."

Andrei slipped through the door and leaned against it. He had to tell her now, get it over with.

"Granny," he said, "I need your help."

"Thought as much," she said, waddling slightly as she made her way back towards her chair by the fire.

"There's something in the street you need to see. Before anyone else does," he added, and she stopped.

Turning, she fixed him with a glittering eye. "What have you brought on my house, boy?"

"Um...I think you'd better come and see."

"Hmpf," she said, but he'd caught her interest, he could tell. "Yurisa, girl, get my outdoor things."

The sullen girl went to the hook behind the door and took down an ancient garment like a blanket with a hood. This was Granny's invariable winter wear when out on her rounds, and the pockets of its inner recesses were said by the village children to contain dreadful mysteries which would turn your blood to ice.

Granny made a great to-do about wrapping herself up against the cold, though Andrei knew perfectly well she could be out of the house in seconds if an emergency summoned. This was vaguely reassuring: if Granny wasn't in a hurry it couldn't be that bad. At last she declared herself ready. Andrei opened the door and she toddled out, followed by Yurisa with a lantern and Andrei himself.

"Well?" Granny demanded. "Brought the bad weather with you, I see. Anything else?"

"Over there," Andrei said unhappily.

"Lift the lantern, girl," Granny commanded, and the light fell faintly onto the stone fountain where it stood just down the road. "I see. Don't tell me you've bought it and had it delivered, because even you aren't that much of a fool when it comes to money."

"It's worse than that," Andrei said miserably. Somehow he'd hoped that it wouldn't be there for Granny to see; that somehow she would have fixed it, just by being there. "It—it follows me." As much evidence as he had of this over the last few days, he still felt a fool saying it.

Granny turned and scrutinized him. "This some sort of a joke?"

"No!"

"Prove it," the apprentice-girl said.

They both looked at her, and she ducked her head so the great heavy fringe hid her eyes again.

"Fair call," said Granny. "Prove it."

So Andrei walked down the road towards the nearest house, thanking his lucky stars that the healer's house was traditionally set well away from the rest of the village by its large and mysterious garden. As he returned, he fancied he could see a resemblance between the two women. Not their faces, but the expression they both shared: not fear, not quite curiosity, but a sort of scientific interest. It came to him that he was the patient, exhibiting his symptoms.

"Mm," said Granny as he drew near again. "Well now, there's a thing I've not seen before. What do you think, girl?"

"You could try smashing it," Yurisa said.

"No!" Andrei was surprised at the strength of his reaction. "It's not the fountain's fault it's following me. I don't want to destroy it, I just want it to leave me alone."

Granny pursed her lips. "You'd better come in and explain as best you can. Through the back door, thank you," she added. "See if you can get your friend here into the barn."

"What about the goats?" Yurisa questioned.

"If there's a situation goats can't turn to their advantage, I haven't met it yet," Granny replied with perfect composure.

"You come in with me and help me get these things off. And I dare say we could all do with a cup of tea, despite the hour."

When they were at last settled around the fire, with Andrei twitching at every sound lest it herald the fountain smashing through the wall, Granny demanded a full history.

Andrei screwed his courage up and told her that he'd been given the sack, rushing on to his immediate re-hiring as she sat ominously swelling in her chair. The look in her eye told him there would be Words about this, but thankfully they were not yet forthcoming. He went on with his story as quickly as possible.

"...so I came home as fast as I could," he ended. "Do you think they'll follow me?"

"Probably some of the way, if the Czar's not got over it by now. It's the duke he'll be focussing on," Granny reminded him. "You're nobody, remember. There's a lot of safety in that. Good thing you thought to stop the thing thumping down hurdy great circles all along your trail, though. About the only sensible thing you've done. Anything else been happening I should know about?"

"Um...Bronya said there's something odd about the Princess Valeska Kira. Her hands are in fists all the time, even when she's asleep."

This lit a spark in Granny's eyes. She leaned forward in her chair. "What's she holding on to?"

"Nothing, as far as I know. Why? Do you think it's important?"

"How do I know? But anyone who's ever raised a child knows to be suspicious of a tightly clenched hand. It's a sure sign of hiding something."

"So what do I do?" Andrei tried not to wail like a little boy.

"Seems to me you'll have to find a way back into the Czar's good books," Granny said. "Either that, or get used to being followed around all your born days."

"You can't do anything?" he asked wistfully.

Granny Sonechka snorted. "Do I look like the Czar of the Seven Steps? Didn't you see him sitting on his throne atop those seven layers? Stone's the base, isn't it? Stone for the earth. Wood for the plants, ivory for the creatures, copper for the likes of us, silver for the merchants, gold for the nobles, and all over gemstones for his own family. Those are the seven estates the Czar has power over. Your friend outside is stone—Czar has power over him in the seventh estate."

Andrei felt nauseous and dizzy. What kind of enemy had he made?

"You want a good dose of the green syrup and straight to bed," Granny advised. "Crack on the head and missing half your meals since—no wonder you're feeling peaky."

"I feel fine," Andrei mumbled, staring at the fire with glazed eyes.

"You *look* like something a goat coughed up," Granny said bluntly.

"All that power," Andrei said. "It's too much for one man."

"You just be thankful it's a man who sits there," Granny said.

"What do you mean?" Andrei said, lifting his head. Granny wasn't one to disapprove of women holding power, and there had been a handful of Czaras over the centuries.

For a moment Granny paused, and then she settled back into her chair, her storytelling look settling over her features.

"A man's got to die, hasn't he? Doesn't matter how good or ill a ruler he is, you've only to wait and time will bring a change. But an immortal..." She sucked in her breath.

"Immortals?" Andrei laughed. Just one of the children's stories, then.

"Don't you laugh at me, boy," Granny said sharply. "It's no laughing matter. Time was, some fools thought they'd persuade Summer to be our Czar and rule forever."

"Sounds like a good idea," Andrei said, putting another log on the fire.

"Are you daft?" Granny demanded. "The dry heat of summer, forever and ever? The land would dry up like a husk and be devoured in fire by the first summer lightning."

"Oh."

"And of course, the other seasons, they weren't at all pleased at the prospect of perpetual banishment, and who can blame them?"

"Perpetual banishment?" Andrei asked, frowning.

"The immortals only walk this earth in their own season," Granny said. "Now if Summer was to take the throne, then it would be summer forever—the others'd be kept out, see? So there was war between the immortals," she concluded, and for a time there was only the crackling of the fire and the soughing of wind in the chimney.

"What happened then?" Andrei asked, though not sure he wanted to know.

"Chaos," Granny said dryly. "Four seasons all battling over the land—what else would come but famine and disaster? So the Throne of Seven Steps was built, and a man enthroned as Czar. So long as mortal man—or mortal woman, if it comes to that—sits on the Throne at the season's turn, we are protected. Which is why enthronements are always on the last night of the season, no matter how many hours or days or weeks since the last Czar died. Because the Throne must be filled by midnight."

"Why leave it so late?" Yurisa's voice out of the dark shadows startled Andrei, and he dropped the log he'd been toying with. "Wouldn't that be an unnecessary risk?"

Granny shrugged. "Tradition. Traditions always have a reason behind 'em, you'll find, but the reason don't always make sense."

"But why didn't the immortals try to take the Throne as soon as the first Czar died?" Andrei asked. "All they had to do was wait."

Granny grinned. "If an immortal ever tries to ascend the

Throne, the Seven Steps will shrink away from their touch. Or so it's said. Never seen it happen myself, of course. Seems to be working so far, mind you—the Czars keep dying. Just like the rest of us."

"Just like the rest of us?" Andrei protested. "The Czar's nothing like the rest of us—he has control of everything!"

"Not everything," Granny snapped back. "Not death, for one thing. Use your noggin, boy. The water and the air are free to us all—though the immortals have their influence there, to be sure—and being only a man, the Czar can't have effect over what he don't know of."

"Why didn't the Czar just order Andrei to come back?" Yurisa asked from her corner.

"Good question," Granny said approvingly. "Three reasons I can think of. One, he don't know his own power, because these days anything that didn't happen five minutes ago is written off as an old wives' tale."

Andrei flushed guiltily and tended closely to the fire.

"Two, Andrei's still got his own will. Seems even that thing out there's got its own will, which is a bit of a mind-stretcher when you come to think of it." She was silent for a moment.

"And third?" Yurisa persisted.

"Three, for all that he's Czar of the Seven Steps and all, Kiril's still thick as two short planks," Granny said. "Now hand me that bottle of green syrup and the spoon. You'll have to doss down on the floor here, Andrei, being as both the beds are taken."

"Doesn't matter. I don't think I'll ever sleep again," Andrei said dismally. He obediently swallowed the syrup and made a face. "Not after that bedtime story of yours."

Granny laughed. "Nothing's changed, Andrei my boy," she said, heaving herself out of her chair. "You just know more about it, is all. Why lose sleep over that?"

But long after the house had settled into what passed for silence so close to the forest, Andrei lay awake, gazing at the

dimming coals, and wondering how he was ever going to get
back on the right side of the Czar.

On the Trail

The next morning proved the truth of what Granny had said about the goats. On heaving open the barn doors to milk them—no harm getting on Granny's good side either—Andrei found them perched on the fountain's upper bowl, taking advantage of the added altitude to help themselves to the hay stored in the loft.

He persuaded them down by the simple means of walking away. As the fountain followed, the goats reconsidered their position and bounded down. By dint of some fancy footwork, he got them out of the door while pushing it closed in what he couldn't help thinking of as the fountain's face.

But not too closed. The last thing he wanted was the thing smashing his Granny's barn to bits in the middle of winter, just because he happened to walk too far away for its liking. He firmly staked the goats' tethers in place, set to work and tried to relax into it. If it wasn't for that monstrosity in the barn it'd be just like old times...

"Andrei?"

He jumped, knocking over the milk pail. A heavily bearded man stood before him, frowning. How long had he been there? How much had he seen?

"You haven't changed a bit," the man said, and suddenly Andrei recognized him.

"Grigori? Is that you under the beard?"

"Not bad, is it?" Grigori asked, stroking it complacently. "Katya says it's the best in the village."

"I'm not surprised," Andrei said, bending down and making a fuss of setting the pail upright. Keep Grigori's eyes away from the barn door... "Good thing the pail was nearly empty! So...you and Katya, eh? I always thought so. Even in school you had an eye for her, as I recall."

Grigori grinned bashfully.

"So what brings you here?" Andrei asked, as casually as he could.

"Katya's...sick in the mornings," Grigori said significantly. "Granny Sonechka has these pastilles—they did wonders for her last time."

"Last time? You mean...?"

"Our little boy's nearly two," Grigori said, beaming with pride.

Andrei stared at his old schoolfellow. They'd shared the same bench at school for years, and now here Grigori was with a wife and a son and another on the way! His hand went to his freshly shaved chin.

"And you?" Grigori asked.

"Um...no. Not yet, anyway," Andrei said, thinking of the necklace he hoped Bronya still wore.

"You should grow a beard," Grigori advised. "Remember Leonid?"

"How could I forget him?" Leonid had been the envy of all the other boys when he'd started a beard at the age of thirteen. Andrei chuckled. "You remember what Teacher used to say?"

"Too bad there's more growth on the outside of his head than the inside," Grigori said in a creaky old voice, and they laughed. There was a creak from behind Andrei, and he froze. The barn door! Grigori was staring over Andrei's head.

"You were saying about Leonid?" he prompted desperately.

"Eh? Oh, yes," Grigori said, apparently focussing on the conversation with an effort. "Beard. Makes you look more mature. Katya tells me that's what made her pay attention to me, in the end. More mature than the other boys, she said."

"Well, I'll bear it in mind," Andrei said, as Grigori's gaze slowly crept back towards the barn. "But I mustn't keep you from your errand of mercy!"

"Hm? Oh, yes!" With one final glance in the direction of the barn, Grigori hurried towards the house and knocked on the back door.

Andrei waited to see Yurisa let Grigori in before he spun back to the barn. Sure enough, the barn door was part open, and the fountain was clearly visible. Hurriedly, Andrei shoved the door closed again, pulled up the goats' stakes and settled the whole operation in place with his back pinned to the door.

He managed a smile as Grigori departed with his little packet of pastilles and a sidelong glance at the door above Andrei's head. Well, that secret was out. It made a second piece of bad news to break to Granny—Andrei still hadn't told her he was in debt to the Howler men to the tune of two and a half eagles.

❄   ❄   ❄

Andrei swallowed the last mouthful of porridge and put down his spoon. "Granny," he said, "I've been thinking."

"About time," she replied amiably. "Let's hear it, then."

"If the Czar is the only one who can stop the fountain following me, then I need to give the Czar a reason to want to, right? I've got to get into his good books."

"Hope you didn't lie awake all night figuring that out," Granny said. "I said as much last night, if I recall."

"As far as I know," Andrei continued, "there are only two things Czar Kiril wants."

"Two?" Granny enquired.

"Assuming he wants to not be a monster, that is," Andrei said.

"I think you can take that for granted," Granny said dryly. "What's the other one?"

"He wants his new wife back. Well, maybe he's more concerned about the son she's carrying, but—"

"He can't possibly know it's a boy," Yurisa said. "There's no way of knowing until the baby arrives."

"And not even then, sometimes," Granny said. "But that won't stop people thinking they can tell, by this or that sign. There's even those who think they can make the chance fall the way they wish, by this or that preparation beforehand."

"But none of them work?" Yurisa asked.

"Course not. Recipe for disappointment. Half the time, anyway. What were you saying, Andrei?"

"The Czarina—whatever sort it is she's carrying, she's disappeared—"

"We know about that," Granny cut in. "We're not up the top of the Long Mountains here, you know—we do get news."

Yurisa got up and collected the empty bowls. Granny settled back in her chair with her cup of tea.

"Duke Maxim might know where she is," Andrei went on. "The Czar thinks so, anyway."

"No help for you there," Granny commented. "Not after what you did to him."

"But..." Andrei said, "The fountain took me more or less north while I was unconscious, and there was a farmer there who said a woman had come through the day before—that's the day she disappeared—travelling in one of those old closed-in sleighs, like noblewomen used. And she was young and beautiful, and...well, travelling of her own free will. In which case...well, I can't go hunting a fleeing woman through the snow, can I? Particularly not one who's, er..." He tried to remember Grigori's expression. "Sick in the mornings."

"Not usually at her time," Yurisa said with a frown, and received a faint nod from Granny in return.

"Well...you know what I mean," Andrei said, hoping to escape an embarrassing degree of enlightenment on the issue.

"So where does that leave you?" Granny asked.

Andrei took a deep breath. "I need to find out how to cure the Czar. Or at least get enough helpful information that he'll change his mind about killing me and make the fountain stop following me."

"Ludmilla!" Granny said triumphantly.

"Ludmilla?" Andrei repeated, baffled.

"That's Granny Ludmilla to you, young man. I knew the name would come to me," Granny Sonechka said with satisfaction. "Haven't seen her since, oh, the last Czar's reign, I would think. She lives up north, near the Lady's Lake."

"What? But I was just—you mean I came all this way south, just to turn around and go back to the north again?" Andrei asked, dismayed.

"She was always interested in what you might call the magical aspect of healing," Granny Sonechka continued, as though Andrei had not spoken.

"You think she could fix the fountain thing?" Andrei asked hopefully.

"Haven't the foggiest. But it'll give you somewhere to head for, anyway. Yurisa, get the bags off the mantelpiece."

Andrei frowned. Bags? Yurisa returned, proffering two little leather bags. Granny took the larger one, which clinked, and nodded sharply at the other.

"Two and a half eagles. You can stop by the Howler man in town on your way."

"How did you know?" burst from Andrei's lips.

"The Howler man told me when he was round here for—when he was here," Granny said, "and in any case your face gave you away in a minute. You're never in debt but you have a constipated look. If the green syrup didn't clear it, it had to be money."

Andrei went beet red.

"I'd grow a beard if I was you," Granny advised. "Cover up a bit of that telltale face of yours."

"Pa never had a beard," Andrei said mutinously.

"And he was a rotten liar, too, same as you," Granny said. "Anyway, why did you give the money to Yurisa?"

"You can't go trotting through town to the Howler man's stall with your big stone friend going after you," Granny said. "So Yurisa will take the money, and meet you on the far side— you take the forest path."

"Meet me?" Andrei repeated, bemused.

"Don't gawp like that, boy. You didn't think *I* was going with you, did you? At my age?"

"But—but—I can't travel with her! She's a girl! People— people will think things," he ended lamely.

"I could borrow my brother's clothes," Yurisa said, her voice so low he barely heard it.

Granny beamed. "No harm in two young fellers travelling together, is there?"

"Won't he mind?" Andrei tried desperately.

"He's dead," Yurisa said stonily.

"And she doesn't know anything about magic," Andrei protested. "You said you didn't, and..."

"This'll be a chance for her to learn, then," the old woman replied placidly. "You're always after me to teach you more and faster, aren't you, girl?"

"About disease, not...whatever this is!" Yurisa said, almost animated for the first time in Andrei's brief acquaintance with her.

"Treat it as a disease, then. Take symptoms. Get a history."

"We can't get a history from the Czar!" Andrei said, his porridge turning to a cold lump in his belly at the thought of barraging that monster with the sort of personal questions Granny was in the habit of asking. "He'd kill us!"

"There's something wrong with that daughter of his, too," Granny said. "Bronya says so, and she's in a position to know, even if she doesn't know what it is she knows. That's two cases. Remember what I told you, girl?"

"One case is an incident, two is an infection, three is an outbreak," Yurisa recited. "You think it's something...catching?"

"I don't know, do I? And nor will you unless you go and find out. Off you go."

Yurisa disappeared up the narrow stairs. The thump of her feet on the ceiling reminded Andrei that she could probably still hear him.

"We can't go into Istvan to talk to Bronya," he said desperately. "Not with things the way they are!"

"Get what information you *can* and take it to Ludmilla for a diagnosis. From what I hear, it's not only Istvan that's been seeing some odd things lately. You didn't see anything odd on your way south?"

"I saw a stone fountain chasing me across the country," Andrei said sourly. "Odd enough for you?"

Granny gave him a reproving look. "You'd best be on your way before Grigori mentions what he saw to that chatterbox of a wife of his and the whole village just happens to stop by for a nosy. This is for you," she added, handing the larger pouch to Andrei. "Travelling expenses."

Andrei gaped. "Granny, you can't just give me your life savings!"

"Give you my life savings?" She cackled with laughter. "Do I look like such a fool? No, these are *your* life savings, my lad. You've been a good boy and sent something home for your granny each week, and seeing as I knew this day would come, it's all gone into the jug on the mantelpiece."

Andrei blinked. "Weren't you afraid someone would steal it?"

Granny snorted. "I may not have a hand with magic, but I know enough ways to make someone's life a misery to them without resorting to that. There isn't a person for miles who'd be fool enough to try robbing me. Now go put your coat on and don't forget a warm muffler. It's a long walk to Yurisa's village, and it's cold out."

"I'll meet you in the thicket just past the bridge," Yurisa said, coming down the stairs with a pack. "Do you know the place?"

"Of course," Andrei said. This was his area, not hers. He knew every hidey-hole and shortcut for miles. "But why are we going to your village?"

"To get my brother's clothes, of course," Yurisa said, glaring at him.

"Yurisa," Granny said, in the voice that meant you didn't want to hear what she was going to say.

Yurisa stopped, halfway through buttoning her cloak.

"Consider the possibility that Luka makes three."

Fire flared briefly in Yurisa's eyes. The door banged, and she was gone.

Granny sighed. "Coat, muffler," she instructed Andrei. "I've got to be off on my rounds. Send me word by a Howler if you get the chance."

She hauled his head down for a peck on the forehead, and departed, the legendary cloak flapping around her.

Andrei groaned. A grumpy girl, a hopeless mission, and his own personal curse waiting for him in the barn. He slipped the pouch into his pocket, put on his coat, and braced himself for the chill wind outside.

❋   ❋   ❋

The wind was even colder than he'd remembered. By the time he arrived at the rendezvous, Yurisa was already waiting, her cheeks whipped red by the wind.

"What took you so long?" she asked.

"Heavy traffic on the forest path," Andrei said sourly. "Every man and his dog's out there. On a day like this!"

"This way," Yurisa said.

"Why not ride?" Andrei suggested.

"On a day like this? We'll get chilled to the bone if we don't keep our blood moving."

Andrei sighed, and they set off into the forest, the fountain blundering along behind.

A sudden gust twined around Andrei's neck, and he wished he'd brought a muffler like Granny said. Only it wasn't very dashing or adventurous, setting out to seek your fortune with a muffler wrapped round your neck because your grandmother told you to.

"Cold today," he gasped.

"My mother would say someone had crossed the Lady," Yurisa said, and Andrei was glad she didn't look at him.

"Do you think," Andrei said, the idea suddenly occuring to him, "do you think when the Czar or the princess or whoever goes on the duty visit each Midseason to the Lady's Lake, or Summer's Meadow or wherever—do you think they actually see them? See the Lady, I mean, and Summer himself, and—"

"How would I know?" Yurisa said bluntly.

"No, well, you'd think someone would say something if they did," Andrei said. "I mean, no one would stop believing in the immortals if people were still meeting them, would they?"

There was a long pause, and Andrei was just about to break it when Yurisa spoke.

"They might. It seems to me most people's beliefs are based on all sorts of silly things, rather than proper consideration of the evidence."

Andrei thought of the farmer convincing himself the fountain hadn't just appeared in his yard, when it obviously had, and decided Yurisa was probably right. He still had his doubts about the imperial family meeting the immortals, though. He sighed and tramped on in a growing silence which Yurisa made no attempt to break.

Once the dull glow of the sun behind the clouds had started on its downward run, Yurisa produced some food from her bundle. They didn't stop, but ate as they walked—too cold to stand still, Andrei decided. At least the fountain served some use as a windbreak.

"So, what made you decide to come across to Granny to apprentice?" Andrei asked as he dusted the last of the lunch crumbs off for the birds. The silence was starting to get to him. "No healer in your village?"

"We have a midwife," Yurisa said.

"But you didn't apprentice with her?"

"Granny Sonechka is the best," Yurisa said, and it was clear that to her, nothing more needed to be said.

Andrei sighed and tried again. "What was it Granny said about one two three?"

"One two three?"

"Outbreaks and so on."

"One case is an incident, two is an infection, three is an outbreak," Yurisa recited.

"So Granny thinks Kiril is one, Valeska is two, and Luka is three?"

Silence again.

"So who is Luka?" Andrei wondered aloud.

"My brother," Yurisa said, in a voice like cold stone.

"The one who died?"

"My only brother."

"I'm sorry," Andrei said sympathetically. He'd never had a brother, or a sister, if it came to that, but... "Bad enough your brother dying, without getting changed into—"

She turned on him, eyes blazing. "My brother was not a monster!"

He put up his hands in surrender. "Sorry! How was I supposed to know? I'm no magic expert. I just need to find out what's going on."

"So you can be a big hero and get on with your life." She wasn't looking at him, but he knew angry when he heard it.

"It's not just that," Andrei said. "There's a girl I really care about who's Valeska Kira's maid and I really don't want anything to happen to her."

"Valeska isn't a monster, is she?"

Andrei thought about this.

"Not more than usual," he said at last. "So you think it's two different things?"

"Not necessarily. The same illness can create different symptoms in different patients. It depends on lots of things—how healthy they were to begin with, their resistance to disease..."

"That would explain why the Czar is—worse," Andrei said. "Because he's older, and frankly he drinks too much, and Valeska is..." He struggled for words.

"Under tight self-control," Yurisa said.

"How did you know?" Andrei asked, surprised.

"She passed through our village with the baron's daughter, Lala, when I was home for Midseason. And before you ask, no, I didn't notice her hands."

Andrei hadn't thought of asking any such thing, but decided Yurisa didn't need to know this.

"Luka thought she was beautiful," Yurisa said. "She even deigned to speak to us. Luka was so excited, he could hardly talk about anything else."

Her voice faded to a gasp at the end, she swallowed hard, and walked faster, battling against the icy wind as though she had a grudge against it. Clearly, that was all he was getting. Andrei hunched into the collar of his coat and tried to make sense of what he'd learned.

To Andrei's surprise, the first place Yurisa took him once they reached her village—once he'd persuaded the fountain to wait among the trees on the forest's edge—was the mortuary house beside the graveyard. The heavy door was unlocked, of course, but it took some effort on Yurisa's part to heave it open.

The hinges let out an uncanny wail, and Andrei found himself wishing they'd walked faster. Visiting a mortuary house in a strange village at dusk was not the best end to a cold, tiring day.

In the dim light of a single oil lamp, Andrei could see only one shrouded figure on the stone slab at the centre of the single room. The village midwife might not be Granny's equal, but she must be a fairly decent healer, he speculated, if they'd only had one death so far this season. People always seemed to die in winter—the most inconvenient time, as the ground was too frozen to dig graves. Hence the mortuary house.

Yurisa gently folded back the rough linen sheet, to reveal a face so like hers Andrei went gooseflesh all over. No need to ask who this was. He stood and waited in respectful silence, quelling the urge to fidget. Yurisa's face wore the softest expression he'd ever seen on it, and he looked away.

"He was always weak," Yurisa said softly. "From a baby. Some seed of death inside him, biding its time."

That didn't seem to fit with the Czar's problem at all. What was Granny thinking?

"How did he...I mean, what did he die of?" Andrei asked cautiously.

"The village bully shouted at him," Yurisa said in a stony voice, "and he just died."

"Just—dropped down dead?"

"Yes."

"By the Lady, what did he *say?*"

Yurisa draped the sheet back in place and turned away. Andrei helped her with the unwieldy door, eager to get out of this room where sadness seemed to condense on the walls with the damp.

"I don't know," Yurisa said, moving rapidly along the nearly invisible path without even looking down. "Does it matter?"

"Does what matter?" Andrei asked, righting himself after a stumble. She might know the path by heart, but it wasn't helping him.

"What Anton said to Luka."

"I dunno. It might."

Yurisa sighed, and changed direction. Stopping outside one of the larger houses, she rapped firmly on the door. The woman who opened it fell back, muffling a cry.

"Where's Anton?" Yurisa demanded.

A young man—no, a boy, Andrei decided—came to see what was the matter, and he too shrank back at the sight of Yurisa on his doorstep.

"What did you say to Luka when he died?" she demanded.

"I—um, I don't remember," Anton said weakly.

"That's a lie," Yurisa said. "Tell me the truth."

Anton looked to the woman for support, but her lips were pressed together tightly. No sympathy there.

"I said—I said...*you're dead*," he mumbled.

There was a painful silence while Yurisa looked daggers at him and he avoided her eye.

"Right," she said at last, and turned away so fast Andrei had to step back in a hurry to avoid being knocked down. He nodded politely to the woman at the door and hurried after Yurisa before she disappeared in the darkness. The door slammed behind him the second he turned away.

"You just walked up and asked?"

"Asking is the simplest way to obtain information," Yurisa said.

"Still, it's a bit...awkward," Andrei said.

"Anton killed my brother," Yurisa said coldly. "Feeling awkward is the least of what he deserves."

It was not Anton's awkwardness but his own that Andrei pitied, but he didn't like to say so. Right now all he wanted was a roaring fire, hot food, and somewhere warm to sleep, but in a recently bereaved home, as an unfamiliar guest? He had the unpleasant feeling that he and awkwardness had not yet parted company for the night.

❄   ❄   ❄

It wasn't as awkward as Andrei had feared. It was worse. A miasma of grief hung over the house like a fog. Yurisa's mother had the quietness of someone whose mind has gone elsewhere, and Andrei didn't have any trouble guessing where. Her only care seemed to be a little pot of anemones she was somehow keeping alive, cosseted in the warmth.

Yurisa's father exerted himself to be hospitable, which was almost worse. Snippets of local gossip which were clearly of no interest to their teller were painstakingly retailed. Who had had twins, what Ony's father had said to him when he lost another job, and the shocking rumours about the neighbouring Baron Boris.

"Living like an animal, they say," Yurisa's father said solemnly.

Andrei looked meaningfully at Yurisa.

"What's his daughter doing?" Yurisa asked.

But there was no gossip about Lala Bora, it appeared. Yurisa gave Andrei a tiny nod. It wasn't much of a lead, but it was something, and it meant not hanging about here, which was all to the good as far as Andrei was concerned.

Early the next morning Andrei stamped up and down outside as Yurisa said her farewells. She appeared on the step and frowned at him. "Aren't you supposed to be wearing a muffler?"

"I didn't bring one. I came away in a hurry," he said defensively.

"I can get you one to borrow," she said, about to disappear inside again, but he shook his head vigorously.

"I'm fine! Granny fusses too much. Come on!"

Yurisa shrugged, and closed the door.

"You're still dressed as a girl," Andrei pointed out.

"I am a girl, and everyone round here knows it," she replied, giving him a look that said "you are an idiot" as clearly as if she'd written it on a sign.

Now he thought of it, anyone who knew the family would probably die of fright themselves if they saw someone who looked so much like the dead boy wandering around in his clothes.

As they reached the edge of the village clearing, Andrei heard a door squeak open, and Yurisa looked back. He turned too, and saw her mother's huddled form moving across the frosty ground towards the mortuary house, with a little bunch of anemones in her hand. As Yurisa turned back he accidentally caught her eye, and wished he hadn't.

"So, we're off to—what's the baron's name again?" Andrei said, by way of diversion.

"Boris."

"Boris's manor, then. And this time, no knocking on the door and demanding information!"

Andrei heard a loud crack and looked over his shoulder. The fountain edged away from a large broken branch, as though wishing to dissociate itself.

He sighed. "Come on, then."

By midmorning Yurisa had begun to slow, her gaze constantly raking the forest about them.

"Looking for something?" Andrei asked at last.

"Somewhere to change. We can't go on much further like this."

"So go behind a tree or something."

She looked directly at him until he started to feel uncomfortable.

"I'll have my back turned," he said, rolling his eyes.

"What about the fountain?"

"It doesn't have a back," Andrei said, and the fountain uttered a little gurgle.

Yurisa looked at it, a little startled, and then wended her way through the frosty underbrush to the largest of the nearby evergreens.

"I'll shout if I see anyone coming," Andrei said, trying to reassure her.

"That would convince them that there's something going on," Yurisa said, and he could almost hear her eyes rolling. "Just greet whoever it is loudly. That will be enough."

It was obvious she thought him something of a fool, and he flushed hotly. He'd show her. This was his mission, after all. She was just tagging along, because Granny told her to. He took up his station on the opposite side of the tree and scanned the trees in a businesslike manner. Cold, dark and deserted. He almost wished he had accepted the offer of the muffler. His throat felt a bit funny.

"Will this do?"

A young man strolled awkwardly around the side of the fountain. Andrei blinked at this sudden apparition, and it resolved into Yurisa.

Andrei gargled. "Fooled me," he managed at last.

Judging by the way her face darkened, this was not the right thing to say.

"You carry this," she said brusquely, and handed him the smaller bundles.

"It's not your, er..." Bad enough having a fountain following him—he didn't want to be carting women's underclothes around the country as well.

"It's food," she said. "We won't be there till dinnertime."

Shouldering her own bundle, she set off, and Andrei hastily followed.

"Shouldn't I be carrying the bigger bundle?" he asked.

"I'm keeping my clothes close," Yurisa said. "In case I need to change back."

"All that is your clothes?" Andrei said in disbelief.

"Quilted petticoats are bulky," she said. "But warm. How do men survive with so little covering their legs?"

"I dunno. We're used to it, I suppose," Andrei said, considering his own legs. "As long as your feet are warm, you're all right."

His own feet were cold and aching, thick socks notwith-standing, long before they reached the grounds of Baron Boris's mansion, and his throat was feeling decidedly raspy. He couldn't blame people for staying in, with this sort of weather, but despite the fountain lolloping along behind, Andrei almost wished they would run into someone. The fountain was not much of a conversationalist, and Yurisa wasn't much more of one.

But all through the day, they trudged along in the silence of the empty road.

For the hundredth time, Bronya wished the state of Valeska's hands did not prevent her working on her embroidery. It was one of the few things that seemed to relax her, and with all the events of the past few weeks, she needed all the relaxation she could get.

Duke Maxim had apparently fled the city the very night of the ill-fated ball, and Valeska's servants had been unable to gain word of him. Nor had she had a word from her father in response to all her messages.

She paced, endlessly, up and down whichever room her routine dictated she be in, and though her face was very often turned away, Bronya suspected Valeska often had tears in her eyes. Her one gently worded suggestion that her lady sit and rest for a moment—for all was being done that could be done—earned her no more than a cold look and a few cold words. Valeska, she was informed, was not so disloyal to her friends as to sit idly and amuse herself while they were in danger.

A discreet cough announced the major-domo's presence.

Valeska whirled towards him. "News?"

"Sergei informs me he has seen Duke Maxim, Your Highness," the major-domo said.

"Where? Is he well? Tell me!"

"The duke is at his town residence, Your Highness," the major-domo said, and something in his manner made Bronya fear what he would say next.

"And is he well?"

The major-domo permitted himself a small smile. "As well as can be expected for a man who has been socializing with His Imperial Majesty."

Valeska frowned. "Maxim has been with my father? But..."

"I understand His Majesty has withdrawn the accusations previously made against His Grace," the major-domo murmured tactfully.

With a long sigh of relief, Valeska sank into a chair.

"But where has he been all this time?"

"I am unable to say, Your Highness. I understand His Grace returned to town three days ago."

Valeska looked up. "Three days?"

"Yes, Your Highness."

She caught her lip between her teeth for a moment. "Thank you. You may go."

The major-domo bowed and departed. Valeska rose to her feet and began pacing again, but slowly now.

"Three days," Bronya heard her whisper. "And not a word to me."

❄   ❄   ❄

"We should have walked faster," Yurisa said, as they eyed the mansion from the cover of a dark night and a thick hedge.

"We should have ridden," Andrei said, wincing as he shifted from foot to foot.

"We'd have frozen," Yurisa reminded him. "It's too late to go asking questions now. We should find somewhere sheltered to sleep and come back tomorrow. We're bound to find someone who'll talk. Perhaps one of the servants."

"The daughter would probably know more, and in any case, why not now?" Andrei urged, the warm glow coming through the winter drapes conjuring up pictures of well-stuffed armchairs before blazing fires. "There's still lights burning in some rooms."

"One room," Yurisa corrected. A shadow passed across the light spilling out onto the little wrought iron balcony, and a moment later, passed back again. A skirted shadow.

"I'll go and ask her," Andrei said sunnily. "She's obviously not about to sleep, the way she's pacing about."

"Weren't you the one saying that we shouldn't—" Yurisa stopped suddenly as the door on to the balcony opened.

They watched in silence as the silhouetted woman lifted her arms and dropped something over the edge of the balcony. Then she darted back in and closed the door.

"Shouldn't?" Andrei prompted.

"Just walk up to the front door and start asking questions. Did you see that?"

"If you mean did I see a young lady come out and lower a rope ladder from her balcony, yes I did. No need to bother with the front door, then."

"You're not going to!"

"Oh come on! How can we pass up an opportunity like that? She's practically inviting us in!"

"And her father's practically an animal! What if he finds you in his daughter's bedroom?"

"He won't. You don't have to come if you don't want to, but I am here in an important cause, and nothing is going to stop me."

"I'll stay with the fountain," Yurisa said. "It has more sense."

Ignoring this last insult, Andrei crept across the garden towards the house, looking back only once to make sure the fountain was staying put. This was a much less manicured sort of garden than the Czar's, with shaggy grass walks instead of gravel. A great improvement as far as sneaking went,

Andrei decided. He swarmed up the rope ladder with little difficulty, and only one creak from the ironwork. He held his breath, but nothing stirred.

Taking a deep breath, he tapped gently at the glass door. It was flung open in a moment and he was drawn rapidly into a room of surpassing pinkness, the door closing behind him. A pink young woman in an even pinker frilly nightgown was clasping her hands in front of him.

"At last!" she said, in a sweet high-pitched voice. "I always knew you'd come!"

"What?" This girl was a stranger to him, he was sure.

"My swain! Let us flee this place together!"

"Er—just a minute."

Andrei went to peek outside the bedroom door, as his brain spun furiously. No sign of life in the darkened corridor outside. It was safe to speak. That'd show Yurisa he wasn't the foolhardy person she thought.

"Now," he said, turning around to find the girl at close range, hands still clasped and face aglow.

"Yes?" she breathed.

"Tell me about your father."

The adoring look dropped off her face, to be replaced by a pout. "He's horrid. He's a beast, and I told him so!"

"When you say *beast*," Andrei queried, "do you mean..."

"Horns and all. Horrid!"

This sounded familiar. "Every time he loses his temper—eh?"

She looked surprised. "Oh, no. Well, yes, the first time. But he's like that all the time, he is really."

Andrei unwound this. It sounded worse than the Czar's case, if such a thing could be. He racked his brains for the sort of questions Granny would have asked. Drat Yurisa, why couldn't she have come along and been useful like she was supposed to?

"I'm Lala," the pink girl coyly put in.

"Nice to meet you," Andrei said automatically. "I'm Andrei."

"I do like your chin," she said. "Much nicer than a prickly old beard."

This was a bit more like it. "Thank you," he said cordially. "Now tell me, how long has this problem been going on with your father?"

"Oh, since *always*," she said breathlessly.

Andrei blinked. "You mean he's always...the horns and all that?" How had a monster's daughter passed muster to be Valeska's lady-in-waiting, however temporarily?

"Oh, *that*," Lala said. "No, that's just lately."

"How lately?"

She frowned. "I don't know. Maybe since Midseason? He was definitely all right when I went away..."

"To the Lady's Lake with Valeska Kira?" Andrei asked.

Her eyes widened. "How did you know?"

"I used to be...part of her household," Andrei said.

"Oh, then you'd know all about her and the duke. It was *so* romantic," she said dreamily, twining a finger in her hair. "Alone in the moonlight, she gave him her heart, and—"

A rhythmic thudding interrupted her, the floor vibrating with it.

"The fountain!" Andrei exclaimed.

"Father!" Lala squeaked.

There was a roar in the corridor outside, and the door burst in.

Three's Company

There was a bright tingling sound as Andrei went through the window, and a painful thump as he hit the insufficiently shrubberied ground below. He lay winded for a moment, listening to the roaring above, then scrabbled to his feet and took off running, hoping Yurisa and the fountain were still where he'd left them.

The fountain uttered a mournful gargle as he approached, which reminded him uncomfortably of wolves.

"Time to go!" he panted, passing them without slowing.

"You think?" Yurisa hissed as she broke into a run. "Someone's coming!"

Andrei looked back to see a lantern bobbing across the garden, gaining on the fountain, which was slowing—because he wasn't running. He ran, reaching the shelter of the tall hedge around the garden and cornering rapidly.

"Hello there!" called the lantern-bearer, and Andrei stopped again.

That wasn't the voice of the bullish Baron, not even close. And it certainly wasn't Lala the Pink, either. He wriggled back to the corner of the hedge for a better view and found their pursuer had almost caught up. The man with the lantern would almost have blended into the night, but for a purple gleam in the lantern light. Andrei's mouth fell open.

"Lovely evening," the purplish pursuer said politely.

Andrei stared blankly at him. He *was* purple. More than that, he was made of purple stone: purple stone from head to toe, it was clear, since all he was wearing was an orange ribbon around his neck. Andrei stared at it.

"Come on!" Yurisa's voice came out of the darkness behind Andrei.

"Porfiry's the name, and, alas, the nature," the stone man said, drawing a long face.

"Eh?" Andrei frowned.

"Porphyry, the reddish-purple stone," Porfiry explained. "I see you've noticed my neckwear."

"Er..."

"I *was* going to wear black, in mourning for my dearest ensemble," Porfiry said in a confidential tone, "but black is just so dreary, especially with all this dark purple! So then I thought—why not orange? It's not too much, you think?"

"Er..." If anything, it was a great deal too little, in Andrei's opinion. "Not at all. It's very...eyecatching."

"I've noticed people can't take their eyes off it," Porfiry said with a wicked grin. "Incidentally, while I don't like to barge in and start throwing around orders, might I suggest we hasten away? The master's gone to get his arquebus, I expect, and he does get up quite a turn of speed."

"Arquebus?"

"A thing like a baby cannon," Porfiry said.

A roar in the insufficient distance seemed to confirm the Baron's hypothetical course of action. The fountain lurched into movement again, heading for the forest with no urging needed. Andrei kept alongside without effort, Porfiry sashaying ahead in a manner more suited to a ballroom.

"What kept you?" Yurisa demanded as she emerged from the undergrowth to join them.

"And you are?" Porfiry murmured, as though this were some sort of elegant tea party. "Or oughtn't I to ask? It's certainly a novel way to elope."

Andrei gaped at him. *Blam!* A single explosion behind them, and they unanimously increased their speed.

"We're not!" Yurisa said in her deepest voice.

"Oh, my mistake! I was sure one of you was a young lady in disguise, although now I come to look at you," he swung the lantern about, inspecting them, "I couldn't say for sure which."

"She is!" Andrei snapped. "I'm Andrei, she's Yurisa."

"There goes that secret," Yurisa muttered.

Blam! But further away now.

"You really ought to consider growing a beard," Porfiry said, stroking his own neat imperial. "And this is?"

"Who?" Andrei asked, looking around.

"Your enchanted friend here," Porfiry said, tapping the fountain's rim with a clink.

"It's just a fountain," Andrei said, trying not to pant too obviously. "It's not cursed, it's just...whatever you are, I suppose."

"Me?" Porfiry exclaimed, clapping a hand to his heart with a clink. "Do I look like a genuine garden ornament?"

"Yes," Yurisa said.

There was a faint pop in the distance.

"Horrors! The master always said I was too decorative, and one day—phut! There I was, and not a stitch left on me, if you'll believe. Such a curse to befall a man with a wardrobe like mine!"

"Tell us about it," Yurisa demanded. "How long has this been the case?"

"And do you cross back and forth?" Andrei put in.

"Dear me! So many questions!" Porfiry looked from one to the other as they ran.

"We're hunting down the curse that's fallen on the Czar," Andrei said.

"Ooh, it hasn't! Now I'd never have learned *that* staying in that utterly forsaken gloom of a house, now would I? I ought to have run away weeks ago, only the chance never seemed to present itself."

"Run away?" Andrei questioned.

"Of course! I'm coming with you for an adventure. I was hoping it would be the circus, but really, I think this might be even better. Now, tell me more about the Czar."

"Information for information," Yurisa put in. "We'll tell you what we know if you tell us what you know."

"Fair's fair," Porfiry said, coming to a halt. "So, what is it with the Czar? What form does it take?"

"Shouldn't we keep going?" Andrei asked.

Porfiry waved a hand dismissively. "He never comes this far."

Andrei and Yurisa staggered to a halt and sat down on the lower bowl to catch their breath. Porfiry seemed as unaffected by the run as the fountain, but stopped courteously and perched beside them.

"You know it takes different forms?" Yurisa said, her breath forming little white puffs in the cold air.

Porfiry shrugged. "It seems obvious, dear girl. Here's the master a monster of sorts, and you couldn't call me a monster, now could you?"

"I suppose not," Yurisa said warily, in case this was held against her.

"You know, the local peasants didn't think much of his disguise at all," Porfiry said cosily.

"His disguise?" Andrei asked, leaning against the fountain's lower bowl. "He tried to disguise *that*?"

"Oh no, not *that*. No, it was the disguise of a decent human being he *used* to wear."

This joke fell a little flat.

"So you're like this all the time?" Andrei asked again, to break the awkward silence.

"Of course!" Porfiry said. "Or isn't it 'of course'?"

"Well, the Czar only changes when he loses his temper," Andrei explained.

"That would be most of the time, from what I've heard," Porfiry said, making a face. "But what does he change into? I'm completely agog!"

"Something quite a lot like what the Baron changed into," Andrei said. "Take it from someone who's seen them both. Up close and personal," he added feelingly.

"What a sight! Considering what happened to my best suit when I was changed, it's just as well I'm not crossing back and forth. Imagine losing an entire outfit every time it happened! Or perhaps it would come back when I changed back—now that would be a relief!"

"So that's one who changes and three—or four—who don't," Yurisa muttered. "Are you sure the Czar was actually changing, Andrei?"

Andrei shuddered. "Unmistakably."

"He couldn't have been like that all along, and then you just noticed when he stood up?"

"There is no way," Andrei said firmly.

"Three or four?" Porfiry put in. "Tell me more! The Czar, the Baron, my humble self, and—who?"

There was an awkward silence.

"Possibly Yurisa's brother Luka," Andrei said, hoping Porfiry would take the hint.

"Oh, my dear, how dreadful! What's his affliction?"

"He's dead," Yurisa said.

Porfiry made a chagrined face. "Oh, I'm so sorry."

"And then there's Valeska Kira," Andrei said, attempting to ease the awkwardness by a rapid change of subject.

"But she hasn't really changed," Yurisa said. "She's just got her hands in fists all the time."

"How odd." Porfiry pursed his lips thoughtfully.

"But not necessarily related," Yurisa said firmly. "Now when did your...condition start?"

"Oh, it must have been..." Porfiry stared off into the wintry woodland. "Yes, a day or so after VK herself passed through. There I was, trying on my best court suit—though when I'd get a chance to wear it at court, who knows—and he barges in, gives a sneering laugh, and bawls, 'Aren't you the decorative fellow! Belong on a pedestal!' And there I was, all over porphyry and my court suit nowhere to be seen."

"Oh!" Andrei sat up in excitement and banged his head on the bowl above. "Ouch. I think I've got something."

"A lump on the head, I should say," Porfiry commented.

"Words," Andrei said excitedly. "That's two cases now where the change has happened right after someone said something to the person who changes."

Yurisa lifted her head and looked at him. "Are you sure that's relevant? Anyone could happen to be talking to someone."

"No, but listen. Boris tells Porfiry he's decorative and should be on a pedestal, and he turns into a statue. Anton tells Luka 'you're dead'..."

"And he dies," Yurisa whispered. "What about the Baron?"

"Lala said she'd called him a beast," Andrei offered.

"And then he changed?" Yurisa queried.

"She didn't say," Andrei admitted. "She didn't say much that was to the point, actually. She seemed to have her mind on, um, other matters." He decided that Yurisa need never know Lala had called him a swain and planned on eloping with him. At this distance, he was rather relieved that her father had intervened.

"Other matters? At a time like that?" Yurisa said sceptically.

"Oh, don't blame Andrei," Porfiry said. "It would take a barrel of gunpowder going off under her to take that girl's mind off romance. She was absolutely starry-eyed over the imperial romance—couldn't have been more excited if the duke had been all over *her* with the honeyed words and the meaningful looks." He heaved a sigh. "Still, it could have been worse.

Imagine the embarrassment if I'd been through the change before Her Imperial Highness's visit! I would have had to wall-
paper myself into a cupboard to avoid her maidenly gaze."

"Or stand very still in the garden," Yurisa muttered.

Andrei frowned. "So was that before or after the Baron's, er,
change?"

"Oh, before, before," Porfiry said airily. "I've rather avoided
his company since his alteration—it hasn't done a thing for his
temper!"

"So if the baron worded you, and Lala worded the baron,
and Anton worded—no, it doesn't make sense," Yurisa said.
"Infection doesn't work like that. Unless of course—"

The two men watched her as her lips moved silently for a
minute.

"It could be," she said at last. "With some diseases, there
are people who catch it but don't get sick themselves. But they
can still infect others. Carriers."

Andrei thought about this. "But if the Baron was a carrier,
then why did he get sick—I mean, cursed? And if he wasn't a
carrier, how did he manage to get Porfiry cursed before him?"

"I don't know!" Yurisa said crossly. "It doesn't make sense.
It's late. I'm going to sleep."

❄   ❄   ❄

Andrei woke to the sound of shouting.

"...like any decent civilized human being!" Yurisa finished.

"What's going on?" Andrei croaked, moving stiffly to a sitting position and cracking the thick frost on his coat. Yurisa
was tending a small fire, her back ostentatiously towards Porfiry.

"I—" Porfiry began, but Yurisa cut in.

"He's naked, and he refuses to put anything on! Tell him he
isn't coming with us like that."

The Wound of Words

Andrei looked at Porfiry, who had his chin in the air. The dark shade of the purple stone made it less obvious, but Porfiry was undeniably a piece of nude statuary.

"You can't very well walk into a village looking like that," Andrei said apologetically.

Porfiry stopped looking offended and stroked his beard. "Yes, I see what you mean. One doesn't wish to cause a riot. But really, what is there to wear?"

Andrei eyed the bundle next to Yurisa. "Well..."

A dreadful grinding choking noise echoed around the clearing, and Yurisa leapt to her feet.

"What was that?"

"It's the cold," Porfiry said. "Poor Wenceslas has got ice in his pipes."

"Wenceslas?" Andrei asked, baffled.

"The fountain," Porfiry said. "I thought he ought to have a name, and since he's hung about with those elegant swags of greenery, I thought...Wenceslas!"

With one final herculean gargle, the newly christened fountain spat out a fist-sized chunk of ice, which embedded itself in a nearby tree.

Andrei flinched. "Ouch. But what's the connection?"

"Wenceslas means wreath," Porfiry said. "You didn't know that?"

"Does it matter?" Andrei said, getting slowly to his feet.

"Names and their meanings are important," Porfiry chided.

"While we're on the subject," Yurisa said, turning back to the fire, "you'd better get used to calling me Yuri."

Porfiry looked puzzled. "I beg your pardon? Didn't Andrei say last night that you..."

Yurisa rolled her eyes. "You can't call me Yurisa while I'm travelling as a man. It would give the whole thing away. Like Andrei did last night. So you'd better call me Yuri."

"Oh, I see. Yes, of course. Yuri it is. Meaning youthful," Porfiry added. "How very appropriate."

"What does Andrei mean?" Yurisa asked, stirring the little pot over the fire.

"Manly," Porfiry said, and stifled a little snicker.

Andrei's hand rasped across his chin. "I need a shave."

Porfiry tsked. "Far be it from me to discourage anyone from their personal grooming, but you may find it hard to shave without any water."

"We have no water?" Andrei asked, seized with alarm.

"There's plenty of water," Yurisa said. "It's just all frozen."

"Then it's not water," Andrei objected.

"Ice is still water," Yurisa said. "It's water in a solid state."

Andrei made a face. "That's totally unhelpful, thanks. Can't we melt some over the fire?"

"It takes a lot of time and fuel," Yurisa said. "We need to make the most of what we've got, and that means drinking it, not using it to pretty up your face."

"Pretty—?" Andrei was speechless, but action did not fail him. Yanking the chunk of ice from the tree, he waved it through the porridge-scented steam rising from the little pot on the fire, and rubbed it on his chin, stifling a gasp at the sting. Flicking out the razor—which seemed positively hot by comparison—he grimly began to shave.

Porfiry uttered a little cry of horror. "My dear boy! You're bound to cut yourself!" He ostentatiously covered his eyes with a hand and turned away as well. "Oh, I can't look!"

"The ice will restrict the blood flow to his skin," Yurisa said calmly. "So you're not likely to see any blood, if that's what's bothering you."

Porfiry turned back. "As a matter of fact, I've never been good with the sight of blood. Particularly not my own. Still, with this chill in the air, Andrei here could probably cut his throat from ear to ear and he wouldn't bleed till spring."

"It is unusually cold," Yurisa agreed. "I was saying only yesterday—no, the day before—that my mother would say on days like this that someone had spoken ill of the Lady."

Andrei's hand slipped, and he nicked his earlobe—which alas, was not as cold as his chin. He felt his skin warm as a drop of blood seeped out.

Porfiry screamed faintly and buried his head in the neighbouring snowdrift.

"Just let it chill," Yurisa advised, "and don't touch it. Silver is a pure metal; you're not likely to get infection from it."

Andrei was staring at Porfiry. "Can he breathe in there?"

"Does stone need to breathe?" Yurisa asked in return.

"No, I don't," Porfiry said, rapidly turning himself the right way up again, "unless I want to speak."

"When don't you?" Yurisa muttered to the fire.

"What was that?" Porfiry enquired, putting his head on one side and tapping vigorously to empty the snow out of his ear.

"So do you still have blood?" Yurisa asked, eyes bright with interest.

Porfiry stopped, head still on one side. "Do you know, I really have no idea."

"A little nick is all it would take to find out," Yurisa said.

Porfiry uttered another little scream. "Experiment on myself? Cut myself open? Oh, my dear, I feel faint." He leaned back, and Wenceslas obligingly splashed him with a faceful of water. He sat up, sputtering.

"Enough of that," Andrei said. "We need to be moving on if we're ever going to get to Granny Ludmilla."

"A clever distraction," Porfiry said, "but it won't do. Don't think I didn't notice."

"Didn't notice what?" Yurisa asked.

"The start he gave when you suggested someone had spoken ill of the Lady," Porfiry said. "Nipped himself and all. Guilty conscience?"

"Don't think *I* didn't notice," Andrei put in hurriedly, "that you're trying to avoid the clothing question."

This drew away Yurisa's attention, as he had hoped it would. Setting the pot aside from the fire, she opened her bundle, fossicked in its interior for a moment, and pulled out a plain homespun petticoat.

"Here," she said, tossing it to Porfiry.

"I can't wear that! It's..."

Andrei sighed. "Woman's clothing?"

"*Plain,*" Porfiry said, with a little moue of distaste.

Yurisa glowered at him. "Take it or leave it—and if you leave it, we're leaving you behind."

Porfiry sighed heavily. "Well, if I must, I must. Although really," he said as he slipped nimbly into the petticoat and adjusted the ties about his waist, "it's all rather Find the Lady."

"Find the Lady?" Yurisa asked.

"The three-card trick," Andrei interpreted. "You know, where the man juggles the cards and you have to guess which one is—"

"Yes, I know, but I don't see the relevance."

Porfiry smoothed the crumpled cloth. "Our little band consists of two gentlemen and a lady, does it not? And we have with us the clothing of two gentlemen and a lady, but—"

"I see," Yurisa said. She scooped porridge into two wooden bowls, and handed one to Andrei. "Better get that into you before your voice goes entirely," she said. "I wasn't expecting hangers-on," she added, handing Porfiry the pot, with the wooden spoon still in it.

His eyebrows rose. "I don't believe I have ever before eaten straight from the—" he began.

Andrei took the pot, handed him the bowl, and took a big spoonful of piping hot porridge.

"You should be careful with hot foods," Yurisa informed Andrei. "You could burn yourself somewhere I can't bandage."

"Indeed," Porfiry said, sipping delicately at the steam rising from his bowl.

"You can't burn stone with porridge," Andrei said, picking up his bundle. "Get it down."

Porfiry looked shocked. "What, abandon my manners like a savage? I think not."

"Besides," Yurisa said, kicking snow over the fire and shouldering her own bundle, "heat can shatter a cold stone."

Porfiry's eyes widened.

"This way," Andrei said, pointing north.

Porfiry turned, blowing on his porridge all the way out of the clearing, the mournful sound competing with the wind in the trees.

At this rate reaching Granny Ludmilla was going to take far too many days for Andrei's liking.

❄   ❄   ❄

"His Grace, Duke Maxim," the major-domo announced, and withdrew.

"Maxim!" Valeska cried, leaping up. "Where have you been all this time? I've been frantic with worry. I thought you'd abandoned me to rot in this house forever."

"Oh? Not worried for my safety, then," the duke observed.

He took a seat, without waiting for an invitation, Bronya noticed. A breach of protocol, but if her lady was prepared to overlook it...

"I might have thought that fleeing for my life would have been enough to engage your sympathies," he continued, "but apparently your place of residence is of greater import."

Valeska drew in her breath and sat down suddenly. "I didn't mean that, Maxim," she said, her tone soft and almost tremulous. "I didn't know what was happening, and I felt so alone... And you didn't—" She broke off.

"Didn't what?" Maxim enquired.

"Nothing."

"No, out with it! I insist on knowing in what particular my behaviour failed to meet with your approval."

"You didn't even tell me you were back," she said reluctantly. "Not even a note. You were carousing with my father before I even heard you were alive," she finished, with a touch of her old waspishness.

"We *are* trying to have you reinstated in the Great Palace, are we not?" Maxim queried. "I could, of course, devote myself entirely to inane chatter in the hopes of amusing you, but I felt my energies might be better spent in procuring the good opinion of the one person who can recall you."

"Oh, Maxim! Have you—did he—?"

"Am I an immortal, that I should work wonders? I had enough ado to cool his displeasure towards myself—which has manifested itself in a rather more violent form than providing me with a home and establishment, as he has for you," he pointed out. His eye caught Bronya's and he smiled.

"Bronya, what are you standing there for?" Valeska demanded. "Go and fetch the box—you know the one."

As Bronya slipped out of the room, Maxim turned to Valeska.

"While we are alone," he said, "I must confess to some grave disquietude."

"Father—?" Valeska halted.

Maxim smiled contemptuously. "I do not doubt myself capable of handling *him*," he said, "but there are other considerations which now occur to me. I would not have it thought, when all is made plain, that I took advantage."

"Maxim, I'm sure you would never—"

"Nor that I had presumed upon your gratitude to improve my own standing," he went on. "Therefore I think it best—much as it pains me—that you should be quite free and untrammelled in your choices. If, when you are mistress of your own fortunes, you think it right, *then* I should naturally have no objection."

"But Maxim, do you mean... I—" Valeska stopped, moved her lips as though she would speak, and then fell silent as Bronya returned.

"Well?" Maxim asked, looking from one to the other. "Am I to be let into the secret?"

Valeska flushed. "Since you were so eager to know what I was doing at the silversmith's the other day, allow me to alleviate your curiosity."

She nodded sharply at Bronya, who presented the parcel to the duke.

"I had intended it as a birthday present," Valeska said, "but it appears you were otherwise engaged in celebrating with my father that day."

"Thank you—Bronya, isn't it?" Maxim said.

Bronya bobbed and murmured that it was.

"You are a credit to your position," Maxim said, his voice smooth and affable. "And a very charming companion, I'm sure."

"Maxim!" Valeska hissed.

"May I not even speak well of another person in your presence?" Maxim asked, a touch of hurt in his fine eyes. But at least they were no longer fixed on Bronya, who slipped into an unobtrusive seat at the side of the room.

"That's not what I—"

"Why should she not be praised for doing her job well?" Maxim said mildly. "It is as well, my dear cousin, to remember to speak well of people, not only...otherwise."

Valeska leaned stiffly back in her chair as Maxim opened the box and glanced at the elegant ornament within.

"Oh, yes, very nice," he said. Putting the box down on the table at his elbow without another look, he chatted lightly of this and that, seemingly unaffected by Valeska's unresponsive demeanour. Bronya watched Valeska carefully but surreptitiously. Her face was white, and her lips seemed unnaturally red, as though bitten.

The duke soon rose to go. The sounds of his departure were still in the hall when Bronya uttered an involuntary "oh..." The box was still on the table.

She turned to see Valeska's gaze move from the box to her. A moment's hesitation, and then a swift gesture of command: take it to him.

Heart quailing, Bronya slipped out, catching up with Maxim just as the footman was about to sweep the front door open for him.

"Your Grace!" she called hesitantly.

He turned and took the box with only half a glance. Half a glance for the box and none for her, to her relief and puzzlement. He slipped it casually in the pocket of his greatcoat and a moment later the door closed behind him.

Bronya leaned against the cold support of a marble barley-sugar column, and tried to think. Something was wrong... but her duty called. She took a deep breath, pressed her cold hands to her burning face, and returned to her duty.

"The duke is out of spirits," Valeska said carefully as Bronya re-entered the room.

"Yes, my lady."

"He has recently suffered a disappointment," Valeska went on, still with that unnatural laborious speech, "which makes him speak a little..." She tailed off.

"Yes, my lady." Bronya bent her head over her embroidery. It did not look to her as though it was Maxim who had suffered the disappointment. But her lady's voice was hoarse—perhaps she was sickening for something. Something else...

❄   ❄   ❄

"You know," Andrei whispered hoarsely, "one day I'd like to arrive somewhere by daylight."

Sparsely peopled as the roads were, they had still needed to take evasive action at times to avoid having Wenceslas seen. Yurisa had tried getting him to skim through the woods just off the path, but the resulting crashing and cracking noises proved too loud for anyone's tastes. So they'd spent the day jumping at every noise that could be someone coming, and diving off the path for all sorts of false alarms.

With all the delays, they could barely see the path in front of them by the time they drew near a village. Andrei carried Porfiry's lantern, but it didn't illuminate much. All he could see was a village square with a well, and the dim glow of firelight in the houses about it.

"Tomorrow," Porfiry advised, "we should tell Wenceslas to simply stay still if anyone comes by."

"Nothing at all suspicious about a fountain suddenly in the middle of the forest," Andrei muttered.

"Suspicious, perhaps," Porfiry granted, "but what has that to do with us? We shall be as surprised as any." He registered dramatic surprise at Wenceslas looming among the trees where he'd been told to wait.

"What's this?" Yurisa asked, and Andrei turned to see a dark column of stone standing in the corner of the square. "There's some sort of inscription—bring the lantern!"

He held it near, and Yurisa squinted at the rough lettering.

"In everlasting memory of Tibor the smith's son of this village aged fourteen," she read, "who freed eleven children from the burning schoolhouse at the cost of his own life."

"Only fourteen," Porfiry marvelled. "What a hero!"

Andrei took off his hat as a mark of respect to the late Tibor, and jumped half out of his skin as a heavy hand fell on his shoulder.

"Who's this, then?" a booming voice enquired. "Don't get many visitors to the village, this time of year!"

"I'm, er, Yur-Yuri," Yurisa said, as they turned to face a big man with a lantern, "and this is Andrei."

The broad face regarded them suspiciously.

"Hat, *Yuri*," Andrei croaked.

Yurisa bit her lip and pulled the hat half off her head.

"And I'm Porfiry," announced a smooth voice beside them, and Andrei noticed for a sliver of a moment that he was bowing. The rest of the moment, and several of those which followed, were occupied in noticing that Porfiry was no longer wearing the petticoat.

"Pleased to meet—" the village man began. He stopped talking, held up the lantern and screwed up his eyes. "What's wrong with your skin?" he said suspiciously.

"Porfiry!" Yurisa said, her voice pitched far too high for a Yuri. "What have you done with my petticoat?"

The big man didn't know who to look at now. His head swung back and forth. "Your...?"

"Sister's," Andrei whispered, but he wasn't sure she heard him. Blast this throat! He'd take a muffler now and welcome it, even if it came with Granny's lecture.

"I mean," Yurisa said, dropping her voice at last, "my sister's—she died, I mean—" Flustered, she dropped her hat, and the thick heavy hair fell loose.

There was an awkward silence.

"Tell me," Andrei said, in the most professional squeak he could manage, "have you had any curse—"

The storm broke on the big man's face. "Don't want no cursed ones here! You clear off, you hear me?"

"But—" Yurisa said.

"Igor, get the dogs," the big man bawled.

This was enough for Andrei. He seized Yurisa by the arm and took off, Porfiry dancing along beside them. Wenceslas closed in as they thudded pell-mell out of the village and into the darkness of the forest, running half blind along the track until the baying of the dogs died away in the distance.

Andrei's throat was whipped raw, and Yurisa was doubled over trying to catch her breath, but Porfiry stood languidly by, tapping his beard with a gentle chink-chink sound which was most annoying.

"Really," he said regretfully, "that could have gone a lot better."

Tale and Trial

Andrei was prevented from expressing his feelings by the now complete absence of his voice, but Yurisa spoke for both of them, and he had to admire the pithy directness with which she spoke.

Within two sentences she had Porfiry apologizing, at three he had resumed the missing petticoat (stashed in Wenceslas's top bowl, as it turned out), and by five he was penitently promising to keep to the forest with Wenceslas hereafter and never try to speak to anyone again, let alone appear in such an inappropriate state.

"And now we'd better get some firewood," she said, "since we're stuck outdoors for another night! And Andrei, I need to borrow your razor."

Andrei's eyes widened.

"For my hair!" she said impatiently. "You saw what happened—we can't risk that happening again. I'll have to cut it off."

"Forgive my interjection," Porfiry said meekly, "but if you are unaccustomed to the use of a razor, I don't recommend starting with it behind your back."

Yurisa frowned. "I suppose you're right. But—"

"I could do it," Porfiry said. "I have some little experience—styling wigs, you know, back when they were in fashion. For household theatricals." He sighed. "Back in the good old days."

Yurisa glowered at him from under her heavy fringe, as if trying to see through the purple stone to the mind beneath. "All right," she said at last, with no great enthusiasm.

Porfiry clapped his hands together. "Excellent! Andrei, my dear fellow, pass me the razor."

"Fire first!" Yurisa said, and there was no argument. Andrei was too cold to care about anything else; and Porfiry was in too good a mood to demur. Indeed, he positively skipped about, shaking deadwood free of the snow and piling it up ready for use.

The fire wasn't quite the roaring blaze Andrei had envisioned—not enough dry wood, for one thing—but the warmth certainly made a difference. They huddled around its meagre crackle in the lee of Wenceslas's bulk, as Porfiry planned the forthcoming cut with mid-air flourishes of the closed razor.

"Just something plain," Yurisa stipulated for the third time. "Like any youth would have. Like Andrei's."

"Are you sure you wouldn't—" Porfiry began.

"No!"

"Very well," Porfiry said, with great reluctance. He opened the razor. "I suppose if I slice the main tail off in one piece, I could dodge up some sort of wig arrangement, in case you need to pretend to be a girl again."

"*Pretend* to be a girl?" Yurisa asked, turning round to glare at him.

Porfiry yelped. "Don't move like that! I nearly had your ear off!"

Yurisa resumed her position. "It's a good idea, though. Tie it up before you cut it and I'll put it in with my other clothes."

Porfiry obliged. "So," he said, clearly beginning to relax and enjoy himself. "If you need to return to your female attire at any time, does that mean your present garments will be available for another wearer?"

"No," she said stonily, and Porfiry raised a perfectly chiselled brow.

Andrei mouthed *brother* behind her back and Porfiry replied with a silent *ah* of comprehension.

"Andrei, perhaps you could tell us a story to while the time away?" he suggested breezily.

It sounded like a good way to get away from the tension, but...

"Erk," he croaked, by way of an explanation.

"Or rather, since you have no voice, I myself could double the roles of barber and raconteur," Porfiry went on smoothly. "How about a tale that will chill the very blood in your veins?"

"I'm chilled enough already," Yurisa growled. "And now my neck's cold. Anyway, I thought you didn't like blood."

"Only the sight of it," Porfiry assured her. "I simply adore tales that wallow in gore. However! Perhaps," and his lips in the firelight crooked in a little grin Andrei was unable to make sense of, "a tale about Lady Spring?"

"Go on, then," Yurisa said, and Andrei nodded.

"*Well,*" Porfiry began, "this all happened a very long time ago, if indeed it ever happened at all. There was a youth, a young and handsome youth—"

"A young youth?" Yurisa interrupted. "What else would he be? It's completely unnecessary to say young if you've already said youth."

"Storytelling is more than the efficient transferral of information," Porfiry said sternly, waving the razor for emphasis. "It should be a painting of words, a music to the ears. And it certainly isn't efficient to interrupt. Where was I?"

"A young and handsome youth," Yurisa said sourly.

"Right. So! There was a young and handsome youth, who spent his days as a gardener. Whether or not he was a good gardener, I don't know, but he was certainly ambitious, and so he begged of the Lady Spring a single lock of her hair. Of course, pieces of the immortals are not to be had for the asking, but he was, as I say, a handsome youth, and the Lady Spring is reputed to be rather softer-hearted than her, er, chillier sister." Porfiry coughed, and threw a sideways look at Andrei, which he pretended not to notice.

"And he was a gardener, when all is said and done," Porfiry continued. "Fling another log on the fire, will you, Andrei? I've got to the fiddly bits."

Andrei obliged, and the flames leapt a little higher.

"Much better. Thank you. Spring being soft-hearted, particularly when it comes to gardeners, and the young fellow being not only a gardener, but a handsome one, it is not perhaps completely surprising that she should have acceded to his request."

"What?" Andrei croaked.

"Did what he wanted," Porfiry amended. "Which is to say, she gave him the lock of her hair, and with it, a strand of her power. Now he could command plants to grow, trees to take root and thrive... She dreamed, so the story says, of this handsome gardener, like a noble knight, spreading her glory throughout the land."

Andrei thought of driving through the woods on a warm spring day, and sighed.

"However," Porfiry said, and the change in his voice somehow made the clearing seem darker and colder, "Spring had reckoned without the fatal plague of ambition which, like a twisting vine, had put down its roots in his heart and twined its way through every part of his being, slowly crushing every bit of goodness in him."

Andrei shivered.

"It began with the little things, as tragedies are wont to do," Porfiry said gently, the flashes of firelight from the razor in his hands slowing to keep time with his speech. "First, accepting gifts from grateful recipients of Spring's bounty. Then witholding said bounty from one who was, perhaps, less than deserving. But then he slid from accepting gifts to expecting gifts, and those who had nothing to offer were left with nothing more. It was hinted, then known for a fact, then stated outright, that even the most undeserving could have what they wanted for a price—and if the price was high enough, others could be kept out and kept down."

Porfiry paused to dust the loose hairs off Yurisa's neck with her hat.

"But then a darker thought arose in his mind," he continued. "For not every plant that Spring blesses is a blessing to those that work the earth. Thorns he could cause to grow, and strangling bindweeds too. He had the power—and he used it. Of course, he only had to use the power once or twice before the mere threat of it was enough. People would pay anything to protect their land from being turned into a thorny waste overnight—they would even give up some of the land itself.

"He grew rich," Porfiry said, "and proud, and scorned even the pretence of being a gardener. Thorns—or the threat of thorns—made much better business. But he had forgotten one thing—for every tragic fall can be traced to the ignorance of some great principle or other. He had forgotten that though he wielded a power which no other human could equal, his power was only a part, a lock, a shred of what Spring's power is. And though she is soft-hearted, she is not weak, and her patience has its limit."

Andrei hunkered into his coat and put another couple of thick sticks on the fire. One of the sparks landed on Porfiry's beard and winked out, leaving no mark on the cool stone.

"She came to meet with him—it is said, in the guise of a poor peasant woman. The moment he scorned her timid and empty-handed request, she threw aside all disguise, and, towering above him like a linden whipped by the storm, she let him feel the dread fullness of her power. The very chair on which he sat sprang into life; it sank roots in seconds through the cold stone of the marble floor, and branches sprouted, pinioning him and piercing him through and through...and so he died."

There was silence for a moment, but for the wailing of the wind in the skeletal trees.

"But the lands he cursed," Porfiry said thoughtfully, "are said never to have grown anything but thorns, ever again, no matter how they were worked upon. The treacherous youth had died—but his curse lived on forever."

"That's not very encouraging," Andrei whispered. "Under the circumstances."

Porfiry shrugged, his face mantled with melancholy.

"That *was* the blood-chilling story, wasn't it?" Yurisa demanded.

The wicked little smile reappeared, and with an abrupt resumption of his usual cheery manner, Porfiry flicked the hat once or twice about Yurisa's shoulders. "There you are, Yuri my boy! Just like Andrei's. What do you think?"

Yurisa looked at Andrei. "Well?"

Andrei nodded. It was a bit neat for a peasant boy's cut, but then so was his. Nothing too gaudy, that was the main thing.

"Thanks," she said gruffly, and pulled on her hat. Then she pulled it off again, and looked inside. "Why is this so prickly?"

❆   ❆   ❆

Valeska Kira sat uncompromisingly upright at her dressing table and watched a reflected Bronya brush the reflection of her hair. The sweeps of the brush were long and slow and smooth, intended to be relaxing, as it had always been before, but on this night it seemed to Valeska as the stroking given to a caged beast that must be appeased. The rigidity of her frame did not soften for a moment. At last, unable to bear a moment more, she put up a hand and blocked the brush mid-stroke.

"That will be all for tonight," she said, her throat tight. "You may go."

"But my lady, your hair isn't—"

"Go!" Valeska half screamed, and Bronya fled, scarcely pausing to lay down the brush.

The heavy door had barely closed behind her hurried retreat when the perfect posture contracted, Valeska's figure convulsed by sobs. Her closed hands drove into her hair, beat on her head, tried to yank out locks they lacked the power to grasp. At last she stilled, and a voice from under the now tangled tresses spoke.

"If no one loves you, it's no more than you deserve."

She lifted her head and caught the eye of her dishevelled reflection. The words slowly ground out of her as she stared herself down in the glass.

"You're just like your father."

Morning found Andrei feeling considerably more cheerful than the night before, mostly because Yurisa had put her training to good use and concocted a syrup for his throat. True, the taste was terrible, and lingering besides, but at least he could talk again. He didn't even mind that she had used the syrup to blackmail him into promising to buy a muffler at the first opportunity. There were worse things than mufflers.

His mood was further improved by their happening across a good-sized hamlet in the early afternoon. He cast a significant look at Porfiry, who stopped, cast up his eyes, placed a hand over his heart, and sighed for good measure, before ostentatiously perching on Wenceslas's lower rim.

"We'll be back," Andrei assured them. The last thing he needed was Wenceslas thundering after him because he felt abandoned.

There was no one about in the hamlet at first sight, but Andrei could hear the clinks, splashes and thumps of human occupation, and a tang of woodsmoke combined with a rather more earthy smell on the breeze.

A man holding a large hammer ducked out of a smoky door-way and nodded to them. If this wasn't a smith, Andrei had never seen one in his life. He gave the smith a cheery good afternoon.

"Visitors, are you?" the smith asked, eyes wary.

"We're looking to buy provisions," Andrei said.

"And a muffler," Yurisa said.

"And a muffler," Andrei agreed. "If you have anyone who deals in that sort of thing."

The smith pulled at his chin, leaving streaks of grey ash in the dark curls of his beard. "Well, not as a general thing in the way of business, but there's an old woman who might have a few things handy. Lost her husband not so long ago," he explained, and led the way.

"You've not lost any others, have you?" Yurisa asked.

Seeing the man look taken aback, Andrei took it on himself to smooth things over. "It's been a hard season in some villages—lots of illness."

The man looked relieved. "No, nothing like that, I'm pleased to say. Just the one loss this season, and he was a good age."

"Have you had anything odd happening lately?" Yurisa asked.

"Odd how?" the smith asked, brows beetling.

"Oh, there are all sorts of rumours flying around," Andrei said, as casually as he could manage. "Talk of monsters and all sorts of things."

The smith looked at him suspiciously. "Happy to say not," he said, and knocked at a weathered wooden door.

The woman who came to answer it was only too happy at the prospect of exchanging some of her old things for money in the hand, and they ended up buying not only a shabby old muffler, but a pair of elderly and baggy leather breeches for Porfiry as well. Provisions she couldn't provide, but she directed them to someone she thought could—first having secured a little something more for the use of her barn for the night.

"Smooth as a sleigh on snow," Andrei said smugly as he and Yurisa carried their newly purchased food to the old barn. "Food, shelter, warm clothes..."

"No information," Yurisa said.

"You're not going to stand there and tell me you're sorry no one's under a curse here?"

"I'm not sorry," Yurisa said. "No healer would want that. But it doesn't get us anywhere."

"Except a day closer to Granny Ludmilla," Andrei said.

"Half a day," Yurisa said. "We could have got a lot further before nightfall."

"We'll leave before dawn tomorrow, then, if that makes you feel better," Andrei said, stretching out luxuriously on the sweet dry hay. "We'll have to anyway, or they'll spot Wenceslas—or Porfiry."

"You should go and get them," Yurisa said.

"Why me?" Andrei asked sleepily.

"I can't go walking arou—" Yurisa stopped. "I can, can't I? Yuri can do whatever he likes."

She slipped out, but Andrei was asleep before she closed the door. He slept on in blissful rest until the moment Porfiry was presented with the breeches, at which point continued unconsciousness became impossible.

❄   ❄   ❄

Porfiry continued to bewail the hideousness of the breeches all through the following morning. Andrei would have let him go back to the petticoat just to shut him up, but his dramatic laments were the only entertainment in an otherwise featureless day. There were no villages, no travellers, nothing to catch the interest; only an endless snowy path to plod down, step after boring step.

At length, Porfiry stopped to draw breath.

"I've had a thought," Yurisa announced.

"Is it about clothing?" Andrei asked, and Porfiry perked up.

"No."

"Good," Andrei said. "Let's hear it."

"We've managed to get a bit of information so far," Yurisa said, "but we don't have a clear idea of how it fits together. We need a systematic understanding of this...thing." She still avoided using the word *curse*, Andrei noticed.

"The rules it plays by," Porfiry said, nodding.

"Exactly," Yurisa said, a spark of enthusiasm lighting in her eye.

"So we walk faster, get to the next village sooner, and hope we get some better answers," Andrei said.

"That's just more information," Yurisa said. "We can't choose what information we get, either. It's just..."

"Playing blind man's buff with one hand tied behind our backs," Porfiry suggested.

Yurisa gave him a startled look. "I suppose you could put it like that."

"And you have some more useful idea than walking faster?" Andrei said sourly.

"We need to conduct some experiments," Yurisa said, and his mouth dropped open.

"But—you—I'm telling Granny!" he exploded.

"Not on *people*," Yurisa said, giving him a look which suggested he was a complete moron. "That would be unethical."

"I haven't heard of it affecting animals," Porfiry said, adding "unless you count Baron Boris, of course."

"And you're not experimenting on Wenceslas," Andrei said firmly.

Wenceslas uttered a deep hollow groan and stopped dead at Andrei's back, almost as though sheltering behind him.

"Wenceslas is an inanimate object. Well, not human, anyway," Yurisa amended.

"Are you sure?" Porfiry asked.

Wenceslas gave an angry gargle.

"I fear I have offended him," Porfiry said. "I do apologize! No one would mistake you for anything but a fountain, however mobile."

Wenceslas subsided, and they moved on down the track.

"If not Wenceslas or animals," Andrei said, brow wrinkling, "what are you going to experiment on? Trees?"

"I mean us," Yurisa said, and both her hearers stopped dead in their tracks. There was a faint chink as Wenceslas bumped into Porfiry.

"In what way is that not experimenting on people?" Porfiry quavered.

"Not experimenting on *other* people," Yurisa conceded. "We are trying to get answers, aren't we?"

Andrei recovered himself. "I would like to make it very clear that I am not volunteering for anything of the sort, and if you so much as think of experimenting on me without my permission, Wenceslas and I are leaving."

"I feel faint," Porfiry announced, draping himself backwards over Wenceslas's lower bowl in a graceful droop.

"There isn't going to be any blood," Yurisa said impatiently. "Just words. We need to test the theory that it's words that are causing this."

Porfiry half sat up, a hand pressed to his chest. "Are you seriously suggesting that we should curse each other?" he asked, eyes wide.

"It's the best way to gain a better understanding of the problem," Yurisa said stubbornly. "I'm not afraid, even if you are."

"I salute your courage," Porfiry said, doing so with a flourish, "but I feel I am definitely cast for the audience in this particular performance."

"Hear, hear," Andrei said. "Bronya accused me of rushing into things without thinking, but let me tell you, I'm not touching this."

"Fine," Yurisa said, chin jutting. "I'll have to do this myself." She took a breath, and the two watchers took an involuntary step backwards.

"Are you sure this—" Porfiry began.

Yurisa closed her eyes and said in a loud, firm voice, "Yurisa, you are stupid."

Porfiry gasped, and Yurisa's eyes popped open. "Did anything happen?"

"No," Andrei assured her.

"Then what did you want to go gasping for?" she demanded of Porfiry. "You're disturbing my concentration. Let me try again." This time she kept her eyes open, but again, nothing happened. She repeated it.

"So what are you expecting to happen?" Andrei asked. "I mean, what are you going to turn into?"

"How should I know?" she answered crossly.

"Andrei's right," Porfiry said, peeping around from behind Wenceslas where he had taken refuge. "You'll have to be more specific. I mean, Boris didn't just call me decorative, he said I belonged on a pedestal."

Yurisa screwed up her face in thought. "What was it...oh, yes. Yurisa, you're as thick as two short planks," she carefully enunciated.

"I can't look!" Porfiry said.

"There's nothing to see—no change, I mean," Andrei corrected himself.

"Maybe you've got the wording wrong," Porfiry said anxiously. "Try it in the first person."

"The what?" Yurisa asked.

"Saying *I* instead of *you*," Porfiry explained.

"Good idea," Yurisa said. "I'm as thick as two short planks."

"Still nothing," Andrei reported.

"A mirror?" Porfiry proposed. "So you can look yourself in the eye when you say it."

"You're getting awfully enthusiastic about this, for someone hiding behind a fountain," Andrei complained. "Anyway, we don't have a mirror, do we? Who would bring a mirror on a journey like this?"

"I would have if I'd had time to pack," Porfiry said. "Yuri?"

"What? Oh, of course not," Yurisa said absently. She was making notes in a tiny book with an even tinier pencil.

"Of course, it doesn't have to be a mirror," Porfiry mused. "Still water? Sheet of ice with black cloth behind it? Shine up the cooking pot—no, I know!" He beamed at them. "Andrei's razor!"

"The razor to the rescue again," Andrei said pointedly. "I'll let you use it, on one condition."

"What's that?" Porfiry asked.

"No more cracks about me not having a beard," Andrei said.

"All right," Yurisa said, an eager hand already extended to receive the razor.

"Porfiry has to agree too," Andrei insisted.

Yurisa gave Porfiry a look.

"Very well," he conceded. "The vein of humour was very nearly mined out in any case."

Andrei handed over the razor, and Yurisa carefully opened it and held it before her eyes.

"I'm as thick as two short planks," she said.

"Nope," Andrei said.

"Yurisa, you're as thick as two short planks," she tried.

"Still no. Didn't we already rule that out?" he asked.

"It pays to be thorough," Yurisa said, and went on to test the other wording she'd tried. Nothing happened, though by this point no one expected it to.

She lifted her eyes from the little notebook. "So it appears that it is impossible to curse yourself."

"Good to know," Andrei said. "Now can we get moving again?"

"Of course." Yurisa shouldered her burden and they moved down the path in silence.

Before half an hour had passed, Porfiry broke out with "All right!"

"All right what?" asked Andrei, startled.

"I'll be an experiment," Porfiry said, striking a dramatically martyred pose, "on one condition."

"Let me guess—no more breeches?" Andrei asked.

"No more breeches," Porfiry agreed.

Andrei looked at Yurisa. A struggle was playing out on her normally inexpressive features.

"You have to wear something," she said at last.

Now the struggle was on Porfiry's features, although it was a lot more vividly depicted. At last, curiosity won.

"Very well," he said. "The petticoat let it be, until some better alternative presents itself. And no calling me stupid. To be ill-dressed is bad enough, but to be an ill-dressed fool would be immeasurably worse."

Yurisa whisked the petticoat out of her bundle and turned her back as he changed. "Ready? All right, then. Um."

"Um?" Porfiry queried.

"I'm trying to think of what to say," she explained.

"Let me," Andrei said. "Porfiry, you're as vain as a girl."

Porfiry uttered a shriek and closed his eyes.

"Calm down, nothing happened," Andrei said. He met Yurisa's unfriendly gaze.

"As vain as a girl?" she asked, pointedly stroking her chin.

"Hey! We agreed no more cracks about my beard!"

"I didn't say a word," Yurisa said. "Anyway, I'm a girl, and I'm not vain. It's a false comparison."

Andrei rolled his eyes. "Fine. Porfiry, you're as vain as Lala."

This time Porfiry's eyes opened wide, and he swatted at Andrei with the old leather breeches.

"How could you? To threaten me with such a fate—without the slightest warning!"

"It hasn't worked, anyway," Andrei said, "so there's no point yelling about it."

"Hmpf!" Porfiry crossed his arms. "I'm not sure I want to go on with this."

"I'm not sure there's any point," Yurisa said, brooding over the little notebook in her hand. "It does appear that you can't be cursed twice."

"Really?" Porfiry beamed. "That is *such* a load off my mind, you can't imagine! I'm invincible!" He struck a heroic pose, the effect of which was somewhat diluted by the petticoat. "Oh, you could experiment on me all day, and I wouldn't mind." He turned to Andrei. "You should try it, you really should! Just think what we could find out!"

"That's exactly what I am thinking about," Andrei said firmly. "The answer is still *no*."

Porfiry pouted. "Well, *I'm* still willing," he said.

"There isn't anything to be gained from testing on you. You would only return a false negative," Yurisa said, setting her chin and setting off down the path once more. "No, if there is any more testing to be done, it'll have to be done on me."

"Such bravery," Porfiry said, pressing a hand to his heart. "You are so manly," he added with a sidewise glance at Andrei.

A chill breeze seemed to pass over Andrei. Up ahead, Yurisa stopped in her tracks. A moment later came the chink of stone on stone as Porfiry clapped a hand over his mouth.

In silence they watched as Yurisa pulled away her muffler, loosened her clothes at the neck, and peered down her front.

"Well," she said, without turning around, and her voice had a timbre Andrei hadn't heard before. "That seems conclusive."

Blessing and Curse

Maxim burst through the dining room door, his fur cloak still swirling about him, lightly dusted with snow.

"There you are, my dear! We must be off at once. Have your maid bring your skates and your outdoor things."

Valeska gazed at him, bewildered, as Bronya tactfully put the fork down on the edge of her lady's plate and averted her eyes.

"Maxim, I've barely begun my meal. Won't you sit down?" Valeska added.

"Didn't you hear a word I said?" Maxim demanded. "Girl, go fetch your lady's skating things. Quick, now!"

Bronya rose, but waited for a sign from Valeska, who was still staring at Maxim.

"Maxim, you know I'm not...that is, that skating is not my preferred outdoor recreation."

Maxim uttered a noise indicative of frustration or contempt—Bronya couldn't quite tell which—dragged a chair away from the table and flung himself into it.

"I have, at great personal cost and effort," he announced, "succeeded at last in persuading His Imperial Majesty to a meeting. I rush straight around here to bring you at once before he changes his mind, and what do I hear? You don't care for skating and in any case you haven't finished your meal."

Valeska half rose in her seat, and Bronya took this as sufficient confirmation of Maxim's orders. She'd barely stepped into the hall when one of the housemaids appeared, and Bronya took the opportunity to pass on the order and return to her lady.

"But why?" Valeska was asking plaintively when Bronya returned to the dining room. "Why such a public place? Even the servants go skating there, I am told."

"One can hardly blame the Czar for preferring a public encounter," Maxim said, "considering the result of your last little tête-à-tête."

Valeska's white cheeks flushed with an ugly reminder of the print of her father's hand.

"No, I suppose not," she said quietly, eyes on her lap where her hands lay clenched.

There was some further delay in the hall while Bronya and the maid got Valeska into her outdoor things, and then they were off at a great speed in Maxim's sleigh, Bronya clutching two pairs of skates.

Her first duty on arriving at the popular frozen pond was to fasten Valeska's skates to her boots, a task made all the more difficult by Valeska standing up every time she saw someone in the distance that might be her father, or a sleigh that had the line of his. But even after Bronya had put on her own skates and joined the princess and the duke on the ice, the Czar was nowhere to be seen.

It seemed to Bronya that practically everyone in the city was there, except the Czar. She kept close behind her lady and just to one side, ready to extend a bracing arm should Valeska seem likely to fall. Maxim was at her other side, his arm closely held in hers, but in Bronya's view he was skating far too fast for his inexperienced companion.

Valeska's attention being constantly elsewhere didn't help either. She was forever tripping on the rough surface of the ice, or lurching ungracefully when Maxim changed the pace—which he did frequently, having a large acquaintanceship to

greet. His manner was impeccable, never forgetting to intro-
duce people to the princess in the appropriate style demanded
by etiquette, but Valeska's mind was clearly elsewhere, and she
made a poor showing. Bronya slunk along behind her, unno-
ticed and unintroduced, and burning with embarrassment by
proxy.

As the afternoon passed the crowds dwindled, the fashionable and unfashionable alike seeking the lights and warmth
of home. The princess and her attendants circled the ice again
and again, until the light slowly faded from the leaden sky, and
even Valeska had to admit that the Czar was not coming.

Maxim insisted on coming in to tea, "to cheer you up," but
Bronya could tell that Valeska would rather have been left
alone to weep the frozen tears banked up behind her eyes.

She exerted herself to be hospitable, however, and ordered
tea in the drawing room as the major-domo relieved Maxim of
his cloak. As Bronya settled Valeska in a chair by the fire with a
rug over her knees, the sound of Maxim's voice came through
the open door from the hallway.

"So cold and reserved," he was saying. "No wonder her father keeps his distance."

No reply was audible, and the next moment the duke himself strolled in, the door closing behind him.

Valeska stood, the carefully arranged rug dropping to the
floor in a heap.

"What did you just say to my major-domo?" she asked icily.

Maxim met her eye without a flinch, and leaned gracefully
against the mantelpiece before replying.

"Eavesdropping?" he murmured. "Hardly the behaviour of
a lady, much less a princess."

"I was not eavesdropping," Valeska protested. "I couldn't
help hearing what you said. How could you say such a thing?
And to a servant!"

"My dear girl," Maxim said, a look of faint surprise upon
his face, as though he'd found a snail in his fish course. "If you

cannot stand to hear a word of critique, how do you suppose you will ever mature into a ruler of any worth? Do you suppose that a Czar—or Czarina—is surrounded entirely by servants who never find the faintest fault with them? You must learn to be less absurdly sensitive. You are not a child any more. Suppose you don't act like one."

"I—I'm sorry," Valeska said, looking away with a little frown pinching her brows.

"Perhaps we could all sit down," Maxim suggested, "instead of standing around in these highly dramatic positions? You don't want to give the servants more to talk about, after all. Besides, you've had a tiring day."

Valeska sank back into her seat and Maxim took the seat opposite, stretching out his long legs towards the fire. Bronya tucked the rug back into place, and hastened to place a table to hand for the tea, which was now being brought in.

Maxim sipped the first cup with a satisfied *ahh*.

"Now," he said, "we've undeniably had a setback today, but we mustn't repine. He agreed to meet us, and that's a step in the right direction, I feel, regardless of the immediate outcome. Now we must decide what approach we're going to take next."

Valeska sat by the fire with her teacup between her lace-mittened hands, and listened.

❄   ❄   ❄

It took some time to revive Porfiry from his dead faint. Even turning him over was no easy task, given his weight, and once he'd begun to regain consciousness he filled the air with such outlandish and extravagant apologies, self-reproaches, and wishes to be rendered into gravel and used to fill holes in the most dismally muddy road that could be found, that it was some time before Andrei had time to take stock of the situation, and by then it seemed too late to be shocked about it.

Yurisa wasn't just pretending to be Yuri now, that's all there was to it.

It was an awkward and silent afternoon, followed by an equally awkward and silent evening around the little fire. Yurisa clearly didn't want to talk, which was almost a relief—at least to Andrei, who had no idea what to say.

Porfiry, on the other hand, was clearly finding the ongoing silence a burden, judging by the way he opened his mouth to speak, closed it again, looked eloquently at one or the other of his travelling companions, and then bit his lip, muttering something to himself in an undertone. Even Wenceslas was silent and lumpen. Andrei had never been gladder of an early night in his life.

Contrary to all his hopes, the next day continued equally silent and awkward. Porfiry kept looking meaningfully at Andrei, and then towards Yurisa, but whatever it was Porfiry wanted him to do, Andrei wasn't interested in doing it. Yurisa announced in a gruff voice that she wasn't going to go into the village this time; she had thinking to do. This was fine by Andrei. He left Porfiry in charge of guarding Wenceslas, and hurried away.

This was a much bigger village than some of the ones they'd been to recently—Andrei could even see an inn sign swinging in the sharp wind, just off the square. A good place for picking up some gossip, he decided, and set off with a brisk step. So intent was he on his goal that he didn't notice the harried-looking woman approaching until he collided with her.

"I'm so sorry!" he said, helping her gather her scattered bags, and retrieving an errant onion from where it had rolled away.

"Not to worry," she said breathlessly. "I wasn't looking where I was going either, I was that bothered about—well, never mind that, you're not interested in my problems."

"Oh, I don't know," Andrei replied, presenting her with the onion. "A problem's like an abcess, my granny says: best not let it build up inside. She's a healer," he added, since the woman looked faintly repelled by the idea.

"A healer!" she said, and seemed relieved.

"Is someone you know in need of a healer?" Andrei enquired sympathetically. It was coming at the curse from a bit of a side wind, but you never knew what you might get.

"No, thank goodness! It's not that at all. No, it's this blasted thing." She fished an item out of her bag and waved it at Andrei.

"Is it supposed to be that shape?" Andrei asked, speculating in fascinated horror as to what the contorted metal implement might be for.

"Of course not! I mean, look at the thing, it's nothing but scrap. And don't tell me it got like that in transport, because it was all wrapped up and the Howlers are always very careful. I didn't even find it was like this till I got it home, and now I've got to track down the Howler man and start the reversal before the time runs out. It's not as though anyone else can start it."

"Last buyer's privilege," Andrei said weakly, thinking of the old bone-backed brush.

The woman looked at the damaged thing in her hand and snorted. "Privilege! Should have sent it unwrapped, then perhaps someone further up the chain would have had the sense to start the reversal and save me the trouble. You all right?" she asked, apparently more cheerful for having got her troubles off her chest.

"Painful memory," Andrei said. Time to change the subject. "Surely the Howler man won't be hard to find? Since you already know where his booth is."

"He's not there any more," she said. "Bet I know where he is, though—gone down to the Golden Goose to see if he can offer his services to the young lady there. What it is to be a step above, eh?"

"Young lady?" Andrei asked absently, mind already on the Golden Goose and its no doubt roaring fire.

"Daughter of some noble or other," the woman said. "I saw her arrive. A carriage drives up like it's the Czar himself and when all's said and done, no one steps out but a girl like one of those pink sugar cakes you eat on the First Day of Spring."

Andrei started. "Pink?" he quavered.

"And nothing but," the woman said, shaking her head. "My girls were mad enough on pink once, but thank goodness they grew out of it."

Andrei moistened his lips. "Do you know what business brings her here?" he asked.

The woman chuckled and dug him in the ribs. "Looking for a man! Well, who isn't, at that age? It's one man she wants in particular, though—says they were all set to run away together and her father interfered. So now she's hauled her poor coachman out in the depths of the season to comb the land for the poor fool. Doesn't seem very—" but Andrei waited to hear no more.

Yurisa's head snapped up as she heard him approaching. "Well?"

"Well?" Porfiry repeated as he came down the track poised on Wenceslas's bowl. "What did you find out?"

Yurisa had her little book all ready.

"Lala," Andrei wheezed.

"What?" Yurisa asked, plainly confused.

"Lala...there," Andrei said by way of explanation, waving a hand weakly in the direction of the village he had just left.

"Lala's there?" Porfiry asked incredulously. "What on earth dragged her out in the middle of—her father's not with her, is he?" he asked, and Andrei could almost have sworn the dark purple stone was paler for a moment.

"No—don't think so." He took a breath. "Pretty sure she would have said."

"Well, what did she say?" Porfiry said. "Tell me all!"

"I didn't see her," Andrei said, his breathing back under control. "It was a woman in the square. She said Lala had arrived at the inn. Well, actually, she didn't say Lala, but she did say it was a noble's daughter all in pink, and—"

"Lala," Porfiry agreed.

"So what else did you find out?" Yurisa asked impatiently.

Andrei looked at her. "You seriously expect me to wander around asking questions in a town which contains Lala? She's hunting me down!"

Porfiry drew in his breath sharply. "What did you do to the poor girl?"

Andrei blushed. "Nothing! It's just—she thinks—well, there was the ladder, you see, and she had already packed, and her father—"

Porfiry stifled a giggle. "You mean to tell me Lala thinks you're eloping with her?" The giggles were completely un-stifled now; they overflowed like a gurgling fountain as he drooped to the ground under the weight of his laughter.

Andrei could feel his face burning red, but whether it was embarrassment, anger, the biting wind, or all three, he couldn't tell.

"That's *it*?" Yurisa demanded, getting to her feet. "You heard she was there and you just ran away? What kind of—" Words failed her for a moment. "You're hopeless!"

Forget the wind; forget Porfiry uttering squeaks of helpless mirth in the snow; this was anger. "You think you can do better?"

"Easily!" she shot back. "No wonder your granny sent me along—you wouldn't get anywhere without me!"

"I'd be talking to Granny Ludmilla by now if it wasn't for you hangers-on," Andrei retorted.

"And you'd have nothing to tell her!" Yurisa said, and flung away through the trees.

"Come back here!" Andrei shouted. "We're leaving—right now!"

She didn't so much as turn around.

"We'll never get to Granny Ludmilla's at this rate," Andrei grouched, sitting down on the rim of Wenceslas's bowl.

"Oh, my stomach," Porfiry groaned weakly. "Who knew that stone could hurt with laughter?"

"I'm not talking to you," Andrei said, and turned away. It was childish, but he didn't care. He was on this mission to make a life for himself and Bronya, not to be laughed at and derided by a couple of people he didn't even ask to come along. He had every reason to sulk.

The darkness of nightfall was nearly complete by the time Yurisa returned.

"Haven't you even built a fire?" she demanded. "Useless, the pair of you!"

"How were we to know you'd be gone so long?" Porfiry asked. "No sense lighting a fire if we're about to depart, is there?"

"I bet you didn't even find anything out," Andrei said, but once the fire was finally lit, he saw a large bruise marking her cheek.

"Yuri! What happened to your face?" Porfiry uttered in alarm.

"My name is Yurisa," she growled.

"But you said we should call you Yuri," Porfiry objected.

"Things have changed," she said savagely. "You don't want to be called lawn ornament, do you?"

Porfiry winced, and fell silent.

"The curse?" Andrei asked, to change the subject. "I mean— in the town?"

"People aren't talking," Yurisa said, not meeting his eye.

"So you discovered nothing," he said, not even trying to hide the smug note in his voice.

"I discovered there's something people are deliberately not talking about," Yurisa countered. "Which is more than you two have managed."

She stood and looked down at Porfiry through the curling smoke of the fire. "I still don't know why you agreed to let him come along. He can't talk to people without starting a riot, and he slows us down. He's no use at all." She wrapped herself tightly in her blanket, settling down with her back to the fire, and that was the end of the night's conversation.

Halfway through the next day's trudge, Porfiry uttered a mournful sigh. As this was the first utterance any of them had made all day, it was startling enough to make the others jump. Even Wenceslas sputtered.

"Very well," Porfiry said, affecting not to notice them glaring at him. "I will begin. Andrei is brave, friendly, and generous with his personal belongings."

"Brave?" Yurisa repeated, eyebrows raised.

"He climbed up a rope ladder into a building he knew to contain a monster," Porfiry reminded her. "And he's come up against the Czar, who I hear was intimidating enough before he, ah, changed. To continue: Yuri is—sorry, *Yurisa* is intelligent, resourceful, and calm."

"Hmpf," was all she said.

"And now that I have begun the ceremonial overtures of reconciliation," Porfiry said, "perhaps you could take my example and we can move on together in the manner of a well-matched team."

He was the lead horse, Andrei immediately thought, trotting in the centre, with Yurisa and Porfiry cantering to each side. His pace quickened at the thought, and it came to him that Porfiry, for all his fooling, was very clever.

"Three things," he said aloud.

"That's traditional," Porfiry said. "One kind word will warm three cold months, they say. Just think what three words will do! And since we are all within a step of each other, they don't have to be written down."

"Porfiry is clever," Andrei began. "And amusing, and..."

"Witty," Yurisa said.

"I was going to say that!" Andrei protested.

"Too late," Yurisa said with something almost approaching a smile. "Porfiry is a peacemaker and good at cutting hair."

Andrei gnashed his teeth for a moment. "Adventurous!" he said at last. "Porfiry is adventurous."

"Oh, I'm blushing," Porfiry said. "Now each other. Go on, my children!"

There was a silence.

"Yuri—sa is...uncomplaining," Andrei began reluctantly. "Mostly."

"Andrei is good at talking to people," Yurisa muttered.

"He's decisive," Andrei went on.

"She!" Yurisa shouted, and they all stopped.

"But you're—" Andrei gestured helplessly. "You know."

"That doesn't make me a man!" she raged. "Porfiry isn't *really* a statue, is he? Boris isn't naturally a monster!"

"Well..." Porfiry murmured.

Andrei remembered his Granny saying the insults that hurt most are those that have a grain of truth in them. He opened his mouth, thought better of it, and closed it again.

"The curse has made me have a man's body, just like it's made Porfiry have a stone body," Yurisa said, a bit more calmly. "But we're still the same people inside."

Porfiry applauded. "Well said, dear girl!"

Yurisa flushed. "You should probably still call me Yuri when people are around," she mumbled.

"She's decisive," Andrei said carefully, "and bold."

"Bold?" Yurisa asked, looking closely and suspiciously at Andrei.

"In a good way," he hastened to add. "Most girls wouldn't have gone off on a quest just like that, and cut their hair and everything."

"Hmm."

"So, that's..." Porfiry did a quick count, fingers whisking

about between the three of them. "Two more for Andrei, Yu-risa."

"I'm thinking," she said, and by the time they stopped to make camp for the night, she had thought of two more: "daring" and "not fussy". The evening passed away as they made lists of three for Wenceslas—even though there was no insult or argument to make up, it was more fun than just staring at the fire, and infinitely more relaxing than listening to one of Porfiry's hair-raising stories.

❄   ❄   ❄

The weather was just as bitter the next day, but it felt warmer as they strode along, Porfiry cracking jokes and telling extravagant tales to while away the hours.

"Can you hear something?" Andrei cut in to the latest tale of scandal.

Porfiry stopped, a little put out.

"What?" Yurisa asked, head cocked.

"Hoofbeats," Andrei said confidently.

"Are you sure?" Porfiry asked, clearly dubious about there being any noise at all.

"Of course he is—he's worked all his life with horses," Yurisa said. "I think I can hear a faint sort of drumming..."

"Who would be going that fa—" Andrei's eyes widened. "Lala! Off the track!"

He flung himself into the woods, whippy little branches slashing at his face, and heard the crash of Wenceslas's bulk shoving through behind him. Off to the side he could hear Porfiry's muffled giggles. He stopped and turned, crouching next to Wenceslas so he could see the path, but remain unseen.

Now that his first panic was over, he wasn't so sure it was Lala. He could only hear one set of hooves, and none of the creaks of harness or carriage body or sleigh runners. Then who...

The thud of hooves drew nearer. Andrei watched, mouth slipping slowly agape, as a centaur—wearing the dark red coat of a Howler courier—cantered briskly down the track.

"Hey!"

His head whipped round. It was Yurisa, stepping out on the path behind the creature. The centaur reined in—no, Andrei corrected himself, there were no reins, he just skidded to a stop—and turned, looking politely back down the track.

"Something I can help you with?" he asked, and then took an involuntary step backwards as Porfiry and Andrei emerged from the forest.

"Howler," he said warningly, indicating the jacket. Not even an outlaw would attack a Howler—the consequences were a penalty not worth paying.

"We just want to ask you some questions," Yurisa said.

"Like how long have the Howlers bred centaurs?" Andrei said, imagining a centaur coachman.

Yurisa cast up her eyes briefly. "It's the curse, Andrei. Centaurs don't really exist. Well—you know what I mean."

The centaur grinned. "I don't know that I'd call it a curse. Bit of a shock at first, of course, but it's been great for work. I mean, horses are wonderful creatures and all, but being a centaur courier is a step beyond. I'm the fastest thing on four legs in the empire. I've cut half a day off my run. Speaking of which..." He began to inch away.

"When did this happen?" Yurisa asked insistently. "And how?"

The centaur scratched his head and whisked his tail about his gleaming sides. "It's been...a few weeks now. My brother and I were...well, showing off, really—he's a courier rider for my uncle too, but he has the eastern run—and the next thing you know...centaur!"

"So your horse...?" Porfiry asked, eyebrows raised.

"Got the fright of his life," the Howler said ruefully. "I fell off, of course, the moment it happened, and then it was all a confused tangle of legs—lucky neither of us broke anything, really."

"What was going on at the precise moment it happened?" Yurisa asked, and sure enough, she had the little book out. "Did somebody say something to you?"

The centaur stared at her and stopped fidgeting. "How did you know? It was some chap who was watching—said that we were practically centaurs."

"We? So there's two of you?" Andrei asked eagerly. A team of centaur coachmen! A matched pair!

"Centaurs, you mean?" the Howler asked. "No, it's just me. As far as I know, of course."

The three travellers stared at him.

"Is there...something I should know?" he asked uncomfortably, sidling a little.

"The man said we—I mean, you," Yurisa fumbled.

"What my friend here is asking," Porfiry took over, "was whether the man's comment was in the singular or the plural."

"Eh?"

"Did he say *you are* or *he is* or *they are* or what?" Andrei interpreted.

The Howler's brow cleared. "Oh! 'Practically centaurs, aren't you?' is what my aunt said he said. I didn't notice myself, I was busy."

The three travellers stared at each other.

"Is my brother in trouble?" the Howler asked anxiously.

"Not at all!" Andrei said heartily. "But you're sure he was talking about both of you?"

"Oh, yes. Tanty wouldn't change details like that. She's a Howler, after all," and he straightened his backs with pride. "We make a living from precision. Speaking of which, I do have a schedule to meet..."

"Of course! Thank you for your time, and may we wish you a safe and profitable journey," Porfiry said courteously.

"Thanks," the courier said, clearly relieved to leave the conversation behind. "Chilly for the season, isn't it?" and he galloped away.

"Fascinating," Yurisa said.

"Isn't it?" said Andrei, who was already mentally altering the necessary harness. The strength of a horse with the intelligence of a man...

"I think we can agree he's the first patient we've encountered who regarded the curse in a positive light," Yurisa went on.

"Wait till he wants to settle down and can't find a nice centaur filly to settle down with," Porfiry said dryly. "I wager he'll change his tune fast enough then."

Yurisa frowned and turned to him. "He couldn't do that. I mean, even if centaurs existed, it—it wouldn't be ethical. I mean, you wouldn't marry a garden statue, would you?"

Porfiry cast his eyes up in horror. "Marry a block of stone? How utterly dull!"

"But you're kind of a block of stone," Andrei argued.

"But never dull," Porfiry said. "And as far as I have discovered to date, there is no such thing as a piece of garden statuary who can make even passable conversation. On the contrary, they are all, without exception, inanimate objects. The idea is beyond the pale, and I simply refuse to discuss it any further."

"That isn't the interesting thing, though," Yurisa said.

"What, Porfiry's marriage prospects?" Andrei asked.

"The centaur's marriage prospects," Porfiry corrected.

"Neither," Yurisa said. "Not even that he thinks being cursed is a good thing—for him at least."

"It did seem odd about his brother," Andrei said slowly.

"Exactly. The words were said about both of them, but only one changed," Yurisa said earnestly. "That is a discovery of great significance."

"Yes, but what does it mean? The curse can only affect one person at a time?" Porfiry asked.

Yurisa hesitated. "Possibly. It's a good theory to be going on with, but..."

"I am not volunteering to be experimented on," Andrei said firmly. "We've been over this before."

"It wouldn't do any good even if you did," Porfiry said sombrely. "We'd need two people to test, and you're the only one of us left uncursed."

They followed the Howler's trail through the thin snow in silence, the wind seeming sharper and the day darker than before.

❊   ❊   ❊

"I still think we should press straight on to Granny Ludmilla's," Andrei groused, following Yurisa through a hanging mist towards the large village of Velika. They had left Porfiry telling Wenceslas a dramatic story in which the hero was made of stone; Andrei only hoped it continued to hold the fountain's attention.

"And tell her what?" Yurisa asked. "Something's going on and we have no idea what?"

"She's the expert," Andrei reminded her.

"Even the best healer needs to be told all the symptoms," Yurisa replied.

It was very irritating, the way she always had an answer which seemed to make sense.

"Fine," Andrei said. "We just keep going into every village between here and her and ask the first person we see for information?"

"Yes." Yurisa waved a hand. "Excuse me!"

A figure materialized out of the low-lying mist, a red-cheeked young woman with big round eyes. "Oh! you startled me." She looked closer at them. "I don't believe I've ever seen you before, either. Not many young men round these parts," and she giggled.

First Lala, then Porfiry, and now this girl. Andrei was devoutly thankful that Bronya wasn't a giggler.

"What brings you to our village, then?" she asked, looking them up and down.

"Have you noticed anything strange happening lately?" Yurisa asked.

The girl's already round eyes opened wider.

"Anything out of the—" Andrei began.

"You need to see Mother Libusa," the girl said hastily, and turned away, beckoning them to follow.

"Mother Libusa? What's her..." Andrei tailed off. Curse? No. Ailment? Not exactly.

"She's the matchmaker," the girl said, and giggled again.

A brisk walk through the foggy street brought them to a comfortably-sized house, standing alone. The girl knocked at the door, and it opened a crack.

"Mother Libusa? There's a pair of young men here, from out of town. They're here about...you know?"

The door was flung wide and they were practically hauled into a warm, brightly lit kitchen. Getting his bearings, Andrei found the girl had not accompanied them in. They were alone with Mother Libusa, who had nothing wrong with her at all that he could see. No horns, no extra limbs, not made of wood or stone, just a short dumpy woman with a beam on her face that could have lit the room without the assistance of the two fine lamps.

"I can't tell you how wonderful it is that you're here," she said, clasping her hands and gazing at them with what seemed like excessive relief. "We don't have many young men in these parts, and let me tell you, it warms the cockles of my heart to know that there are still two brave young men like yourselves willing to do a good turn for your countryfolk."

Andrei, blushing, looked sideways at Yurisa. Had their reputation preceded them? Did Granny have something to do with this?

"Tell me," Yurisa said, getting out her little notebook in a businesslike manner, "how long have you been under this affliction?"

Affliction! That was the word. He must remember it.

Mother Libusa was staring at Yurisa with a strange look on her face. "It's not me, dear," she said. "Did you think it was?"

"Um..." Yurisa said.

Andrei felt for her. There is no tactful way to tell your hostess you thought she was under some kind of hideous curse.

"It's the girls," Mother Libusa said, and there was a calculating look in her eye that Andrei wasn't able to make sense of. "Orphaned twins, and only nineteen years old. But they're not paupers," she assured them.

Andrei's brow hitched itself into a frown. What did money have to do with any of this, when anyone from the Czar down to Luka the peasant boy could be affected?

"Perhaps we'd better see the girls ourselves," Yurisa suggested.

"Well! You are keen." Mother Libusa hesitated for a moment, and then shrugged. "Why not? Might as well get it over with, I suppose. They're through here."

She took up a lamp and led the way to a diminutive staircase which squeezed itself up into the roof of the house. Opening the door at the top, she stood back and let Yurisa in first.

"After you," Andrei said politely at the top of the stairs, but she pushed him through the door with a surprisingly hearty shove, and the next moment came the bang of the door behind him, and the clunk of the key turning in the lock.

"I'll just go fetch the smith," Mother Libusa called from the other side of the door. "Won't be long!"

"Smith?" Andrei asked, but then his eyes adjusted to the gloom of the little attic, and he saw the two girls huddling close together on an old iron bed in the shadows. They had feathers...and beaks.

The Wielder of Words

Yurisa recovered first, fishing her little book out of her pocket and poising her pencil. "I can see your problem," she told the two cowering girls. "Now supposing you tell us all about it. How did it come to be both of you?"

The two girls looked at each other, and then back at Yurisa.

"Kuaaa," the one on the right said.

"Bok," the other added softly.

"Oh," said Yurisa. "You can't talk, is that it?"

"Bok bok bok," the bolder one said, bobbing her head gently.

Andrei finally found his voice. "Yuri, they're halfway to chickens!"

The two feathery girls looked at him reproachfully, and he was conscious of having trampled upon some law of politeness.

"Sorry," he said, automatically. "I suppose I'm not the first person who's said that, am I?"

The girls groaned like—really, there was no other word for it—like broody hens.

"So why didn't Mother Libusa give us the details herself?" Yurisa asked, her broad brow furrowed. "What does she think we can do up here?"

The bolder girl looked significantly towards a shelf in the corner, and then cast a melting gaze upon the two visitors.

Andrei moved closer to the shelf and peered through the

murk. It held four plain iron rings.

"Yuri," he croaked.

"And what did she mean about the smith?" Yurisa wondered.

"Yuri!"

"What is it?"

He held up one of the rings, and had the satisfaction of seeing her jaw drop. She hitched it up in a moment.

"Don't be ridiculous," she told him. "That has nothing to do with it."

"She's gone for the smith," Andrei reminded her. "What for if not to hear our vows? There's no ironwork in here needing fixing that I can see."

Yurisa turned back to the girls. "You can't be serious! What good do you think trapping him into marriage is going to do?"

The girls ruffled their feathers and sighed.

"But marriage isn't a cure!" Yurisa cried.

They regarded her coldly. Clearly, this wasn't the sort of response they were looking for from their intended.

"I say we go out the window now," Andrei said firmly, "before Mother Libusa gets back."

This provoked a flurry of squawks from the prospective brides.

"Not till we've found out a bit more," Yurisa said.

"I'm not marrying both of them," Andrei said. "There are four rings here. Think, Yuri, that's what you're good at."

Yurisa frowned. "You mean—but I can't marry one of them! I'm a girl!"

The feathered girls uttered a horrified squawk as one, and then huddled back on their perches on the bed.

"You may find that difficult to prove, *Yuri*," Andrei said.

Yurisa breathed sharply in and out for a moment.

A door opened and closed below, and a heavy tread sounded on the floor.

She turned to Andrei. "You're right," she said. "The window."

There were no bars, but the two girls were not going to let their prospective bridegrooms get away that easily. The feathers flew, but mercifully their hands had not much grip, and by the time the attic door burst open, Andrei and Yurisa were sliding down the snow-slicked roof, and leaping to the ground.

Andrei started off at a dead run, but a cry from Yurisa turned him back.

"My ankle—landing," she moaned. She tried to stand, but fell again.

He dashed back, got his shoulder under hers, and started to run. A door slammed, and a bellow rent the air.

"The smith—you'd better go on without me," Yurisa gasped.

Andrei made no answer. "Wenceslas!" he shouted desperately. "Wenceslas! Heel!"

A crashing sounded in the distance.

"He'll never get here in time," Yurisa said in despair.

"We need a diversion," Andrei muttered, and a flurry of shouts broke out behind him, followed by a whoop.

"Was that—?" Yurisa said.

"Porfiry? Sounds like," Andrei said, wondering what fresh mischief he had invented now.

Up ahead, the trees squeaked in protest as they were firmly parted by Wenceslas barrelling through.

"Finally!" Andrei said. He half dragged, half rolled Yurisa into the lower bowl, and set a course for the forest, Wenceslas close behind. He risked a glance back, and saw the smith slowed to a stumble, staring blankly at Wenceslas's retreating bulk.

A moment later, both the smith and Andrei had their attention drawn away, this time to the spectacle of Porfiry running mother-naked between the village houses, yodelling and waving something large and white over his head. A solid-looking fellow charged up to him, was promptly enveloped in the white thing, tapped firmly on the head, and de-enveloped, all with Porfiry's customary panache.

"Time to be going," Andrei said, and plunged into the trees.

"What about Porfiry?" Yurisa asked from behind him.

"He'll catch up," Andrei said, and indeed, it was only a few minutes before they were joined by an elated Porfiry, sporting not only the petticoat—which he had wrapped around his head like a turban—but the large white thing draped around him like a statue of old.

"You stole someone's bedsheet?" Yurisa asked.

"Anyone who is fool enough to hang their sheets out to dry in a thick mist deserves whatever comes to them," Porfiry said grandly. "I fancy it rather becomes me."

"I fancy it becomes bandages," Yurisa said. "I've broken my ankle."

❄   ❄   ❄

"Duke Maxim, Your Highness," the major-domo said, the words not even out of his mouth before Maxim had flung into the room and thrown himself down in a chair. The major-domo receded under Maxim's glare, closing the door rather more quickly than his usual dignified pace.

"Maxim! What's wrong?" Valeska asked, her hands pressed close beneath her chin.

"I've had enough of that man!" Maxim said, his fist thumping the elegant wooden arm of his chair.

"The major-domo?" Valeska asked. "What has he—"

"Not him! Do I look like the sort of man who has squabbles with domestics? No—it's your father. He's absolutely—"

"Don't say anything you might regret," Valeska cautioned hastily.

Maxim gave a harsh bark of laughter. "I might have known you'd take his side! I expend every effort on your behalf and he treats you like dirt, but no, you take his side in everything!"

"He is my father," Valeska said. "And the Czar."

"That toy bear you kept in your nursery would make a better Czar!" Maxim snapped. "It was probably a better father to you, as well. You even called it Kiril, as I recall. Even the coldest heart needs something to love, I suppose."

Valeska sat back in her chair, back stiff and lips pressed so closely together they looked almost white. Bronya wanted to reach out, take her hand, say something comforting, but it was a liberty she knew Valeska would not overlook, no matter how distressed.

"Have you still got the mangy old thing," Maxim enquired, "or is it being kept in readiness for the washerwoman's brat?"

Valeska did not answer, her face turned to the fire and her lids blinking rapidly.

"Not that it matters," the duke went on. "Really, why you can't see what's staring you in the face! Do you know what your precious Czar Kiril said today? There was I, pleading for your rights as his firstborn, his child by a lady of rank, and making great ado over all the similarities between you. Not that you've given me much to work with, there," he added in an aside. "If you tried to be a little less uptight I think he'd like you more. Most people would."

Valeska opened her mouth to respond, but he charged on.

"You're both domineering, of course, but he carries it off better. So there I was, talking about how much you look like him—the eyes, you know, and the brow—and he gives this great laugh and says that yes, she's a chip off the old block all right."

Valeska turned to look at him, and her wet eyes were alight. "He said that?"

"He did. His very words were, 'It's a pity she's got such a look of me, or I'd've disowned the bitch by now.'"

Bronya could not restrain a little cry of shock, but Valeska was silent, fallen back in her chair with the blood drained from her face, gazing blankly at the wall.

Bronya started up, but Maxim was ahead of her. In a trice he was on one knee at Valeska's feet, with his hands wrapped around the cold hard lumps of her fists.

"But I'm still here," he said, a warmth in his voice which seemed to drown out the flames crackling in the fireplace. "I've always been here for you, Valeska, and I always will be. You can trust me—you know you can."

Valeska's stiff lips parted. "Maxim..."

"I'm here," he repeated. "After all we've been to each other—all we are—do you think I would abandon you? No!"

"What are we going to do?" she asked, still staring dazedly at the wall.

"We'll get there together, you and I," Maxim promised. "We just need to plan around him—without him. Don't you agree?"

"We need a plan...without him...." Valeska echoed.

Maxim smiled and kissed her hands, and Bronya went to look out the window.

❄   ❄   ❄

It was a distinctly less cheerful group of adventurers that plodded down the road the next morning. Yurisa was grumpy at having to be carried by Wenceslas—wrapped in every garment they could muster to shield her from the cold; Porfiry was grumpy about losing half his sheet to Yurisa's ankle; and Andrei was grumpy about the whole situation having arisen in the first place.

"I told you we should have just pressed on to Granny Ludmilla's," he said.

"I heard you the first three times," Yurisa snapped.

"This time we're doing something about it! No more wandering about asking questions! We go straight on and we stop only to sleep! We'll be there in two days, at that rate."

"I hate to rain on your parade," Porfiry said waspishly, "but you've only got a day's worth of food left. Of course, it's no inconvenience to *me*," he added pointedly.

"We'll have to go into one more village, then," Yurisa said.

Andrei ground his teeth. "Only one! And no asking questions, either. We get in, we get the food, and we get on to Granny Ludmilla's."

There was no argument. Porfiry pulled his damp half sheet a little closer about him, and Yurisa slithered uncomfortably in the lower bowl, trying to get Wenceslas's central pillar between herself and the thin icy rain.

"We can't get there too soon for me," she muttered. "Not with this weather."

"I quite agree," Porfiry said, shaking the droplets off his fingers with an air of distaste. "But—well."

"Well what?" Andrei snapped. "If you've got something to say, say it, don't garland it round with flowery fluff."

Porfiry drew himself up. "Very well. From the very beginning of my association with this undertaking—indeed, from the very beginning of the undertaking itself, if my colleague here is to be believed—" with an incline of the head towards Yurisa, "the weather has been a source of more than seasonable unpleasantness."

"If this is your idea of not talking a lot of fluff, I don't think much of it," Andrei said sourly.

"You know he's right, Andrei," Yurisa put in.

"More than once it has been suggested in jest that this was due to some, er, *person* insulting the Lady; and your behaviour in response to these sallies and flights of wit has rather tended to suggest that you are, in actual fact, the one responsible."

Andrei didn't say anything, but he could feel a burning inside that cut against the cold.

"Which was a very stupid thing to do," Yurisa said.

"As you do not take the trouble to deny it," Porfiry went on, "I take it that such is the case; and that *being* the case—"

"Oh, just get on with it, can't you?" Andrei shouted.

"—you ought to apologize to the Lady in some way, and above all, *soon.*"

"I agree," Yurisa said. "I should have thought of that before."

The burning spilled. Andrei turned to face them, and the icy rain clawed at his cheek. "Apologize? To that cold-hearted bitch? If Winter's so small-minded that she can't take a bit of constructive criticism, *she* ought to be apologizing to *me!*"

Porfiry and Yurisa stared at him in shocked silence. At last Porfiry gathered himself.

"I really think you should not have said that," he said carefully, and, moving to the other side of Wenceslas, he set off at a brisk walk. Andrei hunched into his collar and strode ahead. He wasn't going to let *anyone* start taking the lead or telling him what to do. This was *his* quest, after all.

As the day closed in around them, so too did the forest. The track was still—just barely—wide enough for a large cart to pass through, providing it met nothing coming the other way, but twists and turns hid the track ahead from the travellers' eyes. A dangerous place for driving, Andrei thought, plodding glumly over the rough ground. Uneven terrain, hidden corners—definitely not a place a coachman worth his salt would speed through. Since he was on foot, however, speeding was exactly what he wanted to do.

He had got some distance ahead of the others when there was a gargling yell behind. Andrei whipped round, just in time to see a very dirty man leap out of the trees alongside the path and take a swing at Yurisa with a rusty sword. She threw herself flat and the sword whistled past the rim of Wenceslas's bowl.

"Your money or your life!"

Porfiry hurled himself out from behind Wenceslas and received the next blow on his raised forearm. The resulting clang died away in the fog rising through the trees as Andrei slithered back down the track towards the others. The road-robber flicked his gaze towards Andrei and back. No element of surprise, then...

Porfiry looked at his arm and shrieked. "I've been chipped! You...you wretch!"

"Names ain't gonna hurt me," the dirty man said, his sword swinging from side to side as he tried to keep both Porfiry and Andrei in view. "But cold hard steel is gonna hurt you plenty, if you don't start handing over some eagles!"

"Do I look like I'm carrying eagles?" Porfiry demanded, whisking the half bedsheet away with a flourish. "Where precisely do you imagine I'm keeping them, pray tell?"

"Aargh!" Andrei tried. "A magical stone man and a moving fountain! It must be a curse!"

The road-robber gave Wenceslas scarcely a glance. "Seen stranger things than that this season, let me tell you. Eagles! Now!"

Andrei slipped closer. His razor would be no good against a sword like that, old and rusty as it was. And the fact that he'd managed to chip Porfiry suggested the road-robber had plenty of muscle hiding under that scraggy coat. But perhaps between them...

"You, then," the road-robber said, his gaze flicking across to Andrei. "Or the fathead in the fountain, I don't care, but someone's got to have something and they'd better start handing it over!"

"How dare you call me a fathead?" Yurisa demanded hotly. "Don't you know words—"

The idea was in Andrei's mind and out his mouth before he could think twice. "Call this an ambush? More of a rosebush!"

❄   ❄   ❄

The rosebush had roses; he hadn't been expecting that. They were a sort of dirty pink, and they made Andrei feel very uncomfortable.

"Couldn't you have asked a few questions first?" Yurisa asked. "He's no use like that, is he?"

"There is a time for questions, and there is a time for action," Porfiry declared. "Andrei, I forgive your harsh words about my eloquence."

"I take them back," Andrei replied. "You bought us time by distracting him."

"Well, one does one's best," Porfiry said, trying to look modest and looking only like a Sculpture in Praise of Modesty. "I take it as some consolation that I can now claim to have been wounded in action. Tremendously heroic, don't you think?"

"You were wounded?" Yurisa asked, leaning dangerously far out of the bowl to see.

"A chip in my arm!" Porfiry said, holding the affected arm out for her to see and draping the other dramatically over his eyes.

"That's interesting," Yurisa said, poring closely over the chip.

"What is?" Porfiry asked in trepidation.

"You don't bleed."

Porfiry looked closely at the chip himself. "You're right. I may never see my own blood again!" He beamed.

"Shouldn't we be pushing on?" Andrei asked. "This isn't really the best place to camp, and it'll be dark soon."

"Of course." Porfiry turned to take one final look at the rosebush. "I'm sure it's not healthy for a rose to have blooms at this season," he said, stroking his beard thoughtfully.

"Do you think we should prune him?" Yurisa asked impatiently.

Porfiry uttered a little shriek and clasped a hand to his abdomen.

Andrei sympathized—he felt a bit sick at the thought himself. "We'll just have to leave him and hope for the best," he said, hoping no one would ask him what the best would be.

"Let no one say I am not magnanimous in victory," Porfiry said, and he draped the half bedsheet over the rosebush with a flourish. "With any luck, this will keep the worst of the frost off."

"And what's going to keep the frost off you?" Yurisa asked sourly. "Don't think we haven't noticed that you're half naked again."

"If you hadn't insisted on taking half my sheet," Porfiry riposted, "I might now be only two-thirds naked. Or is it three-quarters? Mathematics was never my strong point."

Still muttering to himself and drawing fractions in the air, he followed the others as they moved on down the darkening track. Andrei looked back from the next turn in the path, and shivered. The sheeted bush was still visible in the low light, with the mist swirling around it giving it almost the appearance of movement. Andrei turned away, and walked on.

❄   ❄   ❄

Andrei insisted he be the only one to go on the (by now very necessary) food-buying expedition. Yurisa fretted over a dozen things she wanted asked, and called another couple after him as he left, but he waved them away. Getting to Granny Ludmilla, that was the main thing. All this question-asking was just groping about in the dark for a lamp which might not even be in the room.

The first thing that struck him as he entered the village was the smell. The second thing was the large number of un-penned pigs, which at least explained the smell. He watched the largest creatures warily as they lounged about near the doors of houses, but they seemed disinclined to move. Still, he was uncomfortably aware of their small dark eyes watching him as he picked his way along.

A group of piglets came rushing towards him and then fled squeaking away when he got too close, one or two sows grunting with an alarm which wasn't quite enough to get them to their feet.

"Hullo there!" Andrei called, and a door creaked down the end of the village's one street. A head poked out, with a pipe poking out of its mouth. A person, at last! Andrei quickened his steps.

"I'm passing through and looking to buy food," he called.

The door opened further, and an old man hobbled out. Andrei drew up and gave him a friendly smile, which was not returned. A well-grown piglet with a dirty stubble of bristles snorted at him, and darted about the old man's feet. The old man took his pipe out of his mouth, aimed a kick at the piglet, and put the pipe back.

"Perhaps a nice sucking pig?" Andrei said, gesturing to the stubbly piglet. It uttered an ear-splitting squeal and ran away.

The old man took his pipe out again. "That's my nephew. Can't eat him. More's the pity."

Andrei's mouth stopped halfway to his next question.

The old man snorted with laughter.

"Your nephew?" Andrei looked back down the street, to a villageful of pigs watching him.

"Can't eat them either," the old man said.

"They're all..." Andrei couldn't quite say it.

"Yep. Real pigs are out the back, if you're—"

"No, I think I've lost my appetite for pork," Andrei said weakly. A whole village...

The old man threw back his head and laughed heartily, though his face was as unsmiling as ever when he had done.

"How did it happen?" Andrei asked.

"One man calls another a pig, he becomes a pig, and from there it's nothing but payback and pigs and more pigs," the old man said.

"You must be very well thought of in the village," Andrei said respectfully. "It's clear no one thought of calling you a pig."

The old man snorted. "Don't you believe it. People in this village have called me any name you can think of, but I'm not turning into a pig for anyone."

This was a new take on curse resistance, but not one Andrei thought Yurisa would be impressed by. "So, um, when did this happen?"

The old man scratched his head. "Just after Midseason, it'd be. Everyone with a bit of a head from the day before—you know how it is—and tempers short. That'd be it. They were all human for Midseason, I remember, because of the princess coming through twice."

"Twice?"

"There and back again," the old man said. "Went past to the Lady's Lake Midseason morning; stayed here that very night and left south again in the morning."

"And have you had any strangers come through recently?"

"'Sides the princess and her lot? No. We don't much care for strangers in this village, though you wouldn't have thought it the way this lot went flocking down to see the princess off." The old man coughed and spat. "Even my nephew couldn't think of anything better to do than go hear half a dozen words from a girl who wouldn't know him again if she saw him and wouldn't care if she did."

"I take it you didn't go, then?" Andrei said cheerily. If there was one thing he'd learned from working under Coachman, it was that it didn't pay to argue with people who were set in their opinions.

"'Course I didn't. Only man in the village who didn't." The old man seemed proud of this.

Something stirred in Andrei's mind. "When you say 'the only man'—do you mean you were the only person, I mean, man, woman or child, who didn't go?"

"That's right. Now are you buying food or—"

But Andrei was gone, streaking away like Winter herself was after him, hurdling pigs with barely a check in his stride.

❄   ❄   ❄

"It's her!" he gasped minutes later, bursting into the spinney where his companions waited.

Porfiry leapt to his feet in alarm, and Yurisa sat up suddenly.

"Lala?" Porfiry asked, eyes wide.

Andrei could only shake his head, bent double, and suck in the freezing air.

"What do you mean, 'it's her'?" Yurisa asked. "And where's the food?"

"Never mind food," Andrei croaked at length, just as Porfiry was getting restive with the wait, and Yurisa was proposing making him write in her little book, if he couldn't come out and say it. "It's the princess—Valeska Kira—it's her words. The curse."

"Don't be silly," Yurisa said promptly. "It was Porfiry whose words changed me, and Boris whose words changed Porfiry, and—"

"Not the change," Andrei said, straightening up slightly and leaning on a snowy branch for support. "The...what do you call it."

"That explains everything," Porfiry said, straight-faced, and Andrei gave him a dirty look.

"What makes people change or not, when they're worded," Andrei went on. "Everyone in that village is a pig except for one man who didn't go to hear Valeska Kira speak when she left after her visit to the Lake. Different people said the words, but only the man who didn't hear her speak didn't turn into a pig."

"When you say that *everyone in that village is a pig...*" Porfiry began.

"Yes. Pig. Four legs, little tail, oinks—pig."

Yurisa waved them into silence. "So your theory is that if the princess speaks to someone, that makes them susceptible to being cursed?"

"Susceptible! That's the word. Listen—" but she waved him into silence again.

Her lips moved silently as she ticked things off on her fingers.

"It's possible," she conceded at last. "It's not proved, because we don't know that many of the afflicted we've seen *were* spoken to by the princess; but it is possible, because we don't know for certain that they weren't."

"What was the point of taking all those notes if you aren't going to look at the little book?" Porfiry enquired.

"It helps my memory to write things down," she said.

"So I imagined, but—"

"To write things down, not to read them later," she added.

"Could we return to the point?" Andrei demanded hotly. "Which is that the heir to the Throne of Seven Steps is making every person she talks to susceptible to being cursed. Including Bronya!"

"We don't know that for certain," Yurisa said calmly.

"Don't we? Think about the villages we've been through! Velika, Zeva, Monik—it's a direct line south from the Lake. It's Valeska Kira's path home from the Midseason visit—down as far as Boris's estate to take Lala home, and then back through your village. And think how many people used her visit as a marker for when the curse started!"

"That could be because not much happens in these villages," Yurisa said.

"I've thought of something," Porfiry announced with great satisfaction.

"For or against?" Yurisa asked.

"Against. What about the rosebush? When would she ever speak to him—as a road-robber, I mean, not a rosebush. Princesses may well speak to rosebushes, although I must say VK doesn't strike me as quite the sort to—"

"The road-robber!" Andrei clapped a hand to his head, which felt surprisingly cold from the outside, given the fire that burned within. "Coachman said there was a road-robber on the way back who tried to assail them, and Valeska Kira stood up in her carriage and drove him back with a withering blast of words."

"I can imagine that," Porfiry said, shivering.

"It has to be the same road-robber," Andrei said. "It has to be Valeska's speech. It has to be."

"It might be," Yurisa said grudgingly. "But we'll have to test it."

"Test it! What do you mean? Find someone we know she's spoken to and turn them into another pig?" Andrei demanded.

"Of course not! But if your theory is correct—*if*—then any village beyond the Lake won't be affected by the curse. Didn't you notice anything when you were passing through on your way south?" she added, more than a hint of criticism in her tone.

"Passing *by*," Andrei corrected. "And I was a bit distracted," he added sourly, jerking his head in Wenceslas's direction.

"You could have provided a lot of useful information if you had just—"

"Yes, yes, all right!" Andrei burned to get on, to take wing, to get to Granny Ludmilla as quickly as possible, if not sooner, to find out how to dissolve this curse, and to get Bronya... His skin crawled.

"Bronya," he said. "I have to get to Bronya, get her to safety! Valeska talks to her every day! The next conversation she has with someone—what if someone shouts at her in the street? She could be—"

"If Bronya wouldn't leave her when she thought VK was under a curse," Porfiry said, "I don't imagine she'll be the sort to turn her back now. That's a point—what about VK's hands? *Is* she under a curse?"

"Never mind that now!" Andrei begged. "Let's get moving!"

"There's no sense in starting back to Istvan now," Yurisa said patiently. "We're days away from there, and only a day or two at most from Granny Ludmilla's. Better to go to her first, and see what help she can give us. After all, the Czar is probably still out for your head."

"And you'll do Bronya no good if you lose it," Porfiry said.

Andrei wavered. "Fine, then! We go straight to Granny Ludmilla's—no stopping by the Lake or anything." He started off.

"Of course," Yurisa said.

Andrei was suspicious. This docile attitude was not what he had come to expect from her.

"And while we stop for food at a village on the way, we can ask if they've had any trouble with the curse," she added.

Andrei groaned, and broke into a run.

Any Port in a Storm

Valeska sprang to her feet as the clatter of speeding horses' hooves echoed through from the courtyard. She flew to the drawing room door, Bronya getting there just in time to open it for her. They had barely reached the hall when they met Maxim, cloaked and booted and dressed for travel.

"I must speak with you," was his only reply to Valeska's greeting. "Somewhere private."

She led the way back into the drawing room and motioned to a chair. Bronya slipped in behind the duke and closed the door, standing ready to block any untimely intruders offering refreshments.

"What is it? Do you have news?" Valeska asked eagerly.

"Both good and bad," he said. "I must leave town at once—I've barely a moment to spare. Your father—unreasonable as ever—has turned against me once more. I am hunted for my life."

"Oh, Maxim! You must go at once—don't think of me," Valeska said. "Go!"

"My dear! Allow me at least to share the good news before I depart, perhaps never to return."

He drew out of an inner pocket a small phial of dark liquid. "I won't say what I went through to gain this, but I will say this: there are still some in this land who are learned in the old powers of magic, and from one such mystic healer I received this. Guard it well," he said, "for in this phial all our hopes are contained."

"What is it?" Valeska asked, beckoning Bronya forward to take the phial her own hands could not hold.

"An elixir to restore your father," Maxim said. "When he knows the service we have done him, he cannot fail to change his mind about us—both of us. He has a generous heart, when all is said and done."

"But how am I to get it to him?" Valeska asked, her eyes feasting on the slim bottle. "You know he—won't see me."

"Nor me, now," Maxim said. "But you are an imperial princess, Valeska. After your father, you have the highest authority in the land, don't you? So use it."

Valeska bit her lip. "I don't see how I can. He'll ask where it comes from, and then he won't take it."

"Of course you don't just send it along with a note saying 'be a good boy and take your medicine'," Maxim exploded. "Of course he won't take it if he knows it's medicine! When has he ever taken medicine in his life, I ask you?"

"Then how...?"

"Have your girl here take it to the Great Palace, and give it to the major-domo with your instructions," Maxim said impatiently. "He can find a chance to get it into the Czar's glass some night or other, when he's had enough not to notice the taste. He's probably done it before, a man in his position, conspiring with the palace healer for the Czar's good. Nothing to it, and the fewer who know about it the better."

"Yes—oh, yes!" Valeska turned to Bronya. "Bronya, you must take this at once. See that you speak to the major-domo, and no one else—no one else in earshot even! And make sure he knows the importance of the timing—we don't want Father noticing the taste and pouring the rest of it away."

Bronya stood staring at the phial in one hand, pleating her dress with the other.

"Please—please, Your Highness, I can't."

"Can't?" Maxim demanded. "It was not a request."

"Bronya," Valeska said, the hurt in her voice sending a pang through Bronya. "Of course you can do this—you must! It's the only way. Do it for me, if not for the Czar. Why wouldn't you?"

"I just...I don't think this is a good idea," Bronya said, the phial growing slippery in her suddenly clammy hands. "What if the Czar should be taken ill by chance that same night— from—from too much wine—how will it look?"

"Am I risking my life to listen to such drivel?" Maxim demanded. "If Her Imperial Highness requires your opinion, girl, she will ask for it. Until such time, it is your duty to remain silent and do as you are told."

"Bronya, please," Valeska began.

"Please?" Maxim said incredulously. "Valeska Kira, remember who you are! It is beneath the dignity of an imperial princess to plead with a servant, let alone one who began a mere brat in the gutter."

He rounded on Bronya. "Everything you are, Valeska Kira has made you—and she can unmake you with a word."

Bronya looked imploringly at Valeska, tears welling. "I've always done everything I could for you, my lady, acted in your best interests, served you well! Please..."

"You've never been disloyal before..." Valeska said slowly.

"And am not now," Bronya began, but Maxim's anger crashed over her pleas, her cautions.

"So you prefer to heed a servant's advice to mine?" he demanded, taking Valeska by the wrist. "After all I've done for you—risking my life again and again!—you would cast me aside at this menial's word?" A bright red spot stood high on each cheek. "Perhaps to complete the humiliation you would care to call her paramour in to flog me?"

"Maxim—no! It isn't—" Valeska tried.

"She has proven herself enemy to your interests," Maxim said, his voice dropping cold and hard, somehow more frightening than the fireworks of his anger. "Choose your ally—her or me?"

Valeska cast one anguished look at Bronya, then seized Maxim's hand between her cramped fists. "Maxim—I need you!"

"So at last you've come to your senses," he said, patting her hands with his unencumbered one. "But this girl—she could still ruin it all. You have let her too deep into your confidence. She has to go."

Bronya dropped to her knees, tears flowing freely. She was not even aware of the phial sliding from her hand and rolling across the floor to rest against Maxim's polished boot.

"My lady! Please don't send me away!" she begged, hands stretched out to the hem of Valeska's dress.

But Valeska's face was buried in Maxim's shoulder. His lip curled in disgust.

"Look at her! Whining and pawing at you!" A strange light came into his eyes.

A few minutes later Valeska sat alone, white and shivering, staring at the phial which stood on the tea table where Maxim had placed it.

When a footman came to mend the fire an hour later, she had him summon the major-domo, who made no bones about accepting the task she gave him. But he did look at her strangely. Or was she acting strangely? What was the normal way to behave when—no, she wouldn't think of it.

"Shall I call Bronya to you, Your Highness?" he asked as he was leaving.

Valeska gave a strangled half laugh and turned away. "You can call, but she will not come. She is gone."

The major-domo opened his mouth, closed it again, and slid discreetly away, already forming a shortlist of candidates for the newly vacant position of personal maid to the imperial princess.

❆   ❆   ❆

The travellers pushed on the next day with barely a pause for Andrei and "Yuri" to shave, passing the Lady's Lake in the first half of the morning. Trees clad in the seasonal semblance of death clung to the sides of the frozen lake like drowning men clutching at their last hope. Andrei kept his eyes averted, and didn't slow his aggressive pace until the Lake was lost behind them.

"We need to get food," Yurisa called weakly from where she rode in Wenceslas's lower bowl.

"We're nearly at Granny Ludmilla's village!" Andrei said. "It can't be much further now."

"There's at least one more village to pass through—or by—before we reach that long-desired spot," Porfiry observed. "We can't possibly reach her before nightfall. And while *I* could walk all day without sustenance—and indeed all night, if it wasn't for colliding with things—the two of you are going to collapse if you don't eat something *soon*."

"I'm half collapsed already," Yurisa muttered.

"But we're so close!" Andrei protested.

"Come, now," Porfiry cajoled. "What good will it do if you arrive at Granny Ludmilla's house and fall dramatically dead on the floor?"

"And anyway," Yurisa added, "you still haven't proved your theory. We're past the Lake now, so *if* you're right, the curse shouldn't have spread this far."

Andrei tried to sigh, but it came out as a groan. "Fine. I'll go into the next village, get food, and ask one question. One! And then we press on."

Securing agreement turned out to be the easiest part of the plan. The village seemed deserted at first. He worked his way down the street, knocking on every door, and finally found a woman who was prepared to sell him some food. She frowned over his head as he waited at the door, and he looked around casually. Wenceslas! Standing at the far end of the street as though he belonged there. He couldn't see Yurisa, but that was little comfort now.

He turned back, a warm smile on his face, and found that his audience had doubled—a younger man with a curiously blank face was wandering towards them.

"An impressive fountain you have here!" Andrei said. "Local baron's gift, was it?"

The woman murmured something inaudible, but the young man's attention was caught. He pointed down the street.

"What's that, then?" he demanded, his voice slow and thick like custard.

"It's a fountain, Damek," the woman said, a little snappishly. "You know what a—"

"Wasn't there before," Damek said, planting his feet apart and glaring at Andrei over crossed arms. Andrei tensed. Simple he might be, but he was seeing things a sight too clearly for Andrei's comfort.

"Don't be silly," the woman said, making a significant grimace at Andrei. "Things like that don't just appear!"

"Wasn't there before," the young man said again, but the glower faded off his face, to be replaced by a secretive smile. "I saw the lady who'll be Czara," he said. "I saw her on First Day."

The woman rolled her eyes. "The princess was in these parts not so long since, for Midseason," she explained to Andrei. "Damek here seems to have caught a sight of her somewhere about—by the Lady's Lake, no doubt—and he's been telling us all about it."

"Wasn't Midseason," Damek said stubbornly. "First Day. With the man. I saw her'll be Czara. He didn't notice, but I saw it in her eyes."

"She's a beautiful lady, isn't she?" Andrei said, smiling at Damek and tactfully not addressing the time discrepancy.

Damek stared at Andrei. "Her teeth are too pointy," he said disconcertingly, and wandered away.

"Sorry about that," the woman said. "Every village has one, they say. Gets an idea in his head and you couldn't shift it with blasting powder. But you didn't come here to talk about Damek. Here's bread and butter, and a bit of cheese."

"Just one quick question," Andrei said, as he tied the provisions into a clean cloth.

"What's that, then?" she asked amiably.

"Has anyone in this village...changed recently?"

The look on her face told him at once that she knew what he meant. His heart sank.

"Isn't it dreadful?" she asked with relish.

"Yes, very," Andrei said despondently, tucking the bundle under his arm.

"I couldn't believe my ears when I heard," she went on chattily.

"Yes, well, I'd better be—"

"And what I say is, and what I said to my husband at the time is, we must be under the special protection of the Lady, I said, seeing as we're the closest village to her Lake."

Andrei arrested his departing movement. "Protection?"

"From the curse," the woman said. "Not a single case in *this* village, though I've heard the village the other side of the Lake is taken something cruel."

Andrei's heart leapt. He was right!

"Tell me," he said, "did the Princess Valeska Kira visit your village when she was in the area for Midseason?"

The woman frowned. "No, she never came quite this far, more's the pity. We're the closest village; it stands to reason here's the place to stay for Midseason. I hear she didn't even stay the whole day—off again the minute she could! Well, that shows you, doesn't it?"

Andrei made vague noises of agreement, unsure of what exactly it showed him, and inched away.

"There's a lot of ill feeling about," the woman went on, a little wedge of frown reappearing between her brows. "There's some who say the healer in the village over yonder is the one responsible." She waved a hand in the direction of Granny Ludmilla's village.

"Responsible?"

"For the curse," the woman explained. "Of course, *I've* never heard any ill of her," she added conscientiously, "but she does know about magic, so they say, and—well, you can't be too careful, can you? We don't want that sort of thing coming here, not right under the Lady's nose, as it were, so there's a group of our men gone over; left this morning."

"What for?" Andrei asked, a cold worm gnawing at his heart.

The woman sniffed. "To put an end to it, of course. You can't let people get away with that sort of thing, putting curses on people!"

Andrei gaped at her. "But...but..." and then he abandoned the attempt, taking to his heels. There was no arguing with a person like that, and what good would it do? They had to get to Granny Ludmilla before what he feared would be a murderous mob. There was no time to get Wenceslas away by stealth; let the woman think what she would. There was no time to waste.

❄   ❄   ❄

They wasted none. Andrei ate as he ran; Yurisa snatched bites of her food while bracing herself against Wenceslas's speedy lurch. Even Porfiry trotted gamely along in silence, focussing on the path ahead. It was gloomy in the dark of the cloudy afternoon, with a bitter wind whipping the dark firs about.

There was a ping.

"What was that?" Andrei asked. "Did you hear something?"

"Felt something," Porfiry said. "A hailstone, if I am not mistaken."

Andrei groaned. "It only needed that! Come on!"

With a roar, the storm broke over them. Yurisa crouched as far under the shelter of Wenceslas's middle bowl as possible, Andrei hunched into his coat until his head was nearly invisible, and Porfiry strode along with head held high, flinching occasionally when hailstones bounced off his face.

After a while, with no sign of the storm abating, Yurisa began scooping up the hailstones from where they collected around Wenceslas's base and flinging them out.

"Shouldn't we seek shelter?" she shouted to Andrei.

"We can't stop!" he shouted back, not even turning.

"It's getting dark," Porfiry pointed out.

"We can't stop now!" Andrei said. "Not for anything!"

"I wasn't suggesting we stop," Porfiry said mildly. "Just that we think about shedding some light on matters."

Andrei groaned.

"I have my lantern," Porfiry went on, "but there's very little oil left in it. Certainly not enough."

"We could make a fire," Yurisa suggested.

"Where, in our hands?" Andrei snapped.

"Or Wenceslas's upper bowl," Porfiry said.

Wenceslas uttered a noise like an iron-shod plough scraping across stone, and Yurisa clapped her hands over her ears.

"Fire cracks cold stone," she reminded them.

"Of course! My dear, what a horrid thought. No fire to go anywhere near Wenceslas, then. Or me," Porfiry added. He patted Wenceslas in a consoling manner and the ominous grinding noises stopped.

"What have we got that we can fire and carry?" Andrei demanded.

"Branches? They'd never keep alight," Yurisa said despondently.

"Does anyone have any spare oil on or about their person?" Porfiry asked.

"What about the butter?" Andrei asked suddenly. "Did we eat all that?"

"Less than half," Yurisa said. "It might do."

Porfiry sighed. "Very well. What must be, must be. I only hope the lantern will be recoverable. It has quite a history. Did I tell you about the time it assumed the role of the Midnight Sun in the play of the same name? My own production," he said, with a tender sigh.

By midnight the last of the lamp oil was gone, and while the butter didn't provide anywhere near so good a light, Porfiry pointed out that they ought to be grateful to his inestimable lantern for turning dairy products into light at all.

"I think the hail is starting to ease," Andrei said, with a ghastly attempt at cheerfulness.

Without warning, Wenceslas shook himself vigorously, sending Yurisa sprawling and a slurry of partially melted hail scything out in all directions.

Porfiry yelped. "A little warning next time, my stony friend! Look at me, I'm a mess."

Wenceslas gurgled apologetically.

"I feel sick," Yurisa said, crawling back up to the rim and putting her head over the edge, just in case.

"Someone's coming!" Andrei hissed in the sudden stillness. They staggered off the path to take shelter in the trees, Porfiry dimming the lamp. As the creak of harness and the hiss of runners drew nearer, Yurisa was quietly sick over the side.

As the large sleigh passed, the starlight glittered on the weapons carried by the servants at front and back. Andrei watched in silence as the burly figures disappeared down the track.

"Did you see that?" Porfiry whispered when the silence of the forest had fallen at last. "Duke Maxim! Travelling at night, too—he must be in a hurry!"

"So are we," Yurisa croaked.

"Come on, then," Andrei said, fighting his way through the undergrowth back onto the path. "Ow! What was—oh, no..."

"More hail?" Porfiry asked incredulously, the stones pinging off his shoulders. "Trust the duke to find his way into the eye of the storm!"

So it continued, wave after wave of hail trying to hammer them into the very ground they needed to cross so urgently.

Two hours later the hail had finally run out, and the butter was running down. Andrei could sympathize: he was feeling more than a little run down himself.

"Shouldn't we be there by now?" he asked for the fourth time.

"The hail will have slowed us down," Porfiry replied for the fourth time.

"I think I can see some light," Yurisa said. "No—it's gone."

"Where?" Andrei asked, and as she pointed he plunged away from the dim circle of Porfiry's lamplight and into the darkness.

"Land ho!" cried Porfiry, raising the lantern with its sinking flame aloft. "And just in time."

"There it is again!" Yurisa said. "Bright light. Do you see it?"

"Not light," Andrei's strained voice came from the darkness ahead. "Fire!"

Porfiry advised caution in the approach, and very nearly had to hold Andrei back with both arms to enforce it. They halted in the trees at the edge of the village and watched the house burn. The burning house was ringed with figures, dark against the leaping flames, but they stood motionless, leaning on shovels and axes.

"Why aren't they putting it out?" Yurisa whispered.

"Because they lit it," Andrei ground out. "They're just... guarding it. To stop anyone getting out."

"Or to make sure it doesn't spread," Porfiry said.

Andrei groaned and leaned against a tree, staring blankly into the darkness. "What difference does it make?" he asked, voice bleak. "We've come all this way to get Granny Ludmilla's advice, and now what are we supposed to do? Go home and tell Granny Sonechka we were a few hours too late?"

"How is my old friend?" a papery voice enquired from the tree above him.

Andrei jumped as though he had been stung; Porfiry yelped and dropped the lantern.

"My lantern!"

"My head!" Yurisa groaned.

"Keep your voices down, there's a mob out there," the voice above suggested mildly.

"Found it!" Porfiry's voice announced a moment later. "And it's unharmed."

"Granny Ludmilla?" Andrei asked, having finally got his breath back.

"In person," the voice replied, "and, as you may be able to tell, in tree. But you haven't answered my question."

"She's, um, she's fine, thank you," Andrei said, and then, remembering his manners, "I trust you're well yourself?"

"Under the circumstances," Granny Ludmilla said, "not bad, thank you."

"Under said circumstances," Porfiry said, "perhaps we could consider adjourning?"

"I suppose I ought to climb out of this tree," Granny Ludmilla said doubtfully. "Come a bit closer, will you, fountain?"

Wenceslas obligingly shimmied up to the tree, and Granny Ludmilla climbed into the upper bowl, clambering down with the occasional bump and mutter.

"Now what did you turn your back for, young woman?" she asked Yurisa as her long limbs found their way from the lower bowl to the ground. "This wouldn't be the first pair of women's drawers you've ever seen."

"Y-you...you can tell I'm...not—?" Yurisa stuttered out.

The firelight glinted on Granny Ludmilla's gangling glasses clinging precariously to the end of her nose. "Weren't you expecting magic? Or why did you come?"

Half an hour later they were huddling into the shelter of a tiny shed Granny Ludmilla kept out in the woods, "for keeping an eye on growing things when the time must be just ripe," she explained.

Andrei was too tired to make any sense of this. He just wanted to sit down.

"You're sure we won't be found here?" Yurisa asked. "Because that crowd didn't look very friendly, and if the local villagers know you've got this place as well..."

"Not to worry," Granny Ludmilla said with her gentle voice. "This little hut is near impossible to find even by daylight if you don't know where it is, and I think it's fairly clear that the villagers prefer to avoid any sort of interaction with armed mobs."

"Cowards," Yurisa muttered.

"Now," Granny Ludmilla said, settling herself comfortably, "tell me everything."

"It's Valeska Kira, and the Czar's got it and everything. Not to mention centaurs," Andrei said.

Granny Ludmilla blinked, and the other two stared at him.

"I feel I should plead in extenuation," Porfiry said, turning to Granny Ludmilla, "that my fellow adventurer here has been running all day and half the night."

"So have you, and you speak prettily enough," she replied.

"Porfiry speaks prettily in his sleep," Andrei said with a yawn.

"I've been riding with Wenceslas," Yurisa said. "And I've been taking notes."

She took out the notebook and gave Granny Ludmilla a brief account of each case in turn.

"It's Valeska Kira, like I said!" Andrei said when she had finished. "Perfectly clear."

"It fits the facts," Yurisa said.

"And now, dear Granny Ludmilla, we look to you to answer our predicament and save the land from this dread plague," Porfiry said, with the sort of flourish usually attached to a bow. "Why are you frowning? I don't like to see you frown. O wise one, speak! and give us guidance!"

"A chance would be a fine thing," she returned, giving him a chiding look over her glasses.

"It is possible the fatigue is loosening my tongue," Porfiry admitted.

"Any looser and it'll fall off. Now I'm sorry to tell you this, but I don't know what will stop this curse."

Andrei struggled up from the floor where he was unaccountably lying. "What? No! You have to—Granny said! And the magic—you knew—with Yurisa!"

"Don't distress yourself. I didn't say I couldn't help you at all. It's true I know about magic," she continued, "but mine is more the magic of the mind."

"What do you mean, the magic of the mind?" Yurisa asked.

"There is the natural world that healers deal with," Granny Ludmilla said. "Using plants and the like to treat the body. There's the world of the supernatural, which is what you're dealing with here. And then there's the world of the human mind, which lies between them—both and neither, you might say."

"You said you could help," Andrei said, clinging to the one strand of all these words which meant there was still hope.

"I can at least confirm that you're on the right track with the princess's words. The evidence is clear enough for anyone, expert or not. But I can't tell you what to do about it."

Andrei slumped, and Yurisa recoiled as though she'd been hit in the face with a brick wall.

Porfiry was not so reticent in his disappointment. "Then we are doomed!" he cried. "I shall end my days in a garden covered in lichens, and Yurisa will be stuck with the deepest voice of any healer in the land!"

"I don't imagine you'd be popular as a midwife," Granny Ludmilla remarked, peering over her glasses at Yurisa, who was still wooden with shock. "But it's always too soon to despair. Granny Sonechka sent you on to someone who's more of an expert; I can do the same."

Andrei lifted his head out of his hands. "You mean—there's someone who knows more than you?"

Granny Ludmilla laughed: a joyfully squeaky sound which shook her tall bony frame. "In this life," she said, "if there's one thing you can be sure of, it is that someone knows more than you. In this case, that someone is Granny Radinka. She's what you might call a specialist."

"Where does she live?" Andrei asked, pulling himself to his feet.

"Presuming that no one has yet set fire to her home and driven her out into the midnight snow," Porfiry added.

"Into the snow would be right," Granny Ludmilla said. "She lives up in the Long Mountains, just above the tree-line where people will leave her alone."

"Northeast of here," Andrei said, sketching a little map in the air in front of him.

"We'll never get there," Yurisa said calmly. "Not till spring, at least."

"She's not right on top of the peak," Granny Ludmilla reassured them. "Hardly a walk through Summer's Meadow, I grant you, but it's passable."

"Even to someone who's insulted the Lady?" Yurisa asked. "Twice?"

Granny Ludmilla's eyebrows rose, and she turned to survey Andrei over her glasses. He avoided her eye.

"She should be above that sort of thing," he muttered. "You know, be..."

"Be a bigger person?" Granny Ludmilla asked. "Believe me, you don't want the Lady to be any bigger than she is already. Words sting. It doesn't matter who you are. Well, you'll just have to apologize, that's all."

"I take it the traditional three kind words will not quite meet the situation?" Porfiry asked.

Granny Ludmilla shook her head gravely. "For a doubled insult, from a peasant to an immortal? Not even close."

"I'm not going to—" Andrei began, but Porfiry prodded him firmly with a foot, and he subsided. Let them say what they liked. They couldn't make him.

"Three kind words *will* be required," Granny Ludmilla said, taking off her glasses and polishing them absent-mindedly on her dress. "But three kind words engraved in a noble metal."

"A noble metal?" Andrei asked.

"Gold, silver, copper at a pinch, though I wouldn't advise it in this case."

"Silver, eh?" Porfiry said thoughtfully.

Andrei looked at him. Porfiry's gaze was fastened on Andrei's chest. Instinctively, he put a hand up over his shirt pocket, as though to shield it from Porfiry's gaze. "No!"

"Have you anything else made of noble metal on or about your person?" Porfiry enquired. "Because I haven't, and—"

"It has to be something of his own," Granny Ludmilla interrupted. "No apologies at someone else's expense! And don't even think of trying to buy the Lady off with a silver coin."

"She's not getting my razor," Andrei said, folding his arms firmly across his chest, so the razor's handle dug in. "My father gave me that. We'll have to find another way."

"There is no other way," Yurisa snapped. "Don't think I'm looking forward to growing a beard. But there isn't any other way. We don't have the money to buy anything else, and we can't get that far into the mountains with the Lady against us. There is no other way, Andrei."

"Spring isn't far off," Andrei argued. "Anyway, if you're so keen on the idea, why don't you two go?"

"Because my ankle is broken and I can't walk," Yurisa said, with a slow patience Andrei found very annoying.

"I believe I could build up a brace on this," Granny Ludmilla said, peering at Yurisa's ankle. "But you'd still not be able to take more than a few steps."

"And if you think I'm going to trek up into the Long Mountains *all by myself*," Porfiry said, "you can think again. The world is a dangerous place, and porphyry is a valuable material. I have no wish to end up as an elegantly tiled floor in some robber baron's castle."

"Robber barons?" Yurisa asked sceptically.

"You never know," Porfiry said firmly, "and I for one do not want to find out. Wherever Andrei goes, I go."

"But where is Andrei going?" Granny Ludmilla asked. "A man who turns down an idea that flatly must have a better one in mind, yes?"

"I thought I'd try talking to Duke Maxim," Andrei said. "He's connected to the imperial family, maybe he can do something about Valeska."

"Forgive me if I am bringing up painful memories," Porfiry said, "but weren't we proceeding on the assumption that he wants to kill you? After all, you may not have flogged him very hard, but you did flog him. In public. That's the sort of thing a proud man finds very hard to forgive."

"He's not that bad," Andrei said, hoping this was true. "He got me a job after Valeska fired me, remember?"

"That was before you whipped him," Yurisa pointed out.

"And I suppose we at least know where he is," Porfiry said thoughtfully.

"We know where he was a few hours ago," Yurisa corrected. "There are all sorts of places he could be by now."

"Heading north in these parts? He's running home to mummy," Porfiry said. "I would, with the Czar out for my blood."

"Mummy being where, exactly?" Andrei asked.

"At her estate, naturally," Porfiry said. "Not far from here. The dowager duchess is the old-fashioned sort: prouder than a Czar of her blood and position, but scornful of comfort and modern foibles of that ilk. Which is probably why the duke doesn't visit that often. He's a man who likes—"

"That's where we're going, then," Andrei said firmly.

"So...instead of consulting the woman who knows all about magic," Granny Ludmilla said, looking steadily at Andrei over her glasses, "you're going to ask the man who has cause to hate you to do you a favour. Although you're not sure what."

Andrei scowled. "I'm not giving the Lady my father's razor. That's final."

❅   ❅   ❅

Maxim's mother's estate was not a grand one—not even as grand as Baron Boris's—but the only word Andrei could find to describe it was *fortified*. The timbers of the palisade were still fresh and pale, which explained the large number of stumps on the approach. Clearly, the old lady was expecting trouble.

"Who goes there?" the man on guard at the gate demanded, as Andrei stepped into view. "State your name and business."

"My name is Andrei and I need to talk to Duke Maxim," Andrei said boldly. Never cower to large menials.

The guard tightened his grip on his pike, and his eyes narrowed to slits in his weather-beaten face.

"How'd you—what makes you think he's here?"

"I saw him on his way here," Andrei said, hastily adding "I'm no blabbermouth! The Czar's after my head, too, but—I have information that might be useful. To the duke as well as myself."

The guard frowned, and thought. "Best come in, then. But don't try anything funny, or you won't have long to regret it."

Andrei strode in, trying to look as unfunny as possible, and was handed over to another menial who took him to the house itself. The forecourt was full of bustle, horses, women with laden baskets, men complaining about a dog that had run away. They wended their way through it without let or hindrance, and came to the great oaken front door.

It opened into a great hall filled with the chilly grandeur of granite. The ceiling seemed a long way away, lost in gloom. In fact, the back wall was crossed by two galleries running between doors on higher levels—a convenient way of crossing from one wing of the house to the other without constantly going up and down stairs, Andrei supposed.

The servant indicated a hard wooden bench against the wall, and disappeared through a side door, leaving Andrei alone.

As his eyes gradually accustomed to the gloom, he saw what Porfiry meant about Maxim's mother being one of the old-fashioned kind, scorning such weak and foolish things as colour and comfort. The furniture was scanty and of hard uncushioned wood, and the great fireplace was failing entirely in its attempt to heat the room.

Andrei shivered and tried not to think of mortuary houses. The floor was stone, the walls were stone...well, except for the tapestries.

One great tapestry hung on each of the two side walls. A prodigious display of wealth, in its way, though he would have preferred a display in the form of cushions. Andrei took a step back and looked up at the tapestry on the left wall. The dim colours resolved themselves into a rather graphic illustration of Porfiry's story about Spring and the handsome young gardener.

Andrei swallowed and turned on his heel. The sound of a
door opening echoed gently around the room, and he looked
up to see someone passing along the gallery halfway up the
back wall. Not Duke Maxim, not one of his servants if the absence of livery was anything to go by, and…not interested in
Andrei, judging by the way the man moved briskly if quietly
across the gallery and into the other side of the house.

Andrei sat down on a bench facing the other tapestry. This
one proved to be of Summer's failed attempt to take the throne
forever, but at least it didn't give Andrei the creeps. Words
that might once have been a golden yellow loomed out of the
darkness at the top of the tapestry.

Andrei squinted up at them. Ah, yes. *Only a human shall
ascend the Seven Steps.* That was what Granny had said, about
the steps withdrawing if an immortal tried to go up them. Or
something like that.

Yet another door opened in a far dim corner—on the ground
floor, this time—and a couple of women in grubby aprons
came through.

"It's enough to make anyone uneasy, her being so near her
time," one said.

"It's a wonder she—" the other one began, and then broke
off as she caught sight of Andrei on his bench. She elbowed
the other, and they disappeared through the same door the
servant had gone through. Who, now Andrei thought about
it, had been gone a long time.

Still, no one was trying to kill him or throw him in a dungeon, which was a good sign. He heaved a sigh, and supposed
he should be thankful he was considered unimportant enough
to keep waiting. It suggested—he hoped—that Duke Maxim
wasn't impatient to revenge himself for the unpleasant events
at the Czarina's Ball.

He was just wondering whether he'd been waiting long
enough to actually see the sliver of light from the slits of win-

dows move across the wall, when the far door on to the highest gallery opened, and Duke Maxim entered.

Andrei leapt to his feet, but before he could make himself known, he heard another door open above, and Duke Maxim stopped, his face changing.

"Garek!" he said. "What brings you—" He ducked, and a crossbow bolt skimmed over him, juddering to a stop in the door.

Andrei froze, but Maxim charged. Moments later the crossbow clattered onto the floor just feet from where Andrei stood. He looked up to where the two men were grappling.

"He'll have changed his mind by now," Maxim panted.

Garek was bigger than Maxim was, by some way, and most of it was muscle, by the looks of it. Having lost his weapon, he was pushing Maxim slowly but inexorably towards the solid wooden railing that edged the gallery.

"I'm his cousin!" Maxim cried, the rail now pressing into his back.

Garek still said nothing.

As Maxim slid further out over the drop to the floor far below, he cried "I'll pay!"

Garek paused only for a derisive snort, and as he did so, Maxim tried to kick him in the belly—no, slower than that, but somehow, Andrei could see, Maxim had got his foot under Garek's broad leather belt.

With a final grimace, Garek shoved Maxim off the railing. In an instant, the satisfied smile jerked off Garek's face, and they were falling together, to land with tangled limbs and a sickening crunch on the granite floor of the hall.

Andrei's gaze had followed their fall, and this movement broke him out of his frozen shell. He drew a couple of gasping breaths, and tried to force his eyes to look at something other than the shattered bones. Dragging his gaze to the floor beside the mangled pair was not much of an improvement, as the pool of blood crept slowly towards him across the stone.

And then Maxim stood up.

Reunion

"Assassinated by a dead man—what an irony," Maxim said, and he wasn't even breathing heavily. He straightened his coat, tucked a stray lock of hair in place, and turned away—only to meet Andrei's horrified gaze.

Their eyes locked for a moment, and then Andrei was away, heaving the oak door open just far enough to slip through, and rushing through the crowded forecourt as though the vengeful Lady herself were behind him. A shout went up as he fled, but the guard at the gate was clearly not expecting to have to keep people in as well as out, and Andrei was clear away and into the forest with not a hand laid on him.

Porfiry was perched elegantly on a stump and clearly in the middle of an elaborate anecdote when Andrei charged through the newly-made clearing. Porfiry leapt to his feet, and then leapt to the side to avoid Wenceslas. Yurisa hung on grimly as Wenceslas smashed his way over the stumps in Andrei's wake. The shouts faded into the distance.

"Where are we going?" Yurisa called to Andrei.

"Away!" Andrei replied, without turning his head.

"Dare one ask how the conversation went?" Porfiry asked as he drew alongside.

Andrei made no reply.

"Well?" Yurisa asked. "What did he say?"

Andrei cut short a hysterical laugh. "Assassinated by a dead man—what an irony!"

"Is he mad?" Porfiry queried. "Or are you?"

"It made sense at the time," Andrei said. "Well, it didn't, but it made more sense than that."

"Whereas you make no sense at all, my dear fellow," Porfiry said.

"I'll explain when we get there!"

"Where's there?" Yurisa asked.

"Somewhere a long way away from here!"

They pounded on in silence until Andrei was wheezing in the cold air, and even then he stumbled on as fast as he could force his legs to carry him, Wenceslas close behind.

"I think I saw something," Yurisa hissed. "In the trees back there."

"What was it?" Porfiry asked, jogging backwards and surveying the trees with a lively interest.

"I don't know, or I would have said," Yurisa said. "I just saw a flicker of white. And it wasn't snow, because it was moving along the ground."

"A face?" Andrei's stomach twisted.

"Too low," Yurisa said. "Maybe—clothes?"

"The duke's livery is royal blue," Porfiry said. "Could it be a shirt?"

Yurisa screwed up her face. "I don't see it any more. I don't think it was a shirt. Not unless the person wearing it was crawling along the ground, which doesn't make sense."

"A shirt worn by a dwarf, or a child?" Porfiry suggested. "Or—ooh! I know! A rather natty person like myself with a tablecloth swathed about their lower reaches?"

"This is no laughing matter!" Andrei panted.

Porfiry turned towards him, opened his mouth to reply, and gasped.

"I saw it! It's beside us now!" He pointed with a rather shaky hand and gulped. "I—I think it's a wolf."

Andrei stopped running and joined Porfiry in backing towards Wenceslas, picking up a fist-sized rock on the way.

"Why should you be frightened of wolves?" Yurisa asked Porfiry. "What damage can teeth do to you?"

"That's a good point," Porfiry said, brightening perceptibly.

"No comfort to you and me, though, Yurisa," Andrei said.

Yurisa sighed. "I'm sure between the three of us—four of us—" as Wenceslas growled, "we can manage one solitary wolf. It's probably young or sick if it's on its own, anyway."

"Shh—it's coming!" Andrei hissed.

They watched warily as the underbrush shook free of its light covering of snow. Out came a long thin muzzle, followed by a long slender leg.

Andrei frowned. Surely, wolves had bigger paws than that?

The underbrush convulsed, and out came an elegant white borzaya, creeping across the icy path towards them with a woebegone look.

Andrei let his breath out with a rush, and dropped the rock from his aching hand.

"You beauty!" Porfiry crooned to the dog. "Someone will be missing you, won't they?"

The dog whined, and looked sadder than ever.

Porfiry put out a hand to it, but it slipped right past him and came to sit at Andrei's feet, where it sighed heavily and looked up at him as though expecting something.

"It likes you!" Porfiry said. "Go on, give the darling a stroke or a scratch behind the ears, Andrei. You can't be so churlish as to refuse when it so clearly wants to make friends. With you, at least," he added, a little miffed.

Andrei stroked the long white fur, and the dog leaned against his leg with a little groan.

"I wonder whose it is," Porfiry said. "All the way out here!"

"There were some men at the estate saying something about a dog that had run away," Andrei said, fondling the dog's long elegant ears.

"Not very intelligent, to run away at this time of year," Yurisa said, and the dog turned to give her a cold look.

"Look, she knows what you're saying!" Porfiry crowed. "Or is it a he?"

"That is a bitch," Yurisa said flatly. The dog bridled.

"Do you think it belongs to the dowager duchess?" Porfiry asked. The dog barked sharply. "Is that a yes or a no, my dear?" He giggled.

Yurisa sighed. "Is it wearing a collar?"

Andrei felt through the fur about the long neck. "No—oh, wait, there is something. Feels like a chain."

"A chain collar on a dog like this beauty?" Porfiry exclaimed. "Some people have simply no taste."

"I mean a chain like a necklace," Andrei said as it slipped between his fingers.

"What a charming thought," Porfiry said. "Now why didn't I think of that? Perhaps because I've never had a dog?"

Andrei fumbled out the thin silver thread from the long fur and followed it around to the front of the dog's neck. "There's something hanging on it," he said.

"Does it have a name?" Yurisa asked, peering over the edge of the bowl.

Andrei held the little sharp thing between his fingers and crouched down for a closer look.

It was a little silver snowflake.

❄   ❄   ❄

"Does it have a name?" Yurisa repeated.

Andrei looked from the snowflake to the dog's long sad face. "Bronya?"

The dog whined.

"What, Bronya like VK's maid?" Porfiry asked, and then he gave a little gasp and covered his mouth.

"What is it?" Yurisa asked, looking from Porfiry to Andrei and back.

"Oh, my dear, I am *so* sorry," Porfiry said, and then, turning around, he addressed himself to Yurisa. "Have a look at that tree over there. Yes, that one with the shrubby thing at its foot. Remarkable, is it not?"

"I don't see anything about it that's any different from a thousand other trees in the forest," Yurisa said.

Porfiry whispered in her ear.

"Oh!" she said. "Yes, I see what you mean. A tree that would repay further study."

Some minutes passed, during which Yurisa stared fiercely at the tree, and Porfiry at the sky, with occasional glances darted back towards Andrei.

Then there was a loud sniff, and Andrei said "You can turn around now."

They turned back to see the dog licking Andrei's face, while he swiped at his eyes with the back of one hand and rubbed her ears with the other.

"My dear fellow," Porfiry said, starting forward, "I am devastated for you, truly!"

"At least she's not dead," Yurisa said.

"Yurisa!" Porfiry gasped, scandalized.

"She's trying to be encouraging," Andrei said with a watery smile. "She's right, it could be worse."

"Still! At such a time—"

"Never mind that," Andrei said, clapping Porfiry on the shoulder and wincing. "We need to get moving."

"I don't think we're being chased any more," Yurisa said matter-of-factly.

"In which case, where are we going?" Porfiry enquired.

Andrei put a hand to his breast pocket. "The Lady's Lake."

He led the little band away, Bronya staying close to his side, and his hand resting on her head.

"I've got a needle you can use for making the inscription," Yurisa offered.

Andrei stopped, and groaned.

"What must be, must be," Porfiry consoled him.

"It's not that," Andrei said dismally, and turned to the others. "How will I ever be able to find three kind words for *her*?"

Porfiry pursed his lips. "Come now, it can't be that bad! There's—"

"No!" Yurisa shouted, and they all turned to her in surprise. "Don't tell him. They have to be his own."

"A good point," Porifry said, with a slight bow in Yurisa's direction. "I am sorry, dear fellow, but the burden is your own."

"How about if I lie through my teeth?" Andrei suggested.

Bronya whined and nudged his hand with her nose.

"The Lady will know," Yurisa said. "You have to be sincere."

Andrei uttered a deep groan and dropped to the ground, his head in his hands.

"I'm sure you can think of something if you put your mind to it," Porfiry said encouragingly. "It's an ill wind, as they say."

"What does that even mean?" Andrei asked.

Porfiry hesitated, and Yurisa cut in.

"It's an ill wind that blows no good," she said. "It means that something has to be very bad before it doesn't do someone some good."

"Yes, well, all I can think of when you say 'an ill wind' is the weather we've been plagued with," Andrei said. "And I don't see how that's blowing anyone any good."

No one seemed to have an answer for this, and a dejected silence followed.

"It makes you glad when spring comes?" Andrei tried.

Porfiry winced. "I'm not sure that's much of a compliment to the Lady, all things considered. Better not try it."

Andrei dragged off his hat, flung it on the ground and ran his hands through his hair.

"Pulling your hair out won't help," Yurisa said.

"Nothing will help!" Andrei snapped. "We're wasting our time. Even if I could find one thing, I'd never find three, and even if I did, I wouldn't mean a word of it."

"So what do you propose?" Porfiry enquired.

Andrei took a deep breath. "I'm going to see the Czar."

There was a silence, broken only by Bronya's whimper.

"A novel approach," Porfiry conceded. "Just to avoid any confusion, we are talking about the same Czar, are we? The one whose last words in your hearing were 'kill him'?"

Andrei glared at him. "*Actually*," he said, "the last words I heard from him were 'after him'—which is why I am still travelling with a large garden fountain. In case it had escaped your notice."

"I don't think Wenceslas will escape anyone's notice," Yurisa said. "Especially not when you get into the city. People aren't used to seeing things like that."

"That's all you know," Porfiry put in. "Who knows what strange results of this curse may not be haunting the streets by now?"

Wenceslas grumbled deep in his pipes.

"It's still risky," Yurisa said.

"What options do we have?" Andrei asked. "Anyway, everyone knows Czar Kiril is angry one day and forgets it the next. He's probably—"

"And angry again the day after that," Porfiry said. "Think of Duke Maxim running home to mummy."

"But I have valuable information," Andrei countered.

Porfiry looked shocked. "You're not going to betray the duke, are you? After what he did for you?"

"Not that," Andrei said, trying to banish the memory of Maxim rising from the floor and adjusting his coat. "About Valeska—remember?"

Porfiry screwed up his face till it looked like a three-dimensional map of mountain ranges. "I suppose," he said at last. "I mean, I know they don't get on, but still! It's not every father who'd welcome the man who tells him his daughter's a walking curse."

"If not worse," Yurisa muttered.

"It's not every father who's looking for an excuse to disinherit his daughter," Andrei said bluntly, and Bronya yelped. "You don't have to come if you don't want to."

"Oh, I'm coming," Porfiry assured him. "Catch me staying away! No, it's you two I'm worried about. I can just park myself in a niche if things get hairy, but you two?"

"The Czar isn't after my head," Yurisa said. "Andrei's the one who's taking the most risk here."

Bronya whined, and pawed at Andrei's leg.

He looked down at her. "What have I got left to lose?"

❉ ❉ ❉

"You still haven't explained what you said about what Maxim said," Yurisa said suddenly, some half hour later.

Andrei looked up from the snowdrift he was trampling through. "What?"

"You said he said something about being assassinated by a dead man," Yurisa said, "and you still haven't explained it."

"In fact," Porfiry added, "you haven't told us how it went at all."

Andrei groaned. "What a day. I went in; I waited; a goon from the Czar showed up and tried to shoot the duke—"

"What?" Porfiry stopped and stared at Andrei.

"Oh, it gets better. This was all up high on a gallery by the roof and then Garek pushed Maxim off the edge of the gallery and somehow he pulled Garek after him and they both smashed on the stone floor—"

"The duke is dead?" Porfiry clapped both hands to his head.

Andrei laughed, a little hysterically. "Not at all! He stood up out of the pile of mangled limbs and blood, and said 'assassinated by a dead man, what an irony.'"

There was a long silence.

"And that's all?" Yurisa asked.

"Then he adjusted his coat—which wasn't bloodied at all any more, now that I think about it—and turned around and saw me and I ran away," Andrei said, feeling a little embarrassed at the anticlimax of this ending.

"And who can blame you?" Porfiry said generously.

"So what did he mean?" Yurisa asked.

"I don't know!" Andrei moodily kicked a lump of snow off his boot. "I didn't fancy asking him to explain. It was...creepy."

"The irony seems plain enough," Porfiry said. "I would say being assassinated by a dead man was tremendously ironic, it's just—"

"—that it doesn't make sense," Yurisa said.

"Because either the duke means that the dead chap, whatsisname—"

"Garek," Andrei supplied.

"Either that Garek assassinated him—the duke—and is himself now a dead man," Porfiry continued, "and really, it was only an attempted assassination—in fact, even that doesn't work, because Garek wasn't dead at the time of the assassination, attempted or otherwise. *Or* he means that Garek has been assassinated by him, and he himself is a dead man."

Yurisa frowned. "But for either of those to be the meaning, Maxim must be dead—surely?"

Andrei shuddered. "As good as dead, after a fall like that. But he isn't. Take it from someone who knows; he isn't. But maybe he should be."

"Dear me, is that a whiff of treason I detect?" Porfiry asked. "You think he ought to be executed for...what? Upsetting the Czar? That's a little dangerous for a man in your position."

"Not executed!" Andrei protested. "It just seems wrong that he didn't die after all that...crush. Unnatural."

"What about this whole business *is* natural?" Porfiry asked of no one in particular.

"Maybe that's it," Yurisa said, leaning forward eagerly. "Maybe it's the curse."

"It doesn't seem like the worst of fates," Porfiry said, brow wrinkling.

"The centaur Howler didn't think the curse was all bad either," Yurisa pointed out.

"True. Ooh!" Porfiry's brow unclenched, and he straightened. "What if he did it himself?"

"You can't curse yourself, remember?" Yurisa said. "We tried that."

"Well, no, yes, I mean—" Porfiry shook himself, dislodging a light dusting of snow, and tried again. "What if he got someone to do it to him, as a sort of safety plan? Get in quick with a curse he could live with, before someone else said something worse?"

Yurisa frowned, and scratched her prickly chin. "But he wouldn't know that he couldn't be cursed twice. Or that he was in danger, being so close to the princess."

Porfiry airily waved these objections aside. "Not everyone needs to know all the facts before they proceed. It's a bold and daring strike! The sort of thing men of destiny are always doing."

Yurisa did not appear convinced. "It's a terrible risk to take. What if—"

"Hoofbeats!" Andrei said, and they hurried to conceal themselves away from the thin line of the path.

A single rider flashed by, going at great speed, and looking neither left nor right.

"The Czar's livery," Porfiry said thoughtfully, rising to his feet again. He opened his mouth, closed it again, and frowned.

"One of the imperial horses, too, by the looks of it," Andrei said, watching as the powerful beast disappeared among the thin trees.

"Maybe the Czar's remembered the duke's mother," Yurisa suggested.

They had not gone much further before another rhythmic thudding sound was heard.

"Hoofbeats?" Porfiry asked.

Andrei shook his head. "Too slow."

"Sounds more like a spade," Yurisa said.

Through the trees ahead, Andrei caught sight of a simple peasant house, alone beside the path, except for the even simpler barn behind. He gestured to the others to stay put, and moved cautiously on down the path, Bronya stepping delicately after him.

There was a man digging feverishly at some distance from the little house, his coat removed and draped over the ground beside him. It was a small hole he was chiselling out of the frozen earth—small but deep, like a grave.

Andrei's heart squeezed tight with compassion for the poor man, but a moment later something struck him as odd. The man's expression was not one of sorrow, but one of fear.

Dreadful imaginings fluttered across Andrei's mind, but another look at the coat dispelled them. There was something under it, something flat and rectangular, far too shallow to be a coffin for even the tiniest of babies. He firmly reined in his imagination's impending leap into the distressing possibilities provided by the curse, and strode forward.

"A hard season for digging!" he called.

The man straightened up with a jerk, decided Andrei and his dog were no threat, and put a hand to his back with a wince.

"That it is! But I'm not taking any chances," he said, leaning on his spade. "I know there's some as say just turn the face to the wall, but what if it comes loose and falls to the floor? Then where are you?" He returned to his digging.

Andrei puzzled over this. "Where are you?" he ventured.

"Looking at a dead man's face," the man said, and dug faster.

There was only one face which would hang on the wall of a house like this. The air went cold, and Andrei's voice sounded a long way off as he asked "The Czar is dead?"

"Didn't you see the courier? Must've just about run over you, I would've thought. Stopped here for a drink of water and told me the lot. Died three days since, and the courier's been heading north with the news ever since."

"How did he die, did the courier tell you?"

The man snorted. "Pretty cagey, he was, but seems clear to me it was rage and drink as did for him. No surprises there," he added, spitting to the side of the hole and continuing to dig.

"It seems likely," Andrei agreed weakly, a vision of Kiril as he last saw him rising before his eyes, a monster thrashing about in a cloud of liquor fumes. "Well, I'd best be on my way."

The man grunted, and carried on digging.

Andrei carried on past the house and then circled back to where the others were waiting.

Yurisa's face was grave. "Porfiry says he thought he saw a black armband on the courier."

"But I can't be *sure*," Porfiry reiterated.

Andrei sighed. "I can. The man up there is burying the portrait of the Czar."

Porfiry clapped both hands to his mouth, and Yurisa looked stunned.

"How touching," Porfiry said at last. "The walls of his simple home will be bare until the Eve of Spring, when another portrait shall take pride of place."

Andrei gave a long, gasping groan.

"Andrei!" Porfiry exclaimed. "Are you all right?"

"He's just realized he's going to have a fountain following him for the rest of his life," Yurisa said.

Andrei looked up. "I'm what?"

"Granny Sonechka said that only Czar Kiril could take the order back," Yurisa explained, "and that'll never happen now."

Andrei subsided with another groan. "That wasn't even what I was groaning about to begin with."

"Although it's possible that the next Czar—or Czara—could," Yurisa said thoughtfully.

"Never mind that now," Andrei said. "The Throne of Seven Steps will be empty for the rest of the season."

"In mourning for the Czar," Porfiry said. "We all know that. What's your point?"

Andrei gave him a long slow stare. "And then what will happen, O Master of Ceremonies?"

"Valeska Kira will ascend the throne on Spring's Eve," Porfiry said, "always assuming that the missing Czarina hasn't popped up with a son by then."

"And then?" Andrei pushed.

Yurisa looked blank.

Porfiry drew in a horrified breath. "The balcony," he whispered.

"And then she'll go out on the balcony of the palace," Andrei said remorselessly, "and *address all the people.*"

❄   ❄   ❄

Moments later, Andrei was up and moving away at a brisk pace.

"Where are you going?" Porfiry called after him.

"The Lake," Andrei called back. "It's the only hope we have left."

"But you don't have three nice things to say," Yurisa said.

Andrei set his jaw. "I'll think of some."

The wind picked up as they moved swiftly east.

"There's a storm coming," Yurisa said. "Shouldn't we take shelter?"

"I don't think there is any to be taken," Porfiry said, looking about vaguely.

"No," Andrei said shortly. "We keep going."

It was more than a storm. It was a blizzard. Wind screamed in Andrei's ears, snowflakes whipped at his face, and he kept going, his expression beneath the muffler growing sourer by the minute. Think of three nice things to say... He couldn't even see Bronya when he looked down, her white fur disappearing into the swirling white.

"Andrei..." came a faint voice from behind.

He turned, squinting through the dancing air to make out the bulk of Wenceslas and the smaller, darker bulk of Porfiry beside him.

"we...for..." the faint voice said. He couldn't tell if it was Porfiry or Yurisa.

"I can't hear you!" Andrei bellowed.

"We have to stop for shelter!" Porfiry boomed as they drew nearer. "This is killing weather!"

Andrei shook his head and turned back into the wind. The sting drew tears into his eyes, and when he blinked them away, the world was lost. Was this the way he'd been going? Was this the way at all?

As he hesitated, Porfiry came up alongside him.

"We can manage," Andrei said, before Porfiry could say anything.

"Wenceslas and I are made of stone," Porfiry said gravely. "You and Bronya can keep warm by moving. But what about Yurisa?"

"What are you suggesting? That we just give up?"

"Not at all. I merely suggest that the warm-blooded members of the party huddle together until the storm passes over. Perhaps in Wenceslas's lee?"

"We're losing time!" Andrei said, desperately trying to see into the swirling space ahead of him.

"Better than losing our lives," Porfiry said gently.

Andrei looked around him. There was no backwards, no forward, just their little group alone in an ever-shifting world.

"All right." Shoulders slumped, he clambered into the lower bowl.

Yurisa shifted to make room for him on the side furthest from the wind. Bronya leapt up and settled herself between them, a warm and comforting presence.

The wind howled, the snow piled up, but it wasn't as bitingly cold as facing into the storm, Andrei had to admit. Porfiry's dark form passed and re-passed as he wandered around the growing drifts.

"What are you thinking?" Yurisa asked at last.

"Three nice things," Andrei said with a sigh. "What about you?"

"Luka," she said.

"Oh."

"I wanted to be a healer because of him," Yurisa went on, staring out into the snow as though she wasn't talking to Andrei at all. "But I can't cure him now."

"Maybe you'll cure somebody else's Luka," Andrei said awkwardly.

The silence lengthened until the echoes of his inadequate words had almost faded from his mind.

It seemed hours later when Wenceslas shook himself, and a shower of snow-clumps peppered the drifts about them.

"Hoy!" Porfiry's voice sounded close by, and a moment later a fistful of snow exploded off the bowl above their heads. "I'll teach you to throw snowballs at me, you great lummox!"

Andrei gave a half laugh.

"Reminds me of—" Yurisa began.

"Oh!" Andrei cried, oblivious.

"What is it? Are you hurt?" Porfiry asked, appearing suddenly to their side.

"Anxious as a hen with chicks," Yurisa said dryly.

"I happen to be the eldest member of this expedition," Porfiry said austerely, "and as such—"

"Wenceslas is probably older," Yurisa cut in.

"Look, don't you want to know what I was going to say?" Andrei demanded.

"Of course, of course," Porfiry said. "We'll discuss seniority another time."

"Snowfights!" Andrei said triumphantly. "That's one good thing about you-know-what!"

"Excellent!" Porfiry said.

"And skating!" Andrei added. Why had this seemed so hard before?

"One more!" Porfiry said, cutting a little caper in the drift piled up at Wenceslas's side.

"Um..." Andrei strained his memory. What else was there to look forward to about winter? "Roaring fires?"

"Not really her doing," Porfiry said.

"Unlike the snow and ice," Yurisa added. "Are you all right? You look constipated."

"Now who's clucking?" Porfiry enquired.

"I'm thinking!" Andrei said. "Not constipated, thank you very much!"

"Because I can give you something to loosen—"

"*Thinking!*" Andrei repeated, and they all fell silent.

He carried on thinking as the darkness became complete, and through the night he drowsed and woke, searching even in his dreams for something he did not know.

The storm had died away by midday. Andrei tried to persuade Wenceslas to act as a snow plough, but since the snow slid into the lower bowl and needed to be scooped out again, progress was slow. At last Andrei threw himself down for a rest on the rim of the bowl, and Bronya gave him a dainty lick on the face.

"I wish I was a tree," he said wearily, rubbing her ears. "Go to sleep in autumn, wake up in spring. A nice long rest. Just what I need."

A moment later he sprang up and went leaping through the snow.

"I fear he may have lost his mind," Yurisa said.

"Rest! Rest!" Andrei cried, frolicking about with Bronya bounding about and barking at him.

"I fear you may be right," Porfiry said in a hushed tone.

"It's the third thing!" Andrei called, all thought of lying down forgotten. "The trees sleep and build up their strength for growing fruit next year, and humans get a rest because nothing's growing and there's such short days anyway and long nights."

"A fine point," Porfiry said judiciously, "though I feel you may need to extract the essence of your rather incoherent statement before attempting to engrave it on the razor. Unless you have extremely small handwriting," he added.

Yurisa had rummaged out her sewing kit, and now drew out a needle. The sun, too weak to rise far in the sky, still managed to glint off the splinter of steel. "Better start writing. We'll be there before long."

❄   ❄   ❄

Valeska's sleigh moved at a subdued pace through the black-draped gates. She sat alone with lips pressed close together, but as she was drawn slowly past, the gatekeeper caught a gleam in her eye. Whether triumph or tears, he could not be sure.

She was met halfway up the grand stair, not by the major-domo, but her late father's chamberlain.

"This way, if you please, Your Highness," he murmured in the low tones suitable to a household in mourning. She followed him up the rest of the stairs, her black crepe train sweeping the snow from the steps as she went.

The fires in the long enfilade of rooms were not lit, the whole palace sunk in chill gloom. Valeska swept ahead of the chamberlain and through the ballroom's double doors, opened as they approached by two black-clad footmen. The line of glass doors on the far side of the room were open to the chill wind sheeting in from the north, with a black-sashed soldier standing guard at each, facing out over the frostbitten gardens.

Valeska turned towards the throne and caught her breath with an instantly suppressed whimper.

Her father's coffin stood at the foot of the Seven Steps, swathed in black velvet. But all the black draperies in the world could not conceal how large the coffin was, how enormously, unnaturally, large. Rallying herself, Valeska paced regally down the room, the chamberlain keeping a suitable step behind.

Her breath was coming as little irregular puffs of steam in the frigid air, stark white against the blackness of that pall, which swallowed all the light the room had to offer. Hesitantly, she reached out and placed one black-mittened hand on the coffin. One hasty blink against the tears and her hand was gone, devoured like all else by that inky cloth. With a gasp she snatched her hand back as though burned, and turned away, heart thudding.

The chamberlain was babbling—still in that undertone, but babbling all the same. Funeral. He was talking about the funeral. Her father's funeral. "...due to the nature of the coffin...arrangements have to be made...delays inevitable...fortunate season..."

Valeska concentrated, and soon took the point of his repetitive phrases. Her father's monstrous coffin would not fit in the vault provided for it. A new vault would have to be constructed, and in the meantime... This, then, was the reason for the open windows, the absence of fire on a bitingly cold day. The funeral was delayed, and they could not risk, as the chamberlain was saying in an apologetic voice, any *unpleasantness*.

She lifted her eyes from their contemplation of the floor and fixed them on the chamberlain. He stuttered to a stop.

"I understand the necessity," Valeska said in a low voice, and he relaxed a little. "In the meantime, I shall occupy my old rooms. Have them made ready."

The chamberlain gave an awkward little dry cough. "Occupation of the imperial suites is traditionally arranged by order from the Throne," he murmured, not meeting her eye.

"Under the circumstances," Valeska countered, her tone sharpening a little, "surely a few weeks is neither here nor there."

"Under the circumstances," he repeated, giving each word weight as he spoke. "Circumstances can change in a few weeks. Nor are all circumstances favourable to your request."

"It was not a request," Valeska said icily. "My father the Czar is dead; I am his heir. What other circumstances do you imagine need consideration?"

"If the Czarina is found..."

"The Czarina is not, and never can be, an heir to the throne," Valeska snapped.

"But her child may well," the chamberlain returned boldly, meeting her eye for the first time. "It's not for me to say, but there are those who knew the Czar's mind in the matter. Those with whom he spoke in his last weeks," he added pointedly.

Red flared on Valeska's cheeks. How dared he?

"Vulgar persons may have fomented misunderstanding between the Czar and those *nearest* to him," she spat, "but he had seen through their machinations and arranged a meeting of reconciliation."

The chamberlain looked surprised. "And when did His Late Majesty meet with you?"

"He was prevented from attending the meeting he had proposed," Valeska was forced to admit, "but rest assured I intend to discover who did him that disservice."

He was frowning now. "What day was this, that the meeting was planned? What time?"

"Eight days ago," Valeska said. "In the afternoon." No need to tell him the place—so easily misinterpreted.

"Impossible," the chamberlain said briskly.

"How dare you?"

"Eight days ago the Czar was away at his hunting lodge all day," the chamberlain said. "No meeting was planned."

Valeska stared at him, the colour draining from her cheeks.

"I can understand the wish to," he gave a patronizing little laugh, "*reframe* the past, but a man like myself can only afford to deal with realities. And the reality, I'm afraid, is that His

Late Majesty the Czar had your household removed to the Little Palace with no intention that it should ever return."

The swelling cyst of pain and rage in Valeska's chest exploded, and two words flew from her mouth as though fired from the mouth of a cannon.

"You *toad!*"

A moment later her shriek was muffled by the velvet of her mittened fists, pressing her lips against her teeth until they bled. The toad hopped rapidly away, going to ground under a black-draped chair against the wall.

Maxim stepped out from the doorway at the far end of the ballroom.

"I think," he said, his voice echoing in the cold stillness of the room, "that it would be best for everyone if you stopped talking."

The Lady of the Lake

"There!" Andrei held the razor out for inspection.

"Your handwriting would disgrace an illiterate chicken," Porfiry said, "but once you tell her what it says, it should be all right."

"Tell her?" Andrei's eyes widened. "You mean she'll actually be there?"

"Of course! What did you think you were going to do, just stroll up and chuck it in the Lake?"

"You can't do that. It would bounce off," Yurisa said.

"And would be entirely inappropriate to boot," Porfiry went on. "You arrive at the Lake, you make your apology—in the appropriate words—and you give her the razor."

Andrei's heart sank. "The appropriate words? How am I supposed to know what the appropriate words are?"

"Fear not!" Porfiry said. "I have done this before, and I will prepare a statement for you to memorize."

"You've *done this before*?" Andrei asked, as Yurisa turned to stare at Porfiry.

"Well, in a manner of speaking," Porfiry amended. "To be scrupulously honest, it was a play I wrote in which someone apologizes to Autumn—"

Andrei groaned.

"—but I based it on what I found in an old manual of etiquette!" Porfiry said. "So it's as close as you're going to get."

"Go on, then," Andrei said. "What's the worst that could happen?"

"Well," Yurisa began.

"I don't want to know!" Andrei snapped.

"Why would you ask a question if you don't want to know the answer?" Yurisa asked.

"Never mind. Let's just—get on with it."

"I'll have to change a few bits," Porfiry said. "Since it's not Autumn we're dealing with. Give me a minute or two."

They trudged on to the accompaniment of Porfiry muttering to himself.

"Right, I think I've got it," he said at last.

Andrei concentrated.

"It begins with *O, Autumn!*" Porfiry said. "Or rather, *O—*"

"Don't say it!" Yurisa said.

"I wasn't going to," Porfiry said. "But Andrei will have to."

"What, you mean say her actual name?" Andrei paled.

"Why not?" Yurisa asked. "You've been free enough with it in the past."

"The invocation is necessary to get the immortal's attention," Porfiry explained.

"Oh, it'll do that," Yurisa said, looking pityingly at Andrei.

Andrei decided he would proffer the razor *closed*. Just in case the Lady got any ideas. "And then?"

"Once she appears, you say, *O most sweet and puissant lady—*"

"Pwissont?" Andrei said dubiously. "That better not be what it sounds like, or she'll kill me for sure."

"It means powerful," Porfiry said reproachfully.

"And sweet?" Yurisa asked skeptically. "Since when is she sweet?"

"It is a form of speech which is as old as time itself," Porfiry said grandly, "to attribute to the one addressed the qualities which you wish them to possess, in hopes that they will come to see themselves that way and act accordingly."

"Like calling someone merciful when you want them to not chop your head off?" Andrei asked.

"Precisely. And coincidentally, it goes on—where were we?"

"O most sweet and...puissant lady," Andrei said.

"Right, right. *Overflowing with mercy, hear the voice of your humble suppliant and accept this, his apology.* And then you go on and declaim the three kind words, in as poetical and eloquent terms as you can possibly manage."

Andrei turned to Porfiry. "Declaim? You think I can just stand there and declaim? I don't even know what declaiming is!"

"Don't worry!" Porfiry said. "I can provide you with a script. You say—what was the first thing?"

"Ice skating," Andrei said.

"You say, *The Lady is so kind as to freeze the waters of the land, permitting us to disport ourselves in ways the other seasons permit not.* What's the next one?"

"Snowfights. And then rest."

"*The Lady is so generous as to bring snow upon the land, bringing joy to the young and those still young at heart, in the games and diversions which only snow provides.*" He took a deep breath. "*The Lady is so nurturing as to bring upon all the living creatures of the earth a season of rest, in which every being from the humblest plant to the Czar himself can husband their strength for the seasons to come.*"

"The humblest plants probably just die," Yurisa said.

"*Don't* say that," Porfiry warned.

"I'll have trouble remembering any of it," Andrei said. He looked down at Bronya and ruffled her ears. "But I'll try. Can you go over it again?"

"Oh, I haven't finished yet," Porfiry assured him cheerily. "You wind up by saying, *Merciful, generous and gentle-hearted Lady, let these kind words blot out the memory of the foolish words unkindly spoken by your suppliant, and let this gift keep these kind words ever near to your memory.* And then you give her the razor."

"And then?" Andrei asked wearily.

Porfiry nibbled on a finger. "And then she goes away...I think."

"You *think*?" Andrei ran a hand through his hair, spattered his face with a little snow, and slapped it vigorously. "Right. Let's do this. O Lady!"

"Only you don't say Lady," Porfiry reminded him.

"I know! I'm just not going to say it yet. How does it go? O Lady..."

They moved on through the snow, Porfiry feeding Andrei his lines bit by bit, and Andrei going over and over them, his mouth tripping and stumbling as his feet moved purposefully on, closer and closer to the Lady's Lake.

❄   ❄   ❄

The cold seemed to intensify as they dragged themselves wearily through the last miles to the lake shore. Occasional dead branches jutted out of the ice, and a cold mist swirled uncomfortably through everything.

Andrei shivered.

"Go on," Porfiry whispered.

Andrei cleared his throat. He took a breath.

"Don't tell me you've forgotten your lines," Porfiry said in the same stagey whisper.

"I haven't," Yurisa muttered. "I could recite them in my sleep by now."

Andrei shot his companions a quelling look and took another deep breath.

"O Winter!" he called, and mercifully his voice didn't break.

There was a silence, devoid of bird-call or lapping water, only the whine of the prying wind.

"What if she doesn't come?" Andrei muttered under his breath.

"Be patient!" Porfiry scolded. "You're not summoning a chambermaid, you know."

They waited. Andrei shifted from foot to foot to try to keep warm; Yurisa chafed her arms vigorously.

"It's getting late," Andrei said at last, trying to keep his voice steady. "I don't think she's coming."

"Maybe it's the wrong place," Yurisa suggested. "The wrong part of the Lake, I mean."

Bronya looked out over the misty ice, whimpered, and tucked her tail firmly beneath her. She pushed closer to Andrei.

He squinted into the fog. "I think I can see something!" A shadow in the distance, moving across the ice.

"Shh!" Porfiry said, flapping his hands in the closest thing to a panic Andrei had ever seen him in.

Andrei stopped squinting and took a breath, feeling slightly ill. Too much staring into the dizzying spirals of the mist, perhaps. But there was definitely someone coming towards them. A tall, thin figure.

"Is that her?" Porfiry tried to gnaw on his knuckle.

"Barefoot on the ice?" Yurisa said in a low voice. "It has to be."

The mists drew back, revealing Winter closer than he'd realized, standing right in front of him, tall and very pale, with hair like black ice. Andrei's mouth went dry. Bronya shivered beside him, but stood her ground.

Winter looked straight into Andrei's eyes, and Porfiry's fine words drained out of his mind.

"I—I'm sorry for what I said," he said, struggling to bring the words out in the face of that unblinking stare. "You bring us ice, which is good for skating, and—and sleighs. And snow for snowfights and snowmen and things like that, and..." He strained after the third thing, not daring to risk a look at the razor he held in one shaking hand. "And you make people rest—and plants and animals, I mean. And I'm sorry I was rude," he added, in case he'd forgotten to mention it before.

He held out the razor, and without taking her eyes off his, Winter reached out and took it. A sharp pain tore at Andrei's fingers, and he looked down instinctively. The skin was gone off his fingertips, just like the time when he was six and Leonid had dared him to touch the chain of the village well without his gloves on. He looked to the razor in Winter's hand, and it was rimed in frost, his fingermarks disappearing as he looked.

Almost against his will, his eyes rose to Winter's unsettlingly beautiful face. Her lips parted in a smile, Andrei's heart skipped a beat in pure terror, and she turned away, the mists swallowing her in moments.

The wind hissed gently about Andrei for some minutes, as he stared after her, wondering if his eyes had played a trick.

"Is she gone?" Porfiry whispered at last.

Andrei turned to find Porfiry had his hands over his eyes.

"Yes," he said. "She was frighteningly..."

"Human?" Porfiry asked.

"No!" Andrei almost shouted. "Frighteningly real."

He turned to Yurisa, who was staring white-faced in the direction Winter had gone. "Did you see her smile?" he asked, trying and failing to speak without a wobble.

She nodded. "Those teeth," she whispered, and then she blinked. "It wasn't just a trick of the light, was it?"

"No." Andrei tried to wipe away the memory of that smile, but his mind stuck to it like fingers to cold metal. Her face was like a human face; that was the frightening thing. And then her perfect lips parted to reveal row on row of spikes, like the predatory mouth of a monster pike.

"There were gaps, that was the strange thing," Yurisa said in an almost dreamy voice. "Wouldn't—"

"I don't want to think about it!" Andrei said, wiping the back of his hand across his eyes as if that could wipe the image away. "We've done what we came to do, so let's get out of here and on to Granny Radinka's before spring makes this all a waste of time."

"After all," Porfiry said, shaking himself, "I don't imagine anyone fancies camping here for the night."

Andrei shivered. "I don't know about you, but I could happily walk all night. As long as it's *away*."

❄   ❄   ❄

The face which Valeska turned as Maxim entered the drawing room was barely recognizable as the same face that had smiled on him at the start of the season. Some women manage to look lovely in their grief; Valeska was not one of them. Her eyes were reddened and puffy, but the rest of her face looked sallow and gaunt.

"Maxim! You've been so long, and I needed you." Putting her arm clumsily through his, she tried to draw him down onto the long chaise beside her.

He shook her off and sat himself in an armchair at a short distance. "Is this your idea of how a Czarina—Czara—behaves? Your mother would never have given way like this. Pull yourself together. You may be within a step of the throne, but you're not going to impress anyone by getting sick and hysterical."

Valeska choked on a sob. "How can you be so cruel?"

"Cruel? Ask that poor toad in the Great Palace if he thinks *I'm* cruel." He leaned forward and patted her on the knee. "Come now! Dry your eyes. Think of all you have to be thankful for. You wanted that woman gone, and she's disappeared. You wanted to be recognized as your father's heir, and what other heir has been presented?"

"Where has she gone?" Valeska whispered.

Maxim frowned. "How should I know?" he demanded.

"I can't help thinking of her. Worrying. What if—what if something terrible has happened to her—because I wished her gone? I never wanted harm to befall her."

"Put that thought out of your mind!" Maxim spoke sharply. "You mustn't think like that. Don't think about her at all. That kind of woman is perfectly capable of looking out for herself. Forget the past. You must only think about the future—think about your goal. You're so close—now is not the time for regrets."

She tried to pull herself together, but her eyes ran tears in spite of herself.

"I mean it, Valeska. Forget the past. Forget her, forget the child. Forget what you did to your father. Forget the maid. Forget that poor fool of a chamberlain."

The tears ran faster. He stood up and leaned over her.

"Don't think about them."

❅   ❅   ❅

The weather had definitely improved, Andrei had to admit, but it was still winter, and climbing into the Long Mountains in winter was not a sensible proposition. Unless you were desperate. Which he was.

They'd travelled as fast as they could, rising before dawn and walking late into the night, as far as the light of moon or stars would light their way. There were few villages this far north, but every place they briefly stopped to purchase much-needed food was the same: suspicious of strangers and determined to avoid any contamination from further south. Even Yurisa had agreed that now was not the time for questions. The sooner they could transact their business and be gone, the happier everyone would be.

Nearly a week out from the Lady's Lake, they were up in the mountains, cold, weary, and from all appearances alone. Andrei looked down at Bronya, her feet wrapped in rags against the cold, and pushed on.

"We must be nearly there by now," Porfiry said for the dozenth time.

"We need to turn left up along here somewhere," Yurisa said. She was braced in Wenceslas's bowl, squinting at the rough map Granny Ludmilla had provided. "Some kind of ledge, maybe? The map isn't very clear."

"I'll keep an eye out," Andrei said, and scratched ferociously at his chin. "Urgh! Why does it have to be so itchy?"

"I was trying not to think about it," Yurisa growled, her hand going up to her own bristly chin, stopping short, and being pulled away apparently by sheer force of will.

"Face it," Porfiry said, draping a cold heavy arm across Andrei's shoulders. "You're just jealous that she's got a better beard than you."

"Shut up!" Andrei snapped, but not faster than Yurisa did.

"Look, I think this is it, between these rocks," Andrei went on, eager to change the subject. "Kind of a wide ledge, like a road, going off to the left."

"North," Porfiry said dismally.

"That's the least of our problems," Andrei said. "I don't think Wenceslas is going to fit through."

"Are you sure?" Yurisa said. "It looks close to me."

"If there's one thing a driver knows," Andrei said, "it's what will and won't fit through a gap. Trust me: he won't go."

Yurisa clambered out and hobbled up to the gap between the rocks. "We could at least try."

Andrei shrugged and walked through the gap, sidling along the road so as to keep an eye on what Wenceslas tried to do. The fountain galumphed briskly up to the gap and smacked into the rock with a thump Andrei felt coming up through the soles of his feet. He sprinted back, Porfiry already throwing himself into the way to stop Wenceslas having another go at it.

"Wenceslas, you can't," Andrei said breathlessly. "You'll hurt yourself. Damage yourself, anyway," he added.

"Or cause an avalanche and kill us all," Yurisa said, leaning on the offending rock with a white face.

"My dear friend!" Porfiry said, running his hand over Wenceslas's rim. "You have chipped yourself! Hadn't I better stay with him?" he asked Andrei anxiously.

"I, um, I'm not sure I can carry Yurisa all that way by myself," Andrei said. She was of sturdy peasant stock, after all, and turning into a boy hadn't made her any daintier. "You'll have to come with us," he went on hurriedly as Yurisa scowled.

Wenceslas growled deep within and sprayed them all with a fine mist of ice.

"You must see, Wenceslas," Porfiry said earnestly, "that our soft friends can't stay with you. They'd freeze, sitting out here in the cold."

"I'm freezing already," Yurisa muttered.

Wenceslas gave a low guttural howl, in which Bronya joined, apparently on general principles. His base seemed to settle in place.

"I promise I'll come back this way," Andrei said, and Wenceslas gurgled mournfully.

"I'm not sure there is any other way," Yurisa said, frowning at the map. "Come on, then."

She put an arm about Porfiry's neck as he scooped her lightly into the air. He plodded off, followed by Andrei, who found himself constantly looking back to check that Wenceslas wasn't trying anything foolish.

It was half an hour of inching along the snowy ledge, tripping on hidden rocks and blundering through drifts, before they reached Granny Radinka's house. It was a low, snow-covered dwelling which could have been mistaken for an outcropping of rock were it not for the warm glow of firelight coming through the tiny windows.

"At last!" Yurisa said. "I'm a mass of bruises."

"Hmpf! Is that all the thanks I get?" Porfiry enquired.

"It's just that Wenceslas is better shaped for carrying," Yurisa explained, stretching stiffly where he'd put her down.

"It is true that I am not well adapted to be a beast of burden," Porfiry conceded. "Perhaps we ought to knock?"

But the little door was already opening, to reveal a tiny bird-like woman, her eyes two dark jewels in a very wrinkled setting.

"Greetings!" Andrei said affably. "Granny Ludmilla sent us. I'm—"

"Get in! Talk can wait till the door's closed," she said.

They obediently squeezed in through the tiny doorway, each passing under her penetrating gaze as they did. She closed and barred the door, and squeezed her way through the now crowded room to put another log and a kettle on the fire.

"Something serious," she said, her voice like the twittering of a bird, "to bring you up here at this time of year. Yes?"

"The Czar's dead," Andrei began, in case she hadn't heard.

She cocked her head on one side. "Czars die, you know. You could say they're chosen for it. That's not what brought you here. And with such...unusual companions," she added, eyeing Porfiry's gleaming dark bulk as he perched on the logpile in the corner.

"They're under a curse," Andrei said, and then it all came out, with corrections from Yurisa, ornamentation from Porfiry, and occasional probing questions from Granny Radinka. Bronya stretched out on the floor by the fire and filled the room with the smell of warm wet dog.

"Very serious," Granny Radinka said, and poured the tea. "You were right to come. Dear me."

"Can you tell us how to stop it?" Andrei asked urgently.

"Can you tell us how to undo it?" Yurisa added quietly.

Granny Radinka pursed her lips and blew on her tea to cool it. "Not all magic can be undone. But the only way to know for *certain* is to try."

"What do we do?" Andrei asked, and they all leaned forward.

"How much do you know about how magic works?" she asked. "Real magic, not just herbalism or manipulating people."

There was a little silence.

"I know a rather ghastly story about Spring and a gardener," Porfiry volunteered.

Andrei shot him an irritated look, but Granny Radinka was nodding.

"You know a little, then."

"You mean that story's true?" Yurisa asked, her face a mask of revulsion.

"Oh, yes. Of course, it was all a very long time ago now. But you know the basic principle: magic comes from the power of the immortals, and in order to wield magic one must have a piece of an immortal."

"Like a lock of Spring's hair," Porfiry said.

"Precisely."

"So we find what Valeska's got and we take it off her," Andrei said, his heart leaping.

"It's not so easy as that," Granny Radinka cautioned. "Magic cannot be stolen or even simply given."

"Then how—?" Andrei asked, frowning.

"Magic can only be given in return for something else," Granny Radinka said. "A trade, if you like."

"But there's no mention of that in the story," Porfiry objected.

"Stories change in the telling," Granny Radinka snapped. "Time goes on, and people leave out bits they don't think are important."

"So what did the gardener give Spring?" Porfiry asked curiously. "What could an immortal possibly want from a gardener?"

"He was a very good-looking young man," Granny Radinka said sedately, "and Spring is fond of young growing things. He gave her a kiss."

"So it doesn't have to be something concrete given in exchange?" Yurisa asked, and Andrei was not surprised to see that she was making notes in her little book.

"No, it doesn't. Furthermore," Granny Radinka said, "in order for the curse—or blessing, it's a matter of perspective as often as not, although this one seems to be weighted rather on the negative side... Where was I? Oh yes, in order for the curse to be ended, as opposed to simply *paused*, the piece that fuels it must return to the immortal."

Andrei's heart sank, and suddenly he felt drained, tired, and worn. "So you're saying in order to stop the curse we need to find out what Valeska's got, find something she's prepared to trade it for, and then get it back to whatever immortal she got it from in the first place?"

"And even then it won't undo the curse," Yurisa said, her voice like the tolling of a bell.

"Won't *necessarily* undo the curse," Granny Radinka corrected her. "It depends on how it was set up. Don't look so downhearted! Just because you can't steal it off her doesn't mean you can't use a bit of trickery."

"Mm," Andrei said, still gloomy.

"You never know," Porfiry said cheerfully, "she might be eager to be rid of it by now, what with all this unpleasantness ensuing."

Andrei snorted.

"Perhaps I should go and tell her the story about the gardener," Porfiry mused.

"We'll have to go," Andrei said wearily. "We have to go back to town and see what we can find out about it—see if there's anything we can do before the season's end."

"Looking on the positive side," Porfiry said with determined cheerfulness, "unless the duke is back in town there won't be anyone there out for your blood, will there? Now isn't that a nice thought?"

❄   ❄   ❄

The black-draped hearse inched slowly down the avenue, the carefully matched black horses straining against their load. Behind it, the drivers struggling to keep their chilled horses at a sufficiently slow pace, wound the cortege.

Every person of rank or wealth was there to pay the Czar honour, shivering in their sleighs, while a handful of stubborn peasants walked behind, hunched into their coats for warmth. Hundreds more lined each street, watching in grim silence as the cortege crawled past.

Directly behind the hearse came the finest equipage in the Little Palace stables, its silver bells replaced with swags of black crepe for the occasion. Maxim had yielded to Valeska's pleas to take the seat beside her, though his own sleigh followed close behind, empty as it was.

She sat staring numbly at the vast black bulk before her, watching the isolated snowflakes flash white for a moment against the cloth and then vanish into its all-consuming darkness. Tears trickled down her face, steaming in the cold stillness. Occasionally she would bite her lip against a sob.

"Stop that," Maxim muttered. "You're making an exhibition of yourself."

"He was my father," Valeska said, in a voice ravaged with emotion. "And now I'll never—"

"Do you think any of them will believe you're sorry to see him go?" Maxim hissed, indicating the watching crowds with a subtle jerk of the head. "After all you said to each other? After all you did? You're not doing yourself any favours with this...overwrought display of grief."

Valeska bowed her head as her face crumpled and the tears fell free. Then, fighting herself under control again, she raised her head, her face a mask as rigid as any of the marble effigies that topped her ancestors' tombs. The teardrops on the lap blanket whitened, and turned to ice.

❅   ❅   ❅

"At last, we are leaving the mountains!" Porfiry groaned. "Have you any idea how my calves are feeling with all this uphill and down we've been doing in the last two weeks?"

"Like rock," Yurisa said.

"Well...yes. What's the matter with her?" Porfiry asked Andrei, as Bronya began to quiver and whine at his side.

"I don't know," Andrei said, frowning. She was practically dancing on the spot, her eyes fixed on the uneven expanse of white snow ahead. He dropped his hand to her head, but as he did so, she took off like a loosed arrow, charging at something it seemed only she could see.

"What on earth is she—" Porfiry began, and then the snow erupted, large chunks of it rising up and dashing away in all directions.

Andrei blinked. "Hares!" he exclaimed. "Look at them all!"

Bronya leapt and snapped in the middle of the furry maelstrom, but Andrei could see no blood, hear no squeals.

Yurisa leaned out of Wenceslas's bowl for a better look. "Huddling together for warmth, probably," she said, "and hoping we wouldn't spot them."

The last of the hares vanished among the drifts and Bronya stood alone in the trampled snow, panting. She sat, howled once, and then, tail down and head hanging, crept back to Andrei's side.

"She seems embarrassed," Porfiry said. "Well, so would I be, if I'd charged that many hares and come back without so much as a mouthful of fluffy white tail."

"I don't think it's that," Yurisa said, frowning thoughtfully at Bronya.

"Can't you see?" Andrei demanded. "Bronya's becoming more...doglike, and she hates it."

Bronya uttered another mournful howl.

"Come *on*," Andrei said, and broke into a run.

Thaw

Dusk was falling as Andrei crossed the little town square, Bronya at his heels. They had made a good distance that day, his arms were full of food, and there was the promise of a warm fire when he got back to their camp. Even the thought of sleeping in the open again was less disconcerting than it had been, now that milder weather had set in. He whistled a few plaintive notes as he slipped into the alley between the inn and the carpenter's workshop.

A window banged open in the inn wall above his head.

"Andrei! My lost love!"

He froze. That voice...those words! He looked up, and sure enough, it was Lala.

"At last I have found you!" she went on, clasping her hands.

Andrei considered bolting, but decided against it. She had a carriage; she had servants—she was bound to find them. Better put a good face on it. Looking down, he caught Bronya's eye. On second thoughts, better get the misunderstanding cleared up as soon as possible.

"Come up here at once," Lala commanded.

He gave Bronya an apologetic look and plodded back towards the inn's door on the town square. He was relieved to see that she was following him, until she nipped him in the leg.

"I can explain!" he hissed, and wondered how.

A large servant in Baron Boris's livery was waiting in the entryway, and led Andrei into the recesses of the building, stopping at an open door.

Andrei stopped too. "A lady's bedchamber? I would never!" he said, hoping the servant hadn't been given any details about how he and Lala had met.

"It's a parlour, oaf," the servant said, shoving him through the doorway with one meaty hand.

Lala rose from the cushioned seat by the window as he staggered in. It was a corner room, Andrei noted, probably the best in the house. Of course. One window overlooking the alley for ambushing passers-by, and three which looked out towards the forest. The lovely faraway freedom of the forest.

"Look, Lala," he said, neatly fending off her embrace. "This is all a misunderstanding."

"Of course it is!" she said radiantly.

"Er—you see that?"

"Of course!" she assured him. "I knew you would never leave me willingly!"

Bronya uttered a low growl, her eyes fixed on Lala's face.

"No—no, I mean, yes!" Andrei cried. "It's been a misunderstanding from the beginning. I was only looking for information!"

Lala put her head coquettishly on one side. "In a lady's bedchamber? La, sir!"

Bronya's head swung around to Andrei, and the growl was much more noticeable.

Andrei took a deep breath. "Fair lady," he began tactfully. Bronya barked, and he winced, but at least she didn't bite him. "I was on a quest to save the woman I love from a terrible curse," he said.

Lala eyed him narrowly. "The woman you love?"

Andrei indicated Bronya, who stopped growling and licked his hand.

"I'm not *stupid*," Lala said. "That's a dog!"

Bronya barked at her, and she sat down with a flop.

"I was too late," Andrei said, and the words burned around his mind. *Too late...*

"You mean to say, you horrid man," Lala said, "that all the time you were uttering sweet nothings to me, you were betrothed to this poor enchanted creature?"

"Not officially betrothed," Andrei admitted, "but my heart was and is hers and she knew it. Knows it. Anyway, I don't remember saying any sweet nothings. I'm not that kind of man, as Bronya will tell you. Would tell you," he amended.

Bronya barked twice, by way of confirmation.

"Oh, you poor suffering darling!" Lala cried, and to Andrei's surprise, she dropped to her knees and wrapped her arms around Bronya. "To be treated thus!"

"So you see, I was only trying to help her," Andrei said. "By finding information about the curse."

"And what would I know about any nasty curse?" Lala demanded.

"Well, your fa—" And then it hit him. "Valeska Kira. She was in your house, after the—no, you travelled with her, didn't you?" He stared in awe at the sulky face before him. "You were there for it all! Tell me! Tell me everything you know!"

Lala sniffed, and turned away. "I'm not talking to you." And then she uttered a piercing scream.

Andrei opened his mouth to demand a cause for this behaviour, before being nearly flattened by the servant barging in.

"A face!" Lala squeaked. "A face at the window!"

The servant strode across and flung the casement open, putting his head and a boulderlike fist through. Then he recoiled, stared for a moment, and then stuck his head back through again. "Porfiry? Is that you?"

"*Porfiry?*" Lala said, and the servant moved away from the window to let her see. "Oh! It is you! I didn't recognize you at first, lurking all purple in the darkness like that. You'd better come in."

"He'll cause a riot," Andrei warned. "People are all on edge about the curse, and Porfiry's...well, look at him."

"He an't properly dressed, either," the servant added.

Porfiry closed his eyes for a moment with a pained expression.

"Don't be silly," Lala said sternly. "Give him the coachman's coat and hat and bring him up at once."

These were duly handed through the window.

"Is Yurisa with you?" Andrei asked.

"Another of your women?" Lala shrilled.

"Yes—I had to bring Wenceslas to see in the window," Porfiry said apologetically. "Rather high foundations this building's got."

"Bring them all in," Lala commanded, and the servant left the room. "I fully intend to get to the bottom of this!"

"You can't bring Wenceslas in here," Andrei said firmly.

Lala looked at him disdainfully. "You can't tell me what to do!"

"He's a nine foot tall garden fountain," Andrei explained. "Even if seeing him didn't cause a riot, he'd never fit in here."

Lala was looking out of the window to make sure Andrei wasn't pulling her leg, when the door opened to admit Porfiry. He had the coachman's tricorne hat pulled well down and Yurisa held up as an extra screen against prying eyes.

Lala stared. "Where's Yurisa?"

"I'm Yurisa," Yurisa said gruffly, as Porfiry put her down in a chair.

"But that's a *girl's* name," Lala said, "and you have a *beard*."

Andrei sighed and settled himself into a chair by the fire. If they were going to make an evening of it, he was at least going to be warm. "It's the curse," he said wearily. "Bronya, Yurisa, Porfiry...your father. The late Czar."

"And you will never *believe* who's at the bottom of it," said Porfiry cosily, settling himself on the window-seat, which groaned under his weight.

Lala looked at him wide-eyed, lips parted slightly with excitement. "Who? Is it Andrei?"

"What? *Me?* Why would I—"

"Well, I just thought," Lala said. "Since you're not cursed and everyone else is."

"Can't be," Yurisa said, looking thoughtfully at Andrei. "Because he's the one trying to end the curse."

Lala sniffed. "Or so he says. Personally, I consider him capable of *anything*."

"It is in fact," Porfiry said loudly, so as to regain the lost attention of his hearers, "Her Imperial Highness Valeska Kira."

"No!" Lala breathed.

"Yes! Absolutely proven, I assure you. When she speaks to someone, they instantly become vulnerable to whatever words may be said to them."

"So you're probably in dreadful danger every moment," Yurisa said, in a conversational tone. "You met her, didn't you?"

"Met her?" Lala said in a horrified squeak. "I travelled with her for *days. Days!*"

"If it's any comfort," Yurisa said, "you're probably not any more vulnerable than anyone who's only had a word from her."

"And you've been lucky so far," Porfiry pointed out. "Just think if your father had happened to say the wrong thing in one of your arguments!"

Lala went pale.

"So you see," Andrei said, taking advantage of the opportunity, "it really is very important for us to find out what happened at the Lady's Lake when you and the princess and the duke were there, because that's when all this began."

"Nothing happened that day," Lala said, pouting at the fire.

Porfiry cocked his head. "Nothing happened that *day*? What about that night?"

"Tell us!" Andrei begged, leaning forward.

"I'm not talking to you!"

"Lala, you must tell us at once!" Porfiry said, using a commanding voice Andrei had never heard from him before.

"You can't tell me what to do! You're just a secretary!" Lala said, and burst into tears, burying her face in Bronya's fur.

"And you're just a—" Porfiry began, stifled by Yurisa's hand suddenly appearing across his mouth.

"That's enough," she growled.

He nodded, and she took her hand away, limping back to her seat.

"You're fast," Porfiry said, mopping his brow.

"Faster than your mouth, which is saying something," Andrei said, settling back into his chair with heart pounding. "You see the danger you're in, Lala?"

"One thoughtless word is all it takes," Yurisa said, and stared at the fire.

"Come now," said Porfiry. "Let's you and I settle down for a nice gossip like the old days, eh?"

Lala just sniffed.

"Wasn't there something about the duke and the princess?" Porfiry wheedled. "It couldn't hurt to tell me about that, now, could it? Don't tell me it happened under our own roof, for I'm certain I should have noticed something!"

"That's what you say," Lala said sulkily. "But you never noticed her hands, did you?"

"A lowly secretary like me was kept more or less at a distance," Porfiry said wryly. "But I knew about her hands from Andrei."

"Much he knows about it," Lala mumbled.

Andrei had to admit that this was true. "I thought it was a curse at first," he began, "but—"

"It's not a curse!" Lala flashed up. "It's love!"

"Love?" Yurisa asked, little notebook out and broad brow wrinkled. "How is—"

"It's his *gift*," Lala said, glowing, and for a moment she was transformed. "She gave him her heart, there in the moonlight, and she's held his gift tight ever since. And I think it's *lovely*," she said defiantly.

A bolt of lightning seemed to flash through Andrei. His eye caught Yurisa's. "A trade," he breathed. "Maxim got it for her, and now..."

"Now he's under a curse," Yurisa said. "Maybe Porfiry was right, maybe he did do it to himself, knowing what her power was."

"The poor fool," Porfiry said in a hushed tone.

"We've *got* to stop her," Andrei said, getting to his feet.

"But in order to do that, we need to know what it is that she's got," Yurisa said reasonably.

Four pairs of eyes moved inexorably back towards Lala.

"What did he give her?" Yurisa asked. "You were there, you must know."

"I'm not telling," Lala said. "Men are all horrible, anyway, and you'll just make it all seem nasty instead of sweet and romantic."

"I'm *not* a man," Yurisa repeated.

"That's what you say," Lala said, throwing a dark look at her. "But I think you must have been, at least a little, because everyone becomes something they already are a bit, don't they?"

"Don't talk such—" Porfiry began, but Yurisa cut him off.

"What do you mean?" she asked, eyes intent on Lala.

"This silly curse that you're all going on about. Father always was a beast, he was really, and so he became a monstery beast, and Porfiry was always ornamental, so he became an ornament, and—and I expect you must have been a bit of a boy really, or you wouldn't have turned into a man," Lala finished.

"But that's ridiculous!" Andrei burst out, but Yurisa was scribbling in her book.

"Pa always said I was like the son of the house," she said. "Luka being so sickly always."

"The seed of death," Porfiry murmured, and she glared at him.

"Aren't we getting a bit off the topic?" Andrei asked. "We still need to know what it is that Valeska's got in her hands!"

"And I'm not going to tell you!" Lala snapped.

There was a silence while Lala glared at those she had out-generalled, and they tried to remuster their forces.

"What about Bronya?" Porfiry asked at last. "She isn't a beastly man, however you look at it."

"I suppose..." Lala said doubtfully.

"Wouldn't you tell Bronya?" he asked persuasively.

"What good would—" Yurisa began, and was quelled by the force of Andrei's glare. "Go on, then," she said, sinking back into her chair and rubbing her injured leg. "Tell the nice doggy."

Lala hesitated.

Bronya turned her big dark eyes on Lala's face, whimpered a little, and allowed one slim paw to touch Lala's arm. Lala gulped, flung her arms around Bronya once more, and snuffled in her ear. Then she sat back, and Bronya licked her tear-stained face.

"Porfiry," Lala said, getting to her feet with dignity. "I shall be leaving for home in the morning. Kindly give orders." So saying, she swept into the adjoining chamber and banged the door behind her.

"Well?" Yurisa asked Bronya dryly. "What did she say?"

Bronya looked at her, and with a curl of her lip, bared one long fang.

❄   ❄   ❄

The fashionable portrait-painter was not at all what Valeska had expected, considering the beauty that flowed from his brush. A small man of insignificant appearance, with colourless hair and watery eyes. He was sweating, despite the leaden chill of the world outside the windows.

She did not stand to receive him, but watched as he caught his easel in the doorway, dropped a stretched canvas, tripped over it, and dropped his tin of brushes with a clatter.

"I'm—I beg your—" He broke off, bowed deeply if hurriedly, and snatched at his breath. "I do apologize—lateness—unavoidably—I hope I haven't inconvenienced you, Your Highness," he finished, bowing again and dropping the tin again as a footman restored it to him.

"Unavoidably detained?" Valeska asked, slowly and clearly, fixing her eyes on him. "By whom, that you could not tear yourself away even to attend on the heir to the Throne of Seven Steps?"

A procession of footmen brought in screens, spare canvases, all the impedimenta of the painter's trade. The painter himself writhed awkwardly beneath Valeska's gaze, but before he found an answer, his attention was entirely distracted by a tall, wide, but curiously shallow box.

"Not that one!" he yelped. "That one was supposed to stay in the sleigh!"

Valeska stood, and all the eyes were on her, figures frozen across the room.

"I insist," she said, "that you explain yourself."

"It's a secret," the painter said miserably, twisting himself into knots.

"If you are wise," Valeska said, "you will not withold secrets from me. This box contains a painting, does it not?"

He nodded.

"A portrait?"

He nodded again.

"I see. The box is to keep the paint from being smudged in transport, is it?"

"Yes, Your Highness," the painter said, suddenly voluble. "The oil takes some time to dry, you see, so—"

"So it is a portrait of the person whose time you believe more valuable than mine, I take it."

He squirmed, staring at the carpet without showing any appreciation of its artistic qualities.

"Show it to me."

"I can't!" he blurted. "He made me promise! It's a secret— he wanted to surprise you!"

"Who?" Valeska demanded.

The painter made a face suggestive of kidney stones.

"Tell me, by all the seasons, or—"

"Duke Maxim," the painter howled, dropping to his knees and clasping his hands beseechingly.

Valeska sat down. "I see," she said musingly, and her face bore no trace of her recent anger.

The nearest footman let out a sigh and started collecting the various items the painter had scattered in his panic.

The painter took a ragged breath. "He made me swear not to tell," he said pitifully. "Oh, please, Your Gracious Highness, don't tell him I told you! He'd be so angry..."

"Well, I would not want to spoil his surprise," Valeska said at last. "Now, as we are running so late already, supposing we make a start?"

"Very good, Your Highness," the painter said weakly. "And has Your Highness given thought to the backdrop preferred?"

"My father chose to be painted against the forest," Valeska said, "but I confess I have not his taste for outdoor pursuits. Perhaps the library—or no, that might be... The garden? No, that won't do..."

"I have several portable backgrounds with me, should Your Highness wish to view them," the painter ventured, still not quite daring to rise from his knees.

Valeska assented to this with a crisp nod, and the next half hour was occupied with viewing one after another, each unrolled, held up for inspection by two long-suffering footmen, rerolled, unrolled again... By the end of that time, the footmen were weary, the painter was a nervous wreck—still kneeling—and Valeska herself was gnawing on a knuckle, hesitating endlessly between each and all of the options.

"Perhaps," the painter ventured at last, "Your Highness would have a commonality of taste with the noble duke?"

"Oh, yes—of course!" Valeska said, clearly relieved. "Yes, that's just what he'd want. He would have been sure to select exactly what he feels I would choose myself—the portraits are to be a pair, after all."

The painter opened his mouth, shut it again, and clumsily rose to his feet.

"That one there," he instructed the footmen. "And fetch the grand chair—I think it's in the hall."

"I will be painted seated on the Throne of Seven Steps," Valeska announced.

"Er, yes—of course, Your Highness," the painter said, uncertainly at first, then with gathering speed. "The chair is merely to set the pose—you wouldn't want to delay the portrait until spring, after all."

"Very well," Valeska said. She watched him putting up his easel, selecting a canvas, setting up his palette. He was still sweating, she noted with distaste, and his hands shook. But she must remember to smile graciously on him, for all the people would see her through his eyes—through his eyes and the deftness of his hand. But how his hand did shake...

❄   ❄   ❄

"Perhaps you should insult the Lady again," Porfiry suggested.

The ice covering the lake which stretched out before them was definitely looking less thick than Andrei was happy with. He eyed Porfiry sideways.

"Perhaps we should go around the long way." Yurisa said.

"That'll take far too long," Andrei said, jigging impatiently in place. "It's just...a bit warmer than we expected, that's all." He tapped the ice at the edge.

"It sounds solid," Yurisa said, "but that doesn't mean it won't be thinner in the middle."

"It'll have to be rock solid to take Wenceslas's weight," Andrei said.

"No need to elaborate," Porfiry said, striking a noble pose. "You delicate wee things go on ahead. My weighty companion and I shall bring up the rear—at a safe distance," he added, seeing Yurisa open her mouth.

Wenceslas gurgled sadly.

"None of that, my dear fellow," Porfiry said, tickling him under the upper bowl. "They won't be out of our sight. And in any case, what's the worst that can happen? You're not going to tell me you're afraid of drowning, now are you?"

Wenceslas made a noise like a frozen waterfall sneezing, and Porfiry beamed at him.

"That's the spirit!"

"Can you make it that far?" Andrei asked Yurisa. "With a shoulder to lean on?"

"Looks like I'll have to," she said gruffly.

Porfiry gave her an arm to climb out of Wenceslas's lower bowl, and then with Andrei's arm under one shoulder and Bronya close at hand on the other side, she gingerly stepped out onto the frozen lake.

For five minutes they inched across comfortingly solid ice.

"Do you think we could move a little faster?" Andrei asked at last. The far side was still unpleasantly far, and he felt uncomfortably exposed away from the trees lining the shore. Even if Lala had given up on her pursuit, that didn't mean their oddly assorted group was safe in open sight.

"A slip could mean another broken bone," Yurisa said. "For either of us."

"Better safe than sorry." Andrei sighed and tried to be patient. At this rate, the sun would reach the other side before them.

"The ice looks darker here," Yurisa said as they approached the middle of the lake. "Be careful."

Their pace slowed further, as Bronya crept ahead of them, testing the ice with her paws.

"Just because she doesn't go through, doesn't mean we won't," Yurisa cautioned.

"Better veer left a bit further," Andrei puffed. Despite the ice below him, the crystal clear day was getting uncomfortably warm.

They moved crabwise round the suspiciously dark area, giving it a wide berth. Andrei stifled the urge to scream with frustration. They'd gone easily the whole width of the lake in terms of distance, but they were barely past midway.

"Can we change sides?" he asked. "My arm is aching."

"Worth a try," Yurisa grunted.

This necessitated a bit of careful sliding around her as she balanced on one leg, which gave him a brief view of Porfiry apparently in deep, if somewhat one-sided, conversation with Wenceslas.

At last he and Yurisa got underway again, and even, Andrei thought, slightly faster than before.

"I say we sit down when we get to the other side," he panted, "and direct Porfiry from there."

Bronya scampered ahead as they neared the shore, momentarily disappearing into the trees and then flashing out again at a more open spot.

"Head that way," Andrei grunted. "Somewhere to sit."

Getting back onto solid ground—uphill and without the aid of Porfiry—was a slippery, uncomfortable business, and Andrei had managed to give his shoulder a painful wrench before they were at last both on shore and sitting on a fallen tree.

He wearily waved his good arm towards Porfiry, a tiny dark figure in the distance. "Is he coming? I can't even see."

Yurisa squinted. "Yes, here they come." She gestured vigorously to Porfiry. "Left. Left! He's just waving, the idiot! Didn't he watch which way we went?"

"Too busy talking to Wenceslas," Andrei said, sitting up and watching attentively.

"Still, anyone would have the sense to avoid the rotten bit," Yurisa said, hand shading her eyes.

"I don't know," Andrei said. "He's always struck me as more of an indoor person."

A loud crack sounded across the ice, followed by a faint splash as Porfiry disappeared.

Andrei leapt to his feet in time to see the much larger splash as Wenceslas keeled over and crashed through the broken ice after Porfiry.

"Don't panic," Yurisa said, putting out a hand to restrain his impulsive movement towards the lake. "Stone can't drown."

"I can't see them," Andrei said anxiously.

"Stone can't float, either," Yurisa said patiently.

"Wenceslas is nine foot tall! Why isn't he sticking out?"

"Lakes are often deep in the middle," Yurisa said.

They waited, three pairs of eyes scanning the fractured surface, but the lake showed no sign of life.

"Something's wrong," Andrei said at last.

"That's them!" an unfamiliar voice shouted.

Andrei whirled to see four burly men emerging from the trees towards them.

"Don't let the dog get away!" the one at the back snapped.

Bronya showed no signs of trying to escape. Her hackles were up, and her teeth were in plentiful evidence. She dived at the first man, nipped him sharply in the hand and received a kick in the ribs that sucked the air out of Andrei's lungs in sympathy. He threw himself into the fray, but it was an unequal fight from the beginning.

After a blow that made his head spin, he received only fragmentary and confusing impressions of what was going on, until everything went dark, with a lurching sense of movement that made him feel horribly sick.

"Told you they'd come this way," said a voice somewhere outside the darkness.

"Why didn't you run away?" a gruff voice demanded, close at hand.

Andrei blinked. Everything was still dark.

"Yurisa?"

"Who did you think it was?" she snapped.

"I can't see anything," Andrei said, feeling about for some proof that the world still existed.

"Ow! That's my bad leg. Stop panicking, will you? You're not blind, it's just dark in here."

Andrei's questing hands felt fur, and a shrill whimper cut across the muffled sounds of movement.

"Bronya!" He found her face, and slipped off the rope which was tightly bound about her muzzle, receiving a lick by way of thanks.

"Why didn't you run?" Yurisa demanded again. "You could have seen I wasn't going anywhere, sitting down with an injured leg."

"You think I'd just run off and leave you to who knows what fate?" Andrei asked hotly. "What kind of person do you take me for?"

"A smarter one than you are," Yurisa said sourly. "What makes you think having company in 'who knows what fate' is going to be any comfort?"

"Together is better than divided," Andrei said, his hands exploring the limit of the space. "I think I've got it."

"Got what?" Yurisa enquired.

"A sense of where everything is."

"Oh, good. Where are we?"

"In an old-fashioned lady's touring sleigh," Andrei said.

"It looked like a box on runners to me," Yurisa said.

"Well, that's pretty much what a touring sleigh was," Andrei admitted. "Back in the days when noble ladies weren't supposed to be seen by anybody who wasn't related to them."

"Why not? Were they under some kind of curse?"

"There is supposed to be a grill for air and peeking out," Andrei said, feeling along one side of the box. "Here it is—oh. It's got something over it on the outside."

The sleigh bounced over something in the path and Andrei's head hit the roof. Stars startled his vision.

"Ouch!" Yurisa said. "What kind of madwoman would want to travel like this? It's like being in a coffin without the comfort of being dead."

"Thank you for sharing that cheerful thought," Andrei said. "Oh, my head!"

"Did you get hit in the head?" Yurisa asked. "Back at the lake, I mean."

"Yes," Andrei said grumpily. "I thought I'd try fighting instead of just sitting there waiting to be captured."

"I still think you should have run away," Yurisa said. "It would have been the sensible thing to do."

Andrei couldn't think of any satisfactory reply to this, and silence fell within the box.

It soon became apparent that food and drink—while freely indulged in by those on the outside of the sleigh—were not to be offered to those within.

"A long journey, then," Yurisa said, "or they would wait to eat when they arrived."

"Oh," Andrei said hollowly.

"But not too long," she added.

"What do you mean, not too long?" Andrei snarled. "It's been too long already."

"It can't be more than a day or two, or they'd risk us dying of thirst," Yurisa said, with a detachment Andrei almost admired.

"What makes you think that's not their plan?"

"If they were going to kill us," Yurisa said, "they would have just killed us and dumped our bodies by the lake."

"What if someone wants to see our bodies as proof we're dead?" Andrei countered, determined to plumb the depths of the awful possibilities.

"Then they would have killed us first, to save any worry about us escaping."

"Something in that, I suppose," Andrei said grudgingly.

"The question is, who?"

"You say that like you think I know the answer," Andrei said.

"Nothing like this has ever happened to *me* before," Yurisa said pointedly.

"For your information, I've never been kidnapped either!"

"But people keep trying to kill you."

"Thanks for the reminder. I'm going to sleep. If I can."

His head was just drooping onto his chest when suddenly Yurisa said "Andrei?"

"Hm?"

"Do you think..."

"Probably not as often as I should," he said. "Or so Bronya tells me. Told me."

Out of the darkness came a whine and a warm moist tongue.

"Do you think—I mean..." She sighed. "There's no point asking. You can't possibly know."

"Go on—try me."

"It's a waste of time."

"I'll just have a sleep, then," Andrei said grouchily. He closed his eyes—not that it made any difference—and had almost dropped off despite the sleigh's uneven path, when Yurisa heaved a sigh and spoke.

"Do you think stopping the curse would actually undo it?"

"What? I—"

"Right. There's no way you could know. And even if it would, what are the chances we'll survive to stop it?"

"I was going to say," Andrei said, "that I see no reason not to hope for the best. Despair is...oh, what's that word?"

"I don't know, do I?"

"I heard Valeska Kira use it one day when she was talking to Bronya. En...something. Means tiring and draining—enervating! That's it. Despair is enervating."

"So it makes sense to assume the best outcome even if you have no logical reason for thinking it more likely?" Yurisa said slowly, as though testing the thought out as she went.

"Um, yes. Probably? Something like that. As Granny always says, don't buy trouble—"

"—when you can get it for free," Yurisa finished automatically.

"Said it to you too, did she?"

"Every day. But I can't help thinking..."

"That's where we differ," Andrei said agreeably.

"If we assume for the present that this curse is one of the ones that can be undone, how much power is there in the undoing? As much as in the curse itself?"

"You think too much," Andrei said, stifling a yawn.

"Or is it limited to the power of the person or people who undo it?" Yurisa went on as though he hadn't spoken.

"What? Look, you are definitely overthinking this. Why even worry about that now?"

"Is it strong enough to undo death?" Yurisa asked, a note of pleading in her voice he'd never heard before.

An image of a sheeted figure in a cold stone room appeared before his mind's eye. "I don't know," Andrei said at last.

Silence fell in the stuffy, swaying darkness. Andrei settled himself as comfortably as he could, and tried to lure his lost sleep back again. But he was wakeful now, wakeful even after the sleigh changed to the slower pace needed for night travel behind men on foot with torches.

As Andrei sat wedged in one corner, one hand resting on Bronya's shoulder, he felt her twitch. He tensed. The next moment he heard a tiny yip and a soft scrabble of claws on the carriage's wooden floor. Andrei relaxed, and wondered what she was seeing in her dreams. Moments later, the sounds of Bronya's sleep were drowned out as Yurisa began to snore. Andrei sat awake and glared into the darkness.

It was not until the next day—after a surprisingly refreshing sleep, Yurisa assured him—that the sleigh stopped for more than a few minutes. There was the sound of several people tramping across cobblestones, with an echoing effect that suggested stone buildings near at hand on at least two sides.

"I wonder where we are," Yurisa said.

Andrei was busily calculating the distance implied by their speed and the number of times they'd changed the horses, when the door to the sleigh suddenly opened, sending a blare of sunlight painfully across his eyes.

They were hustled out, half blinded, Bronya and all, and before Andrei could get his bearings, they were out of the sun again, and moving down a cold stone passageway. A flight of stairs led down to the inevitable dungeon, in which they were unceremoniously dumped without a word.

Andrei looked around. "Well built," he said dolefully. "Let's have a look out that window."

He jammed the toe of his boot into a crevice between two stones and hauled himself up to the little grill by the ceiling. His reward was an ankle-height view of a courtyard with stable servants bustling about the touring sleigh. He scanned the rest of the courtyard and dropped back to the floor at the urging of his aching fingers.

"Did you see anything useful?" Yurisa asked.

"I don't know. It's hard to tell anything from people's shins."

"So you don't know where we are?"

Andrei heard the horses clop slowly off to their stables—round the left there, yes. Wait. How did he know that? He closed his eyes, turning this way and that as he moved through the space in his mind. His eyes snapped open.

"Well?"

"I've been here before," Andrei said triumphantly. "Bringing furniture for storage—back when they weren't fighting, of course."

"Who weren't?" asked Yurisa, brow creased.

"The Czar and the duke," Andrei explained. "There was never much to do at the Little Palace before Valeska moved in, so the Czar loaned our services to the duke a year or so ago, to move some old stuff out here. This is Duke Maxim's estate. Out east of the capital."

"Maxim again," Yurisa said thoughtfully.

"Acting on orders from *her*, no doubt," Andrei said. "You heard what Lala said. Besotted."

"The question is," Yurisa said, "what now?"

And almost as an echo of her voice, there came a long, deep groan from the shadows.

The Child of the Dungeon

Valeska walked slowly down the long gallery, her black crepe dress rustling as it dragged across the carpet. She could not take up residence, not yet, not as things were, but they could not bar the doors against her. She was the heir to the long line of Czars and their Czarinas whose faces looked down at her from the walls of the gallery, stretching into the dim distance of the past.

There was a gap next to her father's portrait, but that did not surprise her. Her father had had her mother's portrait taken down almost as soon as she'd drawn her last breath, and where he'd had it put Valeska had never been able to learn. A small spurt of anger shot through her at the thought, followed by a larger surge when she realized that only Svetlana's disappearance had prevented a painting of that vulgar little upstart taking her mother's place in the procession of faces.

She turned and stood, considering the as yet bare section of wall, and where the light would fall. One would not wish one's portrait to be lost in gloom, of course, but neither was the sunlight good for the oils. Her own portrait here, perhaps, and Maxim's portrait facing. The Czara and her Czarin.

He'd told her that he didn't need any titles from her, but she was determined that he should not remain plain *Duke* Maxim. There had never been a Czarin before, but what of that? When she was Czara she could make what titles she chose. No one would argue with the voice that spoke from the Seven Steps.

The door at the near end of the gallery swung open, and Valeska started.

"I thought I would find you here," Maxim said gravely. He turned to close the door behind him, concealing the object he carried from her view for a moment. Some sort of cage?

"I've been deciding on a place for our por—" Valeska broke off, pressing her lips with one tightly clenched hand. A harsh squawking came from the cage Maxim carried—a birdcage.

"The painter told you," Maxim said, but he did not seem surprised.

Valeska flushed and hastened to divert his attention. "A magpie, Maxim? Now why would you—?"

"What did you say to him?" Maxim demanded, his manner still grim against her hastily constructed gaiety.

"I didn't say anything to him," Valeska said, defensively. She hadn't even threatened him—not really. "Why do you ask?" she asked, an edge of defiance in her voice.

Maxim said nothing, only lifting the cage high so she could see the magpie practically eye to eye. The bird exploded in a flurry of wings and squawking, and in the furore her eyes fixed on one thing that was still: a paintbrush lying in the bottom of the cage.

"What did you say to him, Valeska?" Maxim asked again, his voice deadly quiet.

Valeska gazed at him with horror-stricken eyes. "No—it can't be! I didn't! I was so careful—I—*Maxim!*"

She tried to move closer to him, blindly seeking the shelter of his arm, but the birdcage with its frenzied prisoner seemed always between them. With a sobbing gasp she turned and fled down the gallery, battering herself against the far door until a startled footman opened it. Half falling through, she righted herself and ran on, ignoring the startled faces of all she passed. The black crepe trimmings of her train and sleeves trailed behind her in the wind of her passing, like the draperies of a ghost yet living.

She passed through the Great Palace and its gardens like a demented comet, leaving alarm and exclamation in her wake. Reaching a low white building, unseen from the palace windows, she stopped, breath tearing in her throat. She hooked her forearms through the great handle of the door and dragged it open just far enough for her to slip through. The heavy door closed with soft finality behind her.

A gentle light from a pane in the ceiling diffused across the pale and quiet room within. The walls were bare creamy stone. So was the floor. So was the surprisingly small, delicate sarcophagus at the far end of the small room, resting on a larger plinth to avoid dwindling into obscurity. Valeska flung herself across the room, fell on her knees beside the plinth and leaned her head against the cold stone.

"Mother," she said. "Mother! What have I done?"

At length her breathing steadied. "I've tried so hard to make everything right," she whispered. "Tried so hard to be like you. But the harder I try the more I become like *him*. What am I going to do, Mother? I can't let go now! I *can't*!"

❆   ❆   ❆

Andrei jumped. "What was that?" His mind conjured up ancient prisoners, chained down here till they even forgot the sound of speech.

"There's someone else in here," Yurisa said, peering into the darkness.

"I'll go," Andrei said. "They could be dangerous."

The groan sounded again.

"Not making a noise like that, they're not," Yurisa said. "Sounds like labour pains to me."

"In a dungeon?" Andrei moved warily into the shadows away from the door, letting his eyes adjust to the dimness. "This place is bigger than I thought," he reported. "There's another room back here. And it's warmer, too."

The groans were getting louder and more frequent. Cautiously, he peeked around the edge of the low arch between the two rooms, and saw where they were coming from. Hastily, he scrambled back the way he'd come.

"What is it?" Yurisa asked in alarm.

"There's a woman back there, and she's, um, she's having a baby. I think?"

"I told you so."

"She's very big in front, anyway, and she's got her legs pulled up, and..." He blushed.

Yurisa climbed awkwardly but rapidly to her feet, and Andrei gave her an arm.

"Where's Bronya?" he asked, looking around.

"Didn't she go with you?"

"Bronya!"

There was a gentle yip from the darkness beyond, half buried beneath a heavy groan. They rounded the archway to find the woman had her arm around Bronya, who was nuzzling her face and making little comforting noises.

"Let's have a look," Yurisa said briskly, dropping to her knees at the woman's side.

Andrei turned away, rightly construing this as a professional "us" not involving him.

"No, please," the woman moaned. "Isn't there a woman who could—" She broke off as another pang hit.

"It's all right," Andrei said, turning round and then averting his eyes again. "This is Yurisa, and she's my grandmother's apprentice. As a healer," he added.

"But you're a man! A man can't be—"

"I'm not a man," Yurisa said, as kindly as Andrei had ever heard her say anything. "It's the curse. I don't know if you've heard anything of it over in these parts."

The woman flinched away. "Like Kiril?"

"I haven't turned into a monster," Yurisa assured her. "Just a man."

"So you've seen the Czar?" Andrei asked, wondering where the two could possibly have met.

The woman's answer was delayed as a pang wrung her. Then she gasped a sort of half laugh. "*Seen* him? Whose child do you think this is?"

Andrei stared at her, open-mouthed. "S-Svetlana? I mean, Czarina Svetlana?"

She gripped Yurisa by the hand. "You know about this curse? Tell me—can it pass from father to child?"

"I don't know," Yurisa said, "but we'll find out soon."

Svetlana sank back with a sob of terror.

"Probably not," Andrei said, looking daggers at Yurisa. "Isn't that right?"

"The balance of probability is in that direction," Yurisa said.

"What does that mean?" Svetlana asked Andrei.

"It means the baby probably won't be a monster," Andrei said, as soothingly as he could manage. "The princess hasn't spoken to the baby, has she? No? Well, you're probably all right, then."

"Valeska?" Svetlana asked. "What has she got to do with any of this?"

Andrei opened his mouth to answer, and it struck him that Svetlana might not yet know of the Czar's death.

"I need some hot water and clean cloths," Yurisa said, interrupting his thoughts.

"In a dungeon?" Andrei asked.

"Do what you can!"

She sounded just like Granny on a case. Andrei hastened away to bang on the door, relieved to leave the question of breaking Svetlana's bereavement to her in Yurisa's hands.

The men on the other side of the door were not inclined to listen to his request, but a loud persistence frequently pays off. Andrei's dramatic descriptions of the sufferings of the poor imprisoned woman (feverishly drawn from his thin stock of "the sort of thing Porfiry would say"), drew pity from a passing servant woman, who'd had five of her own, and one backwards, as she proudly informed Andrei. He tried not to think about it, until she returned with a tin bucket of hot water and an armful of worn but clean rags, handed through the doorway under the watchful eyes of the guards.

Andrei carried them carefully back to the scene of operations in the back room. Things seemed to have quieted down a bit. At least, Svetlana was breathing a bit more evenly.

"So...were you kidnapped by the duke?" he hazarded.

"No—he helped me get away," she panted.

So the Czar had been right about that much, at least.

"Why did you leave?"

She rolled her eyes at him. "You've seen the Czar? You have to ask?"

Privately, Andrei felt there were probably ladies of the court who would be prepared to put up with more than a monster for a husband to swank around as Czarina, but apparently Svetlana wasn't one of them.

"Please..." she said desperately. "Kiril mustn't find me."

Andrei tried to think of how to tell her.

"He won't find you," Yurisa said. "He's dead."

Svetlana gazed at her with open mouth. "Dead? Kiril's dead?"

"Died about three weeks ago. Now let's get this baby born, shall we?"

Andrei decided this was his cue to leave. "I'll just..." he muttered, and sidled as far away from the ensuing growls, shouts and swearings as he could get. For a Czarina, Svetlana had an impressive vocabulary. But something niggled at the back of his mind.

"The Czar died three weeks ago," he muttered. "So...he was already dead when Garek carried out his orders. More or less," he amended. His eyes crossed in concentration and his lips moved.

"Push!" Yurisa commanded in the distance.

Andrei put his hands over his ears. It all fit. What Maxim said made sense, if you counted Garek's efforts as an assassination—one complete in all but the minor detail of the target not actually being dead when it was all over. But *only* if Maxim already knew that the Czar was dead.

Except that heavy sleigh couldn't possibly have outdistanced the courier carrying the news, so the Czar must still have been alive when the duke left Istvan. So he couldn't have known the Czar was dead before the courier reached him at his mother's estate. Surely?

But could he still have had a hand in the Czar's death? He had helped Valeska by getting Svetlana out of the way—had he helped her get her father out of the way too? But you can't kill someone from a distance, can you? *Poison*, his mind said, and he wished it hadn't.

He took his hands off his ears and discovered the dungeon had got a lot quieter. His heart thumped. Had Svetlana died? Had the baby been born a monster and killed them all?

He crept up to the archway, and heard Yurisa's voice saying "Well done. A healthy boy."

"A boy? But the healer said..."

Yurisa snorted. "There's no way to know before the baby arrives—and no reputable healer would tell you otherwise."

"But..." Svetlana seemed bewildered. "She was Maxim's own healer! He told me Kiril would do something terrible if he knew it was another girl. That's half of why I left, because..." Her frown sharpened. "That rat bastard lied to me!"

"There's something weird going on here," Andrei said.

"You've only just noticed?" Yurisa enquired.

"Maxim somehow knew the Czar was dead before the courier arrived," Andrei said. "That's what he meant about being assassinated by a dead man."

Bronya licked his hand, and he looked down at her. "And why did his men make such a fuss about capturing Bronya as well as us?"

"I don't know." Yurisa carried on with her work.

"And how did Bronya get this far north, anyway? She can't have trailed us all the way from Istvan." A memory sparked. "They were saying something at Maxim's mother's—when I was going in—about a dog that escaped. Maxim must have taken Bronya with him when he fled, and that's how she..."

"Why?" Yurisa asked practically.

"I don't know, but it's suspicious. He must know she's not really a dog."

"What?" Svetlana looked up from cooing over her fat empurpled baby.

"The dog is actually Valeska Kira's maid," Yurisa explained.

"I thought it was just the Czar changed," Svetlana said, eyes wide, "and now you're telling me it's you and the dog as well? Is anyone here not under a curse? Besides me and my precious little dumpling," she added, going back to making maternal faces at the baby.

"I'm not under a curse either," Andrei said. "But it does seem to be...oh, what's that word Granny uses, when half the village is down with something?

"Epidemic?" Yurisa suggested.

"Starts with a p. Or is it a d?"

"How can you confuse p and d?" Yurisa asked. "They don't sound anything like each other. If it's a p, then prevalent, but if it's—"

"Prevalent! That's it," Andrei said. "And if you ask me, Maxim knows exactly what's going on."

"He got the thing for her," Yurisa agreed, "and that's the root of it, isn't it? He was up there with her at the Lake."

The word *Lake* conjured up an unpleasant flashback to Winter smiling at him, taking the razor and smiling... He curled his hand up with the memory of the pain, and his mouth dropped open.

"Are you catching flies?" Yurisa asked, and elbowed him out of the way.

"Teeth," Andrei croaked.

"Catching teeth?"

"You saw, didn't you? At the Lake. When she smiled. All those teeth!"

"Jagged and irregular," Yurisa said, her normally impassive face showing a hint of flinch.

"Not irregular," Andrei said, his blood coursing faster and faster. "It's just that there were two missing."

Yurisa processed this for a minute, eyes wide in the dim light. "It fits."

"Of course it does! And now we know what we have to do."

"Get out of this dungeon?"

"No—well, yes," Andrei admitted. "But more importantly, get the teeth back to the Lady."

He paced up and down, gnawing on a knuckle.

"What doesn't make sense to me," Yurisa said, pausing for a moment in her tidying up, "is why the duke would give them to the princess in the first place. Why not keep them for himself?"

"Because he's in love with Valeska?" Andrei suggested.

Svetlana snorted loudly, and the baby began to squall.

"Good lungs," Yurisa said approvingly.

When the din was hushed, Svetlana went on. "That man! He's all charm and manners on the surface, but underneath he's as cold as a dead fish, you take it from me. He persuaded me to flee, told me I'd be taken proper care of. Does this look like a proper Czarina's chamber to you? And that old harridan's place wasn't any better! Rich as Summer's gold and prouder than any Czarina, for all that she only married into the royal line, same as me, but you know what her mattresses are stuffed with? Straw!"

"You were staying with the dowager duchess?" Andrei asked, a faint memory stirring.

"In a manner of speaking," Svetlana said sourly. "She didn't join me in the cellar, I'll tell you that much! But Maxim's own estate'd be the first place Kiril would come looking, wouldn't it? He was always a bit suspicious of Maxim. Like I should've been! Ask me, Maxim's never loved anyone in his life."

"Then what would he want with Valeska's heart?" Andrei asked, scratching his head.

"Eat it, like as not," Svetlana muttered, and returned her attention to her son.

"It doesn't make sense. *None* of this makes sense," Yurisa growled.

"Let's look at the facts," Andrei said. "The duke persuaded Svetlana that she had to get away—thus getting this little fellow out of the way as well. Out of the line of succession."

"I'll kill him!" Svetlana snapped. "Yes, Mummy will, won't she, precious?"

Turning his eyes from this slightly disturbing scene of maternal bonding, Andrei continued. "And he seemed to know that the Czar was dead before the courier arrived, which is..."

"Suspicious, certainly," Yurisa agreed.

"But," Andrei said, "if he doesn't love Valeska, why is he clearing her way to the throne?"

"If you ask me," Svetlana sniffed, "he's clearing his own way there."

"He is her cousin," Andrei said thoughtfully.

"But he'd have to get rid of the Czar—" Yurisa objected.

"Who's dead," Andrei pointed out.

"—*and* Valeska. Which would be a lot more difficult," Yurisa argued. "No one was that surprised at the Czar dying suddenly in a drunken rage, but Valeska's young and healthy. Anyway, you're missing the most obvious point."

"Which is?"

"If the duke can't be killed, he's immortal, and immortals can't take the throne. He'd never have done that to himself if he wanted to be Czar."

"True," Andrei said reluctantly. "It's even plastered across the wall in his mother's hall: only a human can ascend the Seven Steps."

"Only a *mortal*," Yurisa corrected.

"*Human* is what it said on the hanging."

They stared at each other, thoughts racing.

"Are you telling me," Svetlana said at last, "that Duke Butter-Wouldn't-Melt-In-My-Mouth is going to try declaring himself Czar and have the steps to the throne disappear right from under his feet?" She laughed uproariously.

"Let's hope so," Andrei said. "And let's hope we can find a way out of here in time to save Valeska Kira's life."

"He might not need to kill her," Yurisa said.

"Another kidnapping?" Andrei said dubiously.

"Or tell everyone who's behind the curse. It might be enough to swing opinion his way."

"With her standing there clutching the teeth for dear life?" Andrei said. "More than enough." He pulled his hair in frustration. "To think I went trotting off to tell him all about it! To ask for his help! And all the time I've wasted, running here and there trying to get someone else to fix it, someone to take responsibility! Ugh, I'm such a child!"

There was a gasp, a silence, and then Yurisa's measured tones.

"Well, at least you got to keep your clothes."

Andrei held tight to Bronya, who was nearly up to his chest, and tried not to faint. Yurisa was saying something, but he couldn't hear her over the buzzing in his ears.

"You aren't going to faint, are you?" Yurisa asked, her face suddenly close to his. "I don't have any sugar for shock." She was bending down to talk to him, he noticed.

He took a quavering breath. "How...how old am I?" His voice! Like a little girl's!

Svetlana looked over from her corner. "About ten, I'd say."

"Maybe," Yurisa said. "Turn to the light."

The next minute she had a hand on either side of his jaw and was peering at his teeth.

"I think I would say nine," she said judiciously, "but well grown for your age. At least you don't have to worry about itchy beard any more." She frowned. "This is all wrong."

Bronya barked vigorously as though agreeing.

"It's not that bad," Andrei said, putting out a hand to stroke her. "Not as bad as finding you'd changed." He gave a watery smile. "If I don't grow out of this, we'll just be a boy and his dog forever."

She whined and licked his face, something which was much harder to avoid at this height.

"That's not what I mean at all," Yurisa said impatiently. "Our conclusions are flawed. We decided weeks ago that it wasn't possible to curse yourself. Remember? I said I was stupid, and nothing happened."

Andrei thought about this. "But Lala said everyone becomes what they sort of already were a bit, and you said you were like the son of the house."

Yurisa brooded. "I suppose... You turning into a child—that makes sense, you must admit. But what about Bronya?"

Andrei looked at Bronya, and a glint in her eye advised him to choose his words carefully.

"She's always been foolishly loyal," he said, "even to those who mistreat her."

Bronya looked guilty, as only a dog with a long nose and large eyes can.

"Doglike devotion?" Yurisa considered this. "I suppose it's possible."

"And that's why it didn't work when you tried it, because..." he waved his little hands, looking for the right words. "There wasn't any stupid in you for the curse to work on. If you know what I mean."

Yurisa flushed a little at the praise, but tried to cover it by much activity with the little notebook. "It's a tenable theory," she said, tucking it away at last.

"Never mind theory now," Andrei said, his piping voice as grim as he could make it. "We've got to get out of here."

"And get to the bottom of this," Yurisa said, brow furrowed. "Because we still don't know for certain that Maxim isn't doing all this for Valeska. After all, why would he give her the teeth in return for her heart if he didn't have a use for her heart? It doesn't seem likely that he would eat it, really."

Svetlana snorted.

Andrei groaned. "So he's causing all this, *or* she is, *or* they both are, *or*...ugh, it's too much! Anyway, it doesn't make much difference now—we need to get out of here no matter who's causing it."

"But are we stopping Valeska or saving her?" Yurisa asked.

Bronya barked.

"Maybe it's both," Andrei suggested. "Maybe it's both for Maxim, too."

"If you're going off after Maxim," Svetlana said, lifting her head, "I'm coming too."

"That would be very unwise," Yurisa said, lips pursed disapprovingly. "You've just given birth, and it's very cold out there—not suitable for newborns at all."

"Although a dungeon's probably not much better," Andrei said. "Maybe we could take you as far as an inn. Why would you want to see Maxim, anyway?"

"Because," Svetlana said purposefully, "I'm going to rip his head off and make him swallow it."

"That isn't possible," Yurisa informed her.

"Really? Well, no harm in trying, am I right?"

"On the contrary," Yurisa said, "the journey could be very hazardous for both yourself and your child. Of course," she added conscientiously, "the discussion is irrelevant unless we can find a way to get out."

Andrei's eyes gleamed. "I know the routine of the stables here. If we wait till suppertime, we can get in, get the horses in harness and get going before anyone is any the wiser."

"But we don't have a way out of this room," Yurisa pointed out.

"Don't think I haven't looked," Svetlana said. "There's only one way in or out of this place, and it's through that door with the big ugly fellow parked outside it."

"How high did you look?" Andrei asked.

"As high as a woman with a boulder for a belly can look," Svetlana said. "What do you think?"

Fired with enthusiasm, Andrei persuaded Yurisa to a "fact-finding mission" around the two rooms, with him standing on her shoulders to peer into the darkened recesses of the ceiling. But Svetlana was right. There was only one way out.

"I *might* be able to wiggle through the window, now I'm this size," Andrei said hopefully.

"Not unless the iron grill disappears," Yurisa said.

"All right then," Andrei said. "We'll have to get out through the door."

"That locked door with the guard outside it, you mean?" Svetlana mocked. "How are you going to do that?"

"We'll have to get him to open it," Andrei replied briskly. "Ideas?"

"Wait till breakfast arrives?" Svetlana suggested.

"He'll be on his guard then," Yurisa objected.

"We need something he's *not* expecting," Andrei agreed.

"We got someone to bring in cloths and hot water when Svetlana was giving birth," Yurisa said. "What if we do that again?"

"I'm having twins?" Svetlana shrieked.

"No, of course not. I meant you could pretend to be having another."

"He'd still be on his guard," Andrei sighed. "We need something really startling."

"You becoming half the size was startling," Yurisa offered.

Andrei drew himself up. "I'm not half the size! I'd have to be a tiny kid to be half as tall as I was!"

"I didn't say half as tall," Yurisa said, "I said half the size. You'd have to be just as wide as you were before to be half as tall *and* half the size."

Andrei shook this off. "Never mind the arithmetic now. We need something startling by suppertime."

Yurisa stared at him thoughtfully until he could hardly concentrate on thinking for the embarrassment of it.

"What if..." she said slowly, "we made him think that you were the baby?"

Andrei looked blankly at her.

"People here know about the curse," she explained, "and they probably know about the Czar. Gossip travels quickly."

"I don't see the connection," Andrei said.

"Svetlana was worried she was going to give birth to a monster, so why not trick them into thinking she has?"

Andrei got it. "A baby that grows unnaturally fast," he said. "That just might work!"

"As long as you don't want me pretending I popped out a baby that size," Svetlana said, eyeing him, "because not even I can scream that loud."

Five minutes later their few preparations were made. Yurisa took a firm grip on the bucket.

"Right," Andrei said, shivering a little despite his burning embarrassment. "Let's get this over with!"

A Race Against Time

With a dull thunk, the guard sank to the ground. Yurisa put down the bucket as Svetlana retrieved her well-swaddled infant from his place of concealment in the corner.

"Quickly!" Andrei hissed, dashing out through the door and up the stairs.

The passageway was clear—everyone would be at their supper. He led the way around to the stable block and into the horsy hay-scented dimness within, Bronya close beside him. Now for some action, now to show his skills—now, in fact, to erase from everyone's mind, but especially his own, the memory of the last few minutes and his baby impersonation.

The stable block held four horses, the antique touring sleigh, and, half lost in the dim light behind it, a compact racing sleigh.

"No way of getting that out—we'll have to take the box again," Andrei said, darting to let the nearest horse out of its stall. Thankfully, it was still wearing its breastcollar. It practically backed itself between the shafts and stood waiting patiently.

Andrei looked around. The harness was kept in excellent order, but...it was hung a lot higher up the wall than he remembered.

"Here—let me," Yurisa said, reaching up over his head and lifting down the shaft bow. "No heavy lifting for you!" she added, glaring at Svetlana.

"Keep an eye out at the door," Andrei suggested, staggering towards the horse with the shaft bow over his shoulder. "Um…" The horse was really very tall, now he came to look at it.

"What do we do?" Yurisa asked, appearing at his shoulder.

"We put this over the top," Andrei said, hefting the shaft bow. "Ends attach to the shafts. No, the other way around!"

"You aren't explaining it very clearly," Yurisa grumbled, from somewhere on the other side of the horse.

"I'm a driver, not an explainer," Andrei snapped back, going for the second horse.

"Did you hear something?" Yurisa said, and the next moment Svetlana shrieked.

"There's someone coming!"

"Into the box!" Yurisa said. "We'll have to leave the other horses."

"One trotter pull a sleigh like that?" Andrei snorted. "It would be faster to run."

"Come on, then!" Yurisa lunged towards the doors, her limp almost forgotten.

Svetlana threw herself through the door with a squeak, clutching her bundle of baby. Bronya darted after her, and Yurisa and Andrei emerged hard on her heels—to find Svetlana standing very still with a pike at her neck. Bronya made a break for freedom but was brought down by a massive fist closing around her hind leg.

"One move, and the baby's an orphan," the man with the pike said levelly.

"But you have orders not to kill us," Yurisa said, which got his attention.

He frowned suspiciously. "How'd you know that? Anyway, accidents happen, right? Who's to know a buried body didn't die in childbed? So if you don't want any *accidents* happening, you'd better move nice and slow back to where you started your little trip. Didn't get far, did you?"

He looked the group over, his unfriendly gaze dwelling long on Andrei's face. "What happened to you? Childbirth unman you?" He guffawed.

"You recognize him?" Yurisa asked, and Andrei could actually see her hand twitching towards the pocket she kept her notebook in. "But he's..."

"Cursed? Acourse he is. But there's no curse that'll make a man vanish out of a dungeon and a kid appear to take his place, is there? 'Sides, he's got the same stick-out ears. Now move!"

"My ears do not stick out," Andrei muttered, but that was all. He trailed after the others, and sat down in a dispirited heap on the dungeon floor. There had to be a way...

Bronya sat next to him and howled. She was taller than him, sitting down.

Andrei sighed. "You're not really helping."

She looked longingly towards the setting sun, and howled again.

West. West, where Istvan lay, where no doubt preparations were in full force for Valeska's enthronement. Someone's enthronement, anyway.

He patted Bronya reassuringly. "Too soon to give up! After all, if he hasn't killed us..." He looked up as a piece of bread appeared through the grill in the door and fell to the floor.

"Why are you dropping bread on the floor?" Yurisa asked the face on the other side, neatly catching the next bit.

"This is all the supper you're getting, after a trick like that," an angry voice returned. Not the guard with a bucket-related headache, Andrei decided, but from the resemblance, possibly a brother? He gave up with a sigh any thought of persuading the guard to let them escape.

"Here." Yurisa proffered a hatful of somewhat mangled bread. "Keep your strength up."

Andrei took a couple of pieces, fed one to Bronya, and manfully chewed his way through the other, trying not to choke on the crumbs.

"We need to get out of here," Yurisa said in a low voice. "Svetlana's milk will never come in properly on a diet like this."

That might not be the least of their problems, Andrei felt, but it definitely wasn't making the top of his list. He sighed. "Got any ideas?"

"Not yet," Yurisa admitted. "Nothing faster than tunnelling through the wall, anyway."

"We could die of old age before we dig our way out," Andrei said.

"It's better than nothing," Yurisa retorted.

"I'll see what I can think of, all right?"

Night fell. He thought, dozed, woke and thought again, got up and paced to keep warm—anxiously followed by Bronya—sat and dozed again, but no workable idea came to him. The night wore on, punctuated by outbursts from the baby.

"He's hungry," Yurisa said reprovingly, in response to Andrei's mutters.

"He's going to stay that way if we can't think of something," Andrei retorted.

By the time the first light of dawn touched the sky, they had all finally dropped off, huddled together for warmth—dog, baby, and all. In the depths of his dream, Andrei heard a voice call his name. He stirred, and lifted his head with a wince.

"Andrei!" the voice was crying. "Yurisa! Bronya!"

Yurisa was awake now too. "Porfiry?"

"Porfiry!" Andrei crawled to his feet, and Bronya scampered over to the grill, putting her forepaws high up the wall and barking ecstatically.

"Bronya!" Porfiry called. "Where are you? Speak up, my dear!"

She redoubled her efforts.

"What's going on?" Yurisa bawled over the noise.

"It's Porfiry!" Andrei yelled back. "I can't see!"

With a brief look of resignation, Yurisa stooped to let Andrei climb on her shoulders. He clung to the grill for balance and looked out. Wenceslas was standing in the courtyard as though he belonged there, with Porfiry taking up a heroic pose beside him.

"Porfiry!" Andrei squeaked. "Over here!"

"Who's there?" Porfiry strode closer, peering down at the grill.

Andrei's eye caught a movement from an outbuilding. Someone else had been wakened by the shouting.

"Look out!"

"Be with you in a moment, whoever you are!" Porfiry carolled cheerfully, turning on the spot and felling his would-be opponent with an almost delicate punch on the chin. The man crumpled into a heap of clothes on the snowy cobbles and stayed there.

"What's going on?" Yurisa demanded.

"It's Porfiry and Wenceslas, and Porfiry just hit someone," Andrei said.

"All safe and well, I trust?" Porfiry enquired, coming back towards the grill.

"Never mind that now—get us out! There's a door—over there." Andrei put a finger through the grill to point. "Then stairs down to your right, and a door at the bottom. Maybe a guard?"

"Guards? Pah!" Porfiry said, jutting his chin. An arrow whistled out of the deep shadows of the courtyard, hit Porfiry in the back, and clattered to the ground. He twisted around, trying to see where it had hit, and then, lower lip jutting, strode into the shadows. He returned bearing a greenish bowman who dangled from the handful of shirtfront grasped in Porfiry's fist.

"That was very rude," Porfiry said sternly. "If it has left a scratch, I shall be most upset," he added ominously, drawing his face closer and closer to the bowman's own. "And you should know better than to wear royal blue with a complexion like that."

The bowman gave a sickly smile, dropped his bow from nerveless fingers, turned up his eyes and went limp. Porfiry stacked him neatly atop his colleague on the cobbles, and turned back to Andrei.

"I shall be with you in just a moment, dear lad!"

He disappeared off the edge of Andrei's field of vision, striding towards the door. There was a loud hammering, and a couple of thumps, and he reappeared.

"Some churlish fellow has seen fit to bar the door," he said, and turned to Wenceslas. "Forward, Wenceslas! Break the door down, if you please."

Andrei had the sense to jump free at this point.

Yurisa groaned. "Well grown for your age," she said ruefully, rubbing her shoulders.

"Quick—back into the other room!" Andrei said, leading the way with a dancing heart. "Wenceslas is going to smash his way in!"

Yurisa retreated as far as the archway, watching with interest as the walls juddered and the ceiling powdered dust in time with the crashing from above.

"I hope he isn't going to break himself," Andrei said anxiously.

There was one rather louder crash, assorted shrieks from within, and then Porfiry's voice saying "Thank you very much. Excuse me, ladies and gentlemen." The shrieks withdrew, and Porfiry's dark glossy face appeared at the grill in the dungeon door.

"We're in here," Yurisa called.

"Excellent, excellent! Stand clear a moment, if you will."

The dungeon door was not, it turned out, anywhere near as strong as the door on to the courtyard. Porfiry broke it down with three charges, and then stepped into the room flicking the dust off his shoulder.

"I hope I have not damaged my finish," he observed, and then he caught sight of Andrei. "And who is this little chap?"

"It's me," Andrei said gruffly, heading for the door. "Andrei. Long story. Tell you later."

"I shall be all ears, I assure you," Porfiry said politely. "And Czarina Svetlana! With a babe in arms! Dear me. I seem to have been missing all the excitement."

"Wenceslas can carry them," Andrei called back down the stairs. "Come on!"

Mother, child, and Yurisa in attendance were barely settled into Wenceslas's by now rather dusty lower bowl when a concerted force of menservants pressed forward out of the house, armed with a motley assortment of weapons. Porfiry braced himself and brandished his fists.

"Better to run," Andrei said, and did so, making a beeline for the forest that lurked as near to the outbuildings as it was allowed. He heard a few horrified cries from the gathered men as Wenceslas heaved himself into motion. Andrei couldn't really blame them. He'd been frightened enough the first time he saw Wenceslas moving. But the leader clouted a few heads and roused them into action, and they broke into an uncertain run.

"I dare say this has already occurred to you," Porfiry said as they plunged onto the forest path, "but a little chap like you won't be able to outrun them forever. Neither, therefore, will Wenceslas and his companions. Perhaps we should have made a break for the stables instead."

Andrei grinned. "Are we out of sight of the men?"

Porfiry looked back. "We are. All the more so once we get to this twisty bit, I should imagine."

"Then we circle round and go back," Andrei said.

"Back to the dungeon?" Porfiry said blankly.

"Back to the stables," Andrei corrected, and, seeing a gap

in the trees large enough not to show Wenceslas's passage, he turned into it.

They made a careful approach from the south-east, creeping up to the back entrance of the stables. There was some commotion within, and a pounding of hooves as the elderly touring sleigh pulled away, heavily laden with the men of Maxim's household.

"Good grief," Porfiry whispered. "I didn't know anyone still used those things. A museum piece!"

"We were brought here in it," Andrei said sourly. "And let me tell you, I don't envy those old noblewomen one bit. Can you see in? Are they all gone?"

Porfiry raised himself cautiously and peered through the window. "All clear!" he hissed.

Andrei slipped in through the open doors. "And there's our racing sleigh ready to hand," he said with satisfaction.

Porfiry chuckled. The one remaining horse whickered curiously from its stall, and shook itself.

"I think the Czarina should stay here," Yurisa said, appearing behind them. "I know it's nearly spring, but that's an open vehicle, and the windchill..."

Svetlana gave a loud sniff and climbed in, plumping herself and the baby in the middle of the single bench seat and jutting her chin in a most stubborn manner. Yurisa sighed.

"Give me a hand with the harnessing, will you?" Andrei asked.

Porfiry abstracted a large bicorne hat from a nail on the wall, set it at a jaunty angle, and hastened to assist Yurisa under Andrei's instructions. The horse was in fine fettle and clearly ready for a run, but Andrei soon discovered why Maxim's men had left this of all horses behind. It wriggled, it stamped, it nipped, and finally it took a mouthful out of Porfiry's recently acquired hat.

"Enough of that," Porfiry said sternly, seizing it by the chin. A rather unpleasant noise announced the horse's failed attempt at biting Porfiry, and its ears went back. "I have teeth too, you know," Porfiry warned. The two of them eyeballed each other while Andrei ducked about with the straps.

He was quivering with suppressed tension, but, to his relief, his hands had not lost the last twelve years of deftness. Porfiry, he suspected, barely knew one end of the horse from the other until one end bit, but unlike the limping Yurisa, he had the strength to hold almost anything in place indefinitely while Andrei fastened the buckles. The contest of wills had been settled, and the horse, though clearly still abounding in ill will, was at least cooperating.

"Everybody in," Andrei hissed as soon as everything was securely in place.

"I doubt there's room," Porfiry said, examining the sleigh with a dubious eye. "I shall have to constitute myself running footman."

Yurisa and Bronya squeezed in either side of Svetlana as Andrei clambered up onto the driver's perch behind. Andrei started the horse with a crack of the whip which sounded like a thunderclap in the stillness of the stables. The sleigh's runners screeched against the stone flags before they were out and onto the snow-covered cobblestones.

The next thing Andrei knew, Porfiry was dashing along beside them, doffing his hat to sundry shouting or screaming maidservants as they surged past. In only a few minutes they sighted their pursuers, labouring on westwards down the forest road.

They had nearly drawn even before they were sighted, and then, with a shout and clamour and the scrape of branches on paintwork, they were past the heavily laden box sleigh, and Porfiry was waving his hat in farewell as they swept around another corner.

"I hope Wenceslas will be all right," Andrei said.

"I shouldn't worry about him," Porfiry said comfortingly. "Unless you're worrying that he'll lead them to you, of course."

"Oh! I hadn't thought of that."

"How did you think I found you?" Porfiry asked. "Singing under every window in the country?"

Andrei took a better hold on the reins—they felt bigger than he was used to. "They'll be too late, anyway. We need to be in town by midnight, before the enthronement." He explained to Porfiry the conclusions they had reached while imprisoned, and Porfiry was suitably impressed.

"One can only hope the horse is up to the task," Porfiry said, eyeing him doubtfully.

"He seems to have a good wind," Andrei said. "But if we're going to reach Istvan in anything like time, we'll need at least three or four changes of horses, and how we're going to get them is anyone's guess."

"I hate to cast a shade on your already gloomy prognosis," Porfiry said after a glance over his shoulder, "but it appears one of those chaps has had the bright idea of riding the horse instead of driving it." He looked again. "Three chaps, in fact."

Andrei looked back, shocked. "You should never ride a—"

"I don't think they care, Andrei!" Porfiry said. "And I don't think your horse can outrun his colleagues, either, considering their relative loads. Would it help if I pushed?"

"More help if you punched," Yurisa said.

"Only don't hurt the horses!" Andrei cautioned.

Porfiry sighed. "I take it that Porfiry's Last Stand is indicated. And I've always wanted to attend an enthronement— the apogee of a social calendar, don't you think?—but never let it be said that I shirked from making a sacrifice for a good cause. Farewell!"

He stopped dead, taking up an elegantly pugilistic stance in the middle of the track.

Andrei turned in his seat. "Join the next circus that passes!" he shouted back, and Porfiry waved, a diminishing figure in the distance.

Andrei settled back in his place and adjusted the reins. He was back in his element. Time to prove himself.

❄   ❄   ❄

"So what is our plan?" Yurisa asked.

"We have to get to the Great Palace before midnight," Andrei replied.

"That's not a plan, that's a goal," Yurisa said.

Andrei rolled his eyes. "We plan to go fast enough to get to the palace before midnight. We'll be on the main road soon—that'll help. And without Wenceslas and Porfiry, we won't look odd."

"With a newborn in an open sleigh, driven by a child and pulled by a cart-horse?" Yurisa asked.

"Well..."

The cart-horse was the best trade he'd been able to make for the riding horse—the riding horse being what they had traded Maxim's beast for. He'd had to let the straps out to their fullest extent, and it wasn't the fastest thing on four legs, but at least, he told himself, it had good staying power, unlike the rather too plump riding horse.

"Even if we do meet the goal of reaching the Great Palace before midnight, what do we do then?" Yurisa asked.

"We have to get into the throne room. I don't know how hard it'll be. There'll be crowds of people there already, but Maxim might have his henchmen keeping an eye out."

"He thinks we're in his dungeon," Yurisa pointed out.

"No harm taking precautions. Anyway, we get in, and we get the teeth off Valeska Kira—"

"What do we offer?" she interrupted.

"Offer?"

"Granny Radinka said that magic can only be traded, not given or sold. What do we offer the princess in return for the teeth?"

"I don't know!"

"And what if she's not there? Which seems more likely, in my opinion," she added.

"If she isn't there, we split up," Andrei said, thinking quickly. "One of us goes looking for her—"

"And makes sure she doesn't give any speeches," Yurisa put in.

"—and the other stays to denounce the duke," Andrei finished.

"Have we got enough proof to denounce him?" Yurisa asked dubiously.

"I've got plenty of denouncing to do," Svetlana said grimly. "Does this little darling look like a girl to you?"

"You stay with the Czarina," Andrei suggested to Yurisa. "No one will listen to a boy like me, and anyway, I know my way around the city. You don't."

"That's sensible," Yurisa agreed. "But there's another problem."

"We're getting worse and worse horses with every trade," Andrei said. "I know. But we've nothing to offer for a trade up."

"Two problems, then," Yurisa corrected herself. "We need to get the teeth back to the Lady before the season changes."

Andrei gnawed on his lip. He hadn't thought of that.

"It's impossible to get that far that fast," Yurisa said, "no matter what horses we have, and even if we do manage to get the teeth off the princess before midnight. So whoever has the teeth will have the same power that Valeska has. Their words will have the same effect."

"I'll take a vow of silence," Andrei said.

"For three seasons?"

"Is there another way?"

The silence lasted a long time.

"There's a storm coming," Yurisa said at last. "From the north."

Andrei looked to his right, and saw a mass of dark clouds racing across the sky. Turning back, he found Yurisa looking at him suspiciously.

"I didn't say anything!" he protested. "I haven't even mentioned her! I've got nothing to do with it!"

"Insult or not," Yurisa said, "I think you'll find you've got a lot to do with this storm. And it's getting dark."

"I can manage. Driving is what I do, remember? And here's the main road!" Andrei said triumphantly. It was deserted—everyone would be at home or in the village square, getting ready to celebrate. "Look, there's a fire—first I've seen."

"It seems a bit childish to me," Yurisa said, watching the spark of orange through the trees as they went past. "Burning a figure of the Lady and dancing around it. Petty. Spiteful, almost."

"Who doesn't feel a bit spiteful after three months of snow and ice?" Andrei asked. "I'm all for dancing around bonfires myself. It's a chance to get warm," he added with a shiver as snow flurried down on his face.

Yurisa adjusted the blanket to give the Czar's son as much shelter as she could. "We still haven't figured out how we're going to get her—Valeska Kira, I mean—to give up the teeth," she mused.

"No. But if I was her, I'd be so glad to get rid of the things I'd take a fistful of mud in exchange."

Yurisa pursed her lips. "That's assuming she is the victim, not the villain here. Anyway, I don't think we should offer a princess a fistful of mud."

"Got any better ideas?"

They relapsed into silence, no sound to be heard through the white-flecked air but the soft thud of four massive hooves on the thickening snow ahead. The fires grew in size and number, but the snow came down faster.

"We're getting closer to Istvan—I think we'll be in time," Andrei said, wishing he was sure. There was no way to tell time in this world of spinning white. "But the horse is tiring—we need to see what we can trade him for in the next village."

"As quickly as possible," Yurisa said.

"You don't need to tell me that!"

Quarter of an hour later, they were moving briskly over the snow in silence.

"Are you sure this was a good idea?" Yurisa asked at last.

"You were the one who insisted we take the offer instead of pressing on to the next village! You've made that forester's season—a cart-horse in return for his donkey!"

The baby raised a thin wail.

Svetlana tutted. "Now don't you go upsetting my precious little sweetums with your snapping! You can always try trading again in the next village."

"For what?" Andrei asked sourly. "A large pig?"

The donkey was a plucky little thing, however, and drew them into Istvan with his furry head still high. As they drew nearer to the Great Palace gates, Andrei could hear a sea of voices and a crackle of fire.

He suddenly cracked the whip over the donkey's head, and it shot past the gate with a shocked turn of speed.

"That was the gate you just passed," Svetlana remarked.

"Manned by one of Maxim's men," Andrei said. "I saw him at Maxim's mother's estate."

"He won't recognize you, then," Yurisa pointed out. "Or me."

"But he might recognize Bronya, and quite likely the Czarina," Andrei said, "and then the fat really would be in the fire."

"Speaking of which, that's quite a fire they've got there," Yurisa said as they skirted the palace complex. "I can see sparks coming up over the roofs of the outbuildings."

"Let's hope they don't catch fire this year, then," Svetlana said. "The last thing I need after all I've been through is my palace burned down."

Andrei turned the donkey down a side alley and suddenly pulled up. "Yurisa, you'll have to take the reins."

"What—me? I don't know how to—" Yurisa began.

"You won't have to do much," Andrei said. "Just turn in at the stable gate down there, pull up, and then turn again for the stable block. You can do that, can't you?"

"Convincingly?"

Andrei hesitated. She had a point.

"What if we make it look like you're teaching me how to drive?" he suggested. "And then I can keep hold of the reins."

"A much more sensible plan," Yurisa said.

She squeezed into the driver's seat, Andrei standing to make room.

"Hands loosely over mine," he said. "Don't grip the reins, whatever you do! Does that look believable, Bronya?"

Bronya yipped, and Andrei grinned. "Let's go!"

He started the donkey again, and it moved on with a little more briskness, scenting a stable near at hand. The guard at the stable gate had started his celebrating a little early, judging by the cheerful and expansive gesture with which he waved them through.

"That was easier than I expected," Yurisa muttered.

"Getting indoors will be the hard part," Andrei muttered back.

Sure enough, as they drew up to the stables proper, a tall and officious fellow with a disapproving face stalked across to them.

"We were not expecting any further vehicles this evening," he said, "and I am sorry to tell you that there is no possibility of your equipage remaining here. If you will turn in the open space provided, you may leave by the same gate."

"Now you listen here, Evgeny," Svetlana snarled, putting her hood back.

"S-Czarina!"

From the look on his face, Andrei decided, here was one guest he hadn't been hoping to see again.

"If you think I've come all this way in my condition just to be sent away again, you'd better change your mind!" she went on. "I don't care if you leave it blocking the sleighs of eight nobles or break it apart for the fire, but it's not going away, and neither am I. Is that clear?"

"I'll...I'll just...over here," Evgeny said weakly, waving them towards a clear place on the side of the stable court.

"Move it!" Svetlana commanded, and pulled her hood back into place with a flick.

Swallowing the words which rose to his lips at her tone, Andrei moved it, drawing up in the place allotted. Yurisa jumped down and helped Svetlana out with as much solicitude as if she actually was Svetlana's servant. Evgeny's eyes widened at the sight of the bundle in her arms.

"See the Czarina's donkey is properly tended to," Andrei told him, taking advantage of the meagre height the driver's seat provided before jumping down.

"Er...yes, of course," Evgeny said, his eyes following Svetlana as she moved towards the side entrance of the palace with Yurisa to support her on one side and Bronya trailing elegantly beside her on the other.

"Now!" Andrei said, and Evgeny jumped. It was a desperate situation, but a good coachman does not leave his horses untended. Or his donkey. He waited to see Evgeny summoning a groom, then darted after the others.

"Ooh, I'm that sore," Svetlana moaned. "I need a hot bath and a bed—a proper feather bed!—and I'm going to see I get them!"

"What about the duke?" Yurisa muttered.

Svetlana straightened. "*After* I've dealt with him."

They mounted the steps to the side door unhindered, but as they reached it, a footman strung about with gold braid stepped out, a fixed social smile on his face.

"I'm afraid I cannot permit—" he began.

"Make way for the Czar's son!" Svetlana proclaimed, holding the baby out before her. The baby, jolted out of his sleep, turned red, opened his mouth and yelled.

The footman gaped, hesitated, and was firmly pushed aside by Yurisa. Svetlana swept through the door like the place belonged to her, and led the way down the corridor, the footman's burblings dwindling into the distance behind.

"This way," she said, turning to push open a door with an assurance which surprised Andrei till he remembered that she had lived in the servants' quarters of the Great Palace for some time before her elevation to Czarina.

Each door—or pair of doors, as they soon became—opened into a corridor that was wider, better carpeted, and frankly sparklier than the previous. They must be getting close... Andrei started running ahead to open the doors for the others. It was better than trailing behind, and if he was supposed to be taken for some sort of pageboy he might as well act like one.

He burst through a pair of gilded doors into a corridor the width of which was dwarfed by the mammoth man standing astride it. Andrei came up short at the sight, and Svetlana stopped just in time to avoid knocking her "pageboy" flat.

"You there!" the man snarled, putting out a thick meaty hand and pointing menacingly towards them.

But...not at him particularly, Andrei thought, and he slipped on, face blank. Just a pageboy going about his duties...

"*And* that dog!" the man grunted with what Andrei took to be satisfaction.

But Andrei couldn't turn back now. He was so close to the grand doors at the end of the corridor. Doors which buzzed with the noise of the crowd beyond. He stole a moment in the doorway to look forward and back. He'd made it into the throne room before midnight...but he was on his own.

The Throne of Seven Steps

Andrei looked around the room, and tried not to gape. He'd thought the Czarina's Ball was spectacular, but this...this was something else. Candles shone from chandeliers above, from girandoles on the wall, by the hundred if not the thousand, and their light gleamed off gold in every direction.

Hardly a man present but had gold braid or medals in profusion; hardly a woman passed but glittered in gold, silver, and jewels. A road-robber could retire in luxury off a single night's work in this room, Andrei reflected. Even the traditional pink sugar cakes laid out on dainty tables along the walls seemed suspiciously sparkly.

The problem, now that he was so short, was figuring out who was present—and more crucially, who wasn't. He looked about for a vantage point but saw nothing besides well-dressed figures, every way he turned.

Andrei cast his mind back to the night of the ball. The only high point in the room was the Throne of Seven Steps, but there was no way he could go up there. Putting what he hoped was an endearing look on his face, and setting his elbows at a discreet but pointed angle, he plunged into the crowd.

After one battering circuit of the room, he leaned against a wall and rubbed his neck, sore from constantly craning to see the faces of the people around him. And what had he managed to discover? Only that the Throne was empty; nothing of who was expected to be seated on it before the night was out. He wiped his forehead with his sleeve. It was hot in here, with a thousand candle flames dancing above, and probably just as many warm bodies packed into the room, and yet there was one daft woman—he'd caught sight of her once or twice—who was cloaked head to toe in furs. Madness!

He took a deep breath and worked his way back into the crowd. A swish of pink satin caught his eye, and he looked up, freezing into immobility as he caught Lala's eye. But her gaze moved on, as did she, and he was left alone in the crowd, heart thudding with relief. She didn't know him! Well, it's an ill wind... He grinned.

Suddenly the forest of skirts and long waistcoats parted for a moment. Only a moment, like the opening and closing of a door, but it was enough. Andrei had an image fixed in his mind of Valeska Kira seated on a gilded chaise not far from the Steps, her eyes scanning the bowing and curtsying passers-by, a pair of muscular bodyguards standing stonily behind her.

So she at least was here. But where was the duke? Andrei looked about, and saw the woman in furs again, passing close by with one hand clasping her cloak. He frowned. It wouldn't be the first time a lady was too proud of her furs to take them off in a warm room—and these were lovely furs, thick and glossy, in shimmering greys—but if there was one thing an ostentatious lady would not neglect to do, it was show her face. Whereas this woman—or at least, Andrei assumed it was a woman—was not only cloaked but hooded.

He stood rooted to the spot for a moment, until a portly fellow barged into him. Andrei muttered an apology and dived into the crowd again, being sure to move in a different direction to the furred figure. He knew that hand. The last time he'd seen it, it was holding his father's silver razor. What was Winter doing here?

Of course, for all he knew, it was traditional for the immortal of the season to attend enthronements. Except the enthronement was always at the end of the season—did one immortal arrive for the enthronement and their successor replace them at the ball which followed after midnight? He hadn't been born when Kiril was enthroned, but all the same, he thought someone would have mentioned it.

The end of the season...and he wouldn't be sorry to see the Lady nor her season go. But she'd be here for at least—he looked up at the gilded clock set into the wall above the orchestra's end of the throne room—half an hour more. Half an hour!

Perhaps they were wrong about Maxim. There was Valeska, clearly still in the role of heir to the throne...but no Maxim. Andrei frowned. Was she plotting alone all this time? No—Maxim had to be involved. The teeth, the kidnappings, the lies...if he'd been doing it for Valeska, he would be here by now, sitting at her side, or standing by her. Unless... Andrei's mind fizzed. Was it Maxim who was being used and discarded by Valeska after all, and not the other way around?

He gritted his teeth and rubbed his forehead again. It didn't make sense. He wished for Yurisa, or even Porfiry, to help him figure it all out. Somehow between the three of them the truth had always been easier to track down. Andrei tried asking himself what questions Yurisa would ask if she were here, and wondered where she was.

With a bang that echoed off the high ceiling, the doors at the end of the hall—the ones Andrei had been ushered through by the major-domo on his first visit—were flung open so hard they hit the walls to either side. The orchestra flailed for a moment before recovering themselves, and the crowd hushed, drawing aside to make way for Duke Maxim. He was gorgeously apparelled in royal blue and golden silk and attended by a dozen footmen whose royal blue livery failed to disguise their essential bulkiness.

Maxim strode up the room towards Valeska's chaise, the crowd parting before him, and leaving a tongue of empty floor down the middle of the room. This might have had something to do with the bulky footmen stationing themselves at regular intervals along Maxim's wake, Andrei thought, peering out through the gap above where two skirts met and jostled for room.

A niggling voice in the back of his mind said that this could still be innocent, it could still be no more than a grand entrance for a man who liked attention, a man who, perhaps, wished to draw attention to...a proposal?

Valeska smiled on Maxim as he approached, and gracefully extended her clenched hand to be kissed. Without a word, without a kiss, without so much as a bow, he turned his back on her, and the music stopped as quickly and suddenly as if they had all disappeared. Andrei frowned. That had to be prearranged. And if the orchestra was taking their orders from Maxim, who else might be? Valeska's hand dropped back to her lap, her face white.

"My people!" Maxim said, and his deep golden voice carried throughout the hall. "I come to you tonight as the bearer of evil tidings."

A shiver of whispering ran round the hall. Andrei stole a look at Valeska. She didn't look worried, he was surprised to see, or even as angry as she had a moment ago. More...concerned?

"No doubt you have heard of—or been so unfortunate as to experience—the dreadful curse which is at present plaguing our land," Maxim went on, and he could hardly have asked for a more attentive audience. You could hear wax drip off a chandelier in that silence. "I have devoted myself, these last weeks and months, to the unearthing of the awful truth, at great personal cost."

Andrei forgot to look at Valeska. The cheek of the man! When all the time—

"I have endured the misunderstanding of him I sought most to serve," Maxim sighed, and Andrei's lips twisted in grudg-

ing appreciation of this masterpiece of truth-curving. "And I
have suffered the anguish of knowing myself too late to save
him. But now I find myself in the most painful position of all."

The crowd moved uneasily. Andrei peered to see Valeska
over the mounds of red taffeta skirt blocking his way. She was
staring straight at Maxim's back, her eyes glittering like cold
stones in her bloodless face.

"It is a grief to myself personally, and to my family pride,"
Maxim said, "but I consider it my duty to tell you that the one
who has been wielding magic against our late Czar and his
people, is her."

With the last words, he spun, throwing out an arm with one
finger pointing accusingly at Valeska. The crowd gasped. Valeska tried to rise, but the bodyguards behind her each placed
a hand on her shoulder and pushed her back into her seat.

"Her every word breathes contagion!" Maxim shouted.

Valeska, eyes blazing, opened her mouth to speak, but the
guards slipped a gag between her lips, silencing her.

"I no less than you shrink to see these things done," Maxim
said, turning back to the uneasy crowd. "Yet it is for our protection, I assure you."

Andrei seized on the words. *Our* protection...so he wasn't
telling them that he was already under a curse. But why not
present himself as Valeska's innocent victim?

"See here her work!" Maxim proclaimed. "A kind and good-
hearted maidservant, whose very loyalty was turned into a
curse against her, as she was proclaimed a dog—*and became
one*."

The crowd gasped as a white dog streaked across the open
floor towards Maxim. Andrei's heart leapt and twisted like a
fish on the end of a line. Bronya!

One of Maxim's goons stepped forward and collared Bronya
as she dove at Maxim. Her teeth snapped shut mere inches
from the duke's hand, and she was dragged out of the room,
Valeska reaching out towards her with a look of anguish on

her face.

"You may look on Valeska Kira and be taken in by her youth, her beauty, or those smiling lips," Maxim continued. "But do not be deceived. Young as she is, she has meddled in dark magics. What beauty lies in heartless ambition, in a tight-fisted grasp of power? You see she holds her magic tokens tightly still."

Valeska glared at Maxim's back and raised her hands to throw, and Andrei pushed between the skirts, fully expecting to see Winter's teeth flying across the room at Maxim. But Valeska's hands stayed closed. She stared at them in horror.

Maxim turned to look at her. His voice grew cold. "And those soft lips poured out the very words that killed the Czar, *her father.*"

Valeska dropped her head and wept. Her tears flashed as they fell, and became dark rivulets on the white silk of her dress.

"Maxim our Czar!" shouted a voice at the back of the crowd. Andrei would have been prepared to bet every stitch he had on that the voice came from a hired throat. Others took it up, the footmen joining in with a volume sufficient to convince the passing hearer that the whole room was in agreement.

He knew he should be doing something, and yet Andrei couldn't let go of the question—why not tell them what Valeska had done to him? Perhaps to avoid any fear of another cursed Czar, and yet...

"It can only be traded," Andrei mumbled, staring unseeingly ahead of him. Valeska had traded Maxim her heart—but what had Maxim traded to Winter? The answer split his mind like a thunderbolt. Maxim wasn't cursed at all. He'd traded his mortality to Winter for her teeth. Which meant... Andrei's stomach turned over.

Winter had mortality. Winter could take the throne, as Summer had failed to do so long ago. She had played Maxim for a fool, just as he had played Valeska, and that was why she was here tonight.

The words of the simple fellow Damek came back to him. "I saw the lady who'll be Czara..." Not the lady, the Lady! "First Day. With the man... He didn't notice, but I saw it in her eyes." He had to mean Maxim, meeting Winter at the start of the season to lay their plot. *Her* plot. Blast it all, Damek'd even mentioned her pointy teeth! Why hadn't he listened?

Panicked, Andrei looked up and down the alley of open floor. He couldn't see her, couldn't see anything but a sea of people calling for Maxim to take the throne. As he pushed his way through the crowd, carefully circumnavigating a large and ornamental sword projecting from a gold-braided hip, another realization hit him. There was no giving the teeth back to Winter now. But he had to get them, get Valeska free of them, and then...

Then what? If there was no other way—and Granny Radinka had mentioned none—he would be burdened with the teeth forever. He would never be free to speak again. He would never be able to tell Bronya that he loved her. His eyes smarted, and he took a shuddering gasp of air. Well. If she didn't know by now, words would never tell her.

Andrei fought his way through the crowd, wriggling this way and that but moving ever closer to the Seven Steps, and the chaise that sat near the foot of them. A plan was forming in his mind, but the timing—the timing was tricky, he had to admit. The Throne had to be filled by midnight...

Maxim, already moving with the dignity he clearly felt befitted a Czar—though in Kiril's time it was the major-domo who had most of the dignity, Andrei reflected—stepped slowly towards the Throne of Seven Steps. He paused by Valeska's chaise, looking at her with a sort of stern sorrow. He quieted the crowd—some of whom were now calling for instant bloody justice—with a calm gesture.

"Justice shall be done," he said resonantly, clearly not addressing Valeska even though he was looking at her. "But it shall not come from anywhere but the Throne of Seven Steps."

And he'd already rehearsed a suitably dramatic judgement, Andrei was prepared to bet. He felt a brief pang for Porfiry, who was missing not only the pageantry of an enthronement, but all this drama as well.

"Keep her," Maxim said to the guards grasping Valeska's shoulders, and they nodded. He turned away, towards the Seven Steps, some already curtseying and bowing to him.

The crowd stilled into silent immobility as Duke Maxim approached the Step of Stone. Andrei tensed. If Granny Sonechka wasn't right about the Steps, if he wasn't right about Maxim, then this was it; all the power falling into the hands of a man as deceptive and treacherous as...Andrei couldn't think what. Kiril seemed pleasantly simple and open by comparison, despite his many failings.

One step would tell Andrei what he must do. A tackle, a denunciation—he'd have to do his best, even if it proved not enough. If Maxim's deathlessness wasn't a curse, then perhaps words could still stop him.

Maxim stood at the bottom of the Steps, and lifted his right foot. Andrei held his breath.

❄   ❄   ❄

Maxim had his eyes fixed on the glittering Throne itself. His foot descended, and he lurched forward. The Step of Stone had withdrawn, and as Maxim staggered towards them, each Step withdrew under the one above until they formed a cold hard cliff dropping from the very foot of the throne itself.

Andrei felt a brief pang of sympathy for Maxim, sprawling on the floor where the Steps had been. He knew from experience the sensation of stepping in the dark onto a step that isn't there. How much worse in a room blazing with light, when you've built everything on that step?

The communal gasp that sucked the air from the room was followed not by the shocked silence that seemed natural, but by a low, mocking laugh that seemed to fill the room and eddy about the chandeliers. Andrei saw heads turn as people tore their gaze from Maxim—now getting to his feet—to search for the origin of that laugh.

She stepped out of the crowd at the far end of the room, her furs dropping to the floor. A wave of cold spread across the room. Not furs to keep the cold out, Andrei realized; furs to keep the cold in.

He squeezed between the half-dazed people around him, keeping low as he wriggled his way to the chaise. The guards were looking over the heads of the crowd at Winter, but they had not relaxed their grip on Valeska's shoulders. Andrei slid to his knees at Valeska's feet. She stirred and looked at him, her face not a mask of misery but misery to the bone.

"I'm here to help you," Andrei whispered. "Please, trade me the teeth."

Valeska's fine brows drew together in a puzzled frown.

"For a kiss?" Andrei asked, looking as sweet and innocent as he possibly could. He could feel the cold intensifying as Winter moved down the room.

Valeska gave a sob, and turned her face away. Surely, she couldn't still want to keep them? It wasn't that, he was sure.

"It's all right," he whispered, and hoped that it would be. "I've got a plan. I've found out about the lore..."

And it was at that moment that he heard echoing in his mind the voice of Pyotr the Howler: *No one's above the Lore, lad.* It might work... It might! If Valeska was still able to trade the teeth, there was a chance. If not; well, at least things couldn't get worse.

"Just for a moment," Andrei urged. "Then you can take them back."

She turned back, looking doubtful. It grew colder. He could see the bumps rising on her skin.

"You can put them in one hand, then," Andrei said feverishly, hardly knowing what he was saying.

"You forgot I have your mortality," a cold, hard voice said close by. "I never forget anything."

Winter speaking to Maxim—she must be practically at the Steps already!

"At least try—before it's too late!" Andrei pleaded.

Valeska looked long and hard at him, while Maxim raged and Winter laughed—that mirthless, mocking laugh. At last Valeska nodded. Andrei leapt to his feet and planted a kiss on her cheekbone, above the gag. There was a tinkle as her hands loosened and the teeth dropped to the floor.

"What's mortal can die!" Maxim shouted, but with a grunt of expelled air he was hurled aside.

"Out of my way!" Winter said. "Let the Steps return."

Andrei swept the teeth up in one hand and got to his feet. Out of the corner of his eye he saw Winter's head rise above the crowd—she was on the Steps!

"Take them back—give me a kiss," he gasped, proffering the teeth again.

Warily, as though expecting them to sting her, Valeska closed one cramped and nail-marked hand over his, and, tearing the gag from her mouth with the other, pressed her lips to his forehead.

Everything tingled for a moment, and the air was rent with a shriek. Andrei looked across the heads of the crowd to see Winter dropping as the Step of Gold disappeared from under her. He glanced down at his empty hands—a man's hands!— and then at Valeska's hands, as empty as his. She smiled at him weakly, her face flooded with relief.

Bronya... But there was no time for sweet thoughts now. Already Winter was rising, as though drawn to her feet by the scream of rage which coursed through her. The onlookers shrank away as she bared her long, sharp teeth. A full mouth now, Andrei saw.

"Wh-what happened?" Maxim asked, his eyes unfocussed as he struggled back to his feet.

"A reversal," Andrei said loudly, stepping out into the open. "The trades of magic that took place have been reversed."

"You," hissed Winter, turning on him. "You did this!"

Andrei grinned. "I did," he said. "With the invaluable assistance of Her Imperial Highness Valeska Kira."

Valeska got to her feet and advanced to the open space at the foot of the steps, the crowd still drawing away from her, just in case... The Steps slid silently back into place behind Winter's back.

"It is over," Valeska said, fixing Maxim with a gimlet gaze. "Including the curse *you* put on me, preventing me from letting go of those cursed teeth!"

"How dare you try to fix your witchcraft on me?" Maxim demanded. "I had nothing to do with any of this. It was all your choice—all along!"

"No, it wasn't!" came a shrill voice in the crowd. Lala, pink and panting, burst into the open. "I was there and I saw it all!"

"You *saw*—" Maxim broke off, and Valeska flushed.

"*You* gave her the nasty things," Lala said, "and you said something about control never leaving her hands, which even then I thought wasn't very romantic, and then," she said, her voice rising, "she gave you her heart! So of course Valeska couldn't let go. You'd cursed her not to, *and* you had her heart."

The crowd murmured uneasily.

"You know how hard it is for a woman to go against the man that has her heart," Lala appealed to the crowds. "She loved him, and she trusted him, and he betrayed her! He betrayed all of us."

Maxim pulled himself together and gave Valeska a melting smile. "Darling," he began.

"Don't you try your honeyed poison on me, you traitor!" Valeska snapped.

He tried to take her in his arms and she slapped him sharply in the face.

The dashing romantic façade collapsed. "It's not my fault," Maxim whined. "*She* did it, she set me up, she took my..."

He froze for a moment, and then made a dash for the Steps.

Andrei took a step forward, knowing he would be too late, but Winter was there ahead of him. She caught Maxim by the neck as his foot descended on the Step of Stone. It stayed firm beneath his feet. Andrei's heart lurched.

"I can take your mortality off you again," the Lady said.

Maxim wriggled, but was unable to free himself. "No!" he said. "I need it."

"Give it to me!" she demanded.

"No! You tricked me!"

"Never?" Winter questioned.

"Never!" Maxim said, taking on as much of his old lordly manner as a man could with an immortal's hand at his throat.

"Very well," Winter said. "Keep your mortality. See what it will do for you."

With a sudden pained gasp, Maxim's face went blue-grey. The Lady took her hand from his throat and gave him a dismissive push. His frozen body crashed to the floor, pieces shattering off and spinning across the marble.

Lala swooned, her limp form being deftly fielded by a handsome young man in a gold-trimmed uniform.

Winter regarded the circle of horrified faces coolly.

"There's a bonfire waiting just outside!" one man cried, recovering himself. "What say we burn the real thing for once?"

This met with a roar of approval which surprised Andrei by its vehemence. He was no lover of Winter himself, but...

"Stop!" Andrei stepped forward, putting himself between Winter and the leader of the new popular movement.

"A world without—the Lady!" a woman shrilled, catching herself just in time. Others took it up.

"A world without the Lady," Andrei bellowed, overcoming the others by sheer volume, "is a world without skating! A world without snowfights! A world without long evenings by the fire, without the long rest of the land and the trees that brings us such fruitfulness in spring!"

He stopped, his chest heaving.

There was a moment it all hung in the balance, and then the man standing poised to seize Winter stepped back, lifting his hands in a sign of surrender. Andrei and Winter stood alone in a circle of faces.

The Lady laughed. "I *am* immortal," she said. "But you are...sweet. One kind word can warm three cold months. And I never forget."

The moment of stillness was broken by a side door bursting open. Svetlana steamed through, ploughing through the crowd with her baby held before her like a weapon or a talisman.

"I claim the throne in the name of my son, only son of the Czar!" she said, erupting into the clearing at the foot of the Seven Steps.

There was a murmur around the room, and more than a few disdainful glances. Winter drifted across to stand at the side of the Seven Steps, out of the centre of things but watching all and being watched by many. Svetlana looked down and saw what remained of Maxim.

"Too late to serve him out, am I?" she asked. "Well, he got what was coming to him and no mistake. Somebody clear that up," she added, waving imperiously at a couple of broad-shouldered footmen. "All you lords and ladies standing about and none of you with a lick of sense. No point leaving bodies on the floor, is there?"

The footmen winced and bent to their task.

"Dump the bits in an outhouse somewhere," Svetlana advised.

"Carry him to the mortuary house," Valeska said. "He was a duke, and of royal blood, despite his treachery."

Svetlana sniffed and shrugged.

"You say you claim the throne in the name of your son," Valeska said. "What is his name?"

Now that Andrei thought of it, he hadn't heard a name mentioned. Perhaps Svetlana had only picked out a girl's name.

Svetlana hesitated for only a moment. "Vladislav!" she announced firmly. "Vladislav Kirov, of course."

The newly named Vladislav puckered his face and grizzled.

"How certain can one be that he has a right to that name?" an aristocratic lady asked, sending the insinuation home with an arch of the brow.

"He is the Czar's son," Valeska said, and heads turned to stare at her. "This woman was my father's mistress, and she no doubt married him for the sake of his position—but she would not be unfaithful."

"Thank you, I think," Svetlana said. "You heard her! This is the Czar's legitimate son and heir!"

"He will not mount the Seven Steps," Winter said, coming forward.

"What business is it of yours, whoever you are?" Svetlana asked angrily. "And who opened a window? It's freezing in here!"

Winter laughed. "Shall I freeze the blood in your veins as I did in Maxim's?" she asked.

"O most sweet and puissant Lady!" Andrei began desperately, but to his surprise Svetlana was smiling at Winter.

"Well, if you killed that two-faced black-hearted bastard, I'm sure we'll be friends," she said.

Andrei's mind boggled at the thought of Winter having anything that could be described as a friendship with anyone.

"But that throne needs filling by midnight," Svetlana went on, "and here's the one to do it!"

"But a Czar must mount the Seven Steps," Winter said.

"And?" Svetlana demanded.

"And a child of—my brother's age cannot do that," Valeska said.

Svetlana sulked.

"And even if he could crawl already," Bronya said quietly, appearing beside Valeska in her right form once more, "he still has an older sister with...more experience of politics."

"Bronya!" Andrei cried in joy. "You're all right! But where's Yurisa?"

"That midwife with a beard?" Svetlana asked. "We were being held in a side room by that goon who stopped us in the passage. All of a sudden her beard disappears and she shouts out 'Luka!' and punches the goon in the eye and disappears. Leaving me and the baby alone with that nasty ox of a fellow. Might have been very unpleasant for me, if she hadn't of hit him so hard. Who's Luka, anyway?"

"Her brother," Andrei said briefly. "Killed by the curse."

"Oh, I *see*. Well, good luck to her," Svetlana said agreeably. "Good at her job, that girl. Mean right hook, too."

"We're running out of time!" Bronya said. "It's nearly midnight. Valeska must take the throne—she's the only possible person!"

"But Valeska killed the Czar," a voice in the crowd objected.

"No, she didn't!" Andrei said. "Of course the duke said she had—he blamed her for everything."

"That's right," said the gold-braided man whose sword Andrei had noticed earlier in the evening. "She can't have done it. If the Czar had been killed by the curse she carried, when it was undone he would...come alive again," he ended lamely.

There were shudders all over the room, and one or two more ladies swooned in their escorts' arms. The image was so clear it might as well have been a tapestry on the wall: Czar Kiril, waking in his great stone sarcophagus, in the cold, in the dark, in a rage.

Two muscular footmen sprinted off to check, while the crowd shivered and rustled and watched the hands of the great clock at the far end of the ballroom.

"The Czar is still dead," Bronya said in a clear, carrying

voice, "because it wasn't the curse that killed him—it was the duke. He knew the Czar was dead before the news reached him, because he was the one who arranged it."

"But he wasn't even in town then," another voice pointed out.

"With poison, he didn't need to be," Bronya said. "With drink and rage and the curse, he knew no one would suspect it was him."

"You seem to know a lot about it," an elderly aristocratic dame said, eyeing Bronya distastefully.

"I was there when he gave Her Highness the poison," Bronya replied composedly. "He told her it was a cure for the curse. She was trying to save her father—not kill him."

The footmen rushed back in, their chests pumping like bellows. Unable to speak, they merely shook their heads. The room buzzed. Focus drew tight about the Steps again. The Czar was still dead. The Throne was still empty, and it must be filled by midnight—five minutes away.

"Valeska our Czara!" Andrei yelled.

"Valeska our Czara!" Bronya cried, and then the room was shaking with it.

Valeska motioned for silence. "There is something I must do first," she said, her hands stiff and clumsy as she worked a solid silver bracelet off her wrist. "Bronya..."

Bronya stepped forward. "My lady?"

The room was silent.

"Bronya is truthful," Valeska said, loud enough for all the world to hear. "She is kind. She is loyal—to a fault—and I ask her to accept my apology."

Whispers billowed around the room as Bronya took the bracelet and bobbed a blushing curtsey. Valeska was taking a risk, Andrei knew, and he respected her all the more for it. To do the right thing was hard enough—to do the right thing when it could cost you everything you ever wanted showed true strength. How much easier to depend on Bronya's silence, or say a word or two in private instead.

Valeska turned to the assembled crowd and raised her voice so that it rang down the hall. A sharper voice than Maxim's, Andrei thought, but one that rang true. No fear of honeyed deceptions here.

"I swear to you today," Valeska said, "that I will cut out my tongue, I will sew my lips together, I will slit my own throat, before I will wield words like swords again. I have seen the devastation words can wreak—my own words, and the words of others—and I will not willingly walk down that road again."

"Valeska our Czara!" the people roared.

Valeska smiled, the warmest, clearest, truest smile Andrei had ever seen on her face, and she curtsied deeply to her people before turning to mount the Seven Steps.

After all he'd seen that evening, Andrei was almost surprised to see the Steps just sit there, for all the world as though they were only inanimate slabs, ready and waiting for any passing foot to step on them.

Valeska reached the Step of Jewels, turned in place, and sat down. The Throne was filled. Midnight struck, and the long pale figure of Winter disappeared.

❊   ❊   ❊

Andrei, Coachman to Her Imperial Majesty Valeska Kira, emerged exuberantly from that noble lady's salon on the first morning of spring, and collided forcefully with a tall drooping fellow in bedraggled powder blue.

"Sorry," he said automatically, and then "Porfiry!"

"What's left of him," Porfiry groaned.

"Those thugs!" Andrei said, incensed.

"Thugs nothing!" Porfiry straightened. "I practically shovelled snow with those pestilential fellows. And then, hoping I might still be in time for the enthronement, I pressed on to the west. Hour after hour! There I was, wading through the midnight snow, charging through like a monument to some great hero, scorning the dread elements around me, when all of a sudden—pouf!"

"You were human again?" Andrei asked, full of sympathy.

"I have always been human," Porfiry said coldly. "Suddenly, alas, I was weak, feeble, cold, wet, bedraggled, and subject to scratches from passing shrubs. Look at my suit! Or rather, don't. Avert your eyes from the tragedy before you."

"I can tell it was a very nice suit," Andrei said.

Porfiry sighed. "*Was* being the operative word. As tremendous as the ensemble was in its prime, it was never suited for cross-country racing by night, nor yet the journey in a soiled wagon which I eventually sank to the depth of accepting—a wagon which I can only assume had been used for the transportation of some more than usually incontinent farm animal."

"You didn't see any sign of Wenceslas?" Andrei asked, with a little twinge of anxiety.

"Would I have demeaned myself to travel in the aforementioned wagon if I had?" Porfiry demanded. "Thrown upon such meagre resources, I am as you see me now, a mere wreck or shell of my former self."

"Have a hot bath and some breakfast," Andrei advised. "Everything will look brighter after that. And perhaps—a change of clothes? I'm sure someone in the palace has something in about your size."

Porfiry drew himself up. "Do you suppose that I have battled my way across the country—on the First Day of Spring, no less!—to present myself to my newly enthroned sovereign while wearing the borrowed and most likely ill-fitting clothing of goodness knows who? On the contrary. This ensemble may be a ruin, but it is the ruin of a court suit fitted to perfection. The ruin of greatness—and, I might add, an eloquent witness to my noble sufferings. Perhaps I shall donate it to the imperial museum. And now, I have been led to believe that this door opens into the Czara's salon. Have I been correctly informed?"

On Andrei's assuring him that he had, and that, moreover, said great lady was at present in said salon, he continued. "I have come here to plead my case before her, on bended knee if I can be sure the seams will not start."

"You...want to be her secretary?" Andrei guessed.

Porfiry started. "By no means. I have done with secretarying, and set my eyes on higher things. I am a national hero now, after all. Master of the Wardrobe was more what I had in mind."

"Then I'm sorry to tell you that Bronya has already been confirmed as the Czara's lady-in-waiting with oversight of wardrobe," Andrei said.

"And have you got your old job back?" Porfiry enquired.

"You are looking," said Andrei, pulling himself up to his full height, "at the Head Coachman of the Imperial Stables."

"Congratulations! And may I say, your beard is coming in very nicely."

"Well, I haven't been able to shave in a while," Andrei said dryly.

"True," Porfiry said. "Yurisa?"

"Shot off home to check on her brother in the middle of the night."

"Oh, of course!"

"She'll go back to carry on her training with Granny, I expect," Andrei added. "After all, it's not every apprentice healer who can claim to have attended a Czarina in childbed."

"On which note," Porfiry interjected, "what has become of Svetlana and her little mite? Has the Czara sent them away?"

"Not at all! Little Vladislav Kirov is presently her heir, after all. She's invited Czarina Svetlana to reside at the Little Palace. With her son. The Czarina's son, that is—the Czara's brother."

"Half brother, to be genealogically precise. Hmm. Well, as the position of Master of the Wardrobe is unavailable—for I should not dream of attempting to unseat dear Bronya, though we shall no doubt consult frequently—I shall settle for being

Master of the Czara's Revels. Or perhaps Social Adviser to Her Imperial Highness the Czarina. Or in due course Tutor to the Heir to the Throne of Seven Steps. Or even all three. It is not for me to say," he concluded with unconvincing humility. "I serve wherever my Czara sends. Do excuse me."

He turned to the door, but it opened before he could knock, and a pageboy slipped out.

"Coachman, the Czara says Lady Bronya wants to see you in the east terrace gardens—straight away."

Andrei nodded and strode off, leaving Porfiry to explain to the pageboy how he wished to be announced when stepping into the room.

Bronya was strolling between garden beds showing the first faint green of spring when Andrei arrived, the sunlight gilding her hair and sparkling off the silver chain about her neck.

Andrei smiled. "The pageboy tells me Czara Valeska said you wanted to see me."

"I do." She took his arm and began to stroll along the nearest path. "You should keep the beard, Andrei. It suits you, somehow."

"Did you summon me to walk up and down in a recently freezing garden just to tell me my beard is nice?" he asked with a laugh.

"I wanted to apologize to you," Bronya said, twirling Valeska's bracelet around her wrist.

"Apologize to me?" Andrei asked, astounded. "What on earth for?"

"Do you remember the last time we two were alone in a palace garden?" Bronya asked.

"The day I gave you that necklace," he said promptly.

"Yes." She sat down on a broad stone seat. "There was something on your mind that day, I know, but I was too preoccupied with what was on my mind, and...I put you off."

Andrei waited, and she suddenly looked up at him with a dazzling smile.

"But now that what was on *my* mind has been settled," she said, "what was on yours?"

It was the work of a moment to seat himself beside her, to put an arm around her waist, to press her close...and to clutch at the seat with his free hand when the whole thing shook.

Bronya looked at him, breathless and laughing. "Did you feel that?"

He looked up. "Wenceslas!"

A jet of water spouted into the air, and the sunlight turned to rainbows all around them.

A Note from the Author

If you enjoyed this book, please consider leaving a review in the review-leaving place of your choice; or recommending it to others you think might enjoy it.

If you'd like to find out more, visit

> `https://deborah.makarios.nz`

where you can sign up to be the first to hear about new releases, read (or follow) the blog, or get in touch directly.

All characters in this book are purely fictitious. However, Duke Maxim exhibits many of the traits of a person engaged in manipulative abuse (also described as subtle abuse, emotional abuse or narcissistic abuse). So if he reminds you of someone...bear that in mind.

Also by Deborah Makarios

Restoration Day

Princess, pawn—or queen?

Princess Lily was born to be queen of Arcelia, where the land itself has life and magic growing in it. Yet she leads a pawn's existence in the shadow of her guardians' control. She dreams of the day when she will take her rightful place in the world.

At last her chance arrives, with a quest for the three Requisites of Restoration Day, the royal rite which renews the life of the land. But she's been hidden away too long...

Stripped of all she thought was hers, Lily will need to do more than cross the board if she is to emerge triumphant as the queen she knows she must be. The land becomes both field and prize in a gripping game—and this time she's playing for her life.

About the Author

Deborah Makarios was raised in the space between worlds and maintains an eccentric orbit.

She found her niche at the age of six when in short succession she read *The BFG*, her first Agatha Christie (*Why Didn't They Ask Evans?*), and encountered her first P. G. Wodehouse (*Something Fresh*—saying "Heh! Mer!" is enough to make her laugh, decades later).

Her personal motto is *tolle et lege*—pick it up and read it—regardless of whether *it* is a Bible, a book, or a jar of homemade marmalade. Her misson is to write books, plays and blog posts like cups of tea: warm, heartening and restorative. She believes in happy endings, the ultimate triumph of good over evil, and always having a clean handkerchief. It is, however, against her religious principles to believe in "normal."

She lives among the largely unsuspecting populace of New Zealand with only two cats, and her brilliant, albeit marginally less eccentric, husband.

Acknowledgements

Though there is but one name on the cover of this book, a number of people have had a hand in bringing it into existence.

My thanks go to all those readers who enjoyed my first book *Restoration Day*, and took the trouble to tell me so. Each of you made my day, and helped me persevere.

Thanks as always to my invaluable beta readers: Kay McKenzie, Roseanne Lupoli, Carol Carr, Ruth Fyfe, Graham Fyfe, and Jess Trethewey.

Thanks also to Avery Neal (author of *If He's So Great, Why Do I Feel So Bad?*) and her colleague for their willingness to assist with beta-reading, even though it didn't work out in the end.

Thanks to John Greenall of the American Driving Society, for his feedback on some of the carriage-driving parts of the narrative. Any errors in the final version are entirely of my own invention.

Thanks to my husband Timothy, without whose practical and emotional support none of this would be remotely possible.

Thanks to my Lord Patron, for the task, the means, and the reassurance.